THE HIGH GROUND

THE HIGH GROUND

Daryl Fisher

iUniverse, Inc.

New York Lincoln Shanghai

The High Ground

iUniverse books may be ordered through booksellers or by contacting:

iUniverse
2021 Pine Lake Road, Suite 100
Lincoln, NE 68512
www.iuniverse.com
1-800-Authors (1-800-288-4677)

This is a work of fiction. All of the characters, names, incidents, organizations, and dialogue in this novel are either the products of the author's imagination or are used fictitiously.

ISBN: 978-0-595-43782-5 (pbk)
ISBN: 978-0-595-88110-9 (ebk)

Printed in the United States of America

To all who went, and especially to those who died,
half-a-world away from home.

Contents

JOURNAL ENTRY

MEMORIAL DAY 1994

Another Memorial Day is upon us. The politicians will make their speeches, many of them quite moving. The cemeteries will be mowed and fresh flowers placed on some of the graves. Flags will fly everywhere, some at half-mast on tall poles, some floating silently in a soft breeze in front of homes where the pain is still felt.

The Indy 500 will be run. Hard-working people everywhere will make plans to get out of town. Barbecues will be fired up. Young boys and girls will go camping and swimming. The oil companies will thoughtfully raise the price of gas, as they always do for the traveling public at this time of year. The weather will be great and everyone I talk to will be enjoying their three-day weekend. Thankfully, I guess, once the dead are buried, the world never skips a beat.

It wasn't that many years ago that I absolutely hated Memorial Day. I thought of it as nothing more than another societal celebration of war, dedicated to reinforcing much of the garbage we see in movies, or read about in books. I was convinced that if civilized man was ever going to get rid of war, then the very first thing we all needed to do was stop glorifying it, especially the dying part.

As time moved on, though, I came to understand the real reason almost every new generation gets to fight in some war someplace is because people, men in particular, actually like it. By that I mean that for many men throughout the ages, going off to fight in a war was the biggest adventure of their lives. They got to travel to places they would have never seen otherwise, prove (or fail to prove) to themselves and others that they were indeed men, and meet all kinds of exotic people, especially of the opposite sex, who would never have popped up in their real lives. They don't call it the spoils of war for nothing.

But after I came to the reluctant conclusion that mankind will keep having wars because a whole lot of people truly enjoy them, not to mention that they have also been historically good for business and very effective at keeping the world's population from exploding, I started looking at Memorial Day in a totally new light. I turned my attention away from the politicians and the profiteers and the tellers of exaggerated war stories, and towards the chiseled cold marble which simply reads, "All gave some, some gave all."

More specifically, I turned my attention to SGT Jack Blevins, KIA Vietnam. He loved good music and quiet conversation. He had taken his R&R in Hawaii just so he could be with his fiancée, a girl he had known since the first grade. Neither one of them could imagine life without the other; WO1 Wally Wakely, KIA Vietnam. He was fearless to a fault and everyone was in awe of the incredible things he could make a helicopter do. He was always flying at tree-top level and no one could believe that a single shot from a rifle on the ground had actually brought him down; SSG Lance Sanders, KIA Vietnam. He was a giant of a man who liked to joke about how his huge frame made him too good a target. He knew everything there was to know about soldiering and he worried more about the lives of the men in his squad than he ever did about his own; PFC Robbie Cline, KIA Vietnam. He was kind and gentle and could hardly wait to get back to his beloved family and pets. His parents were never the same after they were notified he wouldn't be coming home; SP4 Billy Sax, KIA Vietnam. He was so thoughtful and funny, everybody's friend, and not the least bit wor-

ried about making it back to the world in one piece; 1LT Robert Townsend, KIA Vietnam. He never talked down to the men under his command, or asked them to take a risk he wouldn't take himself. He didn't care about winning the war, he just wanted to do the very best job he could; PFC Donny Marx, KIA Vietnam. He was confident everything would be okay once he had been in Vietnam for awhile and gotten used to his new surroundings. He didn't want to crawl over that exposed mound of dirt, but he knew he had no choice; PFC Benjamin Duncan, KIA Vietnam. He wanted to be a good soldier, but he was so frightened when he was in the field that no matter how hard he tried, he couldn't stay focused on the task at hand; Kit Carson Scout Chin Nguyen, KIA Vietnam. His smile was so wonderfully contagious and he was determined to live free, like all men did in America, a country he knew only went to war for the right reasons, and never lost; and SGT James Ketchum, KIA Vietnam. He was easily the most courageous human being I have ever known, and he taught me that life, just like war, is all about finding a way to take the high ground. The day doesn't go by that I don't miss him.

Ten tiny grains of sand on the terrible beach of war, and each of them would have given anything, absolutely anything, to be alive on Memorial Day, 1994.

CHAPTER 1

▼

INDUCTION

Fort Lewis, Washington in early February of 1968 was not a very hospitable place. A decrepit old military bus unceremoniously dumped me and forty or so other inductees off in the middle of the frozen night and some crazed sergeant wearing a Smokey the Bear hat pulled all the way down over his eyebrows seemed determined to keep screaming at us until dawn.

A wet, blowing snow kept falling and my California attire— short-sleeved shirt, cords, tennis shoes and a windbreaker—simply wasn't keeping any of my important body parts warm. Lawrence 'Lippy' Truman, on the other hand, was layered in the proper clothing and appeared to be almost oblivious to a wind chill factor which had to be well below zero.

For reasons completely unknown to me, Lippy had aggressively befriended me the moment I sat down next to him for the hour or so ride from the airport to the Induction Center. He was a year older than me and from New York City, of all places. He was incredibly opinionated and hardly ever stopped talking. He also had frequent spells when he was simply incapable of telling the truth or getting through a whole sentence without saying the word 'fuck' at least once.

Although Lippy, as he insisted on being called, was arrogant, vulgar and a liar, I liked him immediately. That didn't seem to surprise Lippy at all. He apparently was very accustomed to being liked.

"It's you and me, pal," he informed me only minutes into our relationship. "My cousin just got out of basic training in Louisiana and he says it's a fucking piece of cake if you've got a friend you can count on, so if anyone messes with you, you just let me know, okay?" He even made me promise. "I was a New York City Golden Gloves champ, you know," he lied with pride.

Once everyone was off the bus and lined up the way Smokey the Bear wanted, Lippy nudged me hard with his bony little elbow. "Would you knock that off!" he demanded, his voice irritated.

"Knock what off?"

"Your teeth are chattering, man, and it's driving me fucking nuts."

"I can't help it."

"Quiet down there!" screamed Smokey.

"I wonder if we're ever going to get to eat around this fucking place?" Lippy asked me as we stood around in the ankle-deep snow trying unsuccessfully to blow some warmth into our hands.

"Eat?" I said. "How can you even think of food at a time like this? I'm freezing to death here."

"It's all part of the fucking game," Lippy explained. "This clown is trying to break us down. It's the oldest Army trick in the book. It's the same reason they're going to shave our heads tomorrow and make us all wear green underwear. And why do you think our bus just happened to get here at three-thirty in the fucking morning? Mentally and physically, they want to mess with our heads, break us down."

"Well," I said, "if you ask me, they're doing a darn good job of it."

"Supposedly, you can only create a gung ho soldier from the ground up, and the next nine weeks is going to be nothing but one fucking head trip after another. One big crock of fucking...."

Suddenly, Smokey the Bear was right in Lippy's face. "I thought I told you to be quiet!" he screamed, spit flying out of his cloudy breath.

Lippy closed his eyes to avoid being struck and pointed over to me. "You told that guy there to be quiet, sir."

The sergeant glanced over at me and then quickly returned his full attention to Lippy. "A smart-ass, huh?"

"Oh no, sir, not at all, sir."

"Well, young man," said the sergeant, finally lowering his voice, "let me give you some of the best advice you'll ever get."

"Thank you, sir," said Lippy sarcastically, "I'd really appreciate that."

"The very last thing you want to do in the whole damn world is get on my shit list! Do you understand me?"

As Lippy reluctantly nodded his head, I suddenly came to the conclusion that mind games or no mind games, I had had just about enough. I was convinced frostbite was beginning to set in and if I wasn't allowed to go to the bathroom soon, my first act as a United States soldier was going to be a pretty disgusting one.

"Sergeant," I asked politely, "just how long do you think we're going to have to stand around out here in the snow? I'm freezing." Lippy was impressed.

"Well, well, well, you poor little thing," said the sergeant, his large eyes boring in on me. "Cold are you?" I stuck to my guns and nodded my head 'yes'. "Do you know what's real good for that?"

"No," I admitted.

"Running in place!" roared the sergeant. "So get 'em up! Go on! Get those knees pumping! Get 'em up! Now!"

I had no real feeling left in either one of my feet, but I somehow managed to force them off the ground as the sergeant screamed, "Higher! Higher! I want to see those knees touching your chin! Do you hear me?" Actually, much to my surprise, the sergeant was right. Within a minute or so, I was already beginning to feel quite a bit warmer.

"Nice going," Lippy said to me after the sergeant had charged off to police yet another disciplinary problem at the other end of the line, "you've been in the Army five fucking minutes and you've already screwed up. I don't know if I want to team up with you or not."

"Alright now," yelled the sergeant as he made his way back to the center of the formation, "listen up! All of you! Have any of you boys been to college?"

Lippy's eyes lit up. He thrust his hand high into the air and waved it back and forth for all he was worth. "Come on, Ty," he urged me, "get your fucking hand up. This is our chance, man."

"Chance for what?" I asked between gasps for air as I continued to jog in place.

"To separate ourselves from the rest of this fucking rabble. Check out some of these turkeys, man. Hell, I bet most of them haven't even been to high school, much less college. Some of them look like they just walked off a fucking mountain."

I glanced around and only two or three other hands had been raised. "Have you been to college?" I asked Lippy.

"Of course I've been to fucking college," he shot back, obviously hurt that I would even ask. "Now raise your hand!"

"I don't know, Lippy," I said. "Just before I left home, my dad told me that whatever I do, don't volunteer for anything."

Lippy shook his head in disbelief. "They're probably looking for officer material or something, man. You're going to blow it big time! Now get your fucking hand up!"

I reluctantly raised my hand and quickly discovered that jogging in place is much more difficult that way. I kept tipping over towards Lippy and he kept angrily shoving me back where I belonged.

"I only see five hands," bellowed the sergeant. "Come on, I need one more. It don't matter if you graduated or not." No more hands went up, but the sergeant still seemed pleased. "Well," he finally said, "I guess we'll just have to make do with the five of you. Okay, now everyone who's got their hand up, please step forward."

I didn't particularly like the way the sergeant had to force the word 'please' out of his thin-lipped mouth, but I gladly stopped jogging and moved to the front with Lippy.

"Did I say you could stop running in place?" the sergeant screamed at me, and only after I began churning away again did he resume his train of thought. "Alright now," continued the sergeant, "I've got a real treat for you college boys." A huge, sadistic grin slowly spread out all over his acne-scarred face. "You get to spend your first twenty-four hours in the United States Army pulling KP duty! My congratulations to each and every one of you little college smart-asses!"

The rabble behind me and Lippy burst into laughter.

CHAPTER 2

▼

BASIC TRAINING

Basic training wasn't really as bad as I had thought it would be. Regular hours and three square meals a day did wonders for me. It was a little difficult getting used to being yanked out of a warm bed at five-thirty every morning, but I quickly gained five pounds and within a few days I wasn't even homesick anymore.

Poor Lippy, on the other hand, was truly miserable. He seemed to hate just about everything the Army had to offer, including the bland food, the fit and color of the uniforms, the morning and evening physical fitness sessions, all the outdoor drills and most of the classroom training, and he really had a hard time adjusting to wearing heavy combat boots all the time. He came in dead last in the first round of PT tests and he dropped out halfway through the seven-mile hike. The platoon sergeant also told him his wall and footlockers were a disgrace to all soldiers everywhere, past and present.

More alarming than all of that, though, was that Lippy didn't seem to have the slightest interest in learning how to clean a rifle or properly throw a hand grenade, and he absolutely refused to yell "Kill without mercy!" during the bayonet drills. The only thing he really seemed to enjoy was the pugil sticks fights, which allowed him to occasionally beat other trainees to a pulp with a five-foot padded pole.

As my second week of soldiering began, I was getting my first real good night's sleep when Lippy suddenly shook me awake and informed me it was my turn to take over the fire watch. I vaguely remembered the drill sergeant mentioning something about our squad being responsible for some kind of night duty, but I had been too tired at the time to listen very carefully.

"Come on," whined Lippy, "it's your turn to take over. I want to get some sack time, too."

The thought of pulling off my covers and getting out of my warm bunk was almost too torturous to bear. "What do I have to do?" I asked Lippy, still half-asleep.

"Just stay awake in case a fire starts, although I don't know who's going to start a fucking fire at this hour. Oh, yeah, and tell anyone who's jacking off to stop it."

"Right," I said as I struggled to sit up and keep my eyelids from closing.

As Lippy crawled into his bunk, which was below mine, it dawned on me that I was in a room with dozens of soundly sleeping men, and almost all of them were snoring. The racket was incredible. "Why is it so darn cold in here?" I whispered down to Lippy.

"The sergeant said they're going to start keeping all the windows open to help prevent an outbreak of spinal meningitis."

"What's that?" I asked as I blew my dripping nose.

"You don't want to know," Lippy answered with a chuckle, "but I hear it starts with a fucking runny nose."

"Real funny, Lippy. So, I just walk around the barracks or what?"

"Better avoid Webb's bunk."

"How come?"

"Because the idiot sleeps with his eyes open, and it'll scare the shit out of you just like it did me." He began to laugh and it was contagious.

"Knock it off," I told him. "We're going to wake everyone up."

"Can you actually believe we're in the fucking Army?" he asked as he tried to swallow his laughter. "Did you see that goof Jordan in chow formation tonight? There we are, all standing at attention with our feet pointed out, and that fool's got his boots on the wrong fucking feet again. Can you believe anyone can be that dumb? And what about what's-his-ass who volunteered to be Bravo Squad's squad leader? Did you see the look on his lily-white face when he realized the whole fucking squad is black? Hell, he doesn't even know how to shake hands with those dudes. They're going to kill him."

For the next hour or so, Lippy and I chatted away about our first full week in the United States Army. Lippy was still finding it hard to believe he'd actually been drafted. Almost everyone he knew had managed to find a way out, including his best friend. "Bruce is special," explained Lippy, smiling. "I'd bet my ass he's the only guy in the whole fucking country who got out because of athlete's foot."

"You're kidding me?" I said with disbelief. "Since when does athlete's foot keep you out of the Army?"

"Bruce didn't have just any old ordinary case. He cultivated the fucking stuff, man. It was the grossest thing I ever saw. About a month or so before each of his physicals, he'd start soaking the same pair of socks in the sink and then wear them to bed every night—with a heating pad strapped around each foot." I began to laugh. "I used to laugh my butt off at him, too, but he's at home right now in his own bed, and we're wide awake listening to a room full of complete strangers snore their fucking heads off."

Lippy also talked nostalgically about home and how he had loved growing up the only son of show business parents, although, as usual, I wasn't really sure if he was telling me the truth. He said that for more summers than he cared to count, his parents had dragged him all over the famous Catskill mountains and he got to meet just about every entertainment star imaginable. When he casually mentioned that one of his first memories was being bounced on James Cagney's knee, I told him I thought he was full of shit.

"The truth is vastly overrated, Ty, but believe it or else, to this fucking day, Cagney still sends me and my mom a Christmas card."

"What happened to your dad?"

"Oh, he took off years ago. Marriage just wasn't his thing. I was sitting right there in the same room when he told my mom it was a form of death."

"What'd he mean by that?"

"He meant that he was tired of fucking just my mom, stupid."

"Oh. Do you ever see him or talk to him?"

"Naw. Maybe someday when he's all screwed out he'll pop up again, but I stopped holding my breath years ago."

Looking out my window, I could see the morning sun beginning to illuminate Mount Rainier off in the distance. "This sure is a pretty part of the country, isn't it, Lippy?"

"Ty," said Lippy, ignoring my question, "you wanna know what I really hate about the fucking Army?

"What?"

"Standing in all these fucking lines!"

"Boy, I know what you mean."

"You gotta stand in a line for everything around here. To eat, to take a shower, to use the phone, to get into the PX, even to take a fucking dump. All day long, it's just one fucking line after another. Well, when I get out of the Army, I'll tell you one thing, I ain't ever going to stand in another line again for as long as I live!" He thought about what he'd said for a moment, laughed and then added, "Except maybe to spit on Richard Nixon's fucking grave."

CHAPTER 3

▼

THE WHIP

With each passing day, playing soldier seemed to get easier and easier for me. I was making new friends and even getting used to the bitterly cold mornings and the absolutely frigid nights. I was finally allowed to stay in the PX long enough to buy all the cigarettes and candy bars I wanted, and the next afternoon, I received my first piece of mail, a long letter from Amy.

As I read between the lines, I was more convinced than ever that our best days were behind us. She said she was going to keep writing at least once a week, whether I liked it or not, but I knew she wouldn't. Writing letters was second only to getting a bad haircut on the list of things Amy hated most.

But no matter how hard I tried, I still couldn't seem to get the last few hours we had spent together out of my mind. After we had made love for what I think we both knew would probably be the final time, I pulled her so close to me that I could feel her heart beating and silently thanked her for loving me all those years when it had seemed like no one else did. She had been as much a part of my life as the air I breathed, and there was a part of me that worried I might soon start to suffocate without her.

After mail call, I went over to the dayroom and was leisurely playing a game of pool all by myself when Lippy suddenly burst through the door and pranced over to my side. He had a piece of paper in his hand and he slapped it down on the pool table.

"What's that?" I asked as I continued to line up my next shot.

"Have you ever heard of OCS?" He was more excited than I had ever seen him.

"No, I can't say that I have. What is it?"

"It stands for Officers Candidate School, and believe it or else, if you and I sign this here piece of paper, the Army will send us to Georgia and turn us into fucking officers."

"Really?" I asked, not exactly sure I wanted to go to Georgia, or be an officer for that matter.

"I've already signed it," said Lippy, sticking out a pen in my direction, "but you've got to sign the fucking thing, too."

"Wait a minute, Lippy. Who gave you this, anyway?"

"Some officer who was visiting with the CO when I was over policing up the front yard of his barracks. He's a real nice dude, man. He's the first fucking brass I've ever met who actually gives a shit about the enlisted man. I was telling him all about us, you know, how we're best friends, what colleges we went to and everything, and he said this OCS shit is definitely the way we should go. I guess it's a real honor to be asked to go, and he said they'd keep us together throughout the whole fucking thing."

"Now why would the Army want to make us officers, Lippy?"

"Because officers are dropping like flies in Nam."

"That's nice to know."

"But most of them aren't street smart like you and me, man. Come on, we'll make great officers. Our men will love us."

"I don't know, Lippy. There must be a catch."

"There's no catch, man. Go ahead and sign the fucking thing. It's just so they can start all the paperwork. You can always back out later if you want."

"Maybe we should both go over and talk to the guy?"

"Look, man," said Lippy, his feelings obviously hurt, "if you don't want to sign the fucking thing, then don't! Hell, I thought you'd be as happy about this as I am."

"Well, I am, but...."

"But fucking nothing, man, I thought we were a team. I thought we were best friends. I thought it was you and me against the whole fucking Army. I thought...."

"Okay, okay, I'll sign it!" I said as I grabbed the pen and quickly scribbled my name at the bottom of the page. "There, are you happy, now?"

"Thanks, Ty. This is going to be so cool, man. If we've got to be in the Army, we might as well be fucking officers, right?"

"How about a game of pool?" I asked, returning my friend's smile.

"Maybe later. I gotta get this right back to that guy. He's only going to be on the base for another hour or so."

With that, Lippy turned and hurried out of the dayroom and I didn't give the matter a whole lot of thought until almost a week later when The Whip suddenly sent for us.

The Whip was Captain Harold Hopson, and he never went anywhere without a black and white striped jockey's whip in his hand. It was a vicious looking little thing and rumor had it that he had used it more than once on unrepentant trainees who had disobeyed one of his orders.

"What's the CO want with you and me?" I asked Lippy as we fidgeted nervously in the waiting room outside The Whip's office.

"You got me, man. I've been keeping my fucking nose clean."

"I don't much care for The Whip, do you?"

"He's a real asshole, alright, but I guess that's his fucking job. He sure takes his saluting seriously, doesn't he? He snaps those babies off better than anyone on the whole fucking base."

When we finally got in to see The Whip, he was seated behind a big fancy desk stacked high with neatly organized piles of papers. Lippy and I stood at attention until he finally looked up, gave us the poorest excuse for a salute we had ever seen him produce, and told us to be at ease.

"Truman and Nichols, right?"

"Yes, sir," we answered in unison.

"I see you two men have signed up for OCS?"

"Yes, sir," we both said again as we glanced over at each other, relieved that we apparently weren't in any trouble.

"Well, congratulations," said The Whip. "It's a good program. It lets some of you young men get a step up on the ladder and it allows the Army to get an extra year of service out of some of its draftees. Now, what I need you both to do is...."

"Excuse me, sir," I blurted out. "What did you say about an extra year of service?"

"That's right," said The Whip, "both of your tours of duty will be extended for one year in exchange for all the special considerations offered to those attending OCS. I have all the paperwork right here in front of me. It just came through."

"Wait a minute, sir," I said. "I think there's been some kind of mistake or something. No one said anything about an extra year of service." I looked over with alarm at Lippy.

"It's news to me, Ty," said Lippy. "Really."

"Gentlemen," said The Whip, "I assure you, there has been no mistake. The reenlistment officer is required by law to disclose all the provisions of the program during his presentation, and I'm sure he did just that."

"Reenlistment officer?" said Lippy. "He didn't say he was a reenlistment officer, Ty. Honest! And he didn't say anything about another year, either—at least I don't think he did. All he said was...."

"Gentlemen," interrupted The Whip, his voice growing agitated, "I'm very busy here. I called you in to simply finalize this paperwork, and if it's alright with you, I'd like to get on with it."

"I'm sorry, sir," I said, "but there's no way I want to be in the Army for more than two years. I really don't think I should sign any more papers."

"Me neither," Lippy quickly added, but without much conviction.

"Is that so?" demanded The Whip, his face beginning to turn red.

"It's just a misunderstanding, sir," I said. "If I had known...."

"Listen, you little punks," The Whip roared, "a lot of damn time and work has gone into getting you both into OCS, and in goddamned OCS you're going to stay! Am I making myself perfectly clear?"

"He can't make us do anything, Ty."

"The hell I can't," screamed The Whip, sending papers flying as he picked up his whip and slammed it down on top of his desk.

"Please, sir," I pleaded, "I don't mean to cause any problems, I really don't, but my mind is made up. Another whole year in the Army, even as an officer, is simply out of the question."

"And is that how you feel, too, Truman?" demanded The Whip, shaking with anger.

"Well, not exactly, sir," replied Lippy, his voice barely audible. "I guess, you know, well, I could probably put in another year—to be an officer."

"Good," said The Whip. "Now that just leaves you, Nichols."

"I'm truly sorry, sir," I said, glaring at Lippy, who was looking down at his boots, "but I'm afraid my decision is final."

The Whip suddenly shot up out of his chair like an exploding volcano and shouted at me, "Listen, you ungrateful little fool, if you don't immediately sign these papers, I'll make goddamned sure your miserable butt ends up in the scariest fucking rifle platoon in all of Vietnam! Am I making myself perfectly clear?"

As I tried unsuccessfully to get my legs to stop shaking, Lippy leaned over, put his arm around my shoulder and whispered confidently, "Don't you worry, Ty. He can't do that to you."

CHAPTER 4

▼

FIRST CONTACT

I was shivering from a combination of fear and chilling rain as I cautiously trudged through the mid-morning downpour and the dense, chest-high elephant grass. The heavy, oxygen-starved air was unlike anything I had ever experienced back in the world. My lungs were on fire and my limbs ached as I tried to skirt mud-puddles and keep an eye out for the enemy at the same time. My blistered feet hadn't been helped by an extra pair of socks and the leather straps supporting my waterlogged backpack dug painfully into my shoulder blades no matter how often I reached back and tried to adjust them.

Up ahead, Sergeant Ketchum, my squad's Audie Murphy look-alike squad leader, suddenly thrust a clenched fist high into the air, mercifully bringing the whole thirty-man rifle platoon to an unexpected halt. He and Corporal Nunn, his gangly friend and radio carrier, were a good fifteen yards in front of me, walking the dangerous point position for our seven-man squad, which was the lead element for the day's search and destroy mission.

Sergeant Ketchum glanced back over his shoulder and casually motioned for me and another private, Harry Watts, to join him. Harry, who had only been in Vietnam a little over a month himself, was safely hunkered down in the underbrush and in no hurry to move up. But Sergeant Ketchum had barely uttered a word to me since I had been placed under his command, and hoping to impress him, I rushed to his side.

My prompt arrival went unnoticed as the sergeant continued to stare out intently at an ominous looking tree line some fifty yards to our front.

I watched silently as the sergeant fumbled around in a leg pocket on his faded green and black jungle fatigues and yanked out an old, battered compass. With its help, he performed a calculation or two and then entered into a muffled conversation with his friend. I could make out enough of their mumblings to know that the tree line was going to have to be approached and penetrated if we were going to stay on the course the sergeant's last azimuth had dictated.

Their conversation finally broke up and after one last studied appraisal of the dramatic change in terrain, the sergeant turned his attention to me.

"Your name is Nichols, right?" he asked, looking directly at— almost through—me.

His intense eyes scared me. "Yes, sir," I answered nervously. The words were already out of my mouth, but I made a mental note to stop calling non-commissioned officers 'sir'.

"Nichols," he demanded, "what does that look like to you?" He used the barrel of his sawed-off M16 rifle to point out an area of earth in front of his mud-caked combat boots.

I desperately wanted my first answer to a Sergeant Ketchum question to be a correct one. I took a long, hard look at the object he wanted me to identify. "Well, sir," I said, pausing to take a deep breath, "it kinda looks to me like it's a pile of shit."

Sergeant Ketchum impatiently gave me a few moments to change my mind. "Very good, Nichols," he finally said. "Now just what do you suppose a pile of shit is doing way out here in the middle of nowhere?"

I looked back down at the pile of shit. It had obviously been left by a human being and it appeared to be a pretty fresh specimen. I bent over to get an even better view, trying to buy myself a little extra thinking time.

"Nichols," said the sergeant sharply, "for Christ's sake, get your face out of that!" He grabbed me by the arm and straightened me up. "Nichols, that is gook shit, and where you find gook shit, you find gooks. Understand?"

I nodded my head so rapidly my unstrapped helmet almost fell off and Corporal Nunn made an unsuccessful attempt not to laugh.

"Knock it off, Richie," the sergeant ordered his friend. "He has to learn. You walked around with your head in your ass when you first got here, too."

"Sorry, Nichols," said Corporal Nunn.

I nodded my thanks for the unexpected apology.

Sergeant Ketchum took a final drag on the cigarette he had been cuffing in the palm of his hand, field stripped it and stuck the filter in a back pocket. After taking a quick sip from his water canteen, he returned his eyes to the tree line, staring at it and shaking his head. "You better give me the blower, Richie," he said. "I think we're getting in over our heads again."

Corporal Nunn quickly took the handset from the side of the awkward, bulky PRC-25 radio strapped to his back and passed it to Sergeant Ketchum. The sergeant looked up into the exhausted sky where Major McCalley's command helicopter was circling high overhead and pushed down hard on the talk button. "Stallion One, this is Four-Three Alpha, over." There was a pause and then he said, "Roger that, One, but we're standing in fresh gook shit down here." Another pause. "Roger, One, okay. I'll hold the platoon in place and go take a look. Roger that, out." Then he added, "Damn him!" as he tossed the handset back to Corporal Nunn.

"Proceed with caution, right?" Corporal Nunn asked anxiously.

"You got it."

"Screw him!" said the corporal, dramatically snapping his head to the side for emphasis.

"Relax, Richie."

"Damn it, Jim, there's nothing between us and those trees except open ground." He waited for a response from Sergeant Ketchum which never came and added, "A few gooks in the right place and we're in one big hurt!"

"I got eyes," barked the sergeant. "What the hell do you want me to do? If the major says go, we go. He's God, not me." He removed a soaked green towel from around his neck and wrung it out. Then he used it to wipe away some of the water which had accumulated on his face and forearms from the relentless drizzle.

Corporal Nunn eased himself down on one knee, taking a moment's rest from the added weight he was carrying on his back. "I'm getting too short for this shit," he said to Sergeant Ketchum.

"You better call Townsend," the sergeant ordered Corporal Nunn. "Make sure he's clued in and that everyone is good and spread out back there. I don't want any damn cluster-fucking."

The corporal nodded his head, quickly radioed Lieutenant Townsend, the platoon's ground combat officer, and relayed Sergeant Ketchum's message. The lieutenant didn't keep the corporal on the phone very long. It was more or less common knowledge that Sergeant Ketchum ran the show once the transport helicopters had successfully inserted the platoon into enemy territory, and although he checked in with the lieutenant from time to time, it was more out of respect for the chain of command than a need to seek out his advice and consent.

"Everyone's squared away," the corporal informed Sergeant Ketchum.

"Good," said Sergeant Ketchum as he took his rifle off the safety and checked to see if his twenty-round clip of ammunition was snugly in place. "How many frags you carrying, Richie?"

"Three."

"How about you, Nichols?"

I quickly searched my ammo belt and found two. "Just two, I think."

"Give them to Richie."

"Yes, sir," I said as I very carefully detached them from my person and even more carefully passed them over to Corporal Nunn. The thought of all that explosive power hanging from my waist had been worrying me all day long and I was glad to be rid of the darn things.

Sergeant Ketchum looked back over his shoulder and suddenly yelled, "Watts! Damn it, get your ass up here! I need your frags!"

Harry, his heavily camouflaged uniform blending in perfectly with his surroundings and his face streaked with charcoal, reluctantly left the security of his hiding place and slowly weaved his way up to our position.

"Does it really look that bad, Sarge?" Harry asked, his face full of concern.

"Just give me your frags, Watts," ordered Sergeant Ketchum. Harry quickly turned over enough hand grenades to blow up a small bridge. "At least you come prepared," the sergeant told Harry.

"I'm a walking ammo dump," said Harry with pride. "Need anything else?"

Sergeant Ketchum forced a half-smile and began stuffing the extra grenades into every available pocket. He snapped the chin strap on his helmet securely into place and looked over at me. "Nichols," he said calmly, "you and Watts wait here." He turned towards Corporal Nunn, tapped him affectionately on the shoulder and said, "Well, let's go have us a look, Richie."

Harry and I silently dropped to one knee as Sergeant Ketchum and Corporal Nunn bent forward at the waist and slowly sloshed off towards the tree line. It was only my second day in the field, and twelfth in Vietnam, but I could clearly sense the impending danger. I strained my ears for a clue to my fate and watched with concern as Sergeant Ketchum hopped up on a brush-covered mound to get a better view through all the broken branches and fresh undergrowth.

Suddenly, just as Sergeant Ketchum began to point something out to Corporal Nunn, the deafening and terrifying sound of automatic weapons fire was everywhere. Sergeant Ketchum's steel pot flew from his head as he was blown from his perch. I dove headlong into the safety of the muddy earth. How in the world could Sergeant Ketchum be dead, I asked myself. He was everything a soldier could possibly hope to be. Had they actually killed the most important man in the whole platoon?

Mud and debris started kicking up all around me. My God, I thought to myself, are they specifically shooting at me? That can't be, can it?

"Pull back, Nichols!" yelled Harry. "Pull back!"

I didn't move, not a muscle. Someone let out a horrible scream, followed by a panic filled voice yelling, "Help me! I'm hurt bad! Oh, please, somebody help me!"

Now I was really scared. I could actually feel the air just above me being displaced by bullets as I waited in terror for a piece of cold hard steel to crash into my rigid body. My heart was pounding with such force it seemed to be bouncing me off the ground. I could hear someone crying and someone else pleading for a medic. Where was Harry? I quickly glanced behind me, but he had disappeared.

Corporal Nunn was apparently still alive, because I could hear his high-pitched voice frantically screaming into his radio. I looked out towards the tiny mound and saw Sergeant Ketchum's legs moving. Suddenly hope for my salvation, not just the sergeant's, rekindled itself.

When the rapid-fire cracking sounds of the AK47's eased up for a few moments, Sergeant Ketchum leaped to his feet and started hurling hand grenades at his attackers. Then, as if rejuvenated by the momentary lull and angry that someone was actually fighting back, the frightening display of enemy firepower began again, and with even more ferocity.

Unfamiliar whistling sounds preceded a massive shaking of the ground I was clutching and my whole body vibrated as rocket propelled grenades fell from the sky. Chunks of fragmented iron, just as deadly as bullets, flew in every direction. A sharp pain exploded in my ears as each incoming round crashed to earth. The cries and screams of wounded soldiers were now coming from all directions.

I hadn't moved since I had first thrown myself to the ground. I asked myself if maybe now was the time to try and crawl back towards Lieutenant Townsend and the bulk of the platoon? Sergeant Ketchum and Corporal Nunn were only fifteen or twenty yards to my front, but they looked like they were a mile away, and their little mound of dirt couldn't possibly offer enough protection for another body. I told myself I would be dead before I reached them anyway.

There was a decaying tree stump off to my right and I thought if I could only reach it I would have something solid to hide behind. I slowly turned my head and examined the ground I would have to cover. I could never low-crawl that far without being detected, but I simply had to act. I had dumped every fight-or-flight chemical my body possessed into my churning stomach and I could no longer lie perfectly still and play dead.

I decided to make a run for it. Although I had just been told the opposite a few days earlier during an in-country training class, I easily convinced myself that a sprinting target would be more difficult to hit than a crawling one. I yanked off one of the two smoke grenades I was required to carry on my ammo belt, pulled the pin, and rolled it out in front of me. I waited motionlessly until the yellow smoke began to rush out of its canister and form a protective screen.

When everything around me was finally engulfed by yellow smoke, I forced myself to get to my feet. A single shot rang out and I immediately began running as fast as my legs would carry me. I dove headfirst and skidded to a miscalculated stop just short of the tree stump. I kicked and clawed my way the final few yards to safety.

I glanced back over my shoulder and saw the ground all around my old position being raked by enemy bullets. My heart skipped yet another beat as I realized that if I had listened to that instructor and tried to crawl out, I never would have made it.

The thick hunk of decaying wood I was huddled behind proved to be the perfect hiding place and the Vietcong seemed totally unaware of my new location. I quickly took my rifle off the safety for the first time since the platoon had been ambushed. To my horror, I discovered that on one of my two diving encounters with the wet earth, I had jammed the barrel full of mud. If I tried to fire it now, the darn thing might explode in my face.

"Who are you going to shoot at anyway?" I whispered to myself. I had yet to see a single Vietcong and I had only the vaguest idea of where they might be entrenched.

I thought I had calmed down, but when I tried to take a few deep breaths, I found it impossible to do. I was still gasping for air when I discovered it was the sweat on the palms of my hands which was making it difficult for me to grip my useless rifle, not the rain.

It wasn't long before it dawned on me that unless I wanted to spend the rest of the day and maybe all of the night alone and scared to death, I would have to pull further back. Without giving myself time to change my mind, I leaped up and sped off towards where I believed Headquarters Squad to be. I kept reminding myself to zigzag as I ran and stumbled through the high grass and muddy shell holes. I wasn't drawing any fire, but all the zigzagging was keeping me from putting as much distance between me and the Vietcong as I wanted. The hell with the zigzagging! I held my helmet tightly to my head and wildly ran as fast as I could.

A very young-looking soldier from one of the other squads impulsively stood up in the distance and waved me towards him. I clumsily adjusted my course and raced on. As I approached the wild-eyed teenager, I desperately tried to put on the brakes, but the wet, slick surface wouldn't provide the needed traction. My built-up speed carried me past him and the next thing I knew, I was tumbling down into a massive B-52 bomb crater. The nasty fall stunned me, and when I came to my senses, Harry was excitedly slapping me on the back.

"You're okay, Nichols!" he exclaimed. "Way to go, man, way to go! When you didn't move, I thought sure as hell they'd got you." He pounded me on the shoulder and then hugged me tightly.

I looked around and quickly realized half the platoon was using the crater for shelter, with lookouts posted every ten yards or so along the rim. "Ketchum and Nunn are still pinned down up there," I told Harry as I once again tried hard to catch my breath. "We've got to get them some help!"

"The lieutenant is in radio contact with Nunn," explained Harry, "and reinforcements are supposed to be on the way. Ketchum will find a way out, man. He always does."

Harry lit two cigarettes and passed one of them to me. I reached out with a trembling hand and finally managed to grasp it. I took a deep drag and noticed Harry was twitching his nose and sniffing the air around us.

"What are you doing?" I asked him.

"I hate to bring this up, man," he said as he unsuccessfully tried to wave away the air between us, "but you smell like shit!"

"What are you talking about?"

He wrinkled up his face in disgust and pointed to my chest.

I looked down and discovered I had a sizeable portion of crap caked on my filthy fatigues, just above the left pocket. I immediately wiped the revolting substance off, using a bandanna I carried in the webbing of my helmet. A dark, smelly stain remained. I realized I must have dove on top of that pile of shit Sergeant Ketchum had been lecturing me about when the firefight first broke out. I reluctantly pitched my favorite bandanna.

"It's a long story, Harry."

"I bet it is."

I slyly switched my rifle to the other hand, attempting to keep my mud-clogged weapon out of Harry's sight as he waited patiently for me to finish my cigarette and stop shaking.

"You okay now?" he finally asked.

"I think so. I guess I didn't do too good out there, did I?"

"You're alive, man. That means you did great!"

"Are there a lot of guys hurt?" I asked.

"Too many, that's for damn sure. They've radioed for blood, and that's never good."

Inside the crater, I could see four wounded soldiers, one on a stretcher, who were being attended by a single medic who didn't have enough hands to go around. I didn't really know any of the injured very well, but I knew some of their names and had seen or been in brief conversations with all of them.

I had never seen anyone as badly hurt as Donny Marx, the young soldier on the stretcher. He had been shot in the head and what facial features he had left were black and blue and distorted. His chest continued to heave irregularly up and down, but that was the only sign of life.

Suddenly, a light observation helicopter swooped down out of nowhere and made an extremely low pass over our crater. The unusual maneuver drew some sporadic enemy gunfire, but the doorgunner in the bubble-like aircraft refused to shoot back. Instead, the tiny helicopter swung around and quickly returned, this time pulling up and hovering directly above us.

Straight down it came, with the wind from its whirling blades bending vegetation to the ground and sending dust and debris flying everywhere. For a moment, I thought it had been hit and was going to crash right on top of us.

It didn't stop lowering itself until the medic could reach out his arms and touch the skids with his fingertips. Bullets ricocheted off the helicopter's exterior as a doorgunner with a huge wad of tobacco in his cheek reached down and carefully placed four plastic containers of bright-red blood in the outstretched hands of the tiptoed medic.

One of the shiny bags eluded the medic's grasp, dropped to the ground and burst. The medic tightly cradled the three remaining containers and huddled on the ground as the helicopter began its deafening, dusty ascent. With a great roar of horsepower, it slowly rose until it cleared the tree tops and reached the needed height to bend slightly forward and speed off.

The increased enemy gunfire did not let up with the departure of the helicopter and some of the crater's lookouts were wildly shooting back.

"Damn fools," said Harry. "Our guys could be out there for all they know."

I was still marveling at the helicopter aerobatics I had just witnessed, and the unbelievable courage of the pilot and his doorgunner, when the medic yelled up, "Can one of you give me a hand?"

My useless rifle made me the logical volunteer and I told Harry I would go. I quickly slid down the steep crater wall and offered to help. "I need you to take this and hold it up high," explained the medic as he handed me one of the bags of blood. "And whatever you do, don't drop it."

I held the bag high over my head and the thick red liquid immediately started to flow down a clear plastic tube into the arm of Donny Marx.

"Will he be okay?" I asked the medic, who was about to answer when a loud explosion shook the crater.

Donny's heavily bandaged head jerked violently to the side and the one eye which wasn't puffed up and distorted began blinking rapidly. Fear spread over what was left of his face and the medic, calm and collected, responded by gently stroking the side of Donny's head, like a loving mother might do to a frightened child.

"Take it easy, Donny," the medic softly told him. "Everything's alright. We're going to get you out of here. I promise." Donny's eye slowly closed and the medic hurried off to help someone else.

I completed my task in silence, making a conscious effort not to look down at what I knew was a dying young man. I felt ashamed for being so thankful that it was me holding the bag of blood, and not the other way around.

"Thanks," said the medic when he returned. "I can handle it from here."

I wanted to bend down and say something encouraging to Donny, but I couldn't find the words.

Time finally slowed back down and the heavy afternoon rains had come and gone when an excited and out of breath messenger from Lieutenant Townsend scrambled down into the crater and yelled, "Help's here! Help's here! And they've got tanks with 'em! The lieutenant wants everyone who can to follow 'em in and give 'em cover!"

Harry took me by the arm and pulled me close. "You just stay right here with me," he ordered. "We ain't going nowhere. Those damn mechanized guys are crazy. We've got ourselves a nice little view, and believe me, they won't need our help anyway."

Within minutes, four side-by-side armored personnel carriers with huge M50 machine guns blazing away smashed through the small trees and elephant grass and into the heart of the stalemated struggle.

Burly, unshaven GI's wearing torn and stained flack jackets over their shirtless chests manned the vicious weapons and seemed to know exactly what they were doing. Hardened infantry veterans walked briskly behind the mini-tanks, spraying their M-16's and tossing hand grenades. Others were busy firing their M79 grenade launchers, which produced a distinctive thump-like sound every time they pulled the trigger. Together, they almost effortlessly collapsed the enemy resistance.

The first two Vietcong I had seen since the firefight erupted jumped out of a bunker being overrun by our rescuers and began scurrying for better cover. One of the muscular machine gunners, puffing hard on a large cigar, swung his long-barreled weapon around and cut them down in an instant. He removed the cigar from his mouth and let out a bloodcurdling war hoop.

As if to add an exclamation point to the end of the battle, a fleeing Vietcong was struck in the small of his back by a grenade launched from a thump gun. The short, black-haired man, wearing only red boxer trunks and sandals, was blown bloodily in two. Unable to top such a ghastly moment, the day's struggle seemed to die with him.

Only when the battlefield had been totally secured did Harry proclaim it safe enough for him and me to leave the crater and rejoin the rest of the platoon's survivors, who were busy thanking and congratulating the timely reinforcements. We decided to go in search of Sergeant Ketchum and found him casually describing his close brush with death to a small group of infantrymen from the relief column. They were passing around his steel pot, which had a large, jagged bullet hole in the top of it.

"Do one of you guys have an extra smoke on you?" asked one of the soldiers who had apparently been right in the thick of things. His chin and forehead were bleeding from a dozen tiny shrapnel wounds.

I poked around in my damp pack of cigarettes until I found one in decent shape and offered it to him. "Thanks, man," he said.

"Thank you," I said. "If it wasn't for you guys, we'd still be pinned down."

"What the hell were you people up to, anyway?" he asked me. "You ain't going to take no bunkered gook base camp with a tiny ol' rifle platoon. Your command officer nuts or what?"

"I didn't really understand much of what happened out there today," I confessed. "I'm new."

"Well, friend, you ain't ever going to be old in an outfit like yours." He thanked me again for the cigarette, shook his head and wandered off in search of his friends.

Lieutenant Townsend yelled out that the transport helicopters were on the way and would be setting down as soon as the medevacs finished picking up the platoon's dead and wounded. Everyone more or less ignored him and continued to linger about in small groups, rehashing the battle, much like ringside spectators do after a hard-fought prize fight. Those who had some precious water left generously passed around their canteens and others volunteered to help man the stretchers being loaded into the dustoff helicopters.

There was no joy or elation at having finally routed the enemy, nor was there any grief or concern for the eight or nine dead Vietnamese bodies which littered the battlefield. They were unceremoniously searched for valuables and documents and left to the elements for burial.

"Saddle up, men!" ordered Lieutenant Townsend. "Let's get to the pickup zone before it gets any darker."

I looked down at my field watch and realized there was less than thirty minutes of daylight left. It seemed impossible that the hours could have passed so quickly.

Everyone slowly resumed the military roles they had been assigned at the outset of the mission. Sergeant Ketchum reorganized our squad and took the point for the short march to the PZ. Lieutenant Townsend and his Headquarters Squad fell in behind us, and Sergeant Snow and Sergeant Hughes set up their squads to patrol the platoon's flanks.

The clearing Sergeant Ketchum led us to was a spacious one, created months earlier by Army bulldozers that had worked in vain to destroy a jungle which was already showing signs of vigorous new growth. As a hunter-killer helicopter team circled protectively above the platoon, I wondered how many other bloody battles had already been fought in the very same area.

"The ships will be here any minute," explained Lieutenant Townsend once he had managed to gather everyone around him. "No use setting up a perimeter, but keep your eyes open just in case. You did a fine job today, men. The major radioed down that he's extremely pleased with the mission and that he'll have a tub of ice-cold beer waiting for us in the dayroom when we get back to base."

"What's the final count?" interrupted Sergeant Ketchum. There was a lengthy pause as the first real quiet of the day filled the damp air.

"I'm afraid the medic on the dustoff said Marx was dead when they loaded him," said Lieutenant Townsend, "so we had two KIA's. We lost Robinson early, and there's four WIA's, but only one is serious and they're all expected to pull through. The relief column took quite a few casualties getting to us, but I don't have any numbers on them. Everything considered, though, I think we can count ourselves very lucky. It could have been a lot worse."

As Sergeant Ketchum turned and walked away, I heard him tell Corporal Nunn, "Fuck the pep talk."

When the transport helicopters became visible in the rapidly darkening sky, the lieutenant tossed out a yellow smoke grenade, marking the platoon's position. Four Hueys quickly descended in an orderly fashion, landing single file, and the pilot responsible for our squad lifted off the moment all seven of us were safely aboard.

The noisy aircraft made it almost impossible for anyone to verbally communicate once we were off the ground. An exhausted Harry smiled weakly, gave me the thumbs-up sign and closed his eyes. He was almost immediately asleep.

We weren't in the air more than fifteen minutes when we were blanketed by the black, starless night sky. My drenched fatigues made the wind rushing through the open-door helicopter feel all the more cold and biting. My limbs were shaking and my teeth were chattering.

I rested my elbows on my knees and buried my head into my hands. I had never felt so totally alone in all my life. I didn't see how I could possibly survive another three hundred and fifty-some days like the one I had just barely lived through. If I hadn't actually frozen in the face of the enemy, I had sure as hell been scared to death by him. I had managed to go through a day-long life and death struggle without firing a single shot. I had jammed my weapon, run wildly through kill zones, and dove into a pile of shit. My very worst suspicions about myself had been confirmed.

The dim lights of our base were a welcome sight as they became faintly visible from inside Alpha Squad's approaching helicopter. My spirits rose slightly with the knowledge that we were almost safely home.

Total darkness enshrouded the tiny airstrip as our helicopter touched gently down on the appropriate asphalt pad. I nudged Harry awake and my tired legs almost gave way as I climbed wearily out of the noisy aircraft. I was completely exhausted, my mind a blank.

"Ty, look out!" screamed Harry.

Someone jumped me from behind and tightly wrapped both his arms around my chest, abruptly halting my forward motion. I looked back and realized it wasn't Harry. It was one of the helicopter's two doorgunners. "What are you doing?" I demanded.

"You stupid idiot!" screamed the angry doorgunner into my ear. "You never walk behind a helicopter! Another step and you would have walked right through the rear blade!" He pointed out the whirling piece of steel right in front of me.

Harry ran up and convinced the doorgunner to release me into his custody. I stood stunned and disbelieving at the frightening sight as the doorgunner's words finally registered in my sluggish brain. "He damn near killed himself!" the doorgunner yelled at Harry.

Harry took me by the arm and roughly escorted me around to the front of the helicopter and gave me a forceful shove in the direction of our hootch. I shuffled along in silence until Harry finally caught up with me.

"Sorry for pushing you around, man," Harry apologized, "but I swear, you've been trying to get yourself killed all day long, and after awhile, it starts getting on a person's nerves." He put his arm around my shoulder as we walked slowly on through the sticky darkness, the smells of the day's fighting and dying still locked inside my nostrils.

You'll never make it, I thought to myself. You're simply not cut out to be a soldier. There's no way in the world you can live through a whole year of this madness.

"You're going to be just fine, Ty," said Harry, reading my bewildered mind as he would often do in the days and months to come. "Believe it or else, it gets easier. You wait and see. There's ways to survive over here, and if Charlie doesn't get you early in your tour, all the odds turn in your favor."

As Harry went on and on about how twenty or thirty of the enemy were dying for every single American, and how poorly trained and armed the Vietcong actually were, I silently asked God not to let me die half-a-world away from home. And if crying would have helped, I would have done that, too.

CHAPTER 5

▼

THE MASSAGE PARLOR

I took a deep breath, reluctantly returned Harry's lecherous half-smile and helped him push open the heavy glass door of the base massage parlor. Once inside, Harry whirled around and conveniently used the door as a mirror and examined his lean and handsome profile in great detail. He ran a comb through his curly blond hair and stared at length at the reflected image of his face, obviously much impressed with what he saw. Finally satisfied with his appearance, he nodded for me to follow him up to the front desk where we were warmly greeted by a smiling, middle-aged Vietnamese man wearing a multi-colored Hawaiian sports shirt, shiny black slacks and an ancient pair of Ho Chi Minh sandals. He issued us each a numbered card and politely motioned for us to take a seat in the waiting room.

"I thought you said the Army ran this place," I whispered to Harry as we made our way over to the deserted waiting area and sat down.

"It does, Ty," Harry assured me. "The gooks only work here. It's good ol' Uncle Sam himself who makes sure everything's on the up and up. They inspect the joint all the time, keep prices reasonable, pass out the birth control pills, you name it, man. They even have medics come over and check out the girls every week so none of us war heroes go home with elephantiasis."

"Elephantiasis?" I asked with alarm. "What the heck is elephantiasis?"

"Elephant balls, stupid. If you get that, rumor has it that they put you on the good ship Hope and you never get to go home. You just float around and around the world until you die."

"Don't even joke about that, Harry."

The tiny man at the desk put aside his Vietnamese newspaper long enough to call out Harry's number. "Hey," I blurted out, grabbing Harry's arm as he attempted to stand up, "I don't even know how much this is going to cost."

"Would you relax, man? The bath is only ten piasters, but everything else is extra, a lot extra. Just make sure you leave here with at least twenty-five piasters. You'll need that to get into the poker game tonight." I nodded that I understood, even though it was the first time I had heard anything about a poker game.

Harry rushed off and as soon as he was out of sight, I hastily fumbled through my wallet to check on my financial situation. I had colorful military scrip, not Vietnamese piasters. If they were equal in value, and I had no idea if they were or weren't, then I had exactly forty-one piasters on me.

I was wondering what kind of extra I might be offered for six measly piasters when my number was called out. I bravely stood up and walked nervously over to the front desk. I handed the little man ten dollars worth of military scrip and waited patiently while it was carefully counted.

"Take room numbah twelve," he finally said. "Down hall, on left."

Still not certain what I was getting myself into, I shuffled slowly down the hall until I came to door number twelve. I paused for a moment, took a deep breath and knocked gently on the door. Getting no response, I cautiously let myself in, peeking my head around the corner first.

Absolutely everything in the room was white; the color of the walls, the four foot high box-like steam bath, the rubdown table, and even all the washcloths and towels which were neatly stacked in a doorless cabinet below a large handwritten sign which read, 'Maximum Length of Bath One Hour'.

There were no chairs in the room, so I hopped up on the rubdown table and sat down, dangling and kicking my legs apprehensively. I was eager to bury myself under the inviting shower and I quickly gave up waiting for someone to come in and give me instructions on how to use the steam bath. I undressed, turned on the shower as hot and heavy as I could stand it and covered my head with a blob of shampoo.

I was vigorously scrubbing away when a very sweet young girl's voice called out, "I be right there."

In my panic and haste to identify the speaker, I foolishly opened my eyes and filled them with stinging soap. There was no shower curtain to hide behind and I blindly waved around for the towel I had hung on a nearby hook. Unable to locate it, I frantically attempted to rub the painful shampoo from my eyes. Then, with absolutely no warning, two very warm and soft hands started to lather up my back and buttocks.

"I get you clean," said the cheerful voice, "then I put you in steam bath."

"That's alright," I pleaded, "I can do it, really."

"It my job," she replied indignantly. "I like do it."

She very thoroughly lathered up my neck and arms. Then she squatted down and did my legs, feet and finally, my groin. "See," she said, "I do numbah one job."

"Please," I said, "I can do all this."

"You like it, I can tell," she said as she grabbed my now erect penis and giggled. "And you nice looking," she added playfully. "Black hair and little butt my favorite. I think I like you."

"Thank you," I mumbled, the shampoo now in my mouth.

Even though I was twenty-one years old, I was still almost as new to girls as I was to Vietnam, and being complimented and fondled by a girl I had yet to even see was very disconcerting. Before my bloodshot eyes had cleared enough for me to get a really good look at her, she had me rinsed off and squeaky clean.

She took me by the hand and led me to a wooden stool in the steam bath. She was the tallest Vietnamese girl I had seen, with a long, pretty face and a smile which appeared to be a permanent fixture. Her bright red shorts and blouse clung tightly to her thin body and her long black hair draped down, brushing her back.

"I be right back, ten minute," she informed me while snugly wrapping a couple of towels around my neck to prevent any of the uncomfortably hot steam I was cooking in from leaking out the circular head hole. "I come back and give you numbah one rub! You see."

She scampered out the door and I patiently suffered through my first horrible experience of being trapped inside a steam bath. What in the world are you doing in this thing, I asked myself. I envisioned a Vietcong sympathizer rushing into the room with a loaded rifle and blowing me away. I could just see the headlines in my little hometown newspaper: "Private Ty Nichols—killed in his first month in Vietnam while soliciting sex."

Mercifully, the pretty Vietnamese girl returned exactly when she said she would. "You want stay in longer?" she asked, more cheerful than ever.

"Oh, no!" I exclaimed. "No thank you. I've had more than enough."

She opened the escape hatch and asked me to climb up on the rubdown table. I quickly hopped up and stretched out on my stomach. She reached down under the table and dragged out a cardboard box full of assorted oils, creams and powders. She generously applied what smelled like ordinary baby oil all over my back, arms and legs.

"What's your name?" I asked her as she gently ran both her hands up and down the inside of my thighs.

"Tan is my name. What your name?"

"Ty," I finally answered, having to think about it for a few moments.

Her slim frame didn't seem capable of producing the great strength I could feel in her hands as she rubbed and pounded me into relaxation. She seemed in no particular hurry, humming happily to herself as she worked.

I was almost asleep when I heard her seductively ask me to roll over. I timidly did as she said and the thought of being exposed in front of her quickly sent my up-and-down erection back up again.

"You like make love with me?" she asked softly, almost romantically. She smiled and ever so gently stroked my penis. "It sure look like you all ready."

"I'm sorry," I managed to say, "for me that is, but I don't think I have enough money."

"You not need much," she assured me. "Twenty piaster, that all."

"But I'm afraid I don't have twenty piasters. I mean, I don't have twenty piasters I can spare."

"How bout numbah one blow job?" she calmly suggested. "I do that only ten piaster. I do it good, too!"

"Oh, I'm sure you do, but I don't even have ten extra piasters. You see, my friend and me are going to be in this big poker game tonight, and I'm afraid I'll need most of my money for that."

"How much money can you pay?" she asked, slightly disappointed but still smiling.

"To tell you the truth," I said apologetically, "I think I've only got about five or six piasters I can spare."

"That okay, no sweat," she said happily. "I give you numbah one hand job! That only cost you five piaster."

Assuming I was in complete agreement with her resolution of the problem, she immediately began pouring a heavy cream all over my penis. "This feel great," she assured me. "You wait and see."

She confidently squeezed all the blood up into the growing head of my penis and then slowly stroked it three or four times. She generously repeated the whole procedure over and over again and each time it was a little more pleasurable than the last. "I think it time," she announced proudly, reaching for a towel. "It fun for me, too," she added as she watched me climax.

"Thank you," I said after I had taken a few deep breaths and wiggled my toes in an effort to get my tense leg muscles to relax.

"You come see me again soon," she said sincerely. "Please bring more money, okay, and we have much better fun. I promise!"

"You're very nice," I said as I sat up on the table and returned her warm smile. She blushed.

"Bye-bye now. You numbah one GI. Thank you for coming here."

After Tan had turned and energetically strutted out of the room, I took my time putting my clothes back on, amazed and a little alarmed about feeling so good all over. No wonder these places are so darn popular, I thought to myself as I finished lacing up my boots.

I found Harry sitting out in the lobby, waiting impatiently.

"So, come on, man, tell me, how was it?" he demanded as we exited the massage parlor.

I didn't really know how to answer him.

"Hell," he said, "I can tell from that shit-eating grin on your face that you knocked off a little. Did you at least save enough money to get into the poker game tonight?"

"Oh, sure. No problem."

"Good," he said. Then he smiled, put his arm around my shoulder, and added, "There's nothing like a nooner, is there? And it sure as hell beats jackin' off, now don't it?"

JOURNAL ENTRY

337 DAYS TO GO

There are any number of things we all hate to do over here, but being a member of the dreaded shit-burning detail once a week is probably right at the top of most everyone's list.

We share our end of the base with all kinds of support personnel, along with most of the helicopter pilots, their doorgunners and their maintenance people. We're talking at least a hundred people, and they all have to piss and take a crap from time to time.

We only have one field latrine and the stench from its constant use makes some of the putrid rice paddy water we're always wading around in smell like high-priced, state-side perfume. Even worse than that, though, are the two foul-smelling, six-seat base outhouses which everyone has to use when they take a dump. They get more than their fair share of use, too, and by the end of each long day, the dozen metal drums which collect all the urine, excrement and used toilet paper are full, if not overflowing.

Each morning, at the crack of dawn, those heavy, gag-inducing drums have to be yanked and pulled out from the back of each outhouse and unceremoniously dragged a good half-mile or so to a huge trench out by the perimeter which is used for nothing else but burning shit.

Once there, exhausted and out of breath, the designated shit-burners have to shove the drums a final twenty yards or so up to the edge of the crater rim and then very carefully empty their contents into the trench. The last thing a shit-burner wants to happen is to lose control of his drum, have it tumble down one of the steep embankments and then be forced to wade into the muck after it.

This extremely unpleasant duty is rotated between every soldier with a rank of E4 and below and everyone absolutely hates it. The only upside is that on the days you're assigned to be a shit-burner, Sergeant Ketchum doesn't put you on the manifest, so you don't have to go out in the field that morning.

The trick to being a good shit-burner is to get the heavy containers all the way to the trench with most of the crap and piss still inside the drum, and not all over your hands, fatigues and boots. Depending on the volume of urine in each drum, and the expertise of one's dragging partner (some guys consistently create huge waves which slosh all over the place), the slow, miserable trip to the shit-burning trench can be one of the most disgusting experiences imaginable.

You also have to be very careful where you stand after you light the trench on fire, and on a day when the winds are a little tricky, you can end up returning to your hootch smelling worse than the drums.

A few days ago, one of our new sergeants, a guy named Ted Henson, whom I like very much, forever changed all of the above.

Ted is from the East Coast and he's a graduate of one of their big universities—Penn State, I think. He's in his late-twenties and although he tries real hard not to flaunt it, he's much brighter than any of us. He's also married, already has two kids, and he's the first person I've met in Vietnam who is willing to face up to the fact that he's a coward.

"I don't mind admitting it at all," he told me last weekend. "I get so sick to my stomach every time we head out on a mission that I throw up. And my heart never stops pounding, and I mean really pounding, until we're safely back to base."

"I think we all feel like that," I assured him.

"But not like me," he explained with sincerity. "I've been absolutely terrified every single minute of every single day I've been here, and I've decided to get off my ass and do something about it."

"What?" I asked him.

"Tell me what you honestly think about this idea I've got, okay?"

"Sure," I said.

"Everyone hates being on shit-burning duty, right?"

"Absolutely."

"And it takes two men out of the field every day, right?"

"Right."

"And half the time, the job doesn't even get done correctly. Some of the guys turn it into a full day's work just so they can miss the afternoon manifest, some don't completely empty all the containers and really clean them out good, and some can't even keep the fire going until everything's totally burned."

"Yeah," I said, "I've heard the first sergeant complain about all that stuff plenty of times."

"Well," said Ted with genuine enthusiasm, "I've put together a well-written, logically thought out proposal which addresses each of those issues and more, and I'm going to give it to Top and ask him if I can be permanently assigned as the platoon's shit-burner."

"You're kidding?" I asked him in amazement. "You want to burn shit every single day for the rest of your tour?"

"Sure, why not? I'll hire a couple of Vietnamese helpers with my own money and really start burning shit properly around here."

"You're serious, aren't you?"

"You're damn right I'm serious. It's a seven-day-a-week job, I'll organize it better than they ever dreamed possible, and I won't have to go out in the field anymore."

"You really think Top will go for it?"

"He'd be crazy if he didn't."

The next day, after Ted had talked at length with our platoon's first ser-geant about his revolutionary shit-burning scheme, he stopped by my hootch to celebrate his new military occupation.

"He loved the idea!" Ted informed me, so excited someone would have thought he was about to depart on his R & R.

"So," I said, "you're really going to burn shit for the next eleven months?"

"Damn right. Top's going to talk to the major tomorrow, but he said as far as he was concerned, it's a done deal."

"And he didn't try to make you feel like dirt or anything?" I asked him.

"Of course he did, but I was expecting that. He said everyone in the pla-toon knows I'm a chicken-shit and that sooner or later I was going to fuck up out in the field and get someone killed anyway, and hell, he's probably right."

"You know, Ted," I warned him, "I wouldn't be surprised if you get quite a bit of ribbing from the rest of the guys, too."

"I know that," said Ted. "In fact, when I told Sergeant Ketchum I was planning on doing this, the first words out of his mouth were, 'And just what are you planning on telling your kids when they ask you, what did you do in the war, Daddy?'"

"And what'd you tell him?" I asked with interest.

"I just told him that at least I'll be there to tell them something."

CHAPTER 6

▼

WALKING POINT

I flipped on the ancient lamp which illuminated my depressing little room and shuffled over to my unmade bunk. The notebook and pencil I had left on my pillow earlier that morning were still there, demanding my attention. Completely exhausted from the day's search and destroy mission, I plopped down on the foot of the bed, unlaced my combat boots and kicked them off. I let myself fall backwards on my bunk and then slowly rolled over onto my stomach. I had never been so bone weary in my whole life.

The platoon had covered a lot of ground and the relentless heat and suffocating humidity had been almost unbearable, but for a change, there had been no contact with the enemy, and I was grateful for that.

I propped myself up on my elbows, flipped open the notebook and stared down at the blank page. I had been in Vietnam for three weeks, but with the exception of one completed entry, I had barely touched my journal. I still hadn't written my parents or Amy a decent letter, either, although I had tried. I just didn't want to upset anybody, especially my mother. How could I possibly tell her that objectively judging from what I had already experienced, I was almost certain I'd never get out of Vietnam in one piece? Alive just maybe, but not in one piece.

"Got a minute?" asked a familiar voice. Startled, I swung around to identify the speaker and Sergeant Ketchum was standing in the doorway.

"Oh, sure, Sergeant Ketchum. Come on in."

The sergeant spread apart the colored strings of beads which served as my door and stepped inside. It suddenly dawned on me just how short Sergeant Ketchum was. I didn't know why I hadn't really noticed it before, but he was only about five-foot-seven or eight, if that. His lack of height, barrel chest and thick, granite-like limbs only enhanced his indestructible appearance.

There were no chairs, so I sat up and smoothed out a place for the sergeant on my bunk. He nodded his thanks, sat down and offered me a cigarette. I shook my head 'no'. He looked even more tired than I felt, and his sunken eyes and hollow face made him appear much older than his twenty-three years.

"Pretty long day, wasn't it?" asked Sergeant Ketchum.

"It sure was."

"Well, at least we didn't get hit." He yawned and before I knew it, I was doing likewise. "What's your first name, Nichols?"

"Ty."

"Where you from, Ty?"

"California."

"Is that right?" he said indifferently. He took another couple of hits on his cigarette and decided to come to the point. "Ty, I'm going to put you down as our pointman on tomorrow's manifest." I made an unsuccessful attempt to act like the news was no big deal. "Sorry," he continued, "but the newest man always walks the point. It's only fair. I've let you off the hook long enough. I can't trust the clown I've got up there now—he's a pothead—so you're it."

"I understand," I lied.

"Good. Now there's a few rules. They're real simple." He placed another cigarette in his mouth and used the one he'd almost finished to light it. "No booze or drugs, not even grass. I can't afford to have you wandering all over the damn place. We're the platoon's point squad. You've got to have a clear head. Lives depend on it. My life depends on it. And always keep eye-to-eye contact with me. If you can't look back and see me, then you're doing something wrong. If you run across anything that looks suspicious, get my attention and I'll come up and take a look."

"Okay," I finally said, sensing he wanted me to say something.

"And stay alert for booby traps, too. They're usually clearly marked because Charlie doesn't want his own people tripping over one. If you see anything that doesn't belong, like knots in a vine, or a pile of rocks on the side of a trail, pull up until I can check it out. Any questions?"

"No," I lied again.

"Good, but if any pop into your head, let me know." He stood up to leave and I shot up, too. "Relax," he said, softening his deep voice. "It's not as bad as I'm probably making it sound. You'll catch on real quick. Just do the best job you can." He walked bowlegged slowly to the doorway, spread open the strings of beads and looked back at me. "Most of the guys who get hurt over here do it to themselves, and it usually happens in the first few months they're here. Take your job seriously. That's all I ask. And one more thing. I know you're getting pretty tight with Harry Watts. Well, I guess he's a nice enough fellow, but when push comes to shove, he may be a little hard to find—especially with all that camouflage shit he wears. Pick your friends carefully, Nichols. All we've got over here is each other."

"Pointman?" I muttered to myself as the sergeant exited the room. "My God, what next?"

The new morning dawned just as hot and muggy as the day before and the terrain our platoon found itself in was lush and full of dense, double-canopy jungle. Although visibility between squads was really bad, my first couple of hours as a pointman were wonderfully uneventful. Then my luck abruptly changed.

I stopped dead in my tracks and frantically waved for Sergeant Ketchum to join me. The sergeant moved cautiously up to my position, with Corporal Nunn, his loyal RTO, at his side.

"Look at this," I said, grimacing. I pointed down at the bloody remains of a dead Vietcong spread out at my feet. It looked like he had been hit by a rocket from a cobra gunship and quite a few of his body parts were missing. Judging from the stench and discoloration of his torso, he'd also been dead for quite some time. The skin on his young face was drawn tight to his skull, and it was easy to imagine how he was going to look decades later in his lonely grave.

"Nice job, Nichols," said Sergeant Ketchum. "Now search him."

After hesitating for as long as I could, I reached down and rummaged through all the blood-caked pockets on the clothing of the mangled body while Sergeant Ketchum and Corporal Nunn cast their eyes towards the next objective. All I found was a plastic bag filled with some rock-hard rice and a fist full of dirt-stained black and white photographs of individuals I assumed were members of the dead man's family. Sergeant Ketchum wasn't very impressed.

"Okay, Nichols, it looks like there's another dead VC in that little clearing ahead, and one of our scout helicopters is going to try and mark it for you with a red smoke. Be careful, we're getting close. Look for kill zones, dark, shadowy areas, like caves in the middle of nowhere. Charlie likes to clear himself a field of fire and dig in at the other end of it. Be really alert. Look for those kill zones!"

I nodded my head and tried hard to act like the sergeant's words hadn't scared me, but I felt like a frightened mouse being told to go sniff the cheese in a trap.

"This gook's got no gun, no ammo, and not enough food for even one day," said Corporal Nunn to Sergeant Ketchum. "We're being set up."

"Don't you think I know that?" snapped Sergeant Ketchum. "And so does the major. Look at all this air power he's got out here. He's dying for us to make contact. And if this jungle keeps thinning out, we just might end up doing some real damage for a change."

"Sergeant Ketchum," I reluctantly interrupted, "should I keep off the trail?"

"Of course you stay off the damn trail, Nichols! And if you make contact, break it as soon as you can and get the hell back. We're just here to find Charlie. The gunships can blow him away."

Just to our front, a light observation helicopter swooped down and a doorgunner tossed a smoke grenade on top of my next objective. I waited patiently for the red smoke to crawl skyward, swallowed hard and forced myself to move forward. As I put my ears on high alert, all I could hear was my feet squishing around in my soggy boots, which were drenched from the thick and wet knee-deep grass I had been wading around in all morning. Stop thinking about your darn feet and concentrate on your job, I lectured myself under my breath.

It wasn't long before I had the next disfigured body in sight, but it was lying right in the middle of the snaking trail Sergeant Ketchum had told me to avoid. I slowed my pace and strained my eyes for any sight of the enemy. Seeing nothing, I waved for Sergeant Ketchum and dropped to one knee. When he and the corporal arrived they knelt down next to me as I silently pointed out the dead Vietcong.

"Okay," whispered Sergeant Ketchum, "good, now let's see if we can draw some fire." Now why in the world are we going to do that, I wanted to scream at him, but I didn't. "Nichols, I'm going to set up a cross fire, so you'll have to move across to the other side. Be careful and stay close to good cover. Wave to me when you're ready."

I had only the vaguest idea of what the sergeant was talking about, but Corporal Nunn pointed to where I should go and once again, I forced myself to stand up. My heart began to race before I had taken a single step, but somehow I managed to hustle all the way across the clearing without incident.

I proudly waved that I was in position and Sergeant Ketchum raised his hand high into the air and then dramatically dropped it. Just as he had hoped, when he and Corporal Nunn opened fire on the suspected enemy position, it was immediately returned.

I quickly ducked and turned my head, only to be startled by the terrifying sight of a razor-thin Vietcong sniper halfway up a tree above and behind me. Nobody had said a damn thing about snipers.

For reasons completely unknown to me, the sniper didn't seem to be the least bit interested in me, but he had spotted Sergeant Ketchum and Corporal Nunn and he began raking their position with gunfire. One of the very first shots struck the corporal in the back and he cried out as he fell forward and hit the ground. I could see Sergeant Ketchum was confused about where the gunfire was coming from and that he was looking in all the wrong places.

Much to my amazement, I almost instinctively took my rifle off the safety and began shooting at the Vietcong. My fire wasn't very accurate, but it told Sergeant Ketchum what he needed to know and it only took him a few seconds to whirl around and empty a whole clip into the perch the VC was using for cover. Within moments, the lifeless enemy soldier dropped to the floor of the jungle with a loud thud. "Get over here!" Sergeant Ketchum yelled at me. "Now!"

Don't think, just do what the man says, I told myself as I leaped up and charged head down back across the clearing.

"Give me a hand," said the sergeant as he struggled to get a good enough grip on Corporal Nunn to lift him off the ground.

"Take it easy you guys!" said the corporal through clenched teeth as we gathered him up and hastily carried him to the rear, nearly dropping him twice.

Once we were safely away from the gunship bombardment which had just begun, Sergeant Ketchum and I carefully placed the corporal on the ground and Sergeant Ketchum began yelling, "Medic! Medic!"

"It hurts like hell," moaned Corporal Nunn as Sergeant Ketchum gently rolled his friend on his side to examine the wound.

"I think you're going home, Richie," said the sergeant.

"Alive?" asked the frightened corporal.

"It's not that bad, Richie," he assured him. "I think your radio took some of the impact."

"It's really not bad at all," I suddenly felt the need to say. "Honest to God!"

The sergeant glanced over at me and smiled. "By the way," he said, "just where in the hell did you learn how to shoot a gun?"

"Sorry about that," I said, not sure if I should return the sergeant's smile.

Lieutenant Townsend, his RTO and one of the platoon's medics made their way over to Corporal Nunn just as another Cobra helicopter swooped past on its way to make a rocket run.

"How is he?" Lieutenant Townsend asked the medic after he had examined the wound for a few seconds.

"No sweat," the medic said, much to everyone's relief. "Some surgery and he'll be fine."

"Good," said the lieutenant. "There's a dustoff on the way and it should be setting down any minute. Sergeant Ketchum, why don't you hold your people in reserve during the mop up. Go ahead and take care of your RTO. I know you two are pretty close."

"Thanks, sir. I really appreciate that."

Sergeant Ketchum got the medic to get him a stretcher and asked me to help him carry Corporal Nunn to an already waiting dustoff. On the way there, I could still hear some scattered small weapons fire, but it sounded like the hunter-killer teams had pretty much wrapped up the mission.

With the help of the doorgunner, Sergeant Ketchum and I carefully loaded Corporal Nunn onto the dustoff. Once we had him secured inside the aircraft, Sergeant Ketchum yelled at one of the pilots, "Okay, get him out of here!"

"Sorry, Sarge," the pilot yelled back. "We've got another one on the way."

Sergeant Ketchum nodded that he understood and used the extra time to bend down next to Corporal Nunn and whisper something which made the corporal smile. He shook his friend's hand one last time and reluctantly backed away from the helicopter.

"Take care of yourself, Richie," he hollered, using his cupped hands as a megaphone. Corporal Nunn nodded and gave Sergeant Ketchum the thumbs-up sign.

More gunfire erupted off in the distance and I could tell by the expression on Sergeant Ketchum's face that he felt he should be getting back to the rest of the platoon. "Come on, Nichols," he said as he waved goodbye one final time to Corporal Nunn and motioned for me to follow him, "we're not needed here anymore."

We had only gone a few yards when he turned to me and said, "You're a pretty shitty pointman, so as soon as we get a new guy in, you'll be carrying my radio."

"Be your RTO?" I asked, stunned.

"That's right." He stopped for a moment to light a cigarette, lit two instead, and passed one to me. "I'll drop by your hootch sometime this week and let you know what you're getting yourself into."

"Okay."

"You look a little worried."

"Actually" I said, "I think I'll like it."

"Why's that?" he asked with interest.

I paused for a moment and then decided to tell the sergeant the truth. "Because I kind of feel safer when I'm with you."

JOURNAL ENTRY
324 DAYS TO GO

It doesn't take too many twice-daily search and destroy missions to understand how Major McCalley is using our thirty-man light infantry platoon. Put simply, we're the bait.

We're organized, though, as part of a troop, along with a platoon each of Cobra gunships, OH-6 light observation helicopters and Huey transport helicopters. The large American military compound we work out of is also crawling with pilots, mechanics, doorgunners, cooks, clerks, supply people, chaplains, and all the other support personnel necessary to make sure we're healthy and happy bait.

Our base is near a pretty large Vietnamese village, and it's the kind of place most infantrymen in Vietnam would kill to call home. It's about fifty or so miles north of Saigon, but close enough to some of American's largest military bases to be considered relatively safe except for an occasional evening rocket attack.

"Ain't nobody ever going to overrun this place," Harry told me the other day when we were sitting out in front of our hootch writing letters.

"How can you be so sure?" I asked him.

"Look around," he said, "and tell me what you see."

I gazed out at the airstrip and tarmac which consume much of the view from our front door and said, "Helicopters, lots and lots of helicopters."

"Exactly," said Harry. "Now me and you they don't particularly give a shit about. But all those helicopters out there are a different story. They cost millions and millions of bucks, and Uncle Sam don't leave them lying around just anywhere."

Our base certainly is different from the tiny and difficult to defend fire-bases which most infantrymen in Vietnam call home. It has its own out-door movie theater, a regulation basketball court, an Olympic-size swimming pool, a newly constructed chapel capable of serving all denomi-nations, a fancy Officer's Club, an always-hopping NCO Club with live music once a month, a well-stocked PX, sturdy hootches with concrete floors and electrical outlets, and of course, access to plenty of prostitutes. It is truly a great place to be stationed, unless, of course, you're the bait being used to kill as many enemy soldiers as humanly possible.

The way it works is that every morning, at the crack of dawn, at least two scout helicopters fly off towards the troop's area of operation in search of Charlie. When they are accompanied by the same number of Cobra gun-ships, they split off into pairs and became hunter-killer teams. If the pilot of a scout helicopter or his doorgunner spots one or more Vietcong in the open, then the pilot maneuvers his aircraft in such a way as to give his doorgun-ner a shot at blowing them away with his machine gun. If the Vietcong run back into the woods or a bunker, then the aircraft commander in the back seat of the Cobra is asked by the pilot of the Loach to swoop down and destroy the enemy position with an aerial rocket attack. If the Vietcong under fire fight back or appear to be part of a larger unit, or if the area looks suspiciously like it might be a base camp for migrating NVA, or even if there are just some bodies that need counting and searching, then contact is broken off and the infantry platoon—my platoon—is called in to find out exactly what is happening on the ground.

The rifle platoon I belong to consists of thirty men, broken down into four squads of seven, with Headquarters Squad getting the two extra guys, who are medics. Each squad has its own squad leader, RTO, pointman,

Kit Carson Scout, thump gunner, machine gunner, and rifleman/M60 ammo carrier.

When we are on the ground, we work out of a diamond formation, with Alpha Squad, which is my squad, taking the point. Bravo and Charlie Squads are on the flanks, and Headquarters Squad is in the center/rear.

Once the enemy has been located, scout pilots call back to base and brief Major McCalley on their findings. If it looks like a promising opportunity, the major immediately notifies operations and has the rifle platoon scrambled.

Like the rest of the guys, I spend every morning and afternoon, seven days a week, confined to my hootch, anxiously waiting for the scramble siren to go off. The moment its unnerving wail floods my room, I quickly put aside the letters I'm writing or the book I'm reading and reluctantly leap into action.

Standard operating procedure requires that I be fully decked out in all my combat gear and out on the tarmac awaiting the slicks (our transport helicopters) within five minutes of hearing the siren. It only took me a few days to learn to hate the explosion of adrenalin which always seems to accompany the blaring of the siren, and as I scramble out to the tarmac like a crazed World War Two pilot during the Battle of Britain, I always pray for some honorable way to get out of the whole terrifying mess.

When we get into our squad's slick, no one ever really knows what kind of mission we're being asked to undertake, or if we're going to be flying into a hot or cold LZ. It is useless to try and talk and exchange rumored destinations over the deafening sounds created by the helicopter's roaring engine and whirling blades, so everyone just sits in nervous silence and tries hard to act like they're not too scared.

Once on station, we begin to better understand what the day will probably hold for us. If the terrain we circle high above has been liberally sprinkled with red smoke grenades, which identify suspected enemy positions, then our hearts drop into our stomachs and we begin mentally preparing for the worst.

The slicks usually drop the platoon off about a klick—which is a little more than half-a-mile—from the nearest smoke grenade, and since it is in the best interest of the pilots and their aircraft to find a safe and secure landing zone, hot LZ's thankfully seem to be the exception, and not the rule.

When a relatively safe LZ has been identified and marked with a yellow smoke grenade dropped by a doorgunner from one of the observation helicopters, the slicks swoop down and hover a few feet off the ground. Everyone tries to disembark one at a time on each side so they won't screw up the weight distribution and make it harder for the pilot to keep his aircraft stable. The moment everyone is safely on the ground, the Hueys lift off and race back into the security of the sky.

Lieutenant Townsend and Sergeant Ketchum are really good at quickly getting all the squads organized and away from the poor cover found in most LZ's. Within minutes, they have everyone properly spread out and stepping off towards our first objective.

As Major McCalley circles high above the ground in his command helicopter, and with hunter-killer teams at the ready should the platoon get in over its head, everyone walks straight toward the suspected enemy positions.

One of two things always seems to happen. Either Charlie has mysteriously disappeared back into the jungle and the objective turns out to be a waste of everyone's time and energy with most of the platoon getting scared to death for nothing, or we get ambushed and all hell breaks loose.

The Vietcong in our area of operation seem to know how we go about our business even better than we do. They know the platoon is going to walk straight towards the red smoke, and if there are enough of them, and if they're feeling brave and have pretty good cover, they just set up an ambush and wait for us to stroll right into it.

Harry explained it to me this way: "We're bait, pure and simple. McCalley wants us to make contact, even if we have to get ambushed to do it. His reputation as a great leader of men, his next promotion, his whole military career depends on us finding gooks and helping the gunships blow them away."

It's true that the hunter-killer teams can only do and see so much from the air, and for more gunship strikes to be successful, Major McCalley has to have the rifle platoon on the ground to pinpoint targets and keep the Vietcong blocked from escaping. So he drops the platoon off, marches it to where he thinks the enemy is hiding, and waits for us to make contact.

The Vietcong usually don't spring an ambush until we're right on top of them, and then the deadly dance begins in earnest. They blow as many of us away as they can, we gather up our dead and wounded, break contact, and pull back far enough to allow the gunships to swoop down and do their damage, which is always considerable, and then what is left of the platoon goes back in to wipe things up and count the dead bodies.

"You don't much like Major McCalley, do you?" I asked Harry when we were talking all this over.

"He's the reason we've got the highest casualty rate in the whole division," he told me with conviction. "Even his own staff can't stand him. Someone tried to frag him about a month before you got here. Go check out his hootch sometime. It's sitting on top of a huge bunker he's had reinforced twice, and not just to protect him from Charlie, either. He's your typical career officer. Vietnam is the opportunity of his life. Once this war is over, the promotions will be few and far between. If he's going to make his mark, he's going to have to do it now, and he knows it. There's only so much of Vietnam to go around and all the brass are fighting to get over here so they can get in their combat command time and hand out valor medals to each other. I absolutely hate the guy!"

"You better be careful who you say things like that to," I warned him.

He just smiled at me and said, "What the hell are they going to do, Ty—draft me?"

CHAPTER 7

▼

A DAY AWAY FROM THE WAR

The morning was already miserably hot and muggy as I leisurely sat up in my bunk and rubbed the sleep from my eyes. The previous night's rumor of a much awaited stand-down had to be true because there had been no shrieking pre-dawn mission siren to send me leaping out of bed half-awake with a pounding heart and a stomach flooded with nauseating adrenalin.

One of the hootch's mama-sans was squatting next to my foot-locker, methodically polishing my boots. Her almost toothless mouth was vigorously gumming away on a beetle nut, some of its dark red juice escaping from the corner of her lips.

"Thank you for doing work," I said in Pidgin English. The startled old Vietnamese woman, her flesh wrinkled and loose, stared over at me with a quizzical expression, seemingly wondering why my English should be as poor as hers. She only begrudgingly returned my smile.

"I got 'em! I got 'em!" screamed Harry excitedly as he stormed into my room, wildly waving two tiny pieces of paper high over his head.

Out of breath and beaming from ear to ear, he pressed the hard-to-come-by passes to his lips and gave them a loud kiss.

"You got to be kidding," I said, reaching up and grabbing the passes and examining each one to make sure Major McCalley had really scribbled his bold and distinctive signature on them. "Unbelievable," I exclaimed. "How did you do it?"

"Who in the hell cares how, man, let's just get gone! They're only good for the rest of the day and the stand-down could be called off any damn minute."

"You know, Harry," I said, suddenly feeling guilty and a little afraid, "I've only been here a few months, and I'm really not that hip on going into town. Maybe you should take one of the other guys? One of the short-timers?"

"What are you talking about, man? I don't want to go without you. Plus the two-digit midgets are walkin' on eggs. They ain't about to take any damn chances."

"I know I said I'd go, Harry, but ..."

"But nothing', man. Your name's on the fucking pass and you're going!" He reached out and playfully slugged me on the shoulder. "Look, the bennies of war await us, and Lord knows we've earned a few, so enough bullshitting, okay. Throw on some decent fatigues and I'll meet you at the front gate. And take my word for it, we're going to have the time of our lives!" He was out of the room before I could offer any further objections.

Harry and I handed our daylight passes to a burly military policeman at the base checkout point, his lightweight, shiny black helmet pulled so far down on his forehead it almost covered his eyes. His scrawny teenage Vietnamese helper immediately handed him a clipboard with a typed list of names attached to it.

"We don't want any incidents in town," explained the almost neckless MP, "so take it easy and stay on your toes. A couple of guys got stabbed in one of the whorehouses last week."

Harry glanced over at me, suddenly not so anxious to ravish the first pretty Vietnamese girl he could find.

"We don't have to go if you don't want to," I said.

"Are you kidding?" replied Harry, quickly regaining his composure. "It's his job to say shit like that. Hell, he's got his own jeep. He probably drives into town and screws a different broad every night."

The MP smiled, checked off our names and returned the passes. "This gate is closed at twenty-one hundred hours sharp. If you're not back by then, you're AWOL. Understand?" We nodded and the MP waved for us to move along. "Plus the boogie man might get you if you're out after dark," he hollered as we departed.

Leaving the safety of the military compound, Harry and I strolled out onto the dusty shoulder of a decaying two-lane asphalt road and began the long walk into town. We quickly came upon a number of the scattered wooden shacks and bamboo huts where families of most of those who toiled on the base as cleaning women, mess hall help and garbage collectors lived. Half-naked children played in the dirt and ancient, black-toothed grandparents sat around in what little shade there was, supervising the youngsters and watching every move Harry and I made. They only occasionally returned my waves.

"Can you believe people actually live like this?" I asked Harry. Chickens and pigs roamed freely in and out of the dirt floor living rooms and the unclothed children looked like they hadn't bathed since the last monsoon.

"Hell," answered Harry, "these gooks are well-off compared to some of the ones we'll see in town." I shook my head in disbelief. I had no idea human beings lived in such poverty and filth.

The repetitive terrain, with the burnt elephant grass and sparsely scattered trees soon became familiar and only an occasional Saigon cowboy puttering along on a motor scooter would interrupt the monotony of picking up one heavy boot and then the other. Kicking up dust with every step, my first day away from the war quickly turned into pure drudgery as the relentless noonday sun continued to bake the back of my neck.

When we finally reached the outskirts of town, we came upon a large military compound belonging to the Army of the Republic of Vietnam. Three old wooden barracks badly in need of some paint, each capable of housing about fifty soldiers and encircled by a ten-foot-high barbed-wire fence, stood end to end.

The outpost appeared to be almost deserted, with only a handful of guards wearing brand new American-made jungle fatigues stationed at strategic positions. Upon spotting me and Harry, two of the young ARVN's left their posts, and with rifles in hand, strolled up to the fence to check us out.

While mumbling something to one another in Vietnamese, they both tossed us looks which should have been reserved for the enemy, not friends. For no apparent reason at all, they suddenly pointed their loaded M16's at Harry and seemed more than willing to use them.

"Allies," said Harry, tipping his flop hat. One of the grim young soldiers spit through the wire at him. While trying hard not to appear frightened, Harry and I stepped up our pace and pulled away from the armed teenagers as quickly as we could.

"We're supposed to be the good guys, aren't we?" I whispered to Harry, who gave me a condescending pat on the back as he often did when he considered one of my opinions hopelessly naive and said, "Just keep walking, and fast!"

The town itself turned out to be much larger and more sophisticated than I had been led to believe. The streets were wide and paved and lined with old and battered homes. Black market vendors had set up shop in every available nook and cranny, selling bottled soft drinks, assorted brands of cigarettes, transistor radios and just about everything else one might expect to find in a well-stocked American post exchange. Even a few weapons and some ammunition were attractively displayed for the more affluent buyer.

"Where do they get all this stuff?" I asked Harry.

"Most of it probably comes from the crooks who run our PX's. Hell, you'd be surprised how many lifers actually volunteer to serve over here just to make the big bucks. A lot of this shit is stolen, too, and some of it gets here as kick-backs for providing broads and other essential services for the brass. War is big business, man."

Harry noticed me wrinkling my nose and sniffing some of the foul smells which quickly seemed to engulf us. "Look over there," he said, pointing towards the center of town. "Apparently for some damn reason, the founding fathers of this pit-hole decided to locate the city dump right in the middle of everything."

The stench of rotting garbage and the hot, still air was an almost unbearable combination. I continued to swat countless flies off my face only to discover I had made room for others. Some were large enough to be mistaken for bees.

Suddenly, in a cloud of dust and exhaust smoke, a beat-up red and white motor scooter came to a screeching halt a few yards in front of us. A young, razor-thin Vietnamese boy of eleven or twelve, wearing only black boxer shorts and a pair of thongs, was at the throttle.

"Hey, GI's, you want numbah one screw?"

"Say again," I said, sure I had misunderstood him.

"You want numbah one screw," he yelled even louder. "My sister, she numbah one screw. You want?"

"Thanks," said Harry, "but we're just browsing."

"I take you to her. Only twenty-five dollar, American."

"Thanks, but not right now," said Harry.

"She clean. You screw long as you want. Twenty dollar, American."

"Maybe a little later," said Harry.

"Big tits! Does blow job, too. Fifteen dollar, American."

"This is your sister you're talking about?" I asked the young boy.

"Right, my sister. She numbah one screw! Ten dollar, American. No lower."

"No thanks, friend," Harry said firmly.

"You lose," said the boy, shaking his head slowly from side to side. Then he quickly sped off, leaving a thick cloud of gas and oil fumes for me and Harry to try and wave away.

"Can you believe that?" I said. "A little kid pimping his own sister."

"Not only that," said Harry angrily, "but did you hear what the little son-of-a-bitch started out asking for her? Twenty-five bucks, man. Hell, whatever happened to a chocolate bar and a pair of nylons? If you ask me, we got in on the wrong damn war."

We walked on and passed through the town's main open air market where dead chickens still in need of plucking and gutting hung everywhere by their feet on blood-stained clotheslines. Little old ladies in baggy black pajama bottoms paid no attention to us as they leisurely sorted through the seasonal vegetables and fruits, hunting for the best possible buys. There was no red meat displayed anywhere, but assorted seafood was plentiful, including some that was still alive and swimming around in large basins.

"The funny thing about it," said Harry, "is you can get crab, lobster, great shit like that for almost nothing, but if you want a scrawny chicken to fry up, the damn thing will cost you an arm and a leg. I guess it's a delicacy or something over here."

Since the sprawling outdoor market was only a few blocks away from the city dump, every species of insect imaginable was constantly harassing the uncovered food, especially the chickens. No effort was made to even occasionally swat some of the pests away.

"I don't know about you, Harry, but I don't think I could eat something that's had every fly for miles around parked on it all day long."

"If you think a bug-infested chicken dinner, head and all, is bad, you ought to try their rat stew."

"What?"

"Sergeant Snow was telling me about the time some important gook invited him over for dinner. One of the dishes he got served was rice covered with big chunks of boiled rat."

"You're kidding?"

"Nope. I guess meat is so hard to come by over here that lots of gooks have their own rat traps." He broke into a wide grin. "Wilson said he tripped over one once when he was out on a night patrol and it scared the shit out of him. He thought sure as hell he had triggered a booby trap, but instead, there was this rat the size of your boot staring up at him. He said it was the ugliest looking thing he had ever seen, with a tail long enough he could have used it for jumping rope."

"You're making that up."

"No I'm not. You wanna know what Wilson did?" I shook my head 'no'. "He doused the damn thing with a can of sterno, opened the cage door and dropped a match on it. I guess it took off running all over the place, just like a ball of fire. Sergeant Snow got really pissed. They had to pull out of there in a hurry because that flaming rat could be seen for miles around."

"How much further?" I asked, hoping to change the subject.

"Gettin' excited, huh? No problem. It should be right around that next corner."

Madam Pham's teahouse turned out to be a faded yellow concrete box without any of the loud colors or girly posters I had expected to find splashed all over its exterior. With the exception of boarded up windows and a bullet-riddled front door, the two-story house was much like all the other rundown homes and businesses on the block.

Once inside, a long, dark hallway led to a spacious and dimly lit dance floor. While I gave my eyes a moment to get adjusted to the lack of light, a girl I could barely make out took my hand and hustled me off to a table. Her chattering friend followed with Harry.

"You buy a girl drink?" my new companion asked.

"Sure, I guess so." A jukebox playing an old Frankie Lane song blared away in the background.

"The music is just a bit outdated, ain't it?" said Harry, shaking his head.

A chubby, expressionless mama-san, sweating profusely, brought us our drinks. They were a murky, dark brown in color and the tiny glasses they came in looked as though they hadn't been washed in weeks. I reluctantly tasted mine, and although I could make out a small trace of some unknown liquor, it was mostly warm tea.

"Well," said Harry after gulping down his drink, "I ain't here to get drunk anyway."

"You want dance with me?" asked my date.

"Okay."

The girl who escorted me to the uncrowded dance floor appeared to be about twenty years old and was wearing a white, see-through blouse and an extremely short, pink mini-skirt. She was at least a couple of inches under five feet tall and her face was very round and very plain. She was also slightly overweight and apparently had never received any training in how to properly use makeup, because her tiny brown eyes were almost nonexistent behind all the heavy mascara, liner and shadow she had generously applied. She smiled pleasantly enough but the blood-red lipstick caked on her lips made the thought of ever having to kiss her an uninviting one.

She was a much better dancer than me, effortlessly performing a combination twist and jerk right out of American Bandstand. The energy she expended apparently made her extremely thirsty and immediately upon returning to our table she ordered another drink, although she had hardly touched the one in front of her.

"This rot-gut is two bucks a pop," warned Harry. "Let her have a couple, but no more."

"We go to bathroom," said the pretty girl with Harry. "We be right back."

"Oh no you don't," replied Harry, roughly grabbing her by the arm. "No switching, understand? I know all about that shit, and I don't plan on starting all over again with some other broad you send over here." He forcefully returned her to her seat. "Let's get down to business, okay? We've had enough of the preliminaries."

"You in big hurry, huh, GI?"

"Honey," said Harry, "this is our first day off in months."

"Okay, it cost you twenty."

"Ten," calmly offered Harry, who seemed to have a natural flare for dickering.

"The lady never let us work for less than twenty," the girl insisted, pointing out a balding mama-san in her fifties or sixties with great sagging breasts who was busy rearranging bottles behind the bar. "Usually it thirty."

"Ten," repeated Harry. "Take it or leave it. And the same goes for my partner here, too."

The obviously unhappy girl took a few moments to consider Harry's ultimatum and finally said, "Okay, business very slow, but no tell friends. Come on. Follow me."

"Harry," I said, "if it's okay with you, I think I'll pass."

"Come on, man," said Harry as he stood up and grabbed me by the arm, "just close your eyes and pretend she's Annette Funicello."

Harry and I followed the girls over to the bar where we were asked to produce our money. We immediately passed it to the sinister-looking old woman dispensing drinks, who I assumed was Madam Pham. She quickly counted it, gave both of her employees a strong look of dissatisfaction, and handed Harry's girl two room keys.

The grey walls enclosing the steep flight of stairs ascending to the second floor were covered with dated graffiti left behind by American soldiers as far back as 1966. I paused for a moment to read one of the more lengthy contributions, which read: When I die I'm going to heaven because I've already spent my time in hell. A colorful peace symbol, right out of the Haight-Ashbury district in San Francisco, was just below it, and reminded me of how far I was from home.

A blast of heat hit me in the face as Harry opened the door which gave access to the upstairs hallway. "You broads are going to have to chip in and get this damn place a fan or something," said Harry as he wiped the perspiration from his forehead with his sleeve. "No wonder business is the shits. Who in the hell wants to screw around in heat like this?"

Ignoring his words, the girls hustled past him and Harry's pretty prostitute inserted one of the keys into the first door on the right hand side of the hallway.

"You go here," she ordered me and the solemn-faced girl whose name I didn't even know.

"Have a good one," shouted Harry as he and his girl hurried off to a room farther down the corridor.

There was not a stick of furniture in the tiny cubicle I cautiously entered. Two filthy mattresses, one on top of the other, rested on the dirty floor in the center of the windowless room. A couple of almost used up candles were waxed tightly to a coffee cup saucer which I accidentally kicked as I approached the makeshift bed. A water faucet with a rusty on-and-off valve protruded from a jagged hole in one of the walls and an empty wooden pail sat below it.

For the first time since entering the depressing, oxygen-starved room, I forced myself to look over at the young girl standing next to me. Much to my surprise, she appeared frightened and unsure of herself and not at all the confident and professional hooker I had imagined her to be.

With great difficulty she produced a thin-lipped smile and without uttering a word, began to disrobe. She kicked off a pair of thongs and lost another inch in height. With her eyes glued to the floor she unbuttoned her blouse and discarded it. Then she stepped out of her mini-skirt and folded it so carefully and neatly that it seemed to be the one possession she most prized in all the world. She laid it gently down on what had become the foot of the bed and slowly removed her underwear, taking off her black bra last while making a conscious effort to keep her back turned to me.

She sunk to her knees and rolled over into the center of the two-story mattress. She looked up at me with surprise, wondering why I had failed to remove even a single stitch of my clothing. The puzzled expression on her multi-colored face continued as I stared down at her, my mouth open and my feet bolted to the floor.

I had not seen a nude female body for so long that my memory seemed to be playing tricks on me. Her tiny breasts, light colored nipples and shaven vagina made the small, pale body spread out in front of me appear almost formless, and not feminine at all.

How ridiculous this whole thing is, I thought to myself. I don't want to be here, she doesn't want to be here, yet here we are.

I was thankful for the late arrival of what was going to have to pass for an erection and I finally removed my uniform and lowered myself on top of her. As our clammy bodies stuck to one another we exchanged silent half-smiles and quickly made love. We did not kiss, or hold each other, or make any unnecessary sounds. Outside of a moment's disruption in my thought process while I climaxed, my mind struggled without much success to get involved in what my body was doing.

That wasn't making love, I thought to myself. In fact, it had barely been a sexual experience at all. And I was sure it had been even worse for my partner.

I raised myself to my knees, my lungs aching for some fresh, cool air. With my weight off her, she dashed for the waterspout. Squatting and using her cupped hands to capture the water which came out of the pipe in irregular spurts, she splashed her vagina a dozen or so times and then hurried back to her orderly pile of clothes. We both dressed in silence and as rapidly as we could.

"We go downstairs," she said as I finished lacing up my boots. "You wait for friend there, okay?"

I was thirsty so I walked over to the water pipe and turned it on. The murky, rotten egg smelling substance obviously didn't belong in anyone's mouth and I turned the faucet off.

I followed the young girl back down the staircase, her thongs slapping loudly against the heels of her feet. Our short but intimate relationship having ended, she quickly introduced herself to another soldier sitting on a stool at the bar and I returned by myself to our table.

I had always wondered what it would be like to have sex with a prostitute. Now I knew, and it sure wasn't worth a case of elephant balls. I sat in silence and waited for Harry.

I hadn't been seated for more than a few minutes when another mini-skirted girl, this one much younger and prettier than the first, pulled out Harry's vacant chair and sat down beside me.

"You cute GI Joe," she said with a smile. "Your hair shiny black, like mine." She crossed her handsome legs and put her hand on top of mine. "Buy me drink?"

"I guess so," I answered.

She really was lovely, with bright, inquisitive eyes and a stunning figure. "Want to dance?" she asked after ordering her drink.

"No. I'm waiting for a friend."

"How bout we talk? I like talk."

"You're very pretty," I said. "How old are you?"

"I only sixteen," she said proudly, pulling her shoulders back and playfully inviting me to look at her firm young breasts.

"What's your name?"

"Mai," she answered as she reached down under the table and placed a hand on my thigh. "What your name?"

"Ty."

She started giggling. "That very strange name for American," she said.

"Going for seconds, huh?" interrupted Harry as he bear-hugged me from behind. "Hey, this one's a knockout!" He winked at Mai and slumped down in a chair at the table. "So, how long have you been waiting for ol' super-stud here?"

"You already go upstairs?" Mai demanded to know.

"Yes," I answered.

"You numbah ten GI!" she yelled as she jumped up and strutted off.

"I don't think they like you wasting their time," explained Harry. "Anyway, how was it? And I want all the gross details."

"Let's just get out of here, Harry. I've had enough of this place."

"Fine with me, man. I got my rock." He gulped down what was left of Mai's drink and followed me outside.

Instead of retracing our steps, Harry suggested we take a different route through town so we wouldn't miss any of the sights. We passed an open air repair shop littered with countless bicycles and motor scooters rusting away from lack of attention and then came upon a school yard scattered with noisy children enjoying their recess.

"That's a pretty run-down school," I said.

"Take a closer look, man. That ain't' no school. That's a fucking orphanage. Gooks don't usually have red hair, man." He pointed out a young girl with reddish brown hair and freckles. "And that black kid over there with the slanted eyes and kinky hair probably ain't the most popular little dude in this country, either."

A few of the dirty, poorly clothed children spotted us and began scrambling in our direction. When they reached the wire fence which separated them from us they jammed their fingers through the tiny openings and began begging for candy and gum. Neither Harry nor I had anything to give them, but they persisted anyway, tripping over one another as they roughly jockeyed for better position along the fence.

"Honest, gang," said Harry, "we ain't got any goodies."

I picked up my pace and kept my eyes focused straight ahead until the last of the pleas had faded in the distance. Harry finally caught up with me and said, "What in the hell are you all uptight about, man?"

"This war sucks, you know that, Harry?"

"War ain't supposed to be pretty, Ty. Look, man, you gotta kill people to have a decent war, right? Well, once everyone has agreed that blowing each other away is okay, then all the other rules get tossed into the dumper, too. For Christ's sake, why in the hell do you think wars have always been so damn popular down through the years? Because there's no fucking rules, man. Everyone gets to go completely crazy, and it's all perfectly legal."

A freshly scrubbed and waxed military jeep with a spit and polish second lieutenant behind the wheel suddenly pulled up next to us, mercifully interrupting Harry's harangue.

"You men interested in a ride back to the base?" he asked me. "I'm headed that way."

"Thanks, sir," I said, hopping into the backseat before Harry had a chance to turn the generous offer down.

"Well, I ain't walking back all by myself, that's for damn sure," said Harry as he reluctantly climbed in next to me.

"Did you have a good time in town, men?" the friendly officer asked me as he put the jeep into gear.

"It was a super day, sir," answered Harry for both of us. "A really super day!"

JOURNAL ENTRY
313 DAYS TO GO

Today I received the letter from Amy I've been expecting. The fact that it got here a little sooner than I had anticipated, and that she's already engaged to be married to Denny Davies surprised me a bit, but the letter itself is so typically and wonderfully Amy, that I want to write it down in my journal before it gets lost like everything else over here:

Dearest Ty,

I should warn you. This is going to sound a little like one of those Dear John letters that all you guys in Vietnam supposedly live in fear of, but it's really not. Remember, you're the one who broke up with me! Anyway, you were right, damn you. I hate being alone, so I finally broke down and called Denny, just to talk, but before we knew it, one thing led to another, and well, to make a very long story short, I'm kinda engaged. Actually, all I really agreed to do is try it out for six months or so, and if things don't work out, I still get to keep the ring (that's supposed to make you laugh).

Now, as you perfectly well know, you are the love of my life and will probably remain so until the day they plant me into the ground. However, just like you, I'm not totally blind to the fact that we have this incredible ability to bring out the very worst in each other. If you think about things honestly, as I've been doing since you left, then I'm sure you will agree that the only thing that's really kept us together the past couple of years was the great sex. (By the way, as part of your punishment for dumping me and running off to play soldier, you're never going to find anyone better in bed!)

I promised myself to keep this short and sweet, because I know that's what you would want me to do. If there's one thing I know about you, it's that you're not one of those creeps (most guys are like this, by the way) who not only want to get rid of their girlfriend, but they also don't want anyone else to have her, either. So, deep down, I know you're wishing me and Denny the best.

His hair is the wrong color and he doesn't have that little-boy smile which always made me take you back, but he seems to worship the very ground I walk on, and believe it or else, I need that right now. (Plus, as you know, his parents are loaded!)

One more thing. You remember those nude photos you took of me last year that I told you I destroyed? Well, I lied. I kept one of them because my boobies looked so great in it. It's the one you said you liked best, too, so I'm sending it to you. I hope it comes in handy (get it?) every now and then.

Please, please, please, Ty, take the very best care of yourself that you can! You are, and always will be, in my thoughts and prayers. All my love, Amy.

CHAPTER 8

▼

THE BUNKER

The daily afternoon monsoon had already come and gone but the cool night air was still moist and scented with the fertile Vietnamese earth. My perimeter bunker was within sight so I slowed my pace and gazed up at the exhausted sky. No moon, no stars, nothing, I thought to myself. This is definitely Charlie's kind of night.

"Don't take another step!" called out an unfamiliar voice. I stopped abruptly and instinctively raised my rifle to the ready. "What's the damn password?" demanded the voice, which was coming from within the perimeter bunker I had been assigned for the night.

"Snow White," I yelled out.

"Figures," replied the indifferent voice.

I cautiously stepped up to the bunker, dropped down into a catcher's stance and peeked inside. Seated Indian-style on the dirt floor of the heavily sandbagged bunker was a burly black soldier I had never seen before. His unauthorized full beard was the next thing I noticed. He didn't even bother to look up.

"Who are you?" I asked. He ignored the question and continued munching away on the contents of a C-ration tin. "And what are you doing in my bunker?" Still paying me no attention, he shoved another bite of food into his mouth. "Look, whoever you are, you're in the wrong bunker. You're not supposed to be in there."

"It wasn't my fucking idea," he snapped, "and if I was you, I'd get my ass in here before some trigger-happy gook shoots it off."

He was right. I quickly stepped down into the bunker and unbuckled my ammo belt. "Who sent you out here?" I asked.

"Some dude named John," finally came the answer.

"The sergeant of the guard?"

"I guess."

I removed my steel pot from my head and sat down on the cold, damp ground. I placed my ammo belt at my feet, within arm's reach, and rested my rifle on my lap. My unwanted companion, finished with his snack, reached into a fatigue top pocket and produced a pack of cigarettes. He took out some matches, bent forward and lit a cigarette. He inhaled a deep, slow drag, and then cupped the cigarette in the palm of his huge hand.

"Make sure you keep that thing down," I warned him. "Charlie can see a lighted cigarette for miles out here."

"I ain't no fool!" he shot back, scowling at me through his thick, dark eyebrows.

Well, screw you, I thought to myself as I heard footsteps outside the bunker. I grabbed my rifle, raised my head to sandbag level and yelled, "Who goes out there?"

"It's just me, Ty," hollered the familiar voice of Sergeant John Snow. "I'm coming in."

"Okay, John," I hollered back. I put my helmet on and climbed out of the bunker. John, loaded down with a PRC-25 radio and an infra-red nightscope, strolled up to me.

"Everything quiet?" he asked me.

"So far."

"Good. The major wants you to have a radio and a scope up here tonight. Intelligence thinks we're going to get hit."

I grabbed John's arm and pulled him a few yards further away from the bunker. "John, who's the clown in my bunker?"

"Oh, him."

"Yeah, him."

"He got in today. The First Cav transferred him over to us."

"Okay, but what's he doing in my bunker?"

"The old man doubled the guard. It's just for tonight. I told you, they think we're going to get hit."

"That's just great. And you stick me with some rookie."

"He ain't no rookie, Ty. He's been over here longer than you and me put together. Hell, I've heard he's got a Silver Star."

"Really?" I asked, impressed.

"Yeah, he's supposed to be pretty hot shit."

"So, then why'd they give him to us?" I asked, knowing full well that the First Air Cavalry wasn't in the habit of transferring its war heroes to other units.

"I heard he got in some kind of trouble with the brass over there."

"What kind of trouble?"

"I think he got into a big fight or something."

"Geez, John, if he's a trouble-maker, why didn't you give him to Donnally or Thomas tonight?"

"Because they hate black guys," he whispered. "Now damn it, Ty," he continued, his voice back to normal, "here, take these. I'm not going to stand out here bullshitting with you all night. And make sure you call in every hour on the hour." He turned to leave.

"Is the radio already on the right push?"

"Everything's set," he assured me as he began to walk away, "and I'll be in the command bunker if you need me."

"What time do they think we'll get hit?"

"After midnight is the old man's best guess," he answered as he disappeared into the darkness.

I hurried back down into the bunker and handed my fellow perimeter guard the nightscope.

"What the hell do you want me to do with that stupid thing?" he demanded, tossing it off to one side. "It's a worthless piece of shit."

"Intelligence thinks we're going to get hit tonight," I explained.

"Well, don't be getting all excited," he said. "There's never anybody intelligent working in intelligence."

"Some time after midnight probably," I said. My unwelcome companion shook his head and mumbled something I couldn't make out. "Look," I continued, "I guess we're going to be spending the night together—my name is Ty Nichols." I stuck my hand out for him to shake. He ignored it. "Fine with me," I said as I squatted down, made room for the radio and settled in for the night.

"Marcus White is my name," the soldier finally said a good five minutes later as he prepared to light up another cigarette.

"Hey, could I bum one of those from you?" I asked timidly.

Marcus abruptly turned his eyes in my direction and glared at me. "You're shittin' me, aren't you? Tell me you're shittin' me."

"Forget it then."

"We're going to be out here all night long, man," he fumed. "Don't you be telling me you didn't bring your own fucking smokes."

"I'm trying to quit," I explained. Marcus lowered his head and shook it in disbelief. "Hey, it's not easy to quit."

"Shit, you ain't going to quit nothin', except buying your own." He reached into a pocket, probed around for a few seconds, and reluctantly tossed me a cigarette.

I hesitated for a moment and then asked, "Could I borrow your matches, too?"

"Jesus fucking Christ! You want me to smoke the goddamn thing for you, too?" He finally stuck his lighted cigarette out where I could reach it.

"Thanks," I said, lighting my cigarette off his.

"Look, man" said Marcus, pulling back his cigarette, "you want the first watch or what?"

"I don't care."

"You want it or not?"

"Not really."

"Yes or no!"

"Okay, yes."

"Good, you got it," he said as he stomped out his cigarette with his boot and yanked his flop hat down over his eyes.

I finished my cigarette in silence and then reached into my snack pouch for my P-38 can opener and the C-ration tin of pound cake I had been saving for just such an occasion. Marcus heard me opening it. "What the hell are you doing now?" he demanded to know.

"Nothing."

"You're eating something."

"So what?"

"What is it?"

"Pound cake."

He lifted up his flop hat and looked over at me. "Where in the hell did you get pound cake?"

"Want some?" I asked.

He hesitated for a moment, trying to figure out my angle. "You're damn right I want some."

"I tell you what, I'll give you some of it if you pull the midnight watch. How's that?" He immediately thrust out a hand, obviously relieved that I did have an angle. I passed him half my pound cake. "I hear you're a hero?" He ignored the question and shoved a piece of the cake into his mouth. "How come they transferred you over from the Cav?"

"You sure are nosey, man."

"I heard you got into some trouble over there?" Again, he didn't answer. "So, what'd you do?"

He slowly stiffened his back and then locked his intense dark eyes on me. "I beat the crap out of this mouthy white dude who kept bugging the shit out of me!"

I almost choked on my mouthful of pound cake. "Oh," I managed to get out.

"Now, you got any more fucking questions?" I quickly shook my head 'no'. "Good!"

He devoured the rest of his pound cake in one bite and pulled his flop hat back down over his eyes. Much to my relief, he was snoring within minutes.

My shift was nice and uneventful but Marcus wasn't so lucky. I was soundly sleeping when he suddenly jabbed me painfully in the ribs with his elbow and said, "Something is going on out there, man. Get up!"

I grabbed my rifle and was wide awake within seconds. "What's the matter?" I asked.

"Listen, man, just listen."

I strained my ears, but I didn't hear anything out of the ordinary. "Did you radio for a flare?" I whispered to Marcus, who as usual, ignored my question.

"Shit, there it is again, man. You telling me you can't hear that?"

I listened as hard as I could, with the same negative result. "I'll radio for a flare," I volunteered.

"The hell with flares, man. They'll light up our position, too."

I reached over, grabbed the nightscope and diligently scanned the high grass to our left and right and the open ground in front of us. Its fuzzy picture wasn't much help. "It's hard to really tell," I said, "but I don't see anything moving."

"See, I told you the damn thing is worthless."

"We're supposed to call for a flare if we hear anything. It's standard operating procedure."

"Fuck the rules, man, and listen up. Don't you hear that?"

"Hear what?"

"Some mother-fucker is crawling around out there, in that elephant grass, twenty-five yards out, at about nine o'clock."

This time I heard it, and my tightly wound nerves made me feel as if I was teetering on the edge of a high building. "I hear it," I whispered to Marcus.

"Well, it's about time, man! You always been so fucking deaf?"

"What do you think it is?"

"Probably a sapper, maybe two."

"Maybe it's just a rat or something," I said without much conviction.

"It's a rat, alright. A big yellow one in black pajamas and Ho Chi Minh sandals."

"But I still don't see anything," I said as I scoped the area again.

"Try ten o'clock, twenty yards out."

"Jesus, you're right," I stammered as a bolt of unwanted excitement ran through me, "the grass is definitely moving."

"That's a free-fire zone out there, ain't it?" Marcus asked.

"Yeah."

"Then let's kill us a gook or two!"

"Don't you think we better radio in first?"

"No time, man. They can damn near spit on us now."

Marcus flipped off the safety on his rifle, put it on rock and roll, and in one cat-like motion, leaped to his feet and opened fire. My ears, which were still geared to detecting the slightest sound, filled with pain as Marcus emptied a whole clip and began jamming in a second. "There they go!" he screamed. "Run you mother-fuckers, run!"

I jumped up to help him, and sure enough, two scrambling Vietcong were running away from Marcus' fire and bounding over every obstacle in front of them. We both kept on shooting long after the Vietcong had disappeared back into the night.

"I've lost sight of them," I finally said. "How about you?"

"Damn," said Marcus, beginning to laugh, "neither one of us can shoot for shit!"

"I don't think I even came close," I admitted.

"Fuck it, man, who cares? At least we scared the crap out of them."

I joined in on Marcus' infectious laughter until I heard the radio start squawking. "They probably want to know what we're doing up here," I said.

"Damn, that was fun!" said Marcus.

I reached down and picked up the headset. "What in the hell is going on up there?" demanded the excited voice on the radio.

"Hi, John. We just chased off a couple of sappers, that's all."

"Anybody hit?"

"No."

For the next few minutes, John chewed me out good for almost every guard duty infraction imaginable. Not only had we failed to request flares and permission to engage the enemy, apparently Marcus had forgotten to call in during his watch. "Okay, John, okay," I finally interrupted, "we're sorry. It won't happen again. I promise."

"You're damn right it won't! And I want both of you staying awake. They were probably just probing, and they may come back in force."

"Roger that, John."

"Out!" he screamed.

"Boy, they're really hot back at Headquarters," I said to Marcus.

"Fuck 'em."

"They think maybe we were just being probed."

"Could be," said Marcus. "They didn't have any explosives on them, so they weren't after the aircraft."

"You think they'll be back?"

"Only if they prep us a little bit first."

"Rockets?" I asked with alarm.

"Maybe just mortars. Maybe both."

"I hate rockets," I said with emphasis.

"You ain't alone, man."

"Worse than anything."

"I hear you." He took out a couple of cigarettes. "How bout a smoke?"

"Sure, thanks."

He lit two cigarettes and passed one to me. "So, dead-eye-dick, where you from?"

"Say again," I said, surprised by the friendly tone of the question.

"Where you from, you know, back in the world? Damn, you really are fucking deaf, aren't you?"

"So," I said, smiling, "we're going to be buddies after all, huh?"

The stern expression on Marcus' face slowly melted away and he said, "Fuck it, man, why not? Maybe for a couple of hours anyway."

As the early morning hours wore on I found out that Marcus had spent a year or two of his life in just about every major city on the East Coast. He called Baltimore home because that was where his mother lived. I had heard guys talk highly of their mother before, but not like Marcus. His father had disappeared when he was very young and his mother had somehow kept a huge family fed, clothed and out of trouble.

Since my arrival in Vietnam, a lot of guys had shown me snapshots of their wife or girlfriend, but Marcus was the first soldier I had met who proudly pulled out a picture of his mother. He looked just like her, too, having the exact same high forehead, broad nose and severe eyes.

"She told me not to join the Army," Marcus said, blowing out the cuffed match which had illuminated her face. "I should have listened to her."

"It's not been exactly what I expected either," I assured him.

"It ain't just that, man. They've been messing with my head since the day I raised my hand. Hell, I had to go all the way up to the IG just over this damn beard."

"I was wondering how you got to keep that."

"I got sensitive skin, man. I can't shave. If it had been a white dude, no problem, man. They would have said grow it down to your fucking dick!" He looked over and locked his dark eyes on me again, and it made me feel even more uncomfortable than it had the first time he did it. "You don't think you're a racist, do you?"

"What?" I asked, surprised by the question and the way Marcus could be so suddenly filled with rage.

"You heard me, man."

"No," I finally answered. "No, I don't."

"Well, you're wrong, man. All white people are racists. You're born with it. It's in your fucking genes. It's part of your—your cultural heritage."

"Why are we talking about this?" I asked.

"Cause you're acting like you want to be my friend, man, and I don't want no fucking white friends."

"Fine."

"Mamma says every once in awhile, a white person can outgrow being a racist, but I ain't ever seen it. Fact is we scare the shit out of you. You're afraid we're going to walk up and beat you up side the head, or move in next door, or worst of all, fuck your scrawny white women with our big black dicks."

When I looked away from him and didn't respond, I sensed that he felt maybe he had stepped over the line. For a moment, I even thought he was going to apologize. Instead, he reached into his pocket and pulled out his last cigarette. He had been saving it for almost an hour.

"Haven't you ever had a white friend, Marcus?"

"You ever had a black friend?" he shot back.

"No," I admitted, "not really, I guess."

"Who knows," he said with the slightest hint of sadness in his voice, "maybe it's best that way. Fuck it, right?" Then he tossed me his cigarette and his book of matches and pulled his flop hat down on his face. "Wake me at first light, okay?"

"But that's your last smoke, isn't it?"

"You want the fucking thing or not?"

"Sure I want it."

"Then light it up, stick it in your mouth and shut the fuck up so I can get some goddamn sleep!"

JOURNAL ENTRY

305 DAYS TO GO

The best five-card-stud poker player on the base is a soft-spoken, round-faced forty-five year old Kit Carson Scout by the name of Toi Nguyen. Toi's reputation for never leaving the table a loser is well-earned, as is mine for never walking away a winner.

Everybody in the platoon likes Toi, which makes his habitual success at cards easier to take, but no one ever challenges him to play one-on-one except me, and it always brings a smile to his face. He knows I do it for the conversation and he always insists on lowering the stakes to penny, nickel, dime, which he knows I can afford. I meet him at his hootch, usually after the Friday or Saturday night base movie, and we often play way into the morning hours.

Toi has been educated at the University of Saigon and his use and understanding of the English language is better than most of the guys in the platoon. He has some kind of an advanced degree in banking and he and his family were very well-off in the Vietnam of the late 1950's and early 1960's. He's given up a lot to become an ordinary soldier, and although he was offered a high commission in the Army of the Republic of Vietnam, he chose to take command of our Kit Carson Scouts, which unlike him, are all repatriated Vietcong. He is invaluable in that position, especially out in the field, where he seems to know everything there is to know about disarming booby traps and getting captured Vietcong to spill their guts.

Toi's love of country, family and freedom consume his every thought, and unlike me and most every other American in-country, he is fighting to win. To him, the war is a life and death struggle. There are no R and R's and guaranteed rotation after one year for Toi and his loved ones, and his insights into the war and what really is going on in Vietnam never fail to hold my interest.

Our conversation last night went something like this:

"Come in, my card playing friend," said Toi as he greeted me with a warm smile. "Here to lose your shorts again, huh?" I laughed and he politely escorted me over to the table and folding chairs he always borrows from the mess hall for the occasion and motioned for me to sit down. "How was the movie?" he asked.

"You won't believe it," I said, "but the projector actually made it all the way through tonight."

"Remarkable indeed," said Toi. "I thought about going, but I'm afraid your Mr. Jimmy Stewart is not a favorite of mine."

"You're a John Wayne man, right?"

"You have a very good memory," he said as he broke out his poker paraphernalia and carefully counted out ten dollars worth of red, white and blue chips for each of us.

"I feel lucky tonight," I warned him.

"Hope springs eternal, I believe is the saying," said Toi as he passed me my chips and dealt out the first hand.

"What'd you think of today's mission?" I asked.

"Not very encouraging, I'm afraid. They were out there, alright, but not in enough numbers to attack us. They let us pass."

"You really think so?"

"Yes. Maybe we will be able to engage them tomorrow. I think we could have flushed them out today if we would have stayed a little longer. But I understand your major's reluctance to have the platoon out after dark."

"I'm not much for staying out after dark, either," I admitted. "If there's anything I've learned over here, it's that the night belongs to Charlie."

"It's really not as dangerous as you might think," said Toi. "Our firepower is so superior to theirs. We shouldn't be so cautious about putting it to good use, even at night."

"I don't know, Toi. I've only been on one night patrol and that was plenty for me. We set up a bunch of claymores, took cover and an hour later, what seemed like half of Hanoi started marching past us."

Toi smiled and said, "That's exactly what I mean. Much of their movement and supply work takes place at night and that is when we should hit them. Did you blow your claymores?"

I shook my head 'no' and it was obvious that Toi wasn't pleased with that decision. "Have you heard from your wife?" I asked him, trying to change the subject.

Toi's tired eyes lit up and he said, "Yes, thank you, and from one of my brothers, too."

"Which one?"

"Quang."

"Oh, the one who went north to fight with the NVA?"

Toi seemed pleased that I had remembered the name and whereabouts of his favorite brother. "Yes, Quang. I received a lengthy letter from him. Usually it is by word of mouth that I know if he is alive or dead."

"Has he seen the light yet?"

"No, I'm afraid not. Actually, he is much worse now. He is really under their spell. Their propaganda is very good. His letter was full of their slogans."

"Like what?"

"The North is sure you will soon tire of your commitment. I know better, but Quang doesn't. America is an honorable country. Unlike Quang, I have read much of your history. You have always helped those wishing to be free, and you have never lost a war." He paused for a moment to rake in the winnings from the first pot of the night. "A man is not a man if he is not free," he continued. "We Vietnamese are new at being free, but we are *getting better at it every day. Our leaders are not very good at it yet, but they will improve, too. Quang has made a horrible mistake, but I still love him very much."*

"I wish I was as confident of our commitment to stay over here as you are," I said. "Back home, lots of people want us to get out. The antiwar demonstrations are getting pretty big."

That was something Toi didn't want to hear and he cut the discussion short with the words, "America will do the right thing. I am sure of it."

He cheered up immediately when I said, "So, how's Hoa and all those kids of yours?"

"They are all well, thank you. I am a very lucky man indeed. Hoa of course wishes I was closer to home, and it is not good that the little ones are growing up without a father, but like you, I am doing what I must."

Toi has four children, two of them under the age of ten, and their expensively framed photographs are proudly displayed on the same wall which serves as the background for a miniature Buddhist shrine he has erected in his hootch.

Toi is a devout Buddhist and he is always on the lookout for potential converts. He has explained the ten major sins to me on numerous occasions and told me how hard it is for one to get into Nirvana. Qualities like knowledge, unselfishness, perfect self-control, enlightenment, and a kindly attitude are all required, and it seems to me that Toi is already well on his way.

"You should stop giving up your passes and go home more often," I suggested.

"My duty is here, my friend. Your American newspapers are always saying that we Vietnamese are not doing our fair share of the fighting. It is not true. We are good soldiers. Too many of our officers are corrupt, though, that is the problem. Those of us who are not corrupt must work three hundred and sixty-five days a year to correct that."

"Have you ever thought of having Hoa and the children visit you here?"

"It would be a difficult and dangerous journey. Soc Trang is secure, but there is too much unrepatriated countryside between here and there. It is best that they remain where they are safe."

"Tell me about Soc Trang, Toi. You and Hoa both grew up there, didn't you?"

Once again, his kind face warmed and his energy returned as he began to talk of home and family. "It is a very old village which hasn't changed much from the time I was a very young man. I met Hoa when she began attending my school. We were maybe ten, no, nine, I think."

"Childhood sweethearts, huh?"

Toi laughed. "Oh, no, no. We have no such thing here. Falling in love in Vietnam is very different from falling in love in America."

"How so?"

"Well, boys and girls here are not encouraged to spend time with each other as soon as American boys and girls are. We start what you would call dating much, much later than you do."

"How much later?"

"Usually we are in our twenties."

"In your twenties?" I asked, shocked. "You're kidding?"

"As a young man, all my time was devoted to my studies. The same was true of Hoa. We both wanted to go on to the university and if we would have started seeing each other in our teenage years, we would have wasted all of our time thinking about nothing else. I also had to work many hours each day in the rice paddies."

"Yuck," I said, my experiences with foul-smelling, leech-infested rice paddies having not been very good ones.

"I agree," said Toi, smiling, "rice paddies are not very pleasant, and the work is very, very hard."

"Were you and Hoa married in Soc Trang?"

"No, we were married in Saigon. We completed our advanced studies and her parents finally accepted me as a son-in-law. We made our home there until the children began arriving."

"Your girls are all very pretty."

"*Thank you,*" *he said, looking back at their pictures.* "*I had hoped for boys, but now I am very thankful they were girls. I will not someday have to give them to the war.*" *He suddenly looked tired again and he took a deep breath and sighed.* "*You know, my friend, some days I believe it will never end. Thirty years now, all the way back to when the French were here. So many, many dead. And I fear that being raised with war has made us as a people—I can't explain it. But it is wrong to grow up as I have, and as my parents did, and now as my children are. I can only hope it will be different for my children's children.*"

"*It will, Toi, I'm sure of it.*"

"*Only with the help of your wonderful country, my friend.*"

CHAPTER 9

▼

WOUNDED

You never believe it's going to happen to you, and even as the force of the explosion lifted me off my feet and hurled me through the air, I refused to accept the fact that my turn had finally arrived. The initial flash of pain was excruciating, but by the time I had belly-flopped back down to earth, it was nothing more than a dull ache.

Just when I had convinced myself I wasn't dead and everything was probably going to be okay, my side went on fire, as if someone was branding me with a red hot metal poker. I immediately reached back and desperately tried to pound out the flame. I could feel something warm and wet and I thrust my trembling hand in front of my eyes. The sight of my own bright red blood terrified me.

I struggled to my knees and like a dog chasing its tail, I spun around and around, trying to see how bad I had been hit.

Out of nowhere, Sergeant Ketchum hurled the full force of his shoulder into my chest, the way football players do to blocking dummies in practice. The solid blow flattened me.

"Stay down!" screamed Sergeant Ketchum.

"I'm hit!" I screamed back. The words were barely out of my mouth when another enemy rocket propelled grenade exploded into the nearby ground and filled the air with more flying dirt and deadly shrapnel.

"Where's your gun?" yelled Sergeant Ketchum.

"I'm hit! I'm hit bad!"

Sergeant Ketchum spotted my rifle and steel pot and scrambled off after them. Another two explosions further darkened the sky around me. I burrowed deeper into the loose earth and covered my exposed head with my hands. More deafening blasts followed, each one a little closer to my position than the last. Then a whistling piece of fiery-hot shrapnel suddenly slammed into the side of my neck with such force it felt like my head had been blown off. I rolled over and cried out in agony. I instinctively grabbed for the area with all the new pain and my forefinger fell into a bloody hole just below my right ear. "Medic!" I yelled, "medic!" The words were barely out of my mouth when Sergeant Ketchum returned and unceremoniously jammed my helmet back on top of my head and shoved my rifle into my stomach.

"Calm down!" Sergeant Ketchum ordered me, his eyes full of concern. "You aren't dead yet!"

"How bad is it?" I asked, pointing to my neck.

He quickly examined my wound and said, "It's not bleeding too much, so it didn't hit an artery or anything important. You're going to be fine."

I sighed in relief, knowing Sergeant Ketchum wouldn't lie to me. "My back's a mess, too."

He roughly rolled me over and ripped my fatigue top out of my pants. When he didn't say anything, I began to get scared all over again. "It's bad, isn't it?"

He didn't answer as he yanked off the packaged bandage I carried on my ammo belt and tore it open. He covered the wound and strung the cloth cords tightly around my waist. "It's not good, Ty. It's wide and pretty deep, and it may have hit something inside."

"It doesn't hurt too much," I said, trying to be positive.

"Good, because we have to get you out of here. Your radio is all shot up, too, and I've got to get to another one that works. Charlie may try to come over the top any minute. Think you can crawl?" I nodded that I could. "Okay, try to keep up. If you can't, yell."

We had at least the length of a football field to cover to get all the way back to Headquarters Squad and every time I dug the heel of my left boot into the earth to get some traction, a knife-like pain would slice from one side of my back to the other. Sergeant Ketchum knew I was hurting and he kept slowing his pace to make it easier on me.

Mercifully, the rockets had stopped raining down, but there was still plenty of small arms fire filling the air right above us. When we finally reached the bulk of the unit, we could hardly believe our eyes. Dead and badly wounded friends were scattered all over the place. It looked as if at least two-thirds of the platoon had been hit and my own wounds suddenly seemed almost insignificant.

Sergeant Ketchum helped me to my feet and much to my relief, I discovered that walking was much less painful than crawling. Panic-stricken cries for help were coming from every direction, but Sergeant Ketchum motioned for me to follow him as we went in search of Lieutenant Townsend. When we found him, the platoon's only able-bodied medic was feverishly working to keep him alive. Most of the bottom half of his body was missing and he had lost so much blood that he was in deep shock.

"For Christ's sake, Doc," screamed Sergeant Ketchum at the startled medic, "help someone who has a chance!"

Doc reluctantly turned his back on his commanding officer and began working on the lieutenant's radio carrier. "Is his squawk box working?" Sergeant Ketchum asked the medic. Doc got down on all fours and pressed his ear up against the radio. He looked back up and nodded his head 'yes'. Sergeant Ketchum quickly bent down next to the wounded RTO and removed the radio as gently as he could. As he desperately tried to reestablish contact with Major McCalley and the rest of the platoon, I went in search of someone to help.

I didn't have to go far. Shorty Cuff, the lieutenant's machine gunner, and Billy Sax, his ammo carrier, were sprawled out face down in the same pool of blood. Shorty was still conscious, but I was pretty sure Billy was dead.

"Am I dying, Ty?" Shorty asked, his voice almost a whisper, as I gingerly rolled him over.

"I don't think so, Shorty."

"But I'm bleeding really bad. I'm covered in blood."

"I think a lot of it is Billy's."

"Billy's dead, isn't he?"

I reached over and tried to find a pulse in Billy's neck. When I couldn't, I said, "Yeah, Shorty, I'm afraid so."

I removed Billy's blood-soaked flop hat and discovered that a piece of shrapnel the size of my fist had penetrated deep into the top of his head. The jagged entry hole was so wide that I could see where the two sections of Billy's brain came together.

"Damn," said Shorty. "What the hell happened anyway?"

"They threw a bunch of rockets in on top of us," I said as I turned my attention back to Shorty and began systematically searching his body for wounds. "Your shoulder's been hit, Shorty, and your ear looks like it's going to need a bunch of stitches."

"That's all?"

"I think so. Do you hurt anywhere else?"

"No, not really."

I quickly bandaged Shorty's badly damaged ear as best as I could and then turned my attention to his shoulder. It was still bleeding quite a bit so I ripped open another bandage and applied as much pressure to the wound as Shorty could stand.

"Do you think I could have a cigarette?" asked Shorty.

"Sure."

Both of us had one free hand and between the two of us, we managed to get a cigarette lit. I took a single drag and started to feel a little dizzy. I handed the cigarette over to Shorty and tried to shake my head clear.

"You okay, Ty? Hey, Ty, are you okay?"

My eyelids began to get heavy and I could hear my pulse loud and fast deep inside my ears. Shorty said something else, but I couldn't make it out. His voice sounded so very far away.

For the next couple of hours, I faded in and out of consciousness, but when I finally came to my senses, I was thousands of feet above the ground and miles away from the battlefield. The comfortable, familiar 'whump-whump' sound of a helicopter's whirling blades was the first thing I heard, and an IV bottle hanging high above my head was the first thing I saw.

I looked all around and realized that except for the two pilots, I was the only one on the aircraft. That made no sense, plus I didn't recognize either one of the warrant officers. That meant it had to be one of Battalion Aid's speed choppers, and that could only mean I was hurt worse than I thought, and that I was being flown all the way to Long Binh for emergency surgery.

For a moment, I was more frightened than ever, but it slowly dawned on me that if some Army surgeon didn't screw up, then the war was over for me and I was going back to the world. When the co-pilot glanced back over his shoulder to see how I was doing, he must have thought I was crazy, because I was grinning from ear to ear.

Organized chaos began almost the moment the skids on my helicopter hit the ground. At least half-a-dozen III Core medevacs were being hastily unloaded and I was just one of many wounded American soldiers in need of surgery. White-shirted corpsmen were racing back and forth with stretchers and frantically trying to communicate with one another over the deafening roar of all the helicopter engines. Two of them jumped into my chopper and unstrapped my litter. They quickly lifted me out onto the tarmac, secured my stretcher to a gurney and rushed off to help someone else.

A doctor in a surgeon's gown glanced down at my wounds and yelled, "This one can wait!" They were the best words I had heard all day.

A few minutes later, I was rolled up to a strategically placed collection of gurneys where more doctors and nurses were working feverishly to help those who needed it the most. I glanced over at the stretcher next to mine and saw a young man who couldn't have been more than eighteen years old. He was a bloody mess and his whole body was shaking uncontrollably. His head was tilted towards mine and his eyes were wild with fear. I quickly looked away.

When I reached the operating theater, a friendly nurse wearing the thickest pair of glasses I had ever seen greeted me with a warm smile and gently removed all of my clothes and bandages.

"This doesn't look too bad," she assured me. "You're a very lucky man. You're going to be fine, just fine. Where are you from, soldier?" I told her, but she wasn't really listening. She removed a long plastic tube from its paper wrapper and said, "I'm going to catheterize you now."

"What's that?"

"It empties your bladder so you won't get any infections during surgery."

"Oh," I said, still unaware that she was about to shove a plastic tube up my penis. "Hey, what are you doing? Hey, don't do that!" I grabbed her hand and stopped her.

"I'm sorry, but unless you can urinate, this has to be done."

"I can urinate, I can urinate!"

Her face skeptical, she handed me a lightweight bottle with a handle on it. "We don't have all day, you know," she said as I tried harder to pee than I had at any other time in my life—and without any success.

"It's coming," I lied, "it's coming!"

When I awoke from the anesthesia, a young doctor with a stethoscope dangling from his neck was standing over me reading papers attached to a clipboard. The room was dark and crowded with sleeping soldiers, but light would occasionally flood the foot of my bed as nurses shuffled quietly back and forth through a nearby hallway door.

The doctor hung the clipboard on the foot of my bed and began wrapping a blood pressure device snugly around my arm. He rapidly pumped it full of air.

"Am I alright?" I asked when he had finished taking my blood pressure reading. He seemed surprised that I was awake. "Am I going to be okay?"

He removed the strap from around my arm and smiled. "So, young man, how are you feeling?"

"My side sure hurts."

"It should. Here, let's roll you over." He very carefully turned me onto my stomach and checked my dressing.

"Am I going to be okay?" I asked again.

"You're going to be just fine." I was too weak to even mentally celebrate. "We took quite a chunk of iron out of your side. It nicked a kidney, and I'm a little concerned about that, but it could have been much, much worse. You were real lucky." He covered me back up.

"Do I get to go home?"

"I want you to sleep now. We can talk about all that tomorrow."

"What about my neck, sir?"

"No problem. Just some soft tissue damage. And I'll have a nurse come by and give you a little something for your back pain."

"But can't you please tell me if I'm going home?"

"Okay," he said, placing his hand on my shoulder, "just between you and me, you'll be on the first flight out tomorrow morning for Tokyo General. They'll keep you there for a few days, maybe a week. It all depends on how quickly your kidney heals. But if everything goes like I expect it to, you should be home before you know it."

"Really?" I said, thinking it was all too good to be true.

"Really," he said, returning my smile. "The war is over for you, son. Now try to get some rest. You've earned it."

I closed my weary eyes. Wow, I thought to myself, you're actually going to live through Vietnam. Can that really be true? And is everybody back home going to be surprised or what?

The next day, I was gently nudged awake by a nurse calling my name. "Wake up, Ty. Come on, Ty, you need to wake up."

I was so groggy I could barely force my eyelids open. When I finally did, I immediately closed them again to avoid a room filled with the bright afternoon sun. Afternoon sun? That couldn't be right. I was supposed to be on the morning plane to Tokyo. Or maybe that had been a dream? "What time is it?" I asked the nurse.

"It's time to get that back of yours irrigated," she answered. "Starting right now, Dr. Jacobson wants it done three times a day."

"Dr. Jacobson? Is that the doctor who talked to me last night?"

"Probably," she answered as she began to carefully remove my dressing. "Now it's very important that we keep this as clean as possible. And this next part is going to sting a little, but it's the only way we can keep down the risk of infection. The doctor wants it to heal from the inside out."

"It's not stitched up yet?"

"No. That would almost guarantee an infection. There was a lot of dirt and other debris in your wound. It needs to drain for awhile. One of the doctors in Vung Tau will close you up in a week or so."

"Vung Tau?" I asked as the nurse finished taping a new dressing snugly in place.

"Aren't you lucky to be going to Vung Tau this time of the year? It's a wonderful place to recuperate. It's right on the sea. The Vietnamese have used it as a resort area for centuries."

"But I'm going home," I explained to her. "I was supposed to fly to Tokyo this morning." She looked up from her task, obviously surprised. "The doctor told me last night I was going home."

"I don't think so, Ty," she said, appearing to be almost as disappointed as I was, "but would you like to speak to someone about it?"

"Yes, please. I'd really appreciate it if I could."

The doctor who came to my bed an hour or so later was not the same doctor who had visited me in the middle of the night.

"I'm Doctor James, Ty. Nurse Turner says there's been some kind of misunderstanding?"

"I don't get to go home?"

"I'm afraid not. You're being sent to Vung Tau for a few weeks. When you've regained your strength, you'll be returned to your unit."

"But last night, a doctor told me ..."

"I know. Dr. Jacobson mentioned it to me this morning when we were discussing your case. He's only been with us for a few weeks and he forgot to check with me before he spoke to you. Now, if you had been in-country for six months or longer, then I could have probably sent you home. But your records show you've only been here about three months. I'm sorry, but the rules say if it's at all possible, we must return you to your unit."

"I see," I said, trying to hide the fact I was crushed.

"You do understand?"

"Oh, sure."

"Good. Look on the brighter side. You should be as good as new in about a month."

"Thank you, sir."

"I really am sorry," he said as he patted me on the shoulder and departed.

"I'm sorry, too," said Nurse Turner sincerely as she stepped up to the head of the bed and puffed up my pillow. "Now, I want you to sleep. I guarantee you that everything will seem much better after you've had some rest."

Only after she had left and I had placed my pillow over my mouth did I allow myself to start cussing out the gods of war.

CHAPTER 10

▼

NURSE CONDOS

There were a number of very pleasant surprises during my eleven-day convalescent stay in the South Vietnamese seaside village of Vung Tau. War was strictly off limits in Vung Tau and the nights were cool and peaceful and the days long and lazy. For the first time since I had arrived in Vietnam, I was sleeping on clean sheets, my pillow didn't reek of mildew and it even had its own freshly laundered case. There was no gritty dirt to be constantly pushed aside under the covers, no mosquitoes to swat away, no humidity to make me want to take a shower every thirty minutes, and best of all, no incoming mortars or rockets in the middle of the night to scare the crap out of me.

The picturesque ocean was only a stone's throw away from my ward and when I wasn't mesmerized by its strength and beauty, I leisurely dispatched letter after letter reassuring relatives and friends that I was just fine and not to worry about me. I even had time to answer a few Red Cross postcards from some little school kids in Georgia who wanted to be pen pals with a wounded soldier in Vietnam.

Vung Tau also doubled as an in-country Rest and Recuperation Center for American soldiers in need of a few days off from the pressures of the war, and I spent a good portion of my slow-moving mornings and afternoons looking out my window at all the uniformed pleasure seekers, native peddlers, and off-duty nurses in bikinis who dotted the seemingly endless beach.

It quickly became obvious to me that Vung Tau was as secure as Vietnam got and I was definitely in no hurry to regain my strength and be sent back to all the uncertainties and fears of constant combat. With only one exception—the three daily and very painful irrigations of my wound—I was having the time of my military life, and I didn't feel the least bit guilty.

Even the wound irrigation had its upside. It was very carefully, almost lovingly, administered by a nurse in her mid-twenties who had the wonderfully melodic name of Carrie Condos.

During my stay in Vung Tau, Nurse Condos would arrive at my bunk at exactly ten o'clock every morning, four o'clock every afternoon, and once again at ten o'clock in the evening with all the paraphernalia needed to perform the dreaded procedure. At first, I feared her very appearance in the doorway, knowing full well I would soon be biting my lip in agony. But I quickly came to the conclusion that all the pain was more than worth it, just to be in her presence.

Nurse Condos was very matter-of-fact about her duties and her mind often seemed to be miles and miles away, but she was also very cute and had one of those thin yet busty bodies which young men thousands of miles from home in a war zone dream of almost nightly. To her professional credit, she did absolutely everything in her power to cover it up in a baggy and colorless uniform and keep it from becoming a part of any discussion, but the Herculean task was truly impossible.

"You've got to stop doing that," she politely told me on our last evening together as she gently turned me on my side and accidentally touched my erect penis.

"I'm sorry," I apologized sincerely.

"Actually," she said, breaking into one of her rare half-smiles, "I guess I should take it as kind of a compliment, shouldn't I?"

"Nurse Condos?" I asked as she began to carefully remove my bandages, "do you think it would be okay if I called you Carrie?"

"Now why would you want to start doing that?

"I don't know. I just do."

"Only if you promise me that you'll stop getting excited when I touch you."

"I guess I could try."

"Then I guess it would be okay for you to call me by my first name."

When Carrie Condos was performing her duties as a nurse, she was definitely in her element. I could tell she loved it and that she took great pride in doing her job to the very best of her ability. Her every movement seemed to have a purpose, and my every potential discomfort was anticipated and honestly explained. "It's actually looking a lot better tonight," she said, "but I'm afraid it's going to sting even a little bit worse than normal."

"Why is that?" I asked.

"Because there's this one little area that doesn't seem to want to heal as quickly as the rest."

"So, it's worse?"

"Yes, one area is worse. But overall, you're doing much better. Now, are you ready?"

"I guess so," I answered reluctantly.

"Then here we go."

With those familiar words of warning, she began to empty a whole bottle of hydrogen peroxide into my six-inch-long, two-inch-wide wound. Within moments, my whole side felt like it had been torched with a flame thrower. I buried my head into my pillow and tried very hard not to scream. "How are you doing?" she asked with concern as she took a piece of gauze and methodically spread the fire around to every nook and cranny of my wound.

"This must be what it's like to burn in hell," I mumbled between clenched teeth.

"Let's hope you never get to find out," she said as she blew air from her own lungs into my pus-filled wound.

"I think the worst part is over," I said as the pain began to slowly drift away.

"You must be getting pretty sick of this little routine of ours."

"How much longer until you think they can stitch me up?"

"Another two or three days at least. Maybe even more. I'm afraid it's taking a bit longer than the doctors thought it would."

"Really?"

"I'm sorry," she said, obviously meaning it.

"That's alright. I'm not in any hurry to get back to my unit."

"I don't blame you," she said as she worked quickly to apply a new bandage. "But I want you to begin getting up and moving around more than you have. You should be walking at least a mile or two every day out on the beach. Dr. Walters says every time he sees you, you're in bed. I won't be here to make sure you do it, but I want you to promise me you will."

"What do you mean you're not going to be here?" I asked, surprised and alarmed.

"I'm rotating on Monday and they're going to give me the weekend off to get ready. Nurse Matos will be taking over all my duties, including making sure you end up as good as new."

I should have been happy for her, but I wasn't. "You're going home?"

"That's right—finally. Now don't forget, I want you out on that beach walking. Even I go for a little stroll every night after work."

"Could I go with you sometime—before you leave?" I begged her.

She smiled and slowly shook her head from side to side. "I guess I walked right into that, didn't I?"

"Please?"

"I have a strict rule that I don't spend my off-duty time with patients," she said as she gathered up my old bandages and stood up to leave.

"Just one walk on the beach," I pleaded. "Couldn't you make just one little exception? Please?"

She hesitated for the longest time and then said, "Can you promise me there'll be no moves, no romance, nothing? Just a therapeutic walk on the beach."

"I promise. Really!"

She hesitated again, but finally said, "Well, okay, I guess it'd be alright. I'm off duty in about an hour. If you're down on the beach around then, we'll walk."

"I'll be there!"

The moon was out and there were stars everywhere as I struggled to keep pace with the short, quick steps produced by the strong but shapely legs of Carrie Condos. She suddenly came to a stop and kicked at one of the waves which was trying to make its way back out to sea. "You are in really bad shape, soldier," she said as she looked out at the moonlight dancing on the water. "All that heavy breathing coming from you is drowning out the wonderful rhythm of the waves."

"Sorry," I said, thankful that she had stopped and pretty sure she had done so to allow me to catch my breath. "Would you mind if we sat down here for a few minutes before we go on?"

"We're not going on," she said, "we're going back. You've had enough. But we can sit down and rest here for a little while if you like."

"Thanks," I said as I plopped down on the still-warm sand and waited for her to join me.

"Hold down the fort," she said as she unzipped and pulled off the thigh-length windbreaker she had been wearing and tossed it to me. "I'm going to run out and take a quick dip."

I desperately wanted to pull her down into my arms as she stood in front of me, wearing a bright yellow, one-piece bathing suit. I tried to be as discreet as possible, but I simply couldn't take my eyes off her remarkable body. "Knock it off," she ordered me, "or I'll take you back and then go swimming all by myself."

"I'm sorry," I said, repeating the one phrase which always seemed to end up coming out of my mouth when I was around her, "it's just that, well, you look drop-dead gorgeous in that thing!"

"It's the most conservative swimsuit in Vung Tau," she assured me.

"Scary, isn't it?"

She smiled, shook her head like I was just one more hopeless GI and dashed out into the surf. I filled my eyes with her as she ran away from me and dove head-first into the heart of a huge wave.

She quickly started smoothly stroking her arms and kicking her legs like swimming great distances was second nature to her, but I began to worry as she continued to get farther and farther out. She had almost disappeared from sight when I stood up and called out her name.

"I'm fine!" she yelled back from beyond the darkness.

When she finally returned to the beach and scrambled out of the surf, I tried as hard as I could not to gawk at her body, which looked even sexier now that her suit was wet.

She sat down next to me and made no attempt to dry off. "On nights like this," she said between deep breaths, "when God's in his heaven and everything seems so peaceful, it's hard to believe people are dying all around us, isn't it?"

"War must really be hard on a nurse," I said sincerely. "I mean, I can't even imagine it."

She looked over at me with a mixture of surprise and appreciation. "I take that as a real compliment—coming from a grunt."

"Being around people who are hurt frightens me," I admitted. "I just don't think I could do it every day."

"I'm impressed, soldier," she said. "And you're right, nursing certainly isn't for everyone." Much to my regret, she returned her eyes to the sea.

"Have you always wanted to be a nurse?"

"Ever since I can remember. My mother is a nurse, and my sister wants to be a nurse someday, too. I guess it's in the genes."

"Is it hard—I mean becoming one?"

"I went to a special college that taught nothing but nursing. The teachers were very strict. Everything was done by the numbers. It was very, very hard. The hardest thing I ever did—until this."

I pointed out to the ocean and said, "At least you've had the sea nearby during your tour."

"I've only been in Vung Tau for a month," she explained. "They sent me here to chill out, to get my head together before I go home."

"Oh, really? Where were you stationed before?"

"I was assigned to the 93rd Evac in Long Binh."

"Hey, that's where they operated on me."

"I know. I saw that on your work-up sheet. I know one of the surgeons who operated on you. His name is David Kleizer. He's very good, very committed."

"Really? Well, he sure did a great job. I was in and out of there like a shot."

"They do fantastic work at the 93rd. They save a lot of lives. I met so many wonderful people there. It was very difficult to leave."

"You asked to be sent to Vung Tau?"

"Well, not really. I just told them I couldn't take it anymore, and they thought it would be best for me to finish my tour here."

"Was what you did in Long Binh a lot different than what you've doing here?"

"Oh, yeah. Like night and day. This is more of a hospital. The 93rd was, well, it was like a factory. Assembly line surgery, one of the doctors called it. Thankfully, it's different here. I've got the time to let soldiers be people. There, towards the end, I'm afraid they were only bodies. There just wasn't any time. Casualties came in with such regularity, and in such volume, that there just wasn't any time to do all the little things which make nursing meaningful—even fun."

"Assembly line surgery, huh? Wow, that sounds pretty grim."

"It was beyond description, actually. And I was totally unprepared for it. I had spent some time in a stateside emergency room, but that's nothing like being an OR nurse in Vietnam."

"You sure must have seen an awful lot of misery."

"Ty," she said, lowering her voice to almost a whisper, "I've seen young boys in conditions I would have never imagined even in my worst nightmare. They'd come in with wounds I had never been exposed to in the States; bellies that didn't even look like bellies any-more; traumatic amputations of every kind and description; and head wounds that nobody had the time or expertise to deal with. It was so awful, and I'm worried that it's changed me forever." Her facial expres-sion didn't change, but tears began to roll down her cheeks. She imme-diately began to wipe them away with the back of her hand. "Now it's me who's sorry," she said. "Usually, it's you, isn't it?"

"You'll be okay once you get out of this crazy place," I tried to assure her.

"I only wish I could believe that, I really do. But to tell you the truth, I'm a basket case. It's like a part of me has just disappeared, and it's the part of me I've always liked the most."

"Which part is that?"

"The part that cares about every living creature. The part that got me into nursing in the first place. I used to really care about everyone. When one of my soldiers died, I'd cry, and not just for a few minutes, either, but for hours, sometimes days. I cried over each and every one of them. Then a few months ago, I just stopped. I couldn't feel any-thing—I couldn't cry anymore. It's like the best part of me is just as dead as all those poor young boys."

"But you're crying now," I gently reminded her.

She looked over at me and took my hand into hers. "You're right," she said, smiling more fully than I had ever seen her before. "I am cry-ing, aren't I?"

"You sure are."

Then she let the flood gates burst and I sat there with her for what seemed like the longest time, her trembling hand in mine, trying hard to think of the right thing to say, wondering if she knew that I was just as scared and alone as she was, and wishing she would look over at me instead of up at the distant stars and out at the indifferent sea.

JOURNAL ENTRY

276 DAYS TO GO

Chin Nguyen was one of our Kit Carson Scouts.

Kit Carson Scouts are repatriated ARVN soldiers who have once fought on the side of the Vietcong. In Chin's case, he had spent much of his youth believing that Ho Chi Minh's nationalist/communist approach to his country's many problems would someday free him and his large family from a life of endless agricultural drudgery and poverty. "Army outhouse smell better than rice paddy," was the way he described his love for farming.

In late 1968, at the age of twenty-two, Chin reluctantly came to the conclusion that he had been wrong about the communists, and his entire family disowned him. Shortly thereafter, he joined the Army of the Republic of Vietnam. "All my relatives call me traitor," he once told me. "My father shoot me dead if I go home."

When Chin was first assigned to our squad, he spoke very little English, but he spent most of his down hours pestering everyone in the hootch to teach him new words, and it was amazing how quickly he learned. It wasn't long before he sounded like he had spent most of his life in Los Angeles, California, instead of Can Tho, Vietnam.

Chin's private life took a turn for the better, too. He met a pretty young Vietnamese girl named Pham who worked in the mess hall and it wasn't long before they were making plans to be married. Hand in hand, they would often stroll through the compound, oblivious to everyone else they passed and obviously very much in love.

Anything and everything about America excited Chin. The language, the clothes, the music, and especially old television reruns and movies from the 1950's and 1960's. He was convinced that Gilligan's Island was a part of Hawaii and that Doris Day was the most beautiful woman on earth. His favorite exclamation, always delivered with a contagious smile, was "America numbah one!"

One evening, while waiting for someone to fix the base movie projector, Chin looked over at me, his expression much more serious than usual.

"You very lucky GI!" he exclaimed.

"Chin," I said, "I'm sitting on a rock-hard bench thousands of miles from home watching one of the worst movies ever made, and I'm lucky?"

"But when time up," he explained, "you go home to most wonderful country on earth." I nodded that I understood. "I trade you, okay?" he suggested.

"No thanks," I said.

"Too bad," he said with conviction. "I make numbah one American!"

In the field, Chin was invaluable. He was only a few inches over five-feet tall and couldn't have weighed more than a hundred and twenty-five pounds, but he was courageous to a fault and had an uncanny knack for being able to identify enemy ambushes before the actual shooting began. His ability to warn others of impending danger saved countless lives and it wasn't long before he was completely accepted by the entire platoon.

On the day I was wounded in Vietnam, so was Chin. He was placed on the stretcher above mine in a crowded medevac helicopter which immediately lifted off and began racing towards a nearby aid station in a place called Lai Khe.

I could tell by the way Chin's arm hung limply from his side that he was badly hurt. During one of my more lucid moments, I called out his name a number of times, but he never answered.

Once in Lai Khe, I was whisked off the medevac, placed on an even faster helicopter and flown all by myself to a large American surgical hospital in Long Binh, where I quickly received the very best modern medical care.

Chin, however, was unceremoniously trucked to a faraway, overcrowded Vietnamese hospital for ARVN soldiers where he apparently received almost no care at all. He died of his wounds a few days after he arrived.

When I returned to my unit to finish my tour of duty, one of the first people I looked up was Pham. But she refused to talk to me, or to any other American, for that matter. A friend of hers, through an interpreter, explained to me that while Chin's life had hung in the balance, Pham had begged every officer on the base to please have Chin transferred to a good hospital. They all refused, explaining with regret that regulations permitted only American soldiers and their dependents to be admitted to American hospitals.

"America numbah ten!" were the last words Pham ever screamed at me.

CHAPTER 11

▼

BACK TO THE WAR

Sergeant Ketchum and Harry were the only two members of my squad who hadn't been hit on the day I was wounded. Of the twenty-eight guys who had been on the ground that day, twenty-one had been hurt or killed. Custer hadn't done much worse at the Little Big Horn, but when I arrived back at the base, Harry was in better spirits than I had ever seen him.

"The whole time you were gone," Harry explained, "we hardly had to go out in the field at all. McCalley tried as hard as he could, but he couldn't come up with enough replacements to get us back up to full strength. No bait, no fishing. All we had to do was go out on a couple of training missions with the FNG's we did get in, and let me tell you, they must be getting down to the bottom of the barrel back in the States."

"So, you've been sitting around on your butt doing nothing, huh?" I asked.

"Not exactly," he answered with a mischievous smile.

"And just what does that mean?"

"Come with me, Mr. Purple Heart. A picture is worth a thousand words."

"Harry, this is my first night back. I'm exhausted. Not tonight."

"If you don't come now," he warned, "I won't be able to give you an advance showing."

"Advance showing?"

"That's right my friend, and just for you."

"Advanced showing of what?"

"Come on, man. It'll only take you a few minutes."

"What are you up to this time, Harry?"

"It's a secret."

"Give me a hint."

"Okay, T and A."

"What?"

"As in big tits and rock-hard asses."

"Really?" I said, no longer surprised by the way Harry could turn almost any conversation towards the subject of sex.

"Not so tired now, are you? Now come on. We'll be back before you know it, and this time, I've really hit the jackpot!"

Harry's gold mine turned out to be an ancient 16mm movie projector he had purchased from one of the local Vietnamese black market vendors. He had then written to one of his old college fraternity brothers and got him to mail off a half-dozen stag films, which had arrived while I was in Vung Tau.

"I want you to know that last night's premier presentation was a total sellout," Harry announced proudly as he began stringing some film from a round tin can into his movie projector.

"You showed it right here?" I asked. "In the mess hall?"

"And there was standing room only."

"The mess sergeant let you do that?"

"Well, for a small percentage of the take."

"You charged admission?"

"You're damn right I did! Five bucks a head. And I could have asked for a lot more, too. I'm telling you, Ty, this is a fucking gold mine."

"And no one said anything?"

"Not a peep."

"The major and the first sergeant don't care?"

"Well, I don't think they know yet, but when they find out, I'm going to give them this great spiel about how this is really good for morale, etc., and I think they just might go for it. In the meantime, I'm going to milk this baby for every penny it's worth."

"Harry, the major and the first sergeant aren't going to let you keep showing stag films in the mess hall."

"Now I wouldn't be so sure of that if I was you. They're two of the horniest guys on the whole base."

It wasn't quite dark yet, so the black and white picture Harry threw up on one of the mess hall walls was kind of fuzzy and hard to follow, but I could clearly make out what the two naked co-stars of the film were doing most of the time.

"No sound?" I asked.

"I can't get it to work."

"I guess you don't really need it, do you?"

"Exactly," he said, returning my smile. "What's to say? Plus the guys make plenty of noise themselves. And they come up with better lines, too."

I sat down next to Harry and we watched the whole movie, which took all of about twenty minutes. "Well, what'd you think?"

"I could have used some popcorn," I answered, trying to be funny.

"Hey, you know," said Harry, always on the lookout for new ways to make a buck, "now that's not a bad idea. Do you know what the markup on movie house popcorn is back in the world?" I shook my head 'no'. "It's something like three or four hundred percent."

"Anyway, Harry, I will say this. That movie was definitely better than most of the ones they show us around here. How many of them did you say you have?"

"Six."

"Have you checked them all out?"

"Yep."

"Which one's the best?"

Looking just like the little kid he sometimes was, he grinned and said, "Well, to tell you the truth, Ty, they all have more or less the same climax."

Within days of my return, the major had the platoon back up to full strength and much to Harry's consternation, things quickly returned to normal. I had come back with a note from the doctors in Vung Tau saying they wanted me kept out of the field for at least two more weeks to make sure everything healed properly. The note also authorized the platoon's medics to take out my stitches a week from the day it was penned.

I was still finding it difficult to put all my weight on my left leg without a sharp pain shooting through my side and I had started to limp in an effort to compensate for it. Although the limp was becoming my own little red badge of courage, I really couldn't walk any great distance without taking numerous breaks, and nobody wanted me back out in the field until I regained all my strength—with the notable exception of the first sergeant.

First Sergeant Thomas LeMaster spent his working hours at Headquarters, which was sandwiched between the communications shack and his private quarters. The whole area was heavily sandbagged and constantly patrolled by the base MP's. A reinforced concrete bunker capable of withstanding direct hits from mortars and rockets ran underneath all three structures and qualified the tiny complex as a fortress.

Headquarters itself was surrounded by a colorful flower bed which was regularly watered and weeded by the first sergeant himself, and the front yard was carpeted with the only green grass to be found on the entire base. The gravel walkway leading to the front door was also lined with large white rocks which always had a fresh coat of paint on them.

"You look fine to me," said the first sergeant after he had read my note from the doctors, wadded it up and tossed it into his trash can.

"For all I know," he added, "you could have written that damn thing yourself."

"Give them a call," I suggested.

"Okay," said the first sergeant reluctantly, "two weeks, but not a damn day more. We're still short-handed around here. We can't afford any malingerers."

"Thank you," I said, wanting to hit him.

As I was preparing to leave the office the first sergeant suddenly said, "Wait a minute." He swirled his chair around and pulled out a cabinet file drawer. He thumbed around inside it until he finally came to the folder he wanted. He spun back around to face me and opened the folder. "You've been to college, haven't you, Nichols?"

"Yes."

"Can you type?"

"A little."

"How fast?"

"I don't know. Sixty or seventy words a minutes I guess."

He was obviously impressed. "Have you ever done any filing?"

"Sure."

"How about letter writing?"

"Well, I write letters all the time."

"The major likes to verbalize his letters to me instead of writing them out himself. It's very time-consuming for me. Do you think you could do that? You know, write down what he says and then type it up for his signature?"

"I guess so."

"Don't guess, Nichols. Can you do it or not?"

"Yes. I can do it."

"Good. My morning report clerk is on his R and R, so for at least the next week, you report here to me at 0700 hours." I nodded that I understood. "And who knows," added the first sergeant with a smirk, "you just may start feeling a hell of a lot better sooner than you think."

He abruptly motioned for me to leave and returned his attention to the paperwork on his desk.

"Now let me get this straight," said Harry when I got back to our hootch, "you're going to be the major's private secretary?"

"I'm just going to take some dictation," I said, realizing it was the wrong word to use as soon as it popped out of my mouth.

"Dictation?" howled Harry. "Are you going to be in charge of bringing him his fucking morning coffee, too?"

"Hey, it beats getting shot at, doesn't it?" That shut him up.

My first seventy-two hours as the troop's substitute company clerk were three of the toughest days I had spent in Vietnam. The moment I arrived in the first sergeant's sweat shop, I was required to spend as many hours as it took to perfectly type the day's morning report.

The morning report was an official document which identified who had reported for duty that morning and who hadn't. Top explained with great passion that regular inspections demanded that the morning report always be up-to-date and accurate. Depending on who was where, it could be a pretty lengthy document, and absolutely no typing mistakes were allowed. Any error, no matter how slight, and I had to rip the thing up and start all over again.

When I would finally finish the morning report, usually sometime around noon, the first sergeant would immediately pile my in-basket as high as he could with what seemed like hundreds of papers in need of typing or filing or both. When all my work was completed, usually around six o'clock, I was too exhausted to even go to the movie. Mercifully, day four was different.

As soon as I had finished the morning report, Top came over and escorted me back into the major's private office. He told me to sit down, shoved a notebook and a couple of pencils into my hands and said the major would be entering by the back door in about five minutes.

"Do exactly as you're told," the first sergeant ordered me. "And don't speak unless you're spoken to," he added with emphasis as he left the room.

Major McCalley had become an almost mythical figure to me and I waited nervously for my first face-to-face encounter with the man who had so often held my life in his hands. It seemed to me that the major almost deliberately kept his distance from all the members of the rifle platoon and when any of us did manage to catch a glimpse of him, his eyes were usually hidden behind an expensive pair of dark aviation sunglasses.

The only thing I really knew about the man was that he had the most perfect posture I had ever seen. Seated or standing, his shoulders were always pulled back and his chest thrust forward. His lean, muscular body seemed to have been chiseled from stone, and the way he strutted around the base left no doubt that he was very proud of it.

The windowless walls of the major's office were covered with plaques and dozens of framed photographs. As I looked around, it became clear the man really liked getting his picture taken. What was weird, though, was that he always posed the exact same way, with the right side of his face turned towards the camera, and his facial expression never varied. Not a single smile in any of the photographs, just the same stern and steely-eyed glare which gave the distinct impression that he was completely in control of every emotion he possessed.

When the knob on the office door began to turn, I leapt to my feet and stood at attention. The major entered the room and walked briskly to his desk, not acknowledging my presence in any way. He was impeccably uniformed as usual, and his fatigues had been freshly laundered, starched and ironed. His recently shined boots had a glow on them the like of which I hadn't seen since basic training.

He pulled out his chair, sat down at his desk and without looking up, said, "Be seated, soldier." I snapped off a salute which the major didn't return and sat down. "I understand you were one of the young men wounded a few weeks back and that you'll be helping Top out for awhile."

"Yes, sir."

"I take it the healing process is going well?"

"Yes, sir."

"Good. Now, as Top has explained to you, I like to dictate my letters. Do you see all the paperwork in my in-box?"

"Yes, sir." It was piled a good foot high.

"I'm at least a month behind in my correspondence. Let's see if we can put a dent in that." I opened my notebook and raised my pencil to the ready. "One more thing," he said, looking up at me for the first time, "everything you hear or see in this office is absolutely confidential. It doesn't leave this room. Is that understood, soldier?"

"Yes, sir."

"Good, now let's get to work."

He took a letter from the top of his in-box, quickly scanned it and said, "Dear Stan. Thank you for your letter of the twenty-second. You must be very proud that young Stan was accepted into the Citadel. As you know, that was my alma mater and it had a lot to do with making me the man I am today."

The words continued to fly out of his mouth fast and clear, and although I was only able to get about every other one down on paper, I didn't ask him to slow down or stop, and I could tell that he was impressed by that.

When he had finished responding to the letter, he said, "Got all of that?"

"Yes, sir," I lied.

"Good. Now go type it up and get it back to me for my signature as soon as you can."

When I returned in less than ten minutes with a typed letter in hand, the major seemed genuinely surprised that I had completed my task so quickly. He read it carefully for mistakes and when he could find none, said, "It's not exactly what I told you, but it's close enough, and a few of the things you added even make it read a little better. Very good, soldier. This may just work out after all."

For the rest of the week, my routine became very predictable. I would finish the morning report as quickly as I could and then spend the rest of the day and most of the evening with Major McCalley in his office, where an extra typewriter had been stationed. We repeated the same procedure we had established over and over again until we were actually beginning to make a dent in his in-box. The only time we weren't together was when the major was called off to supervise a mission, and even then he tried to delegate most of that responsibility so he could stay focused on his correspondence.

I typed up letters to old friends the major had served with all over the world and fellow officers he had recently met in Vietnam. I also sent letters off to banks, insurance companies, car dealerships, colleges the major's children attended, and even state-side businesses he thought might want his services after his military career was over.

By the end of the week, he was even entrusting me with the complicated correspondence he was carrying on between himself and a number of girlfriends he had stashed away in Hawaii and Japan. The only letters the major wrote with his own hand were to his wife, whose picture was proudly displayed on his desk.

Much to the surprise of both of us, when my week was up, the major's in-box was empty. On our last afternoon together, he actually took off his sunglasses, looked me right in the eye and said, "I want to thank you."

"You're welcome, sir," I said, standing up to leave.

The major waved for me to sit back down. "I know that all the men in the rifle platoon hate me," he said with genuine regret. "That truly bothers me from time to time, but your responsibilities here in Vietnam are much different than mine. It's my job to find the enemy and destroy him, and the better we perform that mission, the sooner this war ends. I'm not a horrible person and when I lose one of you boys, I want you to know that it hurts."

"I think the men know that, sir."

"No they don't. And what's even more painful at times is the fact that they often see me as their enemy, instead of the gooks they were sent over here to kill." He waited for me to respond, and when I didn't, he added, "This is a completely new generation of soldiers, Nichols, and to be quite honest with you, most of them are concerned only with their own safety. Stopping communism in its tracks and hanging Ho Chi Minh up by his balls means nothing to the majority of them. And the truly sad part is that they don't even understand how good they have it. This isn't World War Two, you know, where the enemy had just as much fire power as us and when everyone was in it for the duration. Duty and mission meant something back then. I'm afraid that is no longer the case in this Army of draftees."

He rambled on and on for the next fifteen minutes or so, telling me how he had been trained to be distant and aloof and that the decisions he made out in the field were well thought-out and that he always tried to put the safety of his men first.

Somewhere towards the end of the unexpected speech it dawned on me that the man actually liked me, a little anyway, and that I had started to like him, too. I didn't kid myself, though. I was fully aware of the fact that any opinions I might have on any of the subjects the major had raised were of absolutely no interest to him. But in many ways, the major seemed to be just like the rest of the men I had met in Vietnam, trying the best he could to play the cards he had been dealt.

It was the first and last time the major and I spoke to one another and I know of no other conversation he ever had with anyone else in the rifle platoon. And the last words he uttered before he put his sunglasses back on were, "Keep your head down, Nichols. This may not be much of a war, but the other guys are using real bullets, too, and I don't want to have to conduct a memorial service for you someday."

JOURNAL ENTRY

269 DAYS TO GO

I don't know what was in the chow tonight, but about half the platoon has the runs. For the past five or six hours, we've all been taking turns racing back and forth to the outhouse. Harry says it was probably the chipped beef they put on top of our toast. I think it was the watery grey slime they were trying to pass off as gravy. Thank God I'm starting to feel a little bit better. My stomach isn't so cramped up and I'm no longer barfing and sweating bullets like I was a few hours ago. I sure hope my last trip was the final one. My poor butt is so raw from wiping it with that sandpaper the Army calls toilet paper that I can barely sit down.

Like everything else, though, there was an upside. On my second-to-last visit to the crapper (and boy, that place has never smelled worse, and that's really saying something!) I ended up seated next to Joaquin Sanchez, whom I've never had much of a chance to talk to before. He's a crew chief on one of the transport helicopters and like most everyone else, I'm in awe of his big lover reputation. In fact, most everyone just calls him Lover Boy Joaquin, or LBJ for short. And if the rumors are anything close to being true, then the guy has slept with just about every female on the base, and most of the ones in town, too. Visiting nurses, candy stripers, and the best-looking Vietnamese girls from miles around all seem to end up in his bed. I've seen them coming and going from his hootch at all hours of the day and night and have often wondered what his secret was.

Anyway, as Joaquin and I were squatting there making the most barbaric noises imaginable, he suddenly said, "I hear you got yourself a `Dear John' letter awhile back."

"Who told you that?" I asked him, sure he didn't even know my name.

"Your buddy Harry keeps everybody up-to-date on that sort of thing," he said, grunting and pushing hard again, but with only a blast of gas for all his effort.

"Oh."

"Well, don't let it get you down. Remember, there's always another broad." I nodded my head and he quickly added, "The key is just having the courage to ask. It's so simple. My uncle Alberto taught me that many years ago."

"Your uncle Alberto?"

"You know what Alberto used to do?" I shook my head `no'. "Well, he'd put on his best clothes, go down to the busiest street corner in all of Albuquerque and then just stand there for hours and hours at a time."

"Doing what?"

"Asking every nice-looking woman who passed him by if she would be interested in going to bed with him."

"You're kidding?"

He returned my smile. "Nope. Uncle Alberto is very charming and he'd just politely say, 'Excuse me, madam, but you're very beautiful and I was wondering if I can sleep with you tonight?'"

"Really?"

"Yep. Most of the time he'd get slapped silly, or get chased by a boyfriend, or hit with a purse, or even spit on, but you wanna know what?"

"What?"

"Uncle Alberto got more ass than any other guy I've ever known."

CHAPTER 12

▼

MEDALS CEREMONY

At the morning roll-call formation the first sergeant informed the whole platoon that there would be no afternoon mission. When the cheers had finally died down, he further explained that as soon as everyone returned from the morning mission, we were all to take showers, put on our best set of fatigues and try and get ourselves as spit and polished as possible. We were then to report at exactly 1400 hours to the tarmac for a medals presentations ceremony.

"General Novak is flying all the way up from Saigon to pass out the medals," said the first sergeant, "and I don't want you looking like a bunch of damn hippies. Should any one of you fail to attend the ceremonies, or should any one of you arrive looking like a damn slob, I will personally see to it that your life becomes a living hell. Now, are there any questions?"

"Who's getting the medals?" shouted someone from the back row.

"You'll find that out at the ceremony, won't you?" answered the first sergeant matter-of-factly.

"Awe, come on, Top," pleaded Harry. "Can't you give us a little hint? Who's the latest official war hero?"

"Well, Watts," said the first sergeant with a nasty smile, "I can pretty much guarantee a chicken-shit like you isn't going to get one." Even Harry seemed to think that was funny and he joined in on the laughter. "Now, are there any other questions before we get this on the road?"

"Is the whole base falling out for the ceremony, or is it just us?" asked one of the medics.

"Cooks, clerks, mechanics, everyone," said the first sergeant. "It's not often that we get a visitor of General Novak's rank and importance. So, don't forget, 1400 hours, and looking sharp! Dismissed."

I didn't have a decent set of fatigues to my name and neither did Harry, so we spent a good part of our lunch hour running around the compound begging and borrowing. We were both also badly in need of a haircut and weren't about to shine our mud-caked combat boots, so when 1400 hours rolled around, we inspected each other and decided to just hope for the best. We were greatly surprised when we stepped out onto the tarmac and the first sergeant let us pass. His exact words were, "To tell you two the truth, I expected worse."

Then the long wait began. 1400 hours came and went, followed ever so slowly by 1500 and 1600. It was ninety degrees in the shade, of which there was none, and with the humidity just as high, I was about to give in to heat stroke when the general's helicopter finally dropped down out of the sky and created the first real air movement the platoon had experienced in over two hours.

General Novak really looked the part as he climbed out of his aircraft and aggressively shook Major McCalley's hand. He was about fifty years old and there was a big shiny star centered on the steel pot atop his massive head. He also had a thin, neatly trimmed mustache which reminded me of the one Errol Flynn always wore in his swashbuckling movies.

The major quickly introduced the general to his executive officer, the first sergeant, and some of the warrant officers who had gathered for the ceremony. He then directed him to the podium and microphone which had been set up for the occasion.

"At ease, gentlemen," barked the general. He looked out at the limp and lifeless collection of soldiers and apologized for being late, explaining that all hell had broke loose in one of his sectors and his presence had been required to make sure the whole thing didn't get out of hand. "Anyway," he continued, "it's my great pleasure to be here today to present these well-earned medals to the fine officers and men of Charlie Troop."

"Echo Troop, you idiot," Harry mumbled under his breath.

The first sergeant reached over and handed the general a piece of paper and whispered something into his ear. "If I said Charlie Troop," apologized the general, "I stand corrected. I meant Echo. It's been a very long day." He took out a pair of glasses, placed them securely on the bridge of his thick nose and began to read: "For heroism in connection with military operations against a hostile force in the Republic of Vietnam. On this date, Major William W. McCalley...."

"What in the hell is this?" whispered Harry to me as the general went on and on about all the heroic things Major McCalley had supposedly done on the day so many of us had been wounded. Other members of the platoon seemed just as puzzled, knowing full well that the major hadn't even allowed his command helicopter to land on the ground that day until the whole area had been secured and all of the wounded evacuated. "Un-fucking believable," said Harry, no longer whispering. "That asshole doesn't deserve any medal, and everybody knows it. The only thing he did that day was almost get us all killed."

"His courageous initiative and selfless concern for the welfare of those under his command," continued the general, "significantly contributed to the successful outcome of the encounter. Major McCalley's outstanding display of aggressiveness, devotion to duty, and personal bravery is in keeping with the finest traditions of the military service and reflect great credit upon himself and the United States Army. By direction of the President of the United States, under the provisions of

Executive Order 11045, dated September 19th, 1968, I hereby award the Silver Star for valor to Major William W. McCalley."

"The Silver Star?" blurted out Harry, beating his forehead with the palm of his hand. "Jesus-fucking-Christ! Why didn't he just put himself in for the Congressional Medal of Honor?"

Even I was shocked, and Harry and I weren't alone. You could have heard a pin drop on the rifle platoon's section of the tarmac.

The first sergeant stepped over and handed the general a tiny black box which contained the medal. The general opened it and held the Silver Star and the red, white, and blue ribbon it dangled from up for everyone to see. "Major McCalley," said the general, "would you step forward, please."

The first sergeant and some of the warrant officers applauded, but most of Echo Troop just looked at their neighbors in stunned silence.

The smiling general pinned the medal on Major McCalley's freshly starched fatigue top, shook his hand firmly and patted him on the shoulder. Then, after explaining that he regrettably didn't have the time to read any of the other citations, the general said something about all the heroism which had been displayed on the day the rifle platoon took so many casualties and quickly shook hands with everyone in arm's reach. He then gave the whole troop the 'V' for victory sign and waved goodbye with one long sweep of his hand.

As the general's helicopter began to rev up, he shook Major McCalley's hand one last time and nimbly climbed back aboard his aircraft. He was airborne in an instant and barely out of sight when the first sergeant stepped up to the microphone and announced, "Now, a number of others were put in for medals and commendations. When I call out your name, please come up to the podium as quickly as possible. It's goddamn hot out here!"

Later that night, after wolfing down evening chow and watching the movie, Harry and I went over to Sergeant Ketchum's room to admire the Bronze Star he had been awarded. Harry picked up the citation which went with it, and knowing that it would annoy Sergeant

Ketchum, dramatically began to read: "The Bronze Star Medal with "V" device, awarded for heroism not involving participation in aerial flight in the Republic of Vietnam. On this date, Sergeant James J. Ketchum was serving as a squad leader with his mechanized unit within an area of known enemy activity. As the friendly force proceeded through the treacherous region, enemy movement was detected from a light observation helicopter overhead and the decision was made to pursue the insurgents."

"Knock it off, Watts," said Sergeant Ketchum, finally looking up from the book he was reading. "It's all bullshit and you know it. You've seen it, now get the hell out of here. Both of you. It's getting late."

"Acting with tactical deliberation," continued Harry, "Sergeant Ketchum...."

"I'm not kidding, Watts!"

"Come on, Harry," I said, grabbing the citation from him and returning it to Sergeant Ketchum. "You're just jealous, anyway."

"You know," said Harry as we left Sergeant Ketchum's room, "I may be one of the biggest cowards ever to disgrace an American uniform, but what McCalley did out there today was the most disgraceful thing I've ever seen."

"It's done, Harry," I said. "Let it go. Sergeant Ketchum's right. Medals don't mean anything. All that's really important is going home. Do you know what he told me when he was walking off the tarmac with his Bronze Star?"

"No, what?"

"He said, 'Heroes aren't made in heaven, they're just cornered someplace on earth'."

JOURNAL ENTRY

231 DAYS TO GO

We're not even halfway through November yet and they're already starting to show us old Christmas movies. Tonight it was Frank Capra's "It's a Wonderful Life", starring Jimmy Stewart and Donna Reed. Most of the guys said they had seen it a half-dozen times back in the world, but it was a first for me. And it was a great movie! I still can't get it out of my mind. It was in black and white and it starts out with a young boy saving the life of his brother, who had accidentally fallen into an icy pond while playing with his friends. This turns out to be just the first of numerous people and moments in time which are directly affected by the life of George Bailey (Jimmy Stewart).

As George grows older, he also keeps the druggist from accidentally giving one of his customers a deadly prescription; he gives the money he had saved for his own college education to his brother and sends him off to the university he himself had long dreamed of attending; and he reluctantly takes over the leadership of the family business, a rundown savings and loan company which never makes any money, but makes it possible for many of the citizens of Bedford Falls to live in decent homes which they can someday hope to own themselves.

Anyway, poor George never gets the opportunity to fulfill any of his most cherished dreams. He never gets to attend college, or become a famous architect who travels all over the world constructing airports and grand buildings, and he never makes the kind of money which would allow him the freedom to leave tiny Bedford Falls once and for all.

What George does end up doing, however, is marrying Mary (Donna Reed), a hometown girl who has been crazy about him ever since she can remember, and it isn't long before they're raising a big family in the drafty old Grandville house. Now, how anyone in their right mind can possibly consider a lifetime with Donna Reed (I have always had a crush on her) as anything less than the crowning achievement of their life is beyond me, but that is where the plot finds George Bailey on Christmas Eve, 1945.

To make things even worse, $8,000 of the savings and loan assets have been misplaced and it looks like George is going to end up in jail, his life and reputation shot. In a moment of tearful regret that his life has been so meaningless, he wishes he had never been born.

Then an angel named Clarence, who is desperately in need of acquiring his wings, grants George his wish and the movie begins to show what a world without George Bailey would have really been like. Among other things, his brother would have died at the age of nine and never grown up to be a war hero; Mr. Gower, the old druggist, would have accidentally killed one of his best customers; most of the nice citizens of Bedford Falls would have been forced to live in the slums of Pottersville instead of beautiful Bailey Park; and Donna Reed (this is the only part of the movie I found hard to believe) would have ended up an old maid working in the town library.

The movie ends with George happy and appreciative to be back among the living, mean old Mr. Potter thwarted in his greedy effort to gain control of the Bailey Savings and Loan, and everyone in town over at George's house showering him with money and singing Auld Lang Syne. Clarence also finally gets his wings (he's been trying for 200 years) and he leaves George a note explaining that 'No man is a failure who has friends'.

I couldn't believe how homesick I was when it was over! And wow, what a great theme for a movie, that our friends are invaluable, and that every life makes a huge difference, often in ways we don't even understand. It sure does make a guy think—and want to do the Charleston with Donna Reed.

CHAPTER 13

▼

THE SHAKE AND BAKE

Lieutenant Kenneth Davenport and Private Murray Goldstein were both Americans and they wore the same olive drab military uniform, but that was about all they had in common. The lieutenant had his hair chopped down to almost nothing every week, and Murray hadn't had his touched since he had arrived in Vietnam; the lieutenant's voice was loud and clear, while Murray spoke so softly that he was always being asked to speak up; the lieutenant absolutely hated the enemy and Murray thought the Vietnamese were the sweetest people he had ever met; and the lieutenant truly enjoyed killing human beings while Murray was incapable of harming a fly.

The young, bull-necked lieutenant's stay with the rifle platoon lasted less than a month, but I'm convinced that if Charlie hadn't got him, one of his own men would have. He was a handsome, muscular, and thoroughly dislikable shake and bake who arrived with his own World War Two Thompson machine gun under his arm and the announced intention of immediately squaring away his new command and raising our kill count up to a more respectable level.

"With all the air support you people have," shouted the lieutenant as everyone stood at attention out on the tarmac the day of his arrival, "this outfit ought to be kicking ass and taking names on a daily basis! And I'm going to make damn sure we start doing just that!"

"Listen to that deep drawl," Murray whispered to me and Harry. "Why are idiots like that always from the South? When are they going to figure out soldiering isn't the same honorable profession it was way back in the Civil War?"

"The South doesn't have a monopoly on idiots," I told Murray. "Give him a chance. Maybe it's just talk."

"It better be," chipped in Harry, "because I'm sure as hell not going to walk through any walls for that bastard."

"I really wish we hadn't lost Lieutenant Townsend," said Murray. "He was the only officer I've ever known who didn't think he was God. He sure was special."

"Do you three have something you'd like to offer to this conversation?" shouted the new lieutenant in our direction. We all shook our heads 'no'. "Then shut up!"

The platoon's first objective under Lieutenant Davenport's command was a rural cemetery suspected of also being a Vietcong support center. Charlie seemed to like to set up elaborate bunker systems in graveyards and then stock them with everything from rice to medical supplies. He knew Americans didn't like to hang out with the dead, and he took advantage of it every chance he could.

The platoon was inserted into a lush, marshy clearing and I was carrying Sergeant Ketchum's radio as usual. When I leaped out of my transport helicopter, the added twenty-five pounds of weight on my back immediately buried me knee-deep in the muddy earth.

"Nice going," said Murray as he and Sergeant Ketchum struggled to pull me free. "You gotta look where you're jumping, man," he added, smiling. "This is embarrassing."

"What's the damn holdup?" yelled the new lieutenant as he arrived on the scene.

"No problem," said Sergeant Ketchum. "My RTO just got himself stuck in the mud. We'll have him out in a few minutes."

"No problem?" yelled the lieutenant. "What if this had been a hot LZ?"

"Well, it wasn't, was it, sir?" answered Sergeant Ketchum, not even bothering to look at the lieutenant.

Lieutenant Davenport was obviously displeased with Sergeant Ketchum's answer and the tone of his voice but he only said, "Just get your damn squad squared away, Sergeant. We've got a mission to complete."

"Yes, sir," said Sergeant Ketchum respectfully.

The lead element of the platoon soon had the tombstones in sight and it wasn't long before gunships were swooping down and prepping the area, accidentally destroying a couple of burial plots in the process. When the bombardment finally came to an end, I followed Sergeant Ketchum up to where Murray, who was walking point, had stationed himself.

"Our fearless leaders still bullshitting?" Sergeant Ketchum asked me.

I pushed my radio headset, which was dangling from my steel pot, closer to my ear and listened for a few moments as the lieutenant and the major discussed strategy.

"Yep," I said, "it sounds like they're thick as thieves."

"Those two sure like each other, don't they?" asked Murray.

"Yeah, they're always having some damn meeting," mumbled Sergeant Ketchum.

"I guess even the major needs a friend," I said.

"The war must look pretty good from way up there where the major hangs out," said Murray as he squinted his eyes and glanced up into the bright, cloudless sky where the command helicopter was circling high above us.

"And easy, too," said Sergeant Ketchum.

"About the only thing the major has to worry about over here is catching a case of the clap," said Murray. "It sure must be nice."

Murray had been with the squad for almost four months and his nickname was "Hip", short for hippie. He hated the war with a passion, but he still took a lot of pride in the way he did his job and was one of the few veterans who would volunteer to walk point from time to time. Sergeant Ketchum didn't much care for his politics or sense of humor, but he respected him as a soldier.

"They want us to move forward," I informed Sergeant Ketchum. "One of the helicopters has spotted a wounded VC in the open."

"At least they weren't blowing up the graveyard for hell of it," said Murray as Sergeant Ketchum pumped his fist high over his head, setting the whole platoon in motion.

Although Sergeant Ketchum and I were a good ten yards behind Murray, it was me who first spotted the wounded Vietcong. He was seriously injured, bleeding profusely from wounds to the head and chest. He was sitting on the ground, his head tilted to the side and his back propped up against a small grave marker. I immediately pointed him out to Sergeant Ketchum, who yelled up to Murray to take cover, and the three of us quickly ducked behind a nearby tombstone.

We all took turns peeking our heads out around the corner of the tombstone for a second look. On closer examination, we could see that the Vietcong had what appeared to be a loaded AK-47 lying beside him, within arm's reach.

"He's armed," said Sergeant Ketchum as he yanked a hand grenade off his ammo belt.

"I don't think we'll need that," said Murray.

"You sure?" asked the sergeant.

"Look for yourself," said Murray. "He's in no shape to hurt anyone."

Sergeant Ketchum peeked out around his side of the tombstone again and studied the critically wounded Vietcong for at least a full minute. "Yeah," he finally said, "I think you're right. It looks like we got ourselves a POW."

As we all stood up and carefully began making our way towards the young and probably dying Vietcong, we could see how scared he was, and that he was in a great deal of pain. His frightened eyes seemed to be glued to Murray as he desperately tried to get a clue to his fate.

"We're not going to hurt you," said Murray in a calming voice as we approached closer.

Suddenly the distinctive sound of Lieutenant Davenport's submachine gun began to roar and I almost jumped out of my skin as the lieutenant emptied a full clip into the body of the screaming Vietcong. Blood, flesh, and chunks of the grave marker he had been resting against flew in all directions.

"No!" yelled Murray as he turned around and lunged at Lieutenant Davenport. He grabbed the sparkling clean machine gun, yanked it out of the lieutenant's hands and slammed it into the ground.

Lieutenant Davenport was enraged. "Are you crazy!" he shouted.

"You didn't have to kill him," yelled Murray.

"He was going for his gun, you damn fool!"

"Like hell he was," said Sergeant Ketchum.

"One more word out of you, Sergeant," screamed the lieutenant as he pointed to Murray, "and you'll be in as much trouble as he is!" He reached down, picked up his cherished weapon and carefully inspected it for any damage. "Private," he yelled at Murray, "I'll deal with you when we get back to base!"

"Fuck you!" replied Murray.

"Get him out of here!" the lieutenant ordered Sergeant Ketchum.

Sergeant Ketchum stepped between the lieutenant and Murray and said, "Alright, alright, I'll take care of it. Everybody just cool down, okay?"

With his anger still barely under control, the lieutenant stormed off to examine his first kill. "Make sure you fucking do!" he yelled back at Sergeant Ketchum. "I don't want to see his face again until this mission is over!"

"You shouldn't have grabbed his damn gun, Murray," said Sergeant Ketchum.

"He didn't have to do that," said Murray, fighting back tears.

"I know," said Sergeant Ketchum, "but damn it, that gook was going to die anyway. Ty, you better take Murray back to the PZ. I'll go try to calm down the lieutenant."

"Okay," I said as Murray and I watched in silence as the lieutenant repeatedly kicked the lifeless body of the Vietcong to make sure it was dead.

The dying screams of the enemy teenager were still ringing in my ears as I took Murray by the arm and escorted him to the rear.

JOURNAL ENTRY

217 DAYS TO GO

We held last night's poker game over at Bravo Squad's hootch in Sergeant Hughes' room. Everything was going great—I was up almost ten bucks—and then Harry and the sergeant got into it again.

Sergeant Steven Hughes is a solid, reliable squad leader who most everyone in the troop respects for the serious and competent way he goes about doing his job. He has lived everywhere, but calls the state of Idaho home, and he has a girlfriend in a small town there that he writes to every single day. He is a Navy brat, if there is such a thing, and his father is a pretty important Navy officer who has spent most of his career underwater in nuclear submarines.

Sergeant Hughes is also very opinionated when it comes to politics, having worked very hard trying to get Barry Goldwater elected President of the United States in 1964 when he was only a senior in high school. An autographed picture of his dad energetically shaking hands with Goldwater sits proudly atop his wall locker.

Everybody knows it's best not to talk politics with Sergeant Hughes, but from time to time, it seems to be one of Harry's favorite ways of relaxing.

"So, Hughes," said Harry right after the sergeant had raked in the biggest pot of the night, at least half of it coming from a bluff by Harry which

didn't work, "*have you been reading about the new wave of antiwar demonstrations back in the States?*"

"*Come on, Harry,*" *I pleaded,* "*don't start that up.*"

"*You know how I feel about those people, Watts,*" *said Sergeant Hughes.* "*They're scum. Nothing more, nothing less.*"

"*I don't know about that,*" *responded Harry.* "*I think all they're trying to do is end the war. What's so wrong about that?*"

"*What they're doing, though, is just the opposite,*" *explained Sergeant Hughes.* "*They're giving aid and comfort to the enemy and giving Hanoi the false hope that we don't have the political will to stay the course. They're prolonging this war, Watts, not shortening it.*"

"*You're starting to sound just like ol' Tricky Dickie,*" *said Harry.*

"*President Nixon is a great American, Watts, and it doesn't surprise me in the least that you can't stand him.*"

"*Bobby Kennedy would have blown him away at the polls,*" *said Harry.*

"*If he hadn't got blown away himself, huh, Watts?*"

"*Let's just play cards, okay,*" *said Bert Jenkins, the sergeant's RTO and the best poker player of our foursome.*

"*This war will end,*" *continued Sergeant Hughes,* "*when we stop worrying about what a few cowardly hippies are doing and get on with what we were sent here to do.*"

"*And just why was I sent here?*" *asked Harry.* "*I never have been able to quite figure that out.*"

"*To stop the spread of communism, pure and simple,*" *said Sergeant Hughes.*

"*Get serious, Hughes,*" *said Harry.*

"*I'm dead serious. The spread of communism has to be stopped, and it has to be stopped right here in Vietnam. A more despicable form of government has never existed on this earth—never.*"

"*You don't really believe that crap, do you?*" *asked Harry with a smile.*

"*You're damn right I believe it. There's good and bad in this world, Watts, and communism is as evil as it gets.*"

"Why can't the Vietnamese just decide for themselves how they want to run this armpit of a country?" suggested Harry.

"Because the Reds won't let them decide for themselves. That's the problem. And if you let them get a foothold here, it's just a matter of time before we can kiss off Thailand, Laos and Cambodia, too."

"The ol' domino theory, huh?" asked Harry.

"That's right, Watts, and anyone with a brain can understand it. I can't help it if the whole concept goes over your head."

"You know what your problem is, Hughes?" asked Harry.

"I don't have a problem, Watts. You're the one with the problem."

"And what would that be, Sarge?"

"Your problem is that you're a bleeding-heart liberal. That and the fact that you talk politics just like you play poker, with your head up your ass."

That made everyone at the table chuckle and only encouraged Harry to up the verbal ante. "Those demonstrators you can't stand are going to end this war, Hughes, and when they do, the gooks are going to have the last laugh."

"You should have taken off to Canada with the rest of the scum, Watts," said Sergeant Hughes, truly angered.

"Come on, you two," interrupted Bert, "you're both saying a lot of shit you're just going to regret tomorrow."

"Stay out of this, Jenkins," said Sergeant Hughes. "This fool has been bad-mouthing what we're trying to do over here since the first day he arrived."

"Well," I said in Harry's defense, "sometimes what he says makes some sense."

"Right on, Ty!" shouted Harry.

"And all the people who went to Canada ain't scum, Sarge," interjected Bert. "My cousin is up there right now, and he gave up a whole lot when he made that decision. At least he ain't hiding out in some college or the National Guard like most of his friends."

"A draft-dodger is a draft-dodger, Jenkins," said Sergeant Hughes with conviction.

"Everything's not always so black and white, Sergeant Hughes," I said. "And that goes for you, too, Harry!"

"Come on, Ty," said Harry, "damn it, you can't spend your whole life always sitting on the fence. This idiot is a right-wing nut, and you know it as well as I do. You can't hurt his feelings. He doesn't have any."

"That's it, Watts!" yelled Sergeant Hughes. "Get the fuck out of here! I'm sick and tired of listening to your shit!"

"No problem, Sarge," said Harry, aware that Sergeant Hughes was just about ready to stand up and take a swing at him.

"Now!" yelled Sergeant Hughes.

"Here," said Harry as he stood up and pushed what few remaining poker chips he had left into the center of the table, "buy yourself a fucking clue with them."

"And don't ever step in my room again!" screamed Sergeant Hughes as Harry departed.

After I had cashed out, I found Harry outside the Sergeant's hootch, waiting for me. "Just how come I got so lucky, Harry?" I asked him as we walked back towards our hootch.

"What do you mean, man?"

"Tell me, how come, out of everybody in the whole bloody Army, you picked me to be your side-kick?"

Harry thought about his answer for a moment and then said, "I don't know, man. Why did Roy Rogers pick Gabby Hayes?"

CHAPTER 14

▼

THE HOMESICK NVA

As I reluctantly helped our Kit Carson Scout leader Toi Nguyen search some mangled VC bodies which had been blown away by a Cobra rocket run, we unexpectedly came upon a soldier who wasn't quite dead yet. A huge piece of shrapnel had slammed into the center of his chest and it was hard to believe he was still somehow breathing.

We quickly made sure he had no weapons on him and then propped him up against one of the dirt walls of the destroyed bunker. There was no panic in his eyes and although it was a real struggle for him to talk, he seemed more than willing to try and answer Toi's questions. He was closer to Toi in age than me and for someone who had probably been out in the jungle for months, he was remarkably well-groomed. He didn't even have any dirt under his fingernails.

"What's he saying, Toi?" I asked.

"He is in much pain, and he is very homesick. He has been in the South for a long time."

"Then he's not a VC?"

"No, he is NVA, one of their political cadre. He is down here to help with recruitment and indoctrination. It is too bad he is going to die. There is much we could have learned from him."

"Should I radio for a dustoff?" I asked. "Maybe we could get him back to an aid station and patch him up?"

"No. It is much too late for that. I think he only has minutes to live."

"Are you sure?"

"Yes, I'm afraid so."

"Does he know how bad he's hit?"

"Oh, yes. He knows it won't be long now."

Toi continued to calmly talk back and forth in Vietnamese with the dying soldier until the ashen-faced NVA suddenly lurched forward, arched his back and quietly drew his last breath. Only after Toi had said a short Buddhist prayer did he begin his search for documents. He looked through the man's pockets first and then began digging around in a lightweight backpack.

"What's that?" I asked as Toi pulled out what appeared to be a small notebook.

"This is very interesting," said Toi as he thumbed through the pages. "It is their soldier's oath and some other teaching material."

"What's it say?"

"Many things."

"Like what?"

"Well, it says that each new recruit must swear to defend the Fatherland and sacrifice himself for the revolution. They are to obey their orders and work for solidarity between the Army and the people. They must also pay fairly for what they buy, be nice to women, and there is much, much more."

"So, he was down here to swear in new recruits and stuff?"

"Yes, but he was more valuable to them than that. He was a political officer. It was his duty to inspire all the soldiers in his unit. He was probably a good speaker and very knowledgeable about how Hanoi wants things done. Political officers are only selected from the best of the best. Even though he probably wasn't too involved with military decisions, he was still a very important person."

"What about that letter you took out of his pocket?"

As Toi put aside the notebook and removed the one page letter from its envelope, I reached around the dead man's body and checked his rear pockets. "There's nothing back here, Toi."

"This is very sad," said Toi, his voice tailing off.

"What is it?" I asked as he continued to read quietly to himself and shake his head.

"A letter from his wife. His name was Van."

"Really? What does it say?"

"It is quite long."

"We've got a few minutes."

"Well, if you want."

"Thanks," I said, my morbid curiosity piqued by Toi's sorrowful eyes.

"Her writing is not always very clear, but it begins, 'My dearest husband Van: I have just received your letter. How happy I am! My commander gave it to me this afternoon. I am so lucky that my husband who I love above all others is alive and well. It was the first letter from you to arrive in more than one month. I had become very worried. But now I know you are safe and I will sleep well tonight for the first time in many, many days. I am so sorry to learn of your new struggles. We are often short of food here, too. We have very little meat or fish or salt. But just like you, I keep loyal to the party and to the people. I am sure the liberation will come soon and we will both be full of peace and happiness."

Toi handed me a tiny black and white photograph which had been in the envelope. A very pretty woman in dark pajama-type pants and a white blouse was holding a chubby, round-faced baby that looked to be about a year old, two at the most.

"She goes on to say how proud she is to be marching on the revolutionary path and giving all of her strength and energy to the party," added Toi," shaking his head, "and that when victory is achieved, all loved ones will be united again in peace and glory."

"So, she's NVA, too?" I asked.

"Oh, yes. Very much so."

"Boy, she sounds pretty gung ho, doesn't she?"

"She is probably a member of the political cadre, too. They are very well-trained and their propaganda is very strong, and they believe every word they say. But the letter is not all slogans. The ending is very personal."

"What does it say?"

"You really wish to know?"

"Sure."

"Alright. The last paragraph says, 'How precious your love is to me. I wish you good health and strong energy to live forever. I dream of the day when we can hold each other and you can kiss your little one. I so wish I could be in your strong arms right this very minute. I send you my faithful and profound love. Goodbye to you, my very dear husband. I send you a thousand kisses."

"Wow."

"She will be very sad when she learns of his death," said Toi, obviously moved by the letter.

"How long do you think it will be before she finds out?"

"The VC are very good about gathering up their dead. They will be back soon to get him and the others. Since he is an officer, she will be told quickly. At least I hope so."

"I guess they don't send their bodies back home like we do, do they?"

"No. Only very rarely."

I took another long look at the photograph and then said, "Toi, do you mind if I keep this? I mean, he's not going to be needing it anymore."

"Why would you want such a photograph?" asked Toi, surprised.

"I don't know," I admitted. "I just do."

"Certainly you may keep it. I do not wish to look upon it again."

Later that evening, as I sat in my hootch mindlessly playing checkers with Harry, I ran the day's events back through my head again and again—as I did after every mission. Although I tried, I couldn't seem to stop thinking about the dead VC's wife and little baby, who would now have to grow up without a father.

"What is it now?" asked Harry.

"Huh?"

"You heard me. You're even farther out in left field than usual. What's the problem this time?"

"Oh, nothing."

"Let me guess. You got another Dear John letter, right? Has Jody struck again?"

"No, no, it's nothing like that. I'm just thinking about one of those bodies we searched today."

"They were pretty messed up alright," said Harry. "That one gook didn't even have a face anymore." He grimaced.

"Not him," I said. "There was this other guy—an officer. He wasn't completely dead when we found him."

"So, that's it. You finished off some poor gook and you're feeling guilty?"

"No. He died all by himself. But he had this letter on him, and a picture of his wife and baby." I took the picture out of my shirt pocket. "And for some darn reason, I can't seem to stop looking at it."

"Here," said Harry, grabbing the photograph out of my hand, "let me see that damn thing."

"Cute kid, huh?"

"Hey, this broad ain't bad," said Harry, his eyes lighting up. "Look at the tits on her. They're huge for a gook!"

"Come on," I said, "give it back."

"You still got the letter, too?"

"No. But Toi read some of it to me."

"You know," said Harry, "I think you're spending too much time with Toi. He could be a VC, too, for all we know." He gleefully jumped two of my checkers. "King my ass!" he roared.

I flipped back one of the few checkers I had managed to capture from Harry, who said, "So, what'd the damn thing say?"

"You mean the letter?"

"Of course I mean the letter. Hello in there."

"It was from his wife, and she just really missed him and stuff, that's all. It kind of made me realize how much the other side is suffering over here, too."

"And that never crossed your mind before?"

"Oh, sure, but I don't know, not really, at least not like it did today."

"Well, to tell you the truth, we're not supposed to give a shit. War works best when you really hate the enemy, man. If you want to keep your damn sanity, just keep thinking of them as gooks, dinks and slants. That's what I do, and that's what all of us should be doing. It's just a hell of a lot easier to kill one of them that way. Now, if and when I ever get my butt safely back to the world, then maybe, just maybe, I'll start thinking of them as human beings, but not now."

"I guess you're right."

"And you want to know the only thing you really need to remember about that gook who died out there today—other than the fact that his woman had a great pair of tits?"

"What?"

He leaned over the table, looked me straight in the eyes and said, "That if he had had the chance, he would have slit your throat from one ear to the other without even giving it a second thought!"

JOURNAL ENTRY
213 DAYS TO GO

The last few days, I've been really homesick. I don't know why. Maybe because Christmas is just around the corner? I even thought about writing Amy a letter, but at least I had the good sense not to do that. Instead, last night, after everyone had gone to bed, I went out and sat down on top of the hootch bunker and stared up for a good hour or so at the most beautiful full moon I had ever seen. Although I wasn't exactly sure about time differences, it didn't take my imagination long to come up with the comforting idea that the people I most care about back in the world might be doing the very same thing—looking up at the moon—and I felt less alone.

I've been bothered lately by the fact that I'm starting to forget what some of my family and friends look like. It's the funniest sensation. Until just recently, when one of their names would pop into my head, a vision of what they look like would usually accompany it. But that's not always the case now. Some of their facial features are getting more and more fuzzy. It's actually quite alarming. Maybe there's really something to that 'out of sight, out of mind' thing?

Anyway, after I had finished worshiping the moon and was on my way back to my bunk, I happened to notice that Sergeant Ketchum's room light was still on. I stood out in the hallway for the longest time, wondering if he would mind if I stuck my head inside and said goodnight. He has a strict rule now about his room being off-limits to everyone but himself. He's a very private person and firmly believes that friendships in Vietnam are a liability he can do without, but we've been getting along really well lately. I'm convinced he likes me, although we don't actually talk a lot. The missions throw us together for long periods of time, and although we never say much of anything to one another, the time I spend with him inevitably turns out to be the best part of my day.

I finally decided to chance it, pushed aside the dirty white sheet which serves as his door and stepped into his room. A shadeless lamp near his bed was brightly illuminating the depressing space, but Sergeant Ketchum wasn't anywhere in sight. I hadn't been in his room for some time, but nothing had changed. There were no pictures, posters or nude pinups on the walls—not even a short-timers calendar. All his gear was stacked in neat piles on the floor and his foot and wall lockers had huge, indestructible locks on them.

Just when I was about to step back out into the night, I noticed a half-open book resting on his pillow. I had rarely seen Sergeant Ketchum with a book in his hands and I wondered what kind of reading material might interest him. I stepped over to his bunk and picked up the book. Much to my surprise, it was a collection of writings by a French Algerian philosopher named Albert Camus. As I flipped through the pages, my eyes were drawn to those selections which had been underlined in bright red ink.

The first one read, "One has one's morality. You don't fail your mother. You make certain that your wife is respected in the street, and two men don't jump on a single enemy." The next one said, "It remains to choose the most aesthetic suicide: marriage and the forty-hour week, or a revolver." Another said, "It is not a bad thing that young men, in a young land, proclaim their attachment to these few perishable and essential qualities which provide meaning to life: the sea, the sun, and women in the light."

"I just look stupid," suddenly boomed Sergeant Ketchum's irritated voice from behind me.

I immediately shut the book and quickly returned it to his pillow. "That's a nice book," I said, trying hard to come up with some small talk. "Maybe, you know, I could read it when you're done?"

"What are you doing in here?" he demanded.

"Well, I couldn't sleep, and I saw your light on, so I thought I'd just stop by and say goodnight."

The stern expression on his face began to soften a bit and he stepped over to his bunk and picked up his book. "People think of me a certain way around here," he explained, "and I want it to stay that way. Understand?"

"Oh, sure."

"What I like to read is no one else's business and you shouldn't have been snooping around in my room."

"I'm sorry."

"The less people know about me, and the less I know about them, the better. It's best for everyone that way. It makes some of the tough decisions I get stuck with just a little bit easier."

"I understand."

"Good. Now we better call it a night. I'll see you tomorrow."

"Goodnight, Sergeant Ketchum."

"Here," he said, holding out the book. "Take it and read it. But I want it back when you're done. It's a damn good book. I've had it for a long time."

"Thanks," I said, returning his smile and taking the book from him.

"For what it's worth," he added, "the quote on the last page of the book is my favorite."

I quickly flipped through the pages to find it. It read, "In the brief time that is given to him, he warms and illuminates without turning from his mortal road. Such is man, through the centuries, proud to have lived a single instant."

CHAPTER 15

▼

REST AND RECREATION

The water was cold, as usual, but it still felt good as it trickled down over my tired head and aching body. I had just come off a twelve-hour patrol and I was filthy from head to toe. I was too exhausted to lather myself up with soap, so I just stood there, bolted to the slippery cement floor, waiting patiently for most of the dirt and sweat to be rinsed away. For the first time in my life, I thought it entirely possible to fall sound asleep while standing under a shower.

"So, where do you think we should go?" asked Harry, who was next to me, whistling to himself and energetically shampooing his hair.

"What are you talking about, Harry?"

"You know, on our R and R?"

"R and R?" I said when I had finally finished the last of a series of yawns. "All I want to do is go to bed and get some sleep."

"But we gotta start giving it some thought, man. It's only a few weeks off."

"Now that's not true and you know it," I said. "Neither one of us has put in six months yet."

"But I'm going to get us moved up," Harry announced confidently. "The company clerk and me are really tight."

"Harry, I really don't want to talk about my R and R now, okay?" I forced myself to reach up and turn off the water.

"But if we're going to go to the same place at the same time, it's going to take some planning, man."

"And who ever said anything about taking our R and R's together?" I asked as I took a few weak swipes at my body with a towel and made sure my thongs were securely on my feet for the long hike back to the hootch.

"You mean you don't want to go with me?" asked Harry, sounding hurt.

"It's not that, Harry," I assured my friend as he turned off his shower and grabbed his towel. "I just haven't thought about it much one way or the other."

"But that's what I'm talking about, man," said Harry as we both strapped our towels around our waists and exited the shower. "We need to plan!"

"Harry, not tonight, okay? Please?"

"The choices are really pretty simple," explained Harry, ignoring my plea. "Now, Hawaii is basically out because all the married guys usually put in for it and who wants to go somewhere that's part of the States, anyway?"

"I've never been to Hawaii, Harry. I hear it's really nice. I wouldn't mind going there."

"Hawaii is out, okay? No way do I want to spend a whole week listening to Don Ho music and watching married guys do whatever it is they do for fun."

"Then where do you suggest?"

"How about Hong Kong?" he said, his eyes growing wide. "Talk about a wide-open city. The place never sleeps."

"It's supposed to be really expensive, isn't it?"

"You are so damn cheap, Ty," he said, shaking his head.

"I've been sending most of my money home," I explained. "I don't want to blow a couple of month's pay on my R and R."

"Okay, Hong Kong is out because you're so damn cheap. How about Tokyo?"

"What would we do in Tokyo?"

"The same damn thing we're going to do no matter where we go. Look for broads to fuck!"

"Let's just talk about all this tomorrow," I said as we reached our hootch. "I've really got to get some sleep. I'm beat."

"Now the one place everyone says is really great is Bangkok."

"Bangkok?"

"You haven't heard about Bangkok?" I shook my head 'no'. "Come on, man. Don't tell me you haven't heard about Bangkok?"

"I'm sorry, okay?"

"Just what do you do with your free time, Ty? Stand around playing with mama-san's tits or what?"

"Bangkok is in Thailand," I said. "What else is there to know?"

"Only that you can get yourself screwed around the clock there for hardly anything." I stepped into my room and Harry quickly followed me inside. "And we're not just talking one or two girls. The guys who run the hotels in Bangkok will bring four, five, six different broads up to your room each and every day. A guy can literally screw himself into the ground, and don't forget the very best part."

"What's that?"

"It's cheap!"

"Harry," I said as I kicked off my thongs, dropped my towel to the ground and wearily crawled into my bunk, "maybe it will sound a little more exciting after I've had some sleep."

"Bangkok is a soldier's heaven on earth, man. How about if I just go ahead and sign us up?"

"Now don't go doing that. I need to think about it for awhile, okay?"

"That's what you always say. I need a yes or no, man."

"Where are some of the other places we could go?"

"Well, let's see, there's Taipei, Singapore, Manila, Penang, Sydney, Kuala Lumpur ..."

"To tell you the truth, Harry, I've always kinda wanted to see Australia."

"Australia? Now why in the hell would you want to go there?"

"I hear Sydney looks a lot like San Francisco, only not so old and dirty. It's supposed to be really beautiful, and I think it's almost their summer time, too."

"But R and R's aren't for sightseeing, man."

"Everyone I've talked to says the beaches are just crawling with pretty girls."

"Really?" asked Harry, suddenly interested.

"And I hear they have a place there that helps everyone get dates and have a good time."

"To tell you the truth, I've never given Australia much thought."

"Well," I said as I pulled my blanket up around my neck and turned my back to Harry, "why don't you do that and we'll talk some more about it tomorrow?"

"You know, Ty, maybe you've got something there. At least we'd be screwing round-eyes, and that's a plus. And we could always put in for a second R and R towards the end of our tours—a lot of guys do that. Bangkok could wait I guess."

"Goodnight, Harry."

"Okay, my friend, Australia it is! And you just leave all the details up to me. I'll take care of everything!"

True to his word, less than three weeks later, Harry and I boarded a commercial plane which lifted off from Saigon's busy military airport to the loud cheers and spontaneous celebrations of over two hundred deliriously happy American soldiers.

"Sydney, here we come!" shouted Harry as he slapped me on the shoulder and let out a war hoop which would have put an old Confederate cavalry officer to shame.

As the plane continued to gain altitude, I looked out my tiny window and watched as the sprawling capitol city of the Republic of Vietnam slowly faded away. What a pretty place, I thought to myself, as my eyes tried to take in all the lush surrounding countryside. From high above, it seemed almost impossible that such an ugly war could be going on in such an incredibly beautiful land.

Getting to Saigon to catch the plane had been an ordeal. Harry and I had to come up with our own in-country transportation, and twenty-four hours of sleepless hitch-hiking on semi-secure roads and bouncing around in the back of an assortment of dusty military trucks had left me exhausted and sore all over. Harry, on the other hand, was wide-eyed and still full of nervous energy.

"Okay, listen up," said Harry, yanking me away from the window. Then he reached down into a carrying bag and pulled out a notebook. He opened it and began flipping through its contents. "Now, I figure we'll land in Sydney around 3:30 in the afternoon, their time. Then they'll bus us to the R & R Center. The weather should be gorgeous. You were right, it is their summer time." I began looking out my window again. "Hey," said Harry, tugging on my shirt sleeve, "I went to a lot of trouble to find out all this shit."

"I'm listening," I assured him.

"Alright, now the first thing we do when we get to the R & R Center is exchange our money and rent some decent clothes. They've got a shop right there. Then we spend a good hour or so checking out the dolly catalogue."

"Dolly catalogue?"

"Right. The R & R Center's got cards and pictures of hundreds of broads who want to go out with American GI's. We pick out a few we like and give them a call. It's as simple as that." He could barely hold back his excitement. "A whole week, man. Just think about it. And with broads who actually speak English."

The very modern streets of downtown Sydney, Australia were crowded with shoppers, businessmen and office workers. The city itself was clean and organized and dotted with fancy new buildings. Everywhere I looked, there was normalcy. I marveled at the way no one seemed scared that their next step might be their last, or that the person striding past them might be the enemy in disguise. I wished I could be going wherever it was they were all going.

Harry and I were on the second of three military buses motoring us through the heart of the business district. Thrilled soldiers were hanging their heads out of every available window, taking in the sights and waving and whistling at just about every woman—young or old—they saw.

"Man," said Harry with a lecherous smile, "every broad in this city is wearing a mini-skirt. I've definitely died and gone to heaven!"

When the buses finally pulled up in front of the R and R Center, Harry made sure we were among the first to get out the door and fight our way into the newly constructed building. Once inside, he quickly removed all the money from his wallet and stuffed it in my hand. "You hit the money exchange window," he ordered me, "and I'll get a head start on the dolly catalogue. Any preferences?"

"No, not really."

"How about a couple of stacked blonds?"

"Surprise me."

"Tell you what, we'll do blonds tonight, brunettes tomorrow, redheads the next day, and then start all over with blonds again. How's that?"

"Sounds pretty good to me," I said, returning my friend's smile.

"Boy, I sure hope they make them put down their IQ's on those cards."

"Why?"

"Because I like my women dumb as dirt," said Harry as he hurried off in search of the dolly catalogue.

Our dinner dates for our first night on the town turned out just as Harry had promised, blond and extremely big-breasted. However,

Harry's date was petite and very pretty, while mine was big-boned and very plain.

The restaurant the girls selected proved to be an even worse disaster. Not only was the food terrible and the service non-existent, but our fellow patrons kept bursting into song without any apparent provocation. The girls assured us that singing and eating went hand in hand in Australia and encouraged us to join in the fun. 'Waltzing Matilda' seemed to be everyone's favorite, with 'Greensleeves' a close second. I finally excused myself and spent the most relaxing fifteen minutes of the whole evening hiding in the john.

When I returned to the table, Harry was in the middle of yet another lengthy war story. "It sounds horrid, just horrid," exclaimed Harry's impressionable date, Debbie. "How did you ever endure it?"

"And the nights are even worse," lied Harry. "I live way out on this firebase, in a tent with an empty cargo pallet for my floor. When it rains, and it rains all the time, rats move in and set up house between the boards. It's either sleep out in the mud or share your tent with fifteen or twenty big ol' filthy rats." He spread his hands apart to demonstrate the length of a two-foot rat. "And whatever you do, you have to make damn sure you brush your teeth before you go to bed."

"Why's that?" asked Debbie, hanging on Harry's every word.

"Because once you're asleep, the rats like to crawl up on your face, and if they smell any food in your mouth, they'll try to gnaw right through your lips to get at it."

"Hey, Harry," I said, "I'm trying to eat here."

"Do you live on a firebase, too?" asked Margaret, my date.

"No."

"Oh," she said, obviously disappointed.

"Ty is a real live war hero, though," lied Harry again. "He's been awarded the Silver Star for valor."

"Harry!" I exclaimed, looking at him in amazement.

"Oh, really?" said Margaret, impressed.

"And I've got one of those and a couple of Bronze Stars myself," added Harry proudly.

As Harry began explaining in great detail the imaginary circumstances which led up to the awarding of his first Bronze Star, I politely excused myself and headed back to the bathroom.

When our cab finally arrived back at the hotel, the night was still surprisingly young and Harry had big plans for himself and Debbie. She had agreed to spend the night with him, but only if he changed into something more casual and took her dancing first. Margaret, on the other hand, who was as eager to be rid of me as I was her, mercifully demanded to be taken home the minute dinner was over.

"You really screwed that up," Harry whispered to me as I paid the cabby. "Margaret's tits were even bigger than Debbie's."

I quickly exited the cab and was already getting my room key when Harry and Debbie caught up with me. "Sorry you didn't score, Ty. You will tomorrow night. Just wait and see."

"It's okay, Harry, really."

"Tell you what, I'll share Debbie with you." That made Debbie giggle.

"Look, I'm fine. I'm going to go into the lounge, have a few drinks and call it a night. It's been a long day. You and Debbie have a good time."

"Okay," said Harry, "but how about if we have breakfast together tomorrow? I'll come by your room and pick you up at nine sharp. That way we'll get an early start."

"Fine. Nine o'clock. I'll see you then."

As Harry asked the desk clerk for his room key, I said goodbye to Debbie and made my way into the lounge. It was surprisingly plush and well lit. A few couples were seated at the dozen or so tables which surrounded a deserted dance floor. Soft piano music drew me to the only unoccupied stool at the bar.

As I sat down, I couldn't get over how homesick I felt. But the more I thought about it, the more I realized I was missing Vietnam, not California. I wondered how the platoon was doing. Had the guys been in any serious firefights while I had been gone? Who was carrying Sergeant Ketchum's radio? Did he miss me like I missed him? Had anybody been hurt?

Then I recalled something Mr. Mesquita, my college history professor, had said to me when I told him I had volunteered for the draft. He said, "Just always remember, there are things worth fighting to the death for in this world, but they are very few and far between." Was Vietnam actually becoming something worth fighting to the death for, I wondered? No. It was only a place. But Sergeant Ketchum and the platoon, now that was a different matter. They had become almost like family. In a very real sense, they were now my home in the world, and as much as I was determined to enjoy my Australian R & R, I didn't like being so far away from them.

"Yes, sir, what can I get you?" asked a friendly bartender.

"Oh, the first of about six beers, I guess."

"What kind?" he asked, smiling.

"It really doesn't matter."

By eleven o'clock or so the lounge had really thinned out. Only me and a very nicely dressed, middle-aged gentleman still occupied stools at the bar. He had been staring at me off and on for most of the night and I wasn't surprised when he finally picked up his drink and staggered over to me. "Excuse me," he said, "but you're an American soldier, aren't you?" He plopped down on the stool next to mine.

"That's right."

"I thought so. I see you boys in here all the time. Could I buy you another one of those?"

He seemed harmless enough and I said, "Sure."

"On your holiday, are you?" he asked as he waved for the bartender to bring us another round of drinks. I nodded my head. "I think that's a grand idea, giving all you boys a little holiday in the middle of your tour of duty. I sure wish they would have done that for us in World War Two. By the way, my name is Randolph Covington—even my children call me Randy, though." He offered me his hand and I shook it.

"I'm Ty. So, you were in World War Two?"

"I'm afraid so," he answered as a waitress returned with our drinks. "I was just in logistics, though." We both took a sip from our beers.

"My Dad served in the Second World War, too," I said.

"Is that right?"

"Yeah. He did a lot of island hopping in the Pacific. I don't think he got as far as Australia, though."

"Well, thank him for me someday. I don't know what we would have done without the Americans. We'd probably be sitting here drinking hot saki. Was he an infantryman like you?"

"How'd you know I'm in the infantry?"

"Oh, just a guess," he answered, pausing for a moment to stare off into space. "My son was in the infantry and he also spent some time in Vietnam. You have a few of his mannerisms. It was just a guess."

"Your son served in Vietnam?"

"Yes. Quite a few Australian boys have, you know."

"Where was he stationed?"

"Davey spent most of his time in the northern part of Vietnam, near a city named Hue."

"I hear it can get pretty rough up there. He must have seen his share of the action."

"Yes, he did," said Randolph as he finished his beer and very clumsily placed his empty mug back down on the bar.

"When did he get back?"

"Actually, Davey died in Vietnam," he finally answered. "His body was returned to us about this time last year." Tears began to cloud his already bloodshot eyes as he attempted to sit up straighter in his seat. "Please, accept my apology. This is certainly no way to act."

"I'm really sorry," I said.

"I'm afraid that although I'm quite good at appreciating life's pleasures, I don't deal very well with its tragedies. Now please, finish your beer and allow me to buy you another."

"Let me get the next round."

"Thank you," said Randolph, forcing a smile. "That's very kind of you indeed. We shall drink the night away, and I shall attempt to be a little less emotional."

It was after one o'clock in the morning when I knocked softly on the front door of 1200 Stanley Drive. It was a stunning brick mini-mansion in the suburbs of Sydney and I was really proud of myself for having found it with such ease. A stout, middle-aged woman in her nightgown answered the door after I had knocked a second time.

"Excuse me," I said, "but does Randolph Covington live here?"

"Yes," she answered, obviously worried, "is something the matter?"

"Oh, no, nothing like that," I assured her. "I just drove him home, that's all. He's out in the car. I'll go get him."

I hurried back out to the driveway and helped Randolph out of his car. He was only semi-conscious and needed constant support to keep from falling to the ground. I finally curled both of my arms around his upper torso and more or less dragged him up to the front porch.

"Here," said Mrs. Covington, "let me help you. We'll take him right up to his room."

She grabbed one of her husband's limp arms as tightly as she could and between the two of us, we managed to get Randolph inside the door. We steadied him for the steep ascent leading to his second floor room, and with me pulling and Mrs. Covington pushing, we managed to get him all the way up the stairs and into his room. He was completely unconscious by the time we deposited him on his bed.

"There's some tea on the stove in the kitchen if you'd like to pour yourself a cup," said Mrs. Covington as she began to remove her husband's shoes. "I'll be down shortly."

I voiced my thanks and quickly backed out of the room. On my way down the stairs, I took my first real look at the luxurious interior of the

Covington's huge living room. A collection of stunning landscape paintings caught my eye and I was still admiring them when Mrs. Covington, who had changed into a much nicer robe, entered the room.

"They're lovely, aren't they?" she asked me.

"They sure are!"

She seemed genuinely pleased with my response. "I'll get you your tea."

"Oh, no, please, nothing for me. Thank you anyway."

She smiled and motioned for me to take a seat on the couch. "I can't tell you how much I appreciate you bringing him home," she said as she sat down in a chair opposite of me. "I was beginning to worry. Sometimes Randolph's antics fall far short of being amusing. How ever did you find the house?"

"The bartender at the hotel gave me directions. It was actually pretty easy, except I'm not used to driving on the wrong side of the road."

"I can imagine," she said warmly. "You're an American, aren't you?"

"Yes. I'm on my R and R—from Vietnam."

"Oh, I see," she said, lowering her eyes. There was an uncomfortable pause. "I'm terribly sorry, I don't even know your name."

"Ty Nichols."

"Mr. Nichols, I'm afraid I don't drive. The help has gone home for the night and my daughter is out for the evening. Won't you please spend the night? We have plenty of room."

"Thank you. That's very nice of you, but I can take a taxi back."

"But I insist. It's the very least we can do."

I was about to decline her offer again when the front door was suddenly unlocked and pushed open. In stepped a young woman in a stunning black evening dress and heels so high they immediately drew my attention to her long, sensuous legs. She dropped her keys into her purse and strolled into the living room. She quickly spotted me. Her eyes were strikingly blue and clear.

"Oh, no, Mother," she exclaimed, "not again! How is he?"

"Glynis, dear, this is Mr. Nichols. He's an American soldier and he was kind enough to bring your father home this evening."

"Is Father alright?" she asked anxiously.

"Yes, dear, he's just fine. He's sleeping." She hesitated for a moment before adding, "I've invited Mr. Nichols to spend the night. He drove your father home in our car and…."

"What hotel are you staying at, Mr. Nichols?" interrupted Mrs. Covington's daughter.

"The Fairmount," I answered, wondering what I had done to deserve such a hateful glare.

"I'll take him back, Mother."

"It's awfully late, dear. Please, he could have Davey's room."

The thought of me sleeping in her brother's room further angered Glynis and she said firmly, "You want to return to your hotel, don't you, Mr. Nichols?"

"Yes, please," I said as I stood up to leave.

"Fine, then it's settled," said Glynis as she took out her car keys and showed me the door.

"Thank you again, Mr. Nichols," said Mrs. Covington sincerely. "It was extremely kind of you to go to all the trouble of bringing Randolph home." We exchanged smiles and I hurried off after her daughter, who was already out the front door.

I followed Glynis out to her tiny sports car and watched as she unlocked the passenger door and walked briskly around to the other side of the vehicle. I was fascinated by the easy way she made her body move.

I climbed inside and reached over and unlocked her door. Completely ignoring me, she slid very lady-like behind the wheel, turned on the ignition and stomped on the gas. The car jumped away from the curb and we sped off into the breezy night in the direction of downtown Sydney.

I was thrilled just to be in Glynis' presence as she continued to stare straight ahead, her eyes glued to the road. Her window was cracked open just enough to allow the wind to toss her thick red hair in every direction. She seemed to ooze class and good breeding, which really confused me, considering the fact she was acting like a spoiled snot.

"Must you glare at me?" she demanded angrily.

I quickly looked away and tried unsuccessfully to get interested in the sights which were flying past my window. She was obviously in a great hurry to get rid of me and I forced myself not to look in her direction again until my hotel was in sight.

"Your father's an awfully nice man," I finally said as Glynis waited impatiently at a stop sign. "He's very proud of you, you know—how well you've done in school and everything. He's especially proud of the way you're already done with college. He said you're only twenty years old. You must be really smart."

She ignored the compliment, her face remaining expressionless.

"I imagine he told you his whole life story, didn't he?" she suddenly asked.

"And I guess I told him most of mine, too," I admitted, leaping at the possibility of a conversation.

She didn't speak again, however, until she brought the car to an abrupt halt in front of my hotel. "Then you must know my brother died in that stupid little war of yours," she said, glaring at me again.

"Your dad did tell me that, yes."

"And I do mean your war, Mr. Nichols. It's people like you who make it all possible, you know."

"What are you talking about?"

"I'm talking about the most stupid, worthless war in the history of man!" Before I could say anything, she angrily added, "And how many Vietnamese have you personally killed?"

I threw open the passenger door and stepped out onto the curb. I told myself to just walk away, but instead, I thrust my head back into her car and yelled, "Thirty-three! But that's not counting all the women and children!" I slammed the door shut and stormed off into the lonely night.

JOURNAL ENTRY

203 DAYS TO GO

It's three o'clock in the morning and I can't sleep. I met two Australian girls tonight. One thought I was boring, and the other basically called me a war criminal. Feeling a little down, I decided to place a collect call to Mom and Dad. We're eighteen hours ahead here, so it was about nine in the morning, California time, when Dad picked up the telephone.

At first, I think he thought it was a crank call, but when he realized it was really me, he got all over my case for not writing more often. He did ask if I had fully recovered from my wounds, but then he quickly turned the phone over to Mom.

What is it about fathers and sons? Why don't we spend more time on the same page? Mom says he's just worried about me. I guess when I got wounded, they were notified by telegram. Mom said she was at work and Dad was down at the auto repair place, but the next door neighbor saw some guy in a military uniform put the telegram in their mailbox, and being the nosey old witch she is, she called Mom at work and told her she better come home right away. Poor Mom got all scared and called Dad. The worst part is that apparently when a family got a telegram from the military in World War Two—my parents' war—that meant someone was dead, and I guess Mom and Dad both thought the news was a lot worse than it was.

What a horrible thought, that they had to get all scared like that. I think a lot of us forget just how hard this war is on the people back home. I know I do. At least I have some say in what happens to me, but all Mom, Dad, and Sharon can do is sit around and wait and hope for the best. It must be really awful for them at times.

Mom seemed even more worried about Dad than usual. I guess his blood pressure is worse than it's ever been and his doctor has increased his medication again. Between me getting shot up and Sharon's marriage being on the rocks, there hasn't been a lot of good news coming his way lately. Plus Mom says that although he won't admit it, he hates being retired. I knew that was going to happen, but no one would listen to me. Anyone who slaves away for almost forty years at the same job and only misses about seven days of work over that whole time is going to miss it. He was always the first one to arrive at the shops and the last one to leave. It was his whole life. He loved working on those damn trains.

I still remember how he'd leave for work a lot earlier than I left for school and come home late in the afternoon, tired and not very talkative. He'd eat dinner, usually watch one TV show—Red Skelton and Jackie Gleason were his favorites—and then go to bed early because he had to be up at the crack of dawn.

I guess the days—good and bad—that fathers and sons spend together blend into each other, but there were some good times I hope he remembers as fondly as I do. It wasn't all screaming and yelling and calling me names. For instance, I still remember the night he took me to see the Sacramento Solons play the Portland Beavers at old Edmonds Field. I was only about nine years old, but to this day, I have never seen a more thrilling baseball game. It was a masterful pitchers' duel, with neither team able to score a run until Harry Bright—my favorite player—finally hit a long home run over the left field fence with two men out in the bottom of the twelfth inning to win the game for the Solons.

Now, Dad isn't a big baseball fan and I'm sure he took me to that game more as a favor than anything else. I remember that as he and I and a handful of loyal Solon fans filed out of the stadium, I asked him if he had ever seen such an exciting game. "Exciting?" he said, angry as usual, this time because he was up way past his bedtime, "it's after midnight and they only scored one damn run between the both of them. What was exciting about that?"

Anyway, I think as soon as I get back to the base I'll sit my butt down and try to write him a long letter. A lot of water has gone under the bridge, but I may die in this silly war, and he may pop a blood vessel. The truth is that he was always there when I really needed him, that he always made sure I had everything all the other kids had, and that he hugged me tighter than anyone else when I left for Vietnam.

CHAPTER 16

▼

GLYNIS

The next morning I was sound asleep when a knock on my hotel room door made me stir around in the wonderfully soft sheets which covered my king-sized bed. A second knock woke me up. I reached over and clumsily grabbed the alarm clock next to the bed lamp. My half-open eyes took forever to focus, but when they did, the clock clearly read 9:00 AM. There was yet another knock.

"Okay, Harry, okay. I'm coming!"

I forced myself to sit up and abandon the warm comfort of my bed. Nude, I staggered over to the door, unlocked it and quickly retraced my steps. "It's open!" I yelled as I yawned and crawled back into bed. The door slowly squeaked open as I began pulling up the covers.

"May I please come in?" asked a female voice.

Startled, I whirled around and there was Glynis Covington, standing in the doorway. I quickly looked down to make sure I had pulled the covers at least up to my waist. "Of course," I said.

She stepped inside, but stopped well short of my bed. "I didn't mean to wake you," she said. "I've come to apologize—about last evening."

"Oh, that isn't necessary," I said, still stunned.

"Oh, yes it is," she insisted. "This morning, father told me at great length how kind and thoughtful you were last night, and how important his talk with you was to him. I had absolutely no right to speak to you as I did, and I wanted to tell you so in person. I have no idea what got into me. I'm very sorry."

I tried to think of something clever to say as she stood there bathed in the morning light like an angel, but the only words I could get out of my mouth were, "Thank you."

I was just about to beg her for a date when Harry strolled leisurely into the room, took one look at Glynis and whistled.

"And here I was feeling sorry for you," he said, ogling Glynis's legs.

"Harry," I said reluctantly, "this is Glynis Covington." Glynis politely nodded hello.

"And where have you been all of my life?" asked Harry. Poor Glynis smiled weakly and turned to leave.

"Glynis," I called out, "wait a minute, please."

She turned at the door and said, "I'm already late for work. I really must be going."

"Could I please see you again?" I asked.

The expression on her face softened, but she didn't answer. "I'm truly sorry about last night," she said. "Goodbye."

I would have run after her if I hadn't been naked.

"Wow," exclaimed Harry, "where in the hell did you find that?"

I ignored the question and leaped out of bed. I yanked open the top drawer of my chest of drawers and began a frantic search for my bathing suit. "Darn it," I said, "I know I brought it. Harry, did you bring a bathing suit?"

"Kind of early for a swim, isn't it?"

"She's a lifeguard," I said, still searching.

"So what?"

"Come on, Harry, do you have a bathing suit or not?"

"Yeah, I've got one."

"Then go get it. Hurry!"

"What about breakfast?"

"Get the bathing suit, Harry!" I said as I grabbed my shaving kit and raced into the bathroom.

With Harry's bathing suit for underwear, I was out in front of the hotel hailing a taxi cab by 9:30. I tried as hard as I could to remember the name of the public beach where Mr. Covington had said his daughter worked, but I still wasn't really sure of it when a cab finally stopped and I climbed into the backseat.

"Take me to Bonzai Beach," I told the cabby, taking my best shot.

"Do you mean Bondi Beach?" asked the driver, smiling.

"Right, that's it," I answered as my spirits rose.

It was high summer in Australia and the beaches were crowded with swimmers and sunbathers. I quickly removed my shirt and shoes the moment I got out of the cab and began a stroll right out of one of my favorite dreams. The sand was hot, but a cool breeze full of the energy of the sea pushed me along, and everywhere I looked there were girls, girls, girls. They all seemed to be wearing skimpy bikini bathing suits and quite a few of them had shamelessly discarded their tops. I was wondering why so many of them had forgotten to shave their legs and under their arms when I suddenly stumbled and fell flat on my face.

"Hey, watch where you're going there, mate," said the blimp of a man whose legs I had tripped over.

"Sorry," I said, scrambling to my feet and brushing myself off.

"You're one of those crazy Yanks, aren't you?"

"Pardon me?"

"A bloody American."

"Oh, yes."

"Well, stop walking around out here like you've never seen a woman's bum before! You're going to hurt someone!"

"Yes, sir," I said as I apologized again and hurried on my way.

When I finally found Glynis she was seated alone atop one of the lifeguard towers overlooking a very populated section of the beach. A bright orange cap covered the top of her head and a whistle was strung around her long, Audrey Hepburn-like neck. I settled down in the sand at the foot of her tower and never took my eyes off her.

A full half-hour later, purely by accident, she glanced down and spotted me. "Hi," she said, smiling. That was all the encouragement I needed and I jumped to my feet. "What are you doing here?" she asked.

"Admiring you, actually."

She seemed pleased with my honesty. "How did you find me?"

"Last night, your dad said you spend your summers lifeguarding. I had a little trouble remembering the name of the beach, though."

"I'm sorry, but I really can't talk now. I'm on duty you know."

"Do you get some time off for lunch?"

"Yes, around one o'clock."

"I could come back then, if that's okay?"

She took what seemed like forever to consider my offer and then finally said, "Alright then, one o'clock." It was all I could do not to jump up and down and make a complete fool of myself.

For the next few hours, I swam and swam, and sunbathed and sunbathed, and came to the conclusion that one o'clock in the afternoon would never roll around again. When it finally did, Glynis explained that there was no place nearby which served food, but that she would gladly share her sack lunch with me.

"Your father told me you're going to be a teacher?" I said as we settled down on top of a sand dune and munched on our halves of a ham sandwich.

"Yes, at the end of the summer."

"What subject are you going to teach?"

"History."

"Really? Why history?"

"Because it's the most humanizing discipline of all."

"Is that right?" I said, nodding my head even though I didn't have a clue what she was talking about. "Which grade?"

"Secondary—like your high school."

"Are you going to teach here in Sydney?"

"No. I've taken a position in Perth."

"Perth? Where's Perth?"

"Way over on our western coast. It's much smaller than Sydney. That's part of its charm, actually. It's a wonderful young city."

"Is that in the outback?" I asked.

She smiled. "It's beyond the outback, actually. It's very isolated. That's also part of what makes it so special."

"Have you always wanted to be a teacher?"

"Oh, yes, always."

"I never liked school much," I admitted, "especially high school. It was kinda like a prison, if you know what I mean."

"Prison?" she asked, genuinely surprised.

"Yeah. We all wore more or less what everybody else wore, we all had to eat together, do what we were told, and I couldn't leave until my time was up."

"It rather sounds like you're describing the military to me," she said as she passed me half an orange she had just finished peeling.

"Yeah, come to think of it, I guess the Army's a lot like prison, too."

"You sure have spent a great deal of your life doing things you don't want to do, haven't you?"

"A person's not always free to do exactly what he likes," I said, not particularly thrilled with her observation. "Sometimes, they don't give you much of a choice."

"But there's always choices," she said. "I hope you're not one of those people who are always sitting around waiting for someone else to set them free. It doesn't work that way, you know."

"What are you talking about?" I asked, trying not to raise my voice.

"Freedom is something you must take for yourself. It's never given to you. You Americans are always getting that mixed up. That's why this war you're fighting is so absurd. Americans can't set the Vietnamese free. They'll have to do that for themselves."

"We're just trying to help," I said, raising my voice.

"And how many more people must die before you've helped enough?"

"I got drafted. I didn't ask to go."

"But you didn't insist on not going, did you? They're using you—your body—and you're letting them. Don't you see, without you and others like you, there could be no war."

"They would have sent me to jail if I didn't go! Just how free do you think I would have been in a damn jail?"

"Much freer than you are now, I'm afraid."

I had heard enough. I stood up and said, "You are really easy to look at, maybe even the most beautiful girl I have ever seen in my entire life, but you don't know what the hell you're talking about!"

"Do my words frighten you?" she asked matter-of-factly.

"No, but I think I've had enough sun for one day, thank you."

"And enough of me, too, I take it?"

"Yes!"

"Does this mean you're going to take your marbles and go home?"

With that, I turned and stomped off, my feet going ankle deep into the sand with each angry step.

Later that evening, after we had dinner together at the hotel, Harry talked me into going with him to a singles-only dance at the Rest and Recreation Center. A tiny gymnasium had been cleverly converted into a 1950's big band dance hall and the place was packed to the rafters with horny GI's and Australian girls looking for a good time and maybe even an American husband. The smoke-filled room was decorated with hundreds of colorful balloons and dozens of blown-up photographs from the big band era in the United States. It didn't make much sense considering the fact that everyone in the live band had a Beatles haircut and almost all the music they played was rock and roll.

The girl-to-boy ratio was at least two-to-one and Harry hadn't missed a single dance. When he finally returned to our table, he did so by sliding along at top speed on a thin layer of sawdust. He was out of breath and dripping wet.

"Damn it, Ty," he said as he sat down next to me, "would you get off your sorry butt and stop acting like the whole world has come to an end. It's just like LBJ says—there's always another broad, man. Just look around."

"I know, I know," I mumbled.

"You're not going to mope around here all night long, are you?"

"I'm sorry. It's just that I can't get her off my mind, Harry."

"Well, from what you've told me, she sounds like one of those bloody communists we're supposed to avoid."

"She's right, you know. The war is a joke—a big, sick joke."

"Come on, man. This is your R and R. You're supposed to be having fun, not falling in love."

"I've never met anyone quite like her, Harry. Both of the times we've been together, I've ended up wanting to strangle her. But I'm still absolutely crazy about her. Now how can that be?"

"Leave it to you to be pulling something as stupid as this," said Harry, shaking his head.

"And I'm sure she likes me, too, although she hasn't really done or said a single thing to make me think that way."

"So, what are you saying here? You're not doing one of those love at first sight things, are you? Come on, man, didn't you say that broad just turned twenty years old?"

"She's only a year younger than me, Harry."

"And you're telling me you think you might be in love with her?"

"I know it sounds crazy, but I really think I might be."

"Jesus fucking Christ, Ty. There ain't no such thing as love at first sight! Your hormones are just all screwed up because you haven't been around a pretty girl for God knows how long."

"It's not just the way she looks, Harry. It's the way she thinks, the way she says exactly what's on her mind, her accent, her posture, her...."

"Her posture?"

"Even her feet are cute, Harry."

"This is pitiful," said Harry, dropping his chin on his chest, "just plain pitiful."

"All I know is what I feel, Harry. I can't help it."

"I'm telling you, man, this ain't the time or place for that kind of crap. By the time you get back to Australia—which is never—she'll be married and have a house full of kids. Plus she sounds too damn smart. That's the last thing you need, man. Believe me, broads with brains end up being nothing but trouble."

"I've got to see her again, Harry. But I can't just drop by or call, not after today. I made a complete ass of myself."

Apparently feeling charitable, Harry placed his hand on my shoulder and said, "Look, man, this I know. We've got five, count 'em, five days left in Australia. If this is the greatest broad who ever walked the face of the earth, then you at least better let her know about it."

"You're right," I said, "but how?"

"Well, if I had screwed up as bad as you have, I guess I'd go all the way back to square one."

"Which is?"

"It makes me gag to even say it."

"What?"

"Flowers, man, flowers!"

Coming up with a bouquet of flowers at ten o'clock at night turned out to be no easy task. There were no all-night florist shops listed in the phone book and the cab driver I hailed didn't know of any, either.

"You gotta have them tonight?" the friendly cabby asked me.

"Tonight," I assured him.

"How much you willing to pay?"

When I told him money was no problem, that was all he needed to hear. "Hop in," he said as he flipped on the meter and drove me all the way across town to his mother's house.

For thirty dollars, I got a great cup of coffee and a dozen of the best red and white roses in Mrs. Marjorie Manners' garden. She even personally washed off all the aphids. She also told me that if I didn't have any luck with Glynis, to come back and see her. Her exact words were, "A young boy like you would be just what the doc ordered."

With the flowers hidden behind my back, I stood on the Covingtons' front porch for what seemed like forever before I worked up the courage to knock. When Glynis answered the door, her face was expressionless and my heart dropped into my stomach. I whipped out the flowers, but she made no move to take them.

"Aw, come on, do you have any idea just how hard it is to get flowers at this time of night?"

A warm smile slowly spread across her makeup-free face as she accepted the flowers. "They're quite nice," she said, smelling them. "That was very thoughtful of you."

"Could we please talk?" I begged her.

"I'd like that. Please, come in."

As I sat down on a couch in the front room, Glynis went out into the kitchen and quickly returned with a crystal vase half-full of water for the flowers. She carefully arranged them, placed the vase in the center of the coffee table, and joined me on the couch. "I'm afraid Father and Mother have gone out for the evening. They will be disappointed they missed you."

"Where'd they go?"

"To a movie of all places," she answered. "They haven't done that in ages. Father has been in a much better mood since you two talked. Just what did you say to him?"

"Actually, if I remember right, he did almost all of the talking. I just kind of listened."

"What did he say?"

"Well, he talked mostly about your brother. About how much joy he had brought to his life, and how much he missed him."

"That's so odd," said Glynis softly. "Father has barely mentioned David's name since the day they brought him home to us."

"I got the feeling he enjoyed talking about him."

"Really?"

"Yeah, he smiled the whole time he was telling me about how David used to always sneak out of the house late at night and leave blanket dummies behind."

"He told you about that?" asked Glynis, surprised.

"I guess they were pretty believable dummies."

"They really were," she said, her face suddenly flushed with emotion.

"I'm sorry."

"Oh, that's alright. Just the mention of David's name still makes me fall apart. I'm just so happy Father could talk to you about him. Mother and I have been so worried about him. He's been so lost. We don't know what to say to him. I hope you will spend some more time with him before you leave."

"I will, if you like."

"I would like it very much."

"Boy, I'm sure glad I found you tonight. I thought maybe you'd be out on a date or something."

"Oh, I rarely date. When you try to condense five years of university into less than four, there's very little time for a social life."

"Good!" I said, which brought a quick smile to her face.

"I do things with my parents from time to time, but that's about it."

"Why didn't you go to the movies with them tonight?"

She hesitated before answering. "To be honest, I wanted to be here in case you came by or telephoned. I was beginning to think you wouldn't."

"I knew it. I just knew it!"

"Knew what?" she asked, startled.

"That you like me."

"I do?" she asked with a smile.

"Sure you do," I said as confidently as I could.

"You really think so?"

"I really do."

"And just what have I done to give you that impression?"

"Absolutely nothing! Not one single thing!"

She laughed. "Well, I do admit that I have never sat glued to a telephone before."

"And this is the first time in my life I've ever brought a girl flowers."

"Is that right?" she said, smiling again.

"Do you think that might mean something?"

"I don't know," she answered, allowing me to take her hand into mine.

"Do you think we could spend the next few days trying to find out?"

"You're awfully bold, aren't you?"

"I'm sorry."

"Oh, that's alright. It's quite flattering actually."

"It's just that I'm only going to be here for a few days, and there's so much I want to know about you. Could we go out tomorrow?" Before she could answer, I added, "And maybe the day after that, too?"

She was silent for the longest time, then said in a voice filled with warmth and encouragement, "Nothing would make me happier, Ty. Nothing."

"Really?" I asked in disbelief.

"Really."

Sydney had a hundred-and-one things to see and Glynis turned out to be the perfect tour guide. She seemed to know everything about the city, which she said had come into existence as a British penal colony a couple of centuries earlier. She could trace her people all the way back to the original founders and was surprisingly proud of one of her great, great, great, great grandfathers, a one-legged undesirable whom she said had arrived in chains on the very first boat. And he wasn't just a common pick pocket or down-and-out pauper, either. He was a well-publicized double-murderer who had bludgeoned to death a couple of his mates during a barroom brawl in downtown London. With a straight face, Glynis told me that he had been hopping mad at the time.

Our first full day together was spent in cultural pursuits. She dragged me through every art gallery in the city and topped things off by taking me to an evening performance of the symphony. I actually enjoyed some of the paintings, and three full hours of classical music was made bearable by the strapless, braless and sexy-beyond-belief white evening gown she wore for the occasion.

As I sat next to her in silence and pretended to be enjoying each and every selection, I came to the conclusion that some kind of hormonal imbalance was indeed at work. "Do you realize that dress is driving me crazy?" I finally said, throwing all caution to the wind.

"Good," she answered without even taking her eyes off the musicians, "because that is exactly what it's supposed to do."

For the rest of my R & R, Glynis took it upon herself to make sure I didn't have a spare moment to think about the war and what was waiting for me when I returned to Vietnam. She took me to Sydney's world-famous zoo and coaxed a gorilla with a nasty disposition into spitting at us; we went on a heart-pounding hydrofoil ride across Sydney Bay and then spent that evening dancing until two in the morning on the deck of one of the harbor's cruise boats; we spent most of another day strolling hand-in-hand around Kings Cross, shopping for souvenirs and politely saying 'no thanks' to the young kids trying to sell us drugs; we went to the American play "Hair" and made a conscious effort to talk about its nudity instead of its politics; and every night she took me down to a secluded stretch of Bondi Beach where we swam until we were exhausted and then laid on the sand and worshiped the moon and stars together.

"What would happen if you didn't go back?" she suddenly asked me on our last night together as we sat side-by-side, watching the setting sun slowly disappear.

"What?" I asked, surprised by the question.

"You heard me. What would they do to you if you didn't go back?"

"Well, to tell you the truth, I think they shoot guys who don't go back."

"I'm serious," she said.

"I really don't know. I don't think I've ever heard of someone not coming back from his R and R."

She looked over at me with the most serious expression, almost as if she had a foolproof plan for robbing a bank. "Why don't you be the first?"

"What? Are you kidding?"

"No, I'm not. We could leave for Perth tonight. They'd never find you there. They probably wouldn't even look, would they?"

"Glynis, you know I have to go back. But did I hear you right? If I wanted to, I could go to Perth with you—tonight?"

"Why do you have to go back?"

"For all kinds of reasons."

"Name one good one."

"I don't believe we're even having this conversation."

"Ty, you've already done your fair share. What would possibly be accomplished by you shedding more of your blood for that ridiculous war? And if you go back, I just know you'll be killed. I just know it. Stay here with me."

"And do what, Glynis? Hide for the rest of my life?"

"We could live together," she suggested calmly.

"What?" I asked, stunned.

"You love me, don't you?"

"Glynis," I said, softening my voice, "we've never even talked about that. I can't even get up the courage to kiss you."

"I've noticed," she said. She smiled and put her arms around my neck. "I've been told I'm quite a good kisser, actually. Shall we try?"

Before I could answer, she gently placed her lips on mine. Neither one of us closed our eyes, almost as if we both wanted to witness our first kiss. As her mouth slowly widened, and as her tongue began to dance with mine, I wanted to tell her I had never been kissed more romantically. I closed my eyes first and felt her melt into my arms as our kiss went on and on and on. "You do, don't you?" she asked in a whisper when she finally released her lips from mine.

"Do what?"

"Love me."

"Of course I love you," I said without the slightest hesitation. "I've been absolutely crazy about you since the first moment I laid eyes on you."

"Then don't go back."

I reluctantly broke free of her embrace, took a deep breath and said, "Glynis, I have a family back in the United States that would never understand, and friends in Vietnam I would be letting down if I didn't go back. I have to go back. But when my year is up, maybe...."

"No maybe's, Ty. No, I will not wait for another person I love to return from that horrible war."

"Hey, you just said you love me."

"I did not."

"Oh yes you did. I heard it. You said...."

"And what if I do?"

"Do you?"

She looked over at me with tears flooding her eyes and mumbled softly, "Apparently I do."

I took her hand in mine and said, "Glynis, I'm not going to die in Vietnam."

"And that's exactly—word for word—what Davey said the very last time we ever spoke!"

She suddenly jumped up and took off running towards the waves. When I caught up with her, I spun her around and took her into my arms. "And no matter how much I want to," she said, crying and holding me as tightly as she could, "don't let me make love to you. Please don't let me give my soul to someone I will never see again."

My plane back to Vietnam didn't leave until late the next afternoon and Glynis was worried that I was going to leave her beloved Australia with the false impression that all of its beauty was restricted to its coastal cities, beaches and bays. She was determined that I see some of the great open spaces which made up the vast majority of her island continent, so she packed a picnic lunch and was honking for me in my hotel parking lot at the crack of dawn.

Within an hour of leaving the city limits of Sydney, I was up to my elbows in sheep, cattle and waving fields of grain. Glynis pointed out every native Aborigine we came across and raved about the way they lived off the land without harming it. As we motored along, I learned more than I ever wanted to know about kangaroos, wallabies, dingoes and koala bears.

We had been driving for a couple of hours when she suddenly flew around a corner and abruptly drove off the main road and onto a dusty old horse path which finally took us to a huge field of gorgeous white and yellow wild flowers. She brought her car to a stop right in the middle of the breath-taking floral display.

She bounded out of her seat, marched around to the trunk and pulled out a picnic basket and a colorful homemade quilt her mother had loaned her for the day. As I spread out the quilt, she impulsively kicked off her shoes, raced out into the flowers and ran circle after circle around me. As she pranced and skipped and pleaded for me to join her, I sat down and filled my eyes with her. It was almost as if I had been placed on the planet just to participate in that one glorious moment.

When she returned to the quilt, she threw herself down into my arms.

"It's much too early to eat," she said, out of breath. "Let's make love."

"What did you say?"

"You heard me. You do want to make love to me, don't you?"

"Of course I do. But last night you said …"

"I know what I said last night, and tomorrow I will deeply regret having changed my mind. But that is tomorrow, and unfortunately, all we will ever have is today."

With that, she jumped to her feet and began to unbutton her blouse. She wasn't wearing a bra and when her blouse dropped to the ground, without taking her eyes off me, she slowly pulled down her skirt and stepped out of it. "I hate wearing under-things on a beautiful day like this," she said. "Are you shocked?"

"No," I lied.

Completely without clothes, she said, "Now I am going to stand here, just like this, for another minute or two. I don't want you to take off any of your clothes. I don't want you to say anything. I don't even want you to move. I just want you to look at me. And when you are back in Vietnam, I want you to remember how I look, every inch of me. I am twenty years old and I will probably never look any better than this in my whole life. And unfortunately, I will probably never find anyone to care about as much as I have somehow come to care about you. It is very important to me that you remember me as a man remembers a woman."

When my celestial minute was up, she took a few steps closer to me and said playfully, "I wouldn't be a bit surprised if you are a butt man. In fact, I would bet just about anything that you are indeed a butt man. Shall I show you my flip side?"

"Oh, please."

"Now, I don't want to brag, but I really do have a cute butt. Brace yourself."

When she had finished very slowly turning her even more sensuous backside towards me, I very quietly rose to my feet and stepped up behind her. I gently placed my hands around her thin waist and then inched them up towards her small, firm breasts. As her nipples grew and hardened between my finger tips, she arched her back, sighed and rested her head on my shoulder. She smelled of soap, as if she had just stepped out of the shower.

"I guess I should warn you," she said with reluctance.

"About what?"

"Well, although I have always been somewhat of an exhibitionist, I'm afraid I'm still very much an amateur when it comes to this love making thing."

"So?"

"So, I absolutely hate being an amateur at anything I do."

"You've never made love to anyone before?"

"Well, kind of," she answered with the cutest smile.

"Kind of?"

"Oh, it's much too embarrassing to talk about," she assured me, "especially at a time like this. Let's just say I ... panicked."

"Panicked?"

"Ran out of the room is probably a little more accurate."

"Really?"

"Why do you think I've chosen the wide open spaces to seduce you? If there's a problem, look at all this room to run." She suddenly spun around in my arms, unzipped my pants and maneuvered her hand down into my shorts. "Very nice," she said, her warm fingers all around me. "And very hard, too."

"Can I please take off some of these clothes now?" I pleaded, returning her smile once again.

"You know, I've always kind of wanted one of these things myself," she said, digging deeper into my shorts.

"Is that right?"

"But believe it or not, this is the first one I've ever had a really good grip on. I can't get over how soft the skin is."

"Glynis," I begged, "please, this isn't fair."

"But it is memorable, isn't it? And although I'm positive I will never see you after today, I absolutely insist on you remembering me, and these few hours we have left together, for the rest of your life."

With that, she motioned for me to lie down on my back on the blanket. On the way down, I ripped off as much of my clothing as possible and was just about to complete the task when she asked, "What shall we call it?"

"Call what?"

"You know," she said, smiling mischievously and pointing, "your, you know, your...."

"Penis?"

"Oh, I just hate that word, don't you? And I hate all the other names people use in place of it even more. We're going to need a good nickname."

"Glynis...."

"What's your middle name?"

"Richard."

"No, no, that won't do," she said with a big grin, "then it would be just another dick, wouldn't it?"

"Please don't make me laugh," I begged her. "Laughter is not a real good thing right now."

"Oh, I'm sorry."

As I pulled her up on top of me, she very rhythmically maneuvered the lower half of her body around until we both knew it would take just one little thrust from either of us to become one. Then she squeezed one of my hands as hard as she could and took a deep breath which she didn't seem to have the slightest intention of ever replacing.

As she pressed herself down on me and as I felt myself ever-so-slowly entering her, all I could think of was how incredibly wet and warm she felt. Suddenly, when she realized there was no need to push any further, she released a sigh so loving and tender that I was sure she had been storing it up inside of her since she was a little girl.

I simply could not get enough of her. I buried my face into the soft skin of her neck and explored ever inch of her body my hands could reach. "This is so, so sweet," she said as she wiped away some of the beads of perspiration which had begun to collect on my forehead. "You feel so very good inside of me."

I told her again and again that I loved her. "Enough to stay here with me?" she asked.

"Enough to do whatever it takes to get back to you as soon as I can," I promised.

"No more words," she said as she placed a finger over my lips. "You're in possession of my soul now. It will be what it will be. And the best part of my day is still ahead."

"And what's that?"

"This," she said as she began thrusting herself down upon me with as much force and speed as she could generate. Within minutes she knew I was about to climax and she made sure we were kissing when I exploded in pleasure.

There were only small sounds after that, but with Glynis' wet hair clinging to my face and my lungs beginning to breath normally again, I told her, "You know, ever since I was a little kid, I have been scared of things, all kinds of stupid things. And I have always felt so alone, so trapped inside of my own head. But when I'm with you, I'm totally free of all that. I really can't believe I've found you. It's hard to believe you even exist."

With her head resting on my chest she softly said, "Don't die over there, Ty. Please, just don't die. And someday, if you can, come back to me."

JOURNAL ENTRY

175 DAYS TO GO

I just received my first, and I guess my last, letter from Glynis:

My Dearest Ty,

Thank you so very much for all the wonderful letters which have been arriving at my parent's home every day for the past week. They truly are lovely, and believe me when I say I have read each and every one of them over and over and over again.

I'm so thankful that you have arrived safely back at your base and that all your friends are as you left them. I'm also very pleased to hear that your week in Australia was as special for you as it was for me. Someone once said you can live a whole lifetime in one day if you only live that day properly, and God was kind enough to give us a whole week of those kind of days.

As difficult as this is for me to do, I must now ask you a very, very special favor. I want you to stop writing me.

I know I said it would be O.K. for us to exchange letters when you asked me at the airport, but we had just kissed, and I would have probably agreed to anything at the time. For someone who wouldn't kiss me at all when we first met, you have certainly come a long ways!

Ty, as I'm sure you know, I am madly, wildly, crazy in love with you. But as I told you on a number of occasions, I simply cannot bring myself to wait for another person I love to come home from Vietnam. When Davey died, it completely shattered me, and it almost totally destroyed my parents. I honestly don't believe I could survive losing you to that war, too, and the only protection I have against that possibility is to get on with my life. If I allow myself to spend my every free moment thinking of you or waiting for a letter which may never come, I'm sure I will lose my mind and be good for nothing or no one.

This may be very difficult for you to understand, and it's extremely painful for me to say, but if you truly love me, you will not write me ever again. If you should write, I will not open the letter or answer it. If you should call, I will not speak to you.

I want you to know (and truly believe) that my love for you is very real and that I can't imagine it ever diminishing, but that from this day forward, I am going to make every effort to get on with my life as if we had never met. As terribly selfish at it may sound, I'm afraid it is the only way I can preserve my sanity. However, should you ever return to Australia, I give you my word that I will drop whatever I am doing and race into your arms. My parents will always know where I am, and my heart will always be yours for the asking.

I love you beyond my ability to express it, and I will continue to pray as hard as I can for your safety. If it is meant to be that I will never see your sweet face again, also know that I will miss you every day for the rest of my life.

All my love, Glynis

CHAPTER 17

▼

ROBBIE CLINE

Robbie Cline had only been with Alpha Squad for three days when a single bullet from an AK-47 rifle rang out and ripped into his temple, killing him instantly. Life left his body with incredible abruptness. He was between words, smiling at me, and then suddenly he was on the ground, sprawled out at my feet. I was so stunned I didn't even take cover. I just stood there, staring down at Robbie in utter disbelief.

The expression on Robbie's youthful face hadn't even changed. There was a perfectly round bullet hole just above his left ear, but other than that, he looked just fine. There was no blood, not a single drop. He didn't look dead. He looked anxious to finish his sentence.

I heard someone yell, "Get down, Ty, get down!" and the words registered in my numb brain just in time. I dove for the earth as the air filled up with screaming bullets. As usual, Charlie was head-hunting and I had time to spin around and look for cover. I quickly realized there was none. Only Robbie's lifeless body.

The rounds were getting frighteningly close, kicking up dirt all around me. There was no other choice. And as soon as I had maneuvered myself as close to Robbie as I could possibly get, bullets almost immediately began tearing into his lifeless body. The shockwaves they created in his flesh were so powerful that they seemed to roll right through me, too. One of my ears was pressed to Robbie's back and I could hear the tumbling shells shattering ribs and other bones. Then his still warm blood slowly began to blanket my face. I had never tasted someone else's blood before. It was salty and thick and sickening.

As I squirmed and slithered, I could hear one of the troop's gunships finishing off a rocket dive. My body and Robbie's began bouncing like basketballs as a series of shells slammed into the ground just to our front. I clawed my fingers deeper into the earth and held on for all I was worth. It won't be long now, I tried to convince myself. Charlie doesn't want any part of those gunships. Just hold on a little longer. You're not going to die. You are not going to die!

The ambush ended as abruptly as it had begun. The small weapons fire stopped all at once and I could hear Vietnamese voices moving away from my position as Charlie faded back into the jungle. Stay where you are, I told myself. Don't take any chances. You're more than halfway through your tour. You've got less than one hundred and fifty days to go. Don't let them kill you now.

Moments later, I heard the footsteps of someone scrambling up towards my position.

"You okay, Ty?" shouted the concerned voice of one of the platoon's medics.

"I think so," I managed to get out, "but I can't seem to catch my breath."

"Don't move," ordered the medic as he methodically examined my body for wounds. "Any pain anywhere?"

"No, not really. But why can't I breathe right?"

"Your chest looks fine," said the medic as he continued his search. "I think you just had the shit scared out of you, that's all."

"Help me get up, okay?"

"Take it easy, now," he said as he assisted me up into a sitting position.

After I had sat up for a few minutes, my breathing returned to normal and the medic turned his attention to Robbie. "Unreal," he said as he examined the bullet-riddled body. "This poor guy must have a dozen rounds in him. I don't think he has an ounce of blood left. It looks like a pack of wild dogs got at him."

"Help me to my feet, will you?" I asked the medic.

"Sure," he said as he stood up, reached down with both hands and yanked me skyward.

"Thanks," I said as I leaned most of my weight on him.

"Feeling better?"

"Is everybody else all right?" I asked.

"Yeah, but Ketchum ain't going to like his RTO almost getting blown away. He's gonna be pissed, man."

"Where is he?"

"Back with the lieutenant. He probably doesn't even know this went down. See what happens when he leaves you alone for a couple of minutes."

"I better be getting back there."

"Now just hold your horses for a few minutes. You look damn near as white as the dead guy. You better sit back down."

"I'm fine, really. You got a towel or something? I'd like to get some of this blood off me."

"Sure," he said. "I'll go get you something. I gotta go get a body bag anyway. If you feel up to it, get his tags, okay? I'll be right back."

As the medic scrambled back towards Headquarters Squad, I knelt down next to Robbie's lifeless body. I gently lifted up his boyishly handsome head and removed his dog tags. I closed his eyes and carefully returned him to the earth.

"Robbie, Robbie," I said softly as I shook my head, "if only you had just stayed where you were, you'd still be alive. No one asked you to come over to me and start up a conversation. I didn't want to know where you were from and how nice the weather is this time of year back in the Midwest. You new guys just never figure it out, do you?

You don't like standing out here all alone. You got to talk to someone. You won't stay spread out. You just got to cluster-fuck."

I dropped Robbie's dog tags into my shirt pocket and put one of my hands on his. "You fool," I said, fighting back the tears, "you gave up your life to bullshit with someone you hardly even knew!"

JOURNAL ENTRY

170 DAYS TO GO

It's Grandpa's birthday. He would have been seventy-five today.

The last time I ever saw Grandpa he was in a veteran's hospital in Martinez, California and lung cancer was rapidly bringing a close to his long and eventful life. Because of his weakened condition, and after talking it over with Dad, I decided not to tell him that I had been drafted.

Grandpa was a proud survivor of World War One and he loved to tell anyone who would listen all his vivid memories of the war which was going to end all wars. He would often ramble on for hours with great nostalgia about everything from the nauseating smell of mustard gas to the muddy, rat-infested trenches he had hunkered down in for months at a time along the Western Front. He also liked to talk at length about the horrifying battlefield deaths he had witnessed and how lucky he had been to make it back alive to his beloved home state of Tennessee.

If you were really lucky, he would recite, with great emotion and clarity, the last stanza from his favorite poem, "In Flanders Fields":

> *We are the Dead. Short time ago*
> *We lived, felt dawn, saw sunset glow,*
> *Loved and were loved, and now we lie*

In Flanders fields

The last time he recited those words for me, his eyes grew wetter than usual and he said, "Sonny Boy"—he always called me Sonny Boy—"that was the most god-awful war that ever was."

"It must have really been terrible, Grandpa," I said.

"Those Vietnam boys just don't know how good they got it," he said, scratching the short silver bristles which dotted his poorly shaved face.

"I think you may be right, Grandpa."

He was obviously pleased that I was willing to give credit where credit was due, but he added, "The sad fact of the matter, Sonny Boy, is that those two years I spent across the pond were some of the best times of my whole life."

He sat up a little straighter in his wheelchair, took a deep drag off a cigarette he wasn't supposed to be smoking and changed the subject. "Do you know how many people on this here earth have died in wars, in just this century alone?" I shook my head `no'. "Hell, it only took Hitler about four or five years to knock off fifty or sixty million all by himself. Add in my war, Korea, Vietnam and all the other little wars that are always going on someplace, and I bet we're talking over a hundred million—easy." The number seemed mind-boggling.

I rolled his wheelchair up to his room door but Grandpa motioned for me to take him around the ward one more time. When we got down to the end of the hall, he asked me to stop so he could look out a big picture window at the downpour which was going on outside.

"You know, Sonny Boy," he said, "I don't mind telling war stories. Fact is, I love to tell the damn things—there ain't much else to do in here, anyway. But every generation also owes it to the next to tell some of the truth about war, too. How it ain't all medals and glory; how damn scary the fighting is; how a lot of really good men get killed; how bloody and ugly the dying is; and most of all, how few times it really settles a goddamn thing." He put out his cigarette with his bony, nicotine-stained fingers,

*field-stripped it and carefully placed the filter in his pajama shirt pocket.
"It's always good talking to you, Sonny Boy."*

"I love talking to you, too, Grandpa."

*"You remember the first time your mommy and daddy brought you out
to Tennessee for a visit—the first time I ever laid eyes on you?"*

"I sure do."

"You was only about eight or nine-years-old as I recall."

"Ten."

*"And the very first thing you did was run out by the barn and start play-
ing with the chickens and rabbits."*

*"And the first thing Grandma did was come out, grab the cutest bunny
in the whole hutch, take it over to a tree stump and whop its head off with
an axe."*

*He laughed. "I do recall how upset that made you, but like Grandma
told you, a body's got to eat, Sonny Boy."*

*"And the next day she came out, grabbed a couple of the chickens and
wrung their necks. For awhile there, I thought Granny was the meanest
person I had ever met."*

*"Your grandmother was a fine, fine woman," said Grandpa, smiling.
"Nothin' has really been the same since she passed. Those were good, good
days we had together. She may have killed her share of rabbits and chickens
over the years, but she was the most gentle woman I ever knew. She was a
pacifist, you know—so were all of her people. They were Quakers. None of
them approved of me going off to the war."*

"Dad told me that once."

*"And who knows, maybe they had the right idea. All I know is that I
fought in World War One, your daddy fought in World War Two, and
don't be too surprised if your number comes up pretty soon, too. That Vietnam mess is probably going to get a hell of a lot worse before it ever gets any
better."*

"I won't, Grandpa."

"And if you have to go, you do your best, Sonny Boy, but don't forget, somewhere along the line, make sure you tell that next generation of yours just how god-awful war really is."

"I will, Grandpa," I promised.

CHAPTER 18

▼

AVA, MISSOURI

Days turned into weeks and I still couldn't seem to get Robbie Cline out of my head. Maybe it had something to do with the unnerving fact that our first conversation had also been our last? Or maybe I was just feeling guilty for the way I used Robbie's body to shield my own? Whatever the reason, I wanted to know more about him, where he was from, what he was like, who he had left behind. But everyone I asked always said the same thing; "Robbie who?" It was almost as if he had never even existed.

Then one night as I was about to get on with my life, a grease-covered private I had never seen before strolled up to the table I was seated at in the NCO Club and nervously introduced himself. "My name's Joey Bennett," he said, obviously ashamed of his dirty appearance. "You'll have to kind of excuse the way I look. I haven't had time to clean up or anything yet." I nodded that I understood. "Mind if I sit down?"

"Go ahead," I said as Joey yanked out his shirt from his pants and wiped both of his almost black hands with the only clean part of his uniform he could find.

"Now, you're Nichols, right?" he asked as he pulled out a chair and sat down.

"That's right."

"And you're the one who's been asking around about Robbie Cline?"

"You knew him?" I asked excitedly.

"Sure did. Great guy. I went through in-country training with him. They jeeped us down here together."

"Can I buy you a beer, Joey?"

"Well, thank you," he said with real appreciation. "That would really hit the spot right now."

I signaled one of the Vietnamese waitresses to bring me two beers and said, "You must work on the aircraft?"

"Naw. On the road vehicles, mostly. Every once in awhile I get an APC, though. And I really am sorry about the way I look. They kept us late again tonight. We're really backed up and the old man just ain't cutting us no slack at all lately."

"How did you hear I have been asking around about Robbie?"

"There ain't no secrets in this man's Army, you know that," he said as our beers arrived. He quickly gulped down half of his. "So, what'd you wanna know about poor ol' Robbie?"

"Anything. Everything I guess."

"Well, let's see, he was from the Midwest—a little town in southern Missouri. Near Springfield, I think. I forget the name of it."

"Missouri, huh?"

"Yep. You ever been in that part of the country?"

"No, I'm afraid not."

"Well, Springfield's real close to the Ozark mountains. Real pretty country. Nice people, too. Down to earth, hard-working, religious. The weather can sure get you down, though, especially in the summer. It's humid like you wouldn't believe. You take a shower and five minutes later you need another. It's hard to talk. It's even hard to breathe."

"You say he was from a small town?"

"That's right. And he liked it there, too. Everybody knows everybody else in those kinds of places, and you either love it or hate it. He really loved it."

"You don't remember the name of the place?"

"Sorry. Those towns are all pretty much alike to me. I've seen plenty of 'em. The old folks rock away their days on the front porch or hang out in the town square, sipping on cherry Cokes and shooting the breeze, while most the people our age are trying to figure a way to get the hell out. Robbie was different, though. Like I said, he liked small town life. He was really homesick. And he was pretty scared about being in the infantry, too."

"Really? He said that to you?"

"Well, not in so many words, but it was pretty easy to tell he didn't want no part of it. I know for a fact he was going to try and get his MOS changed the first chance he got. He wanted to be a mechanic, like me. He'd worked on a lot of tractors back home and I was going to put a good word in for him."

"You two were pretty tight then, huh?"

"Oh, not really. But I'm from a small town in Georgia and we had a lot of things we could talk about. You wouldn't know it, but once he got started, Robbie was quite a talker."

"Really?"

"Oh, yeah. He'd go on and on about his animals, especially that dog of his. I guess it was retarded or something. You ever hear of that, a retarded dog?" I shook my head 'no'. "Well, just like retarded people, I guess it was extra loveable. Plus it'd do all kinds of really stupid stuff. Like on really hot days, when all the other animals would be hanging out in the shade, it'd go right out and lay in the sun. Crazy shit like that. Robbie sure missed that damn dog."

"Did he say much about his family?"

"Just that they all got along real well and that they were real worried about him. His dad was a small farmer for a long time, but now he's a barber, if I remember right, and his mom, well, she's just his mom—

you know, a housewife. I think he had two younger sisters, too. And a whole bunch of aunts and uncles."

"Did he have a girlfriend?"

"Naw, I don't think so. Robbie didn't talk much about girls. I think he was a little shy when it came to stuff like that. Anyway, if he did, he never mentioned it. Mostly he talked about his family, growing up in that little town, and his dog. Rascal was the name of the dog." He smiled and shook his head. "Funny the things a person remembers. For the life of me, I can't think of that town's name, but I remember his dog was called Rascal."

There was an uncomfortable pause and he appeared to be all talked out. "Would you like another beer?" I asked.

"Naw, I gotta get cleaned up. It's almost time for the movie."

"I really appreciate you looking me up, Joey." There was another uncomfortable pause.

"You was with him when he got it, huh?"

"Yeah, I was."

"I hear he really got blown away pretty good?"

"Actually, I don't think he knew what hit him."

"Then he died quick, you think?"

"Yes."

"And he didn't have time to get too scared or nothin'?"

"No."

"Good, that's good."

I went to the movie that night, too, but all I really thought about was Robbie Cline. He had been dead for almost two weeks and yet he was just beginning to come alive for me. In my mind's eye, I could clearly see the family farm he grew up on, and the small, safe, picturesque little town where he went to school. I could picture his dad cutting people's hair and his mom hanging out the wash to dry. Worst of all, I could see Robbie, healthy and full of life, strolling along dusty country roads with Rascal bouncing along by his side.

"You want to do what?" Harry asked me as we exited the movie together.

"I want to write to Cline's parents."

"What the hell do you want to do that for, Ty?"

"I don't know. Because Robbie's time in Vietnam mattered—at least to me. I want someone to know that. I want his parents to know he wasn't scared when he died."

"So, it's Robbie now, huh? For Christ's sake, Ty, you only talked to the guy one time in your whole life, and that didn't exactly go too well."

"I'm going to go over and ask the new first sergeant for his address after tomorrow's mission."

"I don't think he's going to let you do that, man."

"Why not?"

"Just don't do it, okay? Let it rest, man. Stop worrying about it. His number just came up. Life belongs to the living. All the words in the world ain't going to help Cline. He's dead, man, and whether you like it or not, he's going to stay that way."

"I know all that, Harry, but writing that letter seems like the least I can do."

"Come in," boomed First Sergeant Andrew Adams the next afternoon as I stood nervously on Headquarters' front porch.

The new first sergeant had only been with the platoon for a few days, but his neatly stenciled name and rank was already on the front door. I removed my hat, stepped inside and made my way over to his desk, which had been shipped in from his last duty station and was fancy enough to belong to an executive in a big, state-side corporation. He continued to shuffle papers back and forth and then finally peeked up at me out of the corner of his eye.

"First Sergeant," I said, "my name is Nichols and I'm with the rifle platoon."

"I've seen you around. What can I do for you?"

"I need your help, First Sergeant."

He sat back in his swivel chair and stroked his handsome, thickly-waxed handlebar mustache, of which he seemed to be extremely proud, and nodded for me to tell him more. I had heard some of the guys say he was easily the most vain man they had ever met and that he considered his power to be absolute. If you wanted his help, you apparently had to begin by kissing his ass. "Everyone says you're the one person to go to with problems," I continued as I smacked away, "and I've got one I'd really appreciate your help with."

"What kind of problem, son?"

"Well, a guy in my squad, a friend of mine, Robbie Cline, was killed a few weeks ago and ..."

"Cline?" interrupted the first sergeant, nodding his head. "Right. I think I saw his paperwork. He wasn't even here a week, was he? What about him?"

"Well, First Sergeant, I'd really like to drop his parents a line and I don't have his address. I was wondering if ..."

"You want that boy's home address?"

"Yes, sir," I answered timidly.

Judging from the pained expression on his face, you would have thought I had just ripped off his mustache. "That's absolutely out of the question!"

"But why?"

"What did you say your name was?" he asked, looking at me like I was a subversive, or nuts, or both.

"Nichols."

"Mr. Nichols," he said sternly, "any correspondence sent to Mr. Cline's surviving relatives will be handled by this office. Now good day." He leaned forward in his chair, lowered his eyes and returned to work.

"But I don't understand," I said. "I just want to write one little letter to his parents."

"The major has already sent the Cline family a personal letter of sympathy," said the first sergeant without looking up.

"Why can't I, too?"

"Young man, the answer is absolutely no!"

"But why?"

"Because you might say the wrong things."

"But I might say the right things, too."

"I'm very busy, Nichols," he said, obviously losing patience with me. "Now good day!"

"Please. This is very important to me."

"The answer is no! And that's final!"

As I left the first sergeant's office, I cursed him underneath my breath. Everyone knew all about those personal letters of sympathy. They were usually nothing more than form letters typed up by the company clerk and signed by the company commander.

"That's it!" I whispered to myself as my spirits suddenly lifted. "The company clerk! Now why didn't I think of that first?"

Specialist Fourth Class Randy Ohida was far and away the most important man in the whole troop. His official title was company clerk, but he had a say in just about everything that happened in the daily lives of the soldiers of the rifle platoon. He was the guy you talked to if you wanted a daylight pass or if you needed to make an emergency telephone call back to the States. He could also get you into the PX after hours and according to Harry, could even set you up with a disease-free prostitute who made house calls. Most important of all, Randy was in charge of scheduling everyone's R and R and doing all the paperwork required to get you on a freedom bird once your year was up.

"Impossible, Nichols!"

"Nothing's impossible for you, Randy."

"It's against the regs, man," he said as he put aside his girly magazine and sat up in his bunk. "No one fucks with the regs, not even me." He removed his thick, black-rimmed glasses and squinted at me. "What time is it, anyway?

"It's a little after midnight. I just got off first-shift guard duty."

"I thought so," he said as he jumped up and stepped over to a huge short-timers calendar nailed up next to his wall locker. "Only ninety-nine more days to go, Nichols," he added as he took a red crayon and colored in the box with the previous day's date on it. "You're looking at a real live two-digit midget!"

"Come on, Randy, I don't want the whole file, just his home address."

"Man, if I get caught doing that, I'm in big trouble."

"Who's going to know?"

"Plus I don't like messing around in a dead guy's file."

"Look, are you going to help me or not?"

"No, Nichols, I'm not," he answered without emotion as he took another issue of some really perverted magazine out of his wall locker and climbed back into bed with it.

"But Harry said you'd help," I lied. That got Randy's attention. Harry supplied him with most of his late-night reading material.

"Harry's in on this?" he asked.

"Yes," I lied again.

"Okay, I'll think about it and get back to you."

"Thanks, Randy. Harry said you'd come through."

I left Randy's hootch knowing he'd get me the address and I decided to go straight to my room and begin writing the letter. Most of what I wanted to say had been bouncing around in my head for days and the words quickly poured out of my pen:

Dear Mr. and Mrs. Cline,

You don't know me. My name is Ty Nichols. I'm a soldier in the same squad your son served in and I was with him on the day he died. He hadn't been with us very long, but all the guys liked him very much. We all want you to know that Robbie never suffered when he was killed, not at all. He was doing his job, and he was doing it well when it happened. He didn't have time to say anything, or be the least bit scared.

One of Robbie's friends recently told me how much Robbie missed and loved you both and how much fun he had growing up in his hometown. He was a very fine person, Mr. and Mrs. Cline, and we all miss him very much. We had a really nice memorial service for him here and we're all so sorry he had to die.

I hope this letter doesn't upset you in any way. I just wanted you to know how thankful I am to have known your son.

Very Sincerely Yours, Ty Nichols

I put down my pen, read the letter at least a half-dozen times to make sure I hadn't said anything stupid, and placed it in an envelope. I wasn't sure if it would make Mr. and Mrs. Cline feel any better, but I did already.

The next morning, on the way back from the mess hall, Randy walked up and tapped me on the shoulder. He motioned for me to follow him and we walked all the way over to the water truck, where a number of the guys were still shaving and brushing their teeth. Only after Randy was sure we couldn't be overheard did he say, "Okay, here's your damn address." He handed me a piece of paper which simply read; C/O General Delivery, Ava, Missouri.

"That's it?" I asked.

"That's all you'll need to get it there. His old man's name is Grover. And don't forget, you don't know how you got this."

"I really appreciate this, Randy."

"No sweat. To tell you the truth, I hate them damn form letters myself. But be careful what you say. The old man put your friend in for the Bronze Star, so his parents probably think he was a war hero."

"Why'd he do that?"

"You die in this outfit, you get a medal," Randy explained. "That's the way they do it. It's supposed to make things easier on the next of kin. And maybe it does. I don't know."

I never expected Robbie's parents to answer my letter and they never did. A few weeks later, though, something even better happened, and the news of it spread through the platoon like wildfire.

I received the bulkiest personal package the mail clerk had ever seen and he made me promise not to open it until he could assemble everyone who wanted to watch. It was meticulously wrapped and postmarked, Ava, Missouri, but when I finally got it open, no one could believe their eyes. Every goodie imaginable had been stuffed inside, including canned hams, jams and jellies, sausages, jars of honey and package after package of chips, cheese puffs, and sunflower seeds, air-tight containers of assorted cookies and cakes, dozens of candy bars and just about everything else any soldier far from home would love to sink his teeth into.

Once it was all laid out on top of my bunk, everyone staked out their claim and the feast began. As I took a big bite from a mouth-watering homemade oatmeal cookie, Harry reached over and handed me something he had found in the very bottom of the package. "I think this is for you, Ty."

It was tightly sealed in plastic and sandwiched between two thick pieces of cardboard. "Look at this, Harry," I said, holding up a beautifully framed photograph of what I assumed was the fireplace in the Cline's living room. On the mantle was a large picture of their only son. His Bronze Star and Purple Heart were mounted nearby. Robbie looked even younger than I remembered.

"That's nice, Ty," said Harry sincerely. "Really nice."

I stared long and hard at the photograph. Then I turned it over and on the back were the very carefully printed words, "To Ty. May God always bless you and keep you safe." It was signed, Mr. and Mrs. Grover Cline.

JOURNAL ENTRY

160 DAYS TO GO

I stepped on something I shouldn't have last weekend and ended up spending Saturday night in the base infirmary. When I awoke on Sunday morning I was still sick as a dog and totally unprepared for the conversation which awaited me. "It's about time you joined the fucking living," boomed an unfamiliar voice. "It's damn near nine o'clock!"

I glanced over through squinting eyes at the bunk next to mine and there was a balding, overweight soldier I had never seen before. "Where's Phillips?" I asked him.

"If you mean that ugly nigger who was here last night, the doc shipped him back to the motor pool a couple of hours ago and gave me his bed."

After rubbing the sleep from my eyes, I looked back over at my new roommate. He was at least forty years old and busy wolfing down his breakfast even though he had a thick plaster cast on most of the hand he was using to shovel in the food. "You missed your morning grub," he mumbled between bites.

"What time did you say it was?" I asked him, feeling even weaker than I had the night before.

"Man, this is the life, ain't it?" he said, ignoring my question. "This hand oughta keep me out of the fucking chow house for at least a good *month. No more cooking, no more pots and pans to wash, hell, they're even talkin' about sending me home early. Luckiest damn accident I ever had. What the hell's wrong with you?"*

When I didn't answer, he asked me again. "I got bit by a snake," I finally said.

"Jesus Christ! No shit? One of those poisonous ones?"

"Yeah."

"Was it one of those really big ones, you know, the kind that can squeeze the life out of a guy?"

"No. It was a small one."

"Where'd it bite you?"

"On the ankle."

"Is it all swollen up and everything?"

"Yeah."

"Man, I hate fucking snakes! They really give me the creeps."

I closed my eyes, but my neighbor was still full of questions. "You're one of those infantry guys, right?"

"Yes."

"So, did it happen when you were walking around out in the field?"

"Yeah," I lied, having actually been bit while returning from the latrine.

"You didn't see it or nothing, huh?"

"No."

"You just stepped right on the fucking thing, huh?"

"That's right."

"So, how long you think they're going to let you stay in here?"

"I don't know. They didn't say."

"Well, if I was you, I'd milk that snake bite of yours for all it's worth. Ain't no fucking gook going to put a bullet in you while you're in here, if you know what I mean." I nodded that I understood. *"So, what's it like to be in the fucking infantry?"*

"Look," I said as politely as I could, "I think I'm going to try and get a little more sleep. Maybe we can talk later? I'm really bushed."

"You know," he said, "they were going to make me a fucking grunt years ago, too, but I've got really high blood pressure. Hell, half the time I'm dizzy as can be. I guess I really need to lose some weight—at least that's what everyone keeps saying—but hell, that's a lot easier said than done when you're around food all day long like I am." He quickly devoured the last of his powered eggs and washed them down with a couple of loud gulps of coffee. "Anyway, where's my fucking manners? My name's Jake. What's yours?" He held out a big bushy hand for me to shake.

"Ty," I said as he squeezed most of the blood out of my hand.

"Where you from back in the world, Guy?"

"California."

"You're shittin' me," he said, obviously elated. "Which fucking part?"

"Sacramento."

"Well, I'll be goddamned! Now ain't that something? I was born and raised in Frisco. We're fucking neighbors."

"Is that so?"

"How bout that? Small world, ain't it?" I nodded my head. "You ever been to the City, Guy?"

"Sure. Lots of times."

"What'd you think of it?"

"I like it."

"Really? Well, personally speaking Guy, I hate the fucking place, and I think you'd probably hate it, too, if you actually had to live there. My old man was born and raised there, but he finally said the hell with it a couple of years back and moved him and the old lady down to L.A. He just got fed up with all the fucking hippies and queers." He paused for a moment to pick up and sniff a slice of orange, the only edible thing left on his plate. "Yes-sir-re, all them damn queers used to drive me nuts, too. I'm GI from head to toe, and I can't stand queers. And talkin' about perverts, my sister—her name is Joyce—is really into this religious thing and she says God is getting all the queers to go live in Frisco for a reason. You know what it is?" I shook my head 'no'. "Well," he continued, "accordin' to Joyce, it's all right there in black and white in the Bible. And she oughta know, too,

because that girl's head is always in the fucking Bible. Anyway, accordin' to Joyce, once God gets all the damn queers good and settled in, there's going to be one hell of an earthquake, one about twice the size of the big one back in 1906, and all the queers are going to be washed out to sea and drowned." He looked over at me for a response. "And believe me," he added with conviction, "good ol' Joyce knows exactly what she's talking about. She's a very, very religious person!"

CHAPTER 19

▼

LIFE IS NOT FAIR
OR JUST

Jack Blevins was the rifle platoon's shortest short-timer and he never let anybody forget it. He was a giant of a man, weighing close to two hundred and fifty pounds, although his large-boned, six-foot-four inch frame seemed to handle every ounce of it with effortless ease and grace. He had thick, jet-black hair, which he was always combing, and a flaming-red mustache, the color of which Harry, who was secretly jealous of Jack's good looks, was convinced came right out of a bottle.

"No way is someone's hair that black and his mustache that red," Harry was always telling anyone who would listen. "He's dyeing one or the other."

"He claims that hair genes and beard genes are two different things," I explained, "and that all the males in his family are the same way."

"Bullshit!" was Harry's answer.

Jack had been in Vietnam for over eleven months, and with less than thirty days to go, he began holding a nightly hootch ceremony where he would dramatically cross out yet another day on the huge short-timer's calendar which hung above his bunk. The reason most everyone attended wasn't to listen to Jack gloat and watch another day bite the dust, but rather to sit back and enjoy the best stereo sound system on the entire base.

Jack was really into music, especially jazz, and while most of the GI's I knew blew their pay on booze, cigarettes, poker and prostitutes, Jack sank almost every dime he made into fancy state-of-the-art stereo equipment which he purchased by mail order all the way from Japan.

"I'm getting all this shit for less than half-price," he would often proudly tell me as I watched him add yet another speaker or turn-table or receiver to his 'wall of sound'. "It's quality shit, too, and if I waited until I got back to the States and tried to buy it retail, it'd cost me a small fortune."

Jack looked after his stereo equipment in much the same way soldiers were supposed to take care of their weapons. He was always cleaning and shining and securing it. Above all else, each component had to be religiously protected from the constant heat and humidity, and when the system wasn't up and running, it was meticulously packed away and covered with a thick, clear plastic blanket which he had sent to him all the way from his home state of Colorado.

When Jack wasn't buried in his stereo equipment catalogs, carefully analyzing his next potential purchase, you could easily get him to talk about the other great love of his life, his wife to be, Donna. There were dozens of pictures of her all over his hootch, including five or six which had been taken only a few months earlier while they were in Hawaii on Jack's second R and R with her. With the exception of her dark, sultry eyes, her facial features weren't particularly attractive, but she was as strikingly well-put-together as Jack and she seemed to love posing on sun-drenched beaches in skimpy bathing suits for his camera. Although I enjoyed stopping by to listen to Jack's stereo, it was the sexy pictures of Donna which inevitably drew me into his cubicle.

"You've got the hots for my woman, don't you, Ty?" Jack asked me one night with a smile as I found it almost impossible to take my eyes off one of her photographs.

"You're darn right I do," I freely admitted.

"She's a lot of fun to look at, isn't she?"

"Man, is she ever! When are you two getting married?"

"Probably a month or so after I get back. But feel free to eat your horny little heart out!"

"How long have you been engaged?"

"Since our first R and R together. I wanted to wait until I was safely back in the world, but you know girls, they want that ring as soon as they can get it. I didn't give it to her, though, until the last time I saw her. I ordered that from Japan, too."

"Where'd you meet?"

"Oh, way back in first grade. Not many couples can say they had their first kiss during recess."

"That's a great story," I said, returning Jack's smile.

"And it's true, too."

"You know, Jack, if I was you, and had a girl like Donna waiting for me, I'd stop going out in the field. I bet you could talk Lieutenant Alberti into finding something for you to do back here. He knows how short you are, and he really likes you."

"I know, and believe me, it's been months since I took any chances. But I signed up to do a year over here, and a whole year I'm going to do. Plus who would carry the lieutenant's radio?"

"I still think you're crazy to keep going out there if you don't have to."

"Things have been pretty quiet lately. I'll be okay, Ty."

Less than a week later, the platoon was scrambled out late in the afternoon to check on a suspected enemy base camp deep in the heart of the Iron Triangle. By the time we arrived on station and reached the red smoke grenades which marked our objective, there was less than a full hour of daylight left and everyone was cursing the major for the late start.

"This is no place to be once the sun goes down," Sergeant Ketchum told me as he brought our squad to a halt and grabbed for the handset on the PRC-25 radio I was still carrying for him.

"Stallion One," he said into the handset, "this is Four-Three Alpha, over—Roger that, One, but this elephant grass is getting awfully high and thick. What do you want us to do now?"

The words were barely out of his mouth when the ambush began. I immediately dove for the safety of the earth and the abruptness of my descent ripped the radio handset out of Sergeant Ketchum's hand. The sergeant quickly dropped to one knee, gathered up the handset and re-established radio contact.

I glanced to my left, where Headquarters Squad had been standing around, to see what the lieutenant and his people were doing. If they were going to pull back, I knew we should start preparing to do the same thing.

They were all hugging the damp earth, just like me, with one exception. Jack was still standing straight up, almost as if he was bolted to the ground. He was clutching his face and bright red blood was gushing between his fingers.

"Get down! Get down!" I could hear the lieutenant yelling at Jack, but he seemed to be frozen in place, terrified that he had been hit in the face. When he finally took his hand off his cheek and placed it in front of his eyes, he screamed in a way that sent a wave of fear throughout my whole body. It was almost as if it had come from a wild animal. "Get down!" yelled the lieutenant again and again, too far away from Jack to grab him and force him to the ground.

For maybe the first time in his life, the height and strength of Jack's magnificent body was working against him. He just stood there, way above the top of the elephant grass, like an ancient redwood tree, a perfect target for even the worst shot. And the Vietcong just kept shooting at him. Round after round crashed into his arms, legs and torso, making him lurch and scream, but he simply refused to fall. As Sergeant

Ketchum and I watched together in horror, Jack just kept looking at his blood soaked hand.

Sergeant Ketchum finally leaped up and heaved a couple of grenades out in front of Jack's position and that seemed to quiet the enemy fire for a few moments. Only then did Jack finally collapse to his knees and very slowly fall face-forward into the ground. Both of the platoon's medics and the lieutenant scrambled to Jack's side, but I could tell by the looks on their faces that there was nothing they could do.

With Sergeant Ketchum screaming at our machine gunner to cover our retreat, the Vietcong suddenly doubled their efforts to overwhelm the platoon with small weapons fire and everyone began a serious effort to scramble back to positions easier to defend.

I could see the lieutenant and one of the medics trying as hard as they could to drag Jack's huge body back with them, but without success. I knew from experience that a dead body seemed to weigh twice as much as a live one when you tried to pick it up or drag it, and I wasn't surprised when they finally gave up the hopeless task. They were the last two people to get all the way back to a circular stretch of moss covered boulders where Sergeant Ketchum thought the platoon could hold out until reinforcements arrived.

When darkness fell, the platoon was still pinned down and all the major could promise over the radio was that help in the form of two infantry companies was nearby and that he was going to do everything he could to get them into the fight.

The lieutenant ordered the platoon to form a defensive perimeter, with everyone at least ten yards apart from his neighbor, except for squad leaders and their RTO's, who were to remain together at all costs.

"What's that?" I whispered to Sergeant Ketchum when I heard the first of a series of clicking sounds that scared me half to death.

"That's right," said the sergeant, "this is your first real time out in the field after dark, isn't it?"

"It kinda sounds like those little frog clickers we used to play with back home when I was a kid."

"Very good, Ty, because that's exactly what it is."

"You're kidding?"

"They don't have any radios," explained the sergeant, "so when it's quiet like this, a lot of the VC around here communicate with each other with clickers."

"How do they do that?"

"I don't really know. Probably a certain number of clicks means they're going to move up or back, right or left. Most likely, though, it just lets them know approximately where they're all at. Plus I think they like the fact that it scares the shit out of most Americans."

"Do we shoot at where the clicks are coming from?"

"No. They'd like us to do that. We're not going to do anything to give away our position until help gets here, unless they get really close." He took his steel pot off, placed it in the crease of two boulders and used it as a pillow as he slid down and rested the back of his head on it. "Nudge me if anything starts up. I'm going to try and get a little sleep."

Sleep, I felt like yelling at him, how can you possibly think of sleep at a time like this? We're in the middle of nowhere, probably surrounded by VC, and it's pitch-black! The sergeant yawned and closed his tired eyes.

After I finally got used to the clicking sounds, I let my thoughts return to Jack. I had never seen anyone die like that before. Why hadn't he dove for cover? He knew better than to stand around in a kill zone. And he wasn't the kind of person to freeze. Plus he was a veteran and he knew all the little tricks which were supposed to keep guys alive. It just didn't make any sense. Maybe something really crazy happens when you get hit in the face? And what was this going to do to Donna? How was she ever going to get on with her life after this?

"Thinking about Jack?" asked Sergeant Ketchum, who wasn't sleeping after all.

"Yeah."

"Me, too. He was a good man. The lieutenant is going to be lost without him. I think he's the only RTO he's ever had."

"Why do you think he just stood there?"

"I don't know. But each of us has something that scares us shitless. Maybe getting hit in the head was the one thing Jack couldn't handle."

Over the radio, I could hear the lieutenant requesting to speak to Sergeant Ketchum. "The lieutenant wants you," I said, giving him the handset.

"This is Four-Three, over," said the sergeant. He listened intently for a full minute or more and then said, "Well, that sounds like a pretty good idea to me. Might as well go for it. Roger that, out."

"What's up?" I asked.

"The major has radioed for some fixed wing help and they should be on station in about twenty minutes."

"Jets?"

"That's right."

"What are they going to do?"

"A Napalm drop."

"But those clickers sound awfully close to us."

"Well, it's either that, or keep waiting for help, which might get here too late if there's as many gooks out there as I think there are. They might get brave and try to overrun us any minute."

"So what do we do?"

"We just sit here and watch the fireworks show. You ought to be able to hear everything that's going on over the radio once the jets get on station."

Sure enough, within a half-hour, two of the cockiest young fighter pilots in the United States Air Force joined the push and requested a bunch of technical information which went over my head. What I could make out, however, was that the major and the lieutenant weren't all that sure about how to get the Napalm dropped exactly where they wanted it.

"Just leave that to us," one of the pilots assured the lieutenant, "but let's get on with it. I've got the best blow-job in Nam waiting for me back at the base."

With that, the word was passed along to hunker down and get ready for an air strike which most everyone without access to a radio thought was going to be a bomb drop, not Napalm.

I could clearly see the lights of the two jets, in an I-formation, as they roared down towards the platoon's position. The lead aircraft dropped its load less than fifty yards to the front of where Sergeant Ketchum and I were hiding and night suddenly turned to day. The first of two rolling firestorms lapped up the enemy positions and I could hear the hopeful cheers of my friends mixed in with the death screams of burning Vietcong.

As I looked up into the brightly lit sky, I could see the two jets break off and turn in opposite directions. "I'll bet you got crispy critters coming out your ears down there," were the last words I heard one of the pilots scream into his radio.

For the next few hours, there were no clicking sounds at all, and when the first of the two infantry companies finally arrived, everything seemed to be pretty anti-climactic. They formed a corridor which enabled the platoon to reach our PZ without incident and as soon as Jack had been located and bagged, everyone boarded their extraction helicopters and headed home.

I wasn't on the helicopter which flew Jack's body back to the base, but I was sitting in his room later that night, holding my favorite picture of Donna, when Lieutenant Alberti came by to pack up all of Jack's gear and personal effects.

"You better get out of here now, Nichols," the lieutenant said. "This is never any fun."

"Maybe you could do it tomorrow, sir?" I suggested, knowing that the lieutenant was closer to Jack than anyone else in the platoon and noticing that he had been crying.

"We try to do it right away," explained the lieutenant. "It's best for everyone that way."

I hid the photograph of Donna—she was waving so happily to Jack as he took her picture—behind my back, knowing that I wanted to keep it, although not really knowing why. Maybe because she was just such a joy to look at, so unashamedly feminine and always smiling from way deep down inside, or maybe because I cared about Jack more than I had known.

"Go on, now, Ty," said Lieutenant Alberti softly. "Get to bed. We've got another big day ahead of us tomorrow. You're going to need all the sleep you can get."

"Do you want some help with all that heavy stereo equipment, sir?" I asked as I stood up, still keeping Donna's picture out of the lieutenant's sight.

"No thanks, Ty," he said, clearing his throat and trying hard not to start crying again as he pulled a huge bundle of letters from Donna out of Jack's wall locker. "And please, stop hiding that damn picture behind your back. It's okay with me if you keep it."

"Oh, thank you, sir. Thank you very much."

As the lieutenant slowly thumbed through some of Donna's countless letters to Jack, I heard him mutter something but I couldn't make it out. "Say again, sir," I said.

"It's all my fault," he said, his voice breaking and still not much more than a whisper. "He was too short to be out there. If he would have asked, I would have shut him down. But he didn't ask. Hell, he shouldn't have had to ask. What could I have been thinking? It's just that he was so good at what he did. I didn't think anything would happen to him. And there was no one else I trusted with the radio. Plus I just liked having him out there with me. But now he's dead, and it's all my fault. I should have known better. I could have prevented it. I should have shut him down. How could I have been so selfish?"

"It's really no one's fault, sir."

"Yes it is!" he screamed, raising his voice in anger for the first time since I had known him. "Don't you understand? He'll never get to see her again, and it's all my fault! Now damn it, Ty, get the hell out of here!"

JOURNAL ENTRY

103 DAYS TO GO

In Vietnam, there are two things an infantryman wants to do each and every day. First, he wants to avoid making any contact with the enemy, and second, he wants to receive at least one letter.

Mail call is everything and any day a soldier gets a letter from a loved one, even if it's just from an aunt or uncle, is a good day. Letters are the only tangible proof that someone back in the world still cares and that you haven't been totally forgotten. They are also a status symbol. The more letters you get, the more envied you are, and for quite awhile, no one in my platoon was more envied than Larry Pierce.

Larry was a quiet, unassuming thump gunner who had been in the platoon for more than a month before most of the guys even knew he was here. He was painfully shy and for the longest time he never spoke to anyone unless he was spoken to first. Even his physical features blended into the surroundings. He was just kind of boring looking, if that makes any sense. Although no one tried all that hard, those who did found it difficult to even make eye contact with Larry. If he wasn't looking down at his boots, he was usually staring off into space, lost in his thoughts.

"That guy is really weird," was the phrase I most often heard when Larry's name came up in a conversation.

After Larry had been with the platoon for awhile, everyone more or less knew who he was and what squad he belonged to, but remembering his name was still a problem for most everybody. Not only didn't he have any friends, he also didn't seem to be in much of a hurry to make one, either.

To be honest about it, no one much cared one way or the other about Larry Pierce until rumors started circulating that he was receiving two, and sometimes three, letters each and every single day. Not only that, but he was also apparently getting packages filled with all kinds of goodies, too.

"Like what?" I finally asked Julio Romero, who bunked with Larry.

"Cookies, candy, canned fruit, big ol' salami's, sunflower seeds, you name it," said Julio. "He even got a homemade apple pie last week."

"You're kidding," I said, absolutely amazed. "A homemade pie got here in one piece?"

"I don't know how, but it did. And get this, most of his letters smell like they were postmarked in some French whorehouse, too."

It was definitely time to talk to Danny DeAnda, the platoon's mail clerk to see exactly what was going on. "It's all true," Danny swore to me. "The guy may have the personality of a fence post, but he's putting everyone around here to shame when it comes to getting letters and packages."

"Who's he getting them from?" I asked.

"That's the real mystery," answered Danny. "They all pretty much come from the same place, Wichita, Kansas. But except for the ones from his mother, there's no name above the return address. Your guess is as good as mine."

"I hear all the letters are perfumed?"

"At least one every day is, and not with just any old ordinary crap, either. This is expensive, classy stuff. I've never smelled anything quite like it. Hell, I spend most of my day sniffing Pierce's damn letters."

"Maybe he's got a real sexy girlfriend or something?"

"Pierce? And in Wichita, Kansas?"

As time went by, Larry's popularity skyrocketed and everyone began hanging out at his hootch. He also turned out to be a lot smarter than he looked. He started charging everyone fifty cents to sniff his letters, and a buck to keep an empty envelope for the night, and business was brisk. He even put together a five-dollar-a-head pool he said he'd split with anyone who could come up with the correct name of the perfume.

Finally, a meeting was called to get to the bottom of things and I was elected to make a Herculean effort to quickly become Larry's first real friend in Vietnam. And it turned out to be a very easy and rewarding task.

"You're supposed to find out about the letters, right?" Larry asked me after the second time I invited him to attend the nightly base movie with me.

"Yeah," I admitted. "We're all pretty jealous."

"What's the big deal, anyway?"

"Are you kidding? We'd all kill to have a girl back in the world who wrote us at least one letter every single day and poured expensive perfume all over it."

Larry smiled and said, "It has been a lot of fun, everybody being so interested and all, and she really is a special lady."

"So, who is she?" I begged him. "Tell me all about her. Do you have a picture?"

"Look, if I tell you, and you tell everyone else, they're all just going to be disappointed."

"Why?"

"Just take my word for it, you're all going to be disappointed."

"Larry, we're all dying to know. Please, please, please."

He finally gave in and said, "Okay, I'll tell you, but I'm not going to tell anyone else. If you want to, that's up to you, but I don't really think it's anybody else's business but mine."

"Come on, Larry," I said with anticipation, "spill it."

"Alright. All the perfumed letters, and most of the packages, come from my Nana."

"Your Nana?" I said, shocked.

"That's right, my Nana."

"You don't mean your grandmother, do you?"

"Yes."

"You're putting me on, right?"

"Nope. I just happen to have the greatest grandmother in the whole wide world."

"But what about all the sexy perfume on the letters?"

Larry smiled and said, "Well, when I was real young, in grade school, my parents busted up and I lived with my Nana for about seven years. Every morning, when she'd wake me up for school, the first thing I smelled was this wonderful perfume she always wore and I really came to love it. I still do. All I have to do is take a little whiff of it and I think of her, and of growing up happy and wanted. She knows that when I smell her perfume, I think of her, and home."

"So, there's no sexy girlfriend?"

"Nope. Just my Nana, although she still thinks of herself as a pretty sexy lady."

Larry and I went back to my hootch and swapped granny stories until well after midnight. I admitted that everyone would probably be pretty disappointed to find out who was really sending Larry most of his letters and packages and we agreed it was probably best just to leave everything as it was. So, I told all the guys that Larry was too tough a nut to crack and that he would appreciate it if we all just tried to mind our own business and get a life.

A little over four months later, just before Larry was transferred to another unit on the base, his perfumed letters and packages of goodies suddenly came to an abrupt halt. Everyone in the platoon was sure that Jody had struck again and that like so many other girls with boyfriends in Vietnam, even Larry's sexy lady had tired of waiting and found someone else.

The truth was actually much sadder. Larry's beloved Nana had died of congestive heart failure at the age of eighty-three.

CHAPTER 20

▼

GRAVES REGISTRATION

The monsoon season had arrived and I had never seen anything quite like it. It rained so hard, especially in the afternoons, that I often couldn't see fellow squad members who were just a few yards ahead or behind me. The heavy downpours only lasted for a couple of hours each day, but the constant precipitation which preceded them and lingered long after they passed had saturated the earth and left standing water everywhere. Rice paddies were overflowing, local streams were threatening to flood and there didn't seem to be a dry foot of earth in the whole area of operation. Every mission suddenly became a struggle just to keep dry and stay out of situations which might require the support of grounded hunter-killer teams.

"The old man has finally come to his senses," announced Sergeant Ketchum with a rare smile as he stepped into my room. "He's giving us the whole day off, and probably tomorrow, too."

"You're kidding?" I said, happily putting aside the rifle I was cleaning.

"Nope. You got any plans?"

"No, not really," I answered, surprised to be asked a question like that by Sergeant Ketchum. "I guess I'll play around with my journal for awhile and maybe go to the PX. Why?"

"Well, I've got to go down to Long Binh and I need someone to ride shotgun. Want to come?"

"What's in Long Binh?" I asked, even more surprised by the invitation.

"Graves registration. I've got to identify a body."

Yuck, I thought to myself, and my reluctance to be part of that distasteful task apparently showed on my face. "You won't have to go in," Sergeant Ketchum assured me. "You can stay out in the jeep if you want."

"Gee, I don't know, Sergeant Ketchum."

"Look, I've got to get on the road. You wanna come or not?"

"Well, okay, I guess so."

"Good. I'll go over to the motor pool and check us out a jeep and be back here in about thirty minutes. Better take your flak jacket just in case." With that the sergeant turned and accidentally bumped into Harry, who was just entering my room.

"Hi, Sarge," said Harry. "Have you heard the good news?"

Sergeant Ketchum nodded his head and quickly disengaged himself from the clumsy embrace. "Thirty minutes, Nichols," he reminded me as he hurried off to get us a jeep.

"How long will we be gone?" I yelled after the sergeant without getting a response.

"You and Ketchum got a date or what?" Harry asked me.

"He wants me to ride down to Long Binh with him."

"Really? What the hell for?"

"I don't know. To look at dead people, I think."

"Dead people?"

"Graves registration."

"Jesus Christ. You sure you wouldn't rather join me for a little boom-boom over at the massage parlor?"

"You know, Harry, he's never asked me to do anything with him before. I wonder why he picked today?"

"Who the hell knows with Ketchum. But don't be getting your hopes up, man. The guy isn't capable of having a real friend."

"Anyway, I told him I'd go, so I guess I'm going. What do you think graves registration is like?"

"I don't know, I don't want to know, and don't be telling me anything about it when you get back, either!"

I wasn't all that excited about motoring away from the safety of the military compound and Sergeant Ketchum sensed my nervousness. "Long Binh is one of the safest places in Nam," he assured me, "and the road in and out is as secure as it gets."

"Have you been there before?"

"Sure, lots of times. Just relax and enjoy the sights."

Heavy rain quickly turned into nothing more than a light, warm drizzle as the sergeant and I checked out at the base gate and sped off towards Long Binh. The road was newly paved and crowded with fellow travelers. Dangerously overloaded old buses and recklessly driven, exhaust-puffing motor scooters with young but seemingly experienced drivers at the throttle dominated both lanes. All the rain had made the fertile countryside lush and beautiful, and as we put more and more miles between us and the base, the war grew distant, almost non-existent. The surprising normalcy of life and the beauty of our surroundings was an unexpected treat.

"Gee, Sergeant Ketchum, this is almost like a Sunday drive back in the world."

"My name is Jim," he said with emphasis.

I looked over to make sure I had heard the sergeant correctly, but his eyes were glued to the road. "The closer you get to Saigon," he explained, "the more state-side everything seems. Up north, though, it's a totally different ball game. I was stationed up around the A Shau valley for awhile and it's hell on wheels up there. Real jungle—lions, apes, you wouldn't believe it. And the graves registration they had makes the one in Long Binh look like a palace. During Tet they were using these huge trucks to bring in all our dead. They just dumped them down a chute where some poor guy with a power hose tried to clean them up. Then they toe-tagged them and stuffed them in body bags for the trip home."

"You were here for Tet?"

"Yeah. This is my second tour. And this one is for eighteen months."

I was shocked. I couldn't believe anyone, not even Sergeant Ketchum—Jim—would want to spend one more day than he had to in Vietnam, and I was sure that no one in the platoon knew this was his second tour. As usual, what I was thinking was apparently written all over my face and Sergeant Ketchum quietly added, "I have my reasons."

We were still a half-hour or so out of Long Binh when the sky suddenly turned black as night and the rain began coming down in buckets. Our jeep had no top so we quickly broke out our ponchos, but we were soaked to the skin before we managed to get them on. "It rains like this now and then in Texas, too," said Sergeant Ketchum with a rare smile, "and to tell you the truth, I love it."

"Well, you can have it," I said. "I'll take sunshine any day."

"You sound just like my wife."

Sergeant Ketchum had never mentioned a wife, either. "You're married?"

"Yeah. Going on four years."

"Really? You got any kids?"

"Not yet. My wife isn't into kids. She thinks having them will ruin her body. She lives in fear of stretch marks and things like that." He hesitated for a moment and then added, "Wanna see a picture of her?"

"I sure do!"

He dug out his wallet and passed it to me. I shielded it from the rain with one hand and opened it up with the other. It was overflowing with pictures of the same striking blond and she had the kind of curvy figure and fresh young face that would make any man homesick.

"She's something else, isn't she?" the sergeant asked proudly.

"Wow, she sure is!"

"Thanks. She's the reason I came back over here."

"Now that makes absolutely no sense," I said as I continued to flip through the photographs. "I sure wouldn't have volunteered to spend eighteen months away from a girl as pretty as this."

"It's hard alright, but I'll probably make the Army my career, and this is where the money is right now. I make twice as much here as I would back in the States. I get my regular pay, plus combat and flight pay, and there are no expenses. I can send almost every penny home. If I was in the States, I'd be lucky to be an E4, where here I'm already an E5 and I'll be an E6 before I leave."

"Where'd you meet her?" I asked as I handed the sergeant's wallet back to him.

"She lived right around the block from me when we were teenagers. Her home life wasn't much better than mine—her old lady was always slapping the crap out of her. We didn't get serious, though, until we were juniors in high school. I was pretty hot shit in football and she never missed one of my games."

"Really?"

"I know it sounds pretty corny, but that's the way it happened."

"You were a big football star, huh?"

"Hey, in Texas—especially Dallas—you either play football or you're a nobody."

"I was pretty good in baseball back in California."

"Figures," he said, smiling.

The American military compound at Long Binh had absolutely everything a soldier far away from home could possibly want: lots of teahouses with plenty of pretty prostitutes; night clubs that were already in full swing in the late afternoon; a PX big enough to pass for a department store; a library; a walk-in VD clinic; an indoor movie house with a marquee; and even lighted basketball and tennis courts. Sergeant Ketchum made a special effort to give me the scenic tour, and every block seemed to house a new wonder.

"War's hell, ain't it?" said the sergeant.

"What's a person got to do to get stationed here?"

"Well, to begin with, you gotta know someone a lot more important than me."

"Look over there," I said, pointing out what appeared to be a nine-hole miniature golf course. "Is that what I think it is?"

"How's your putting stroke?" asked the sergeant as I shook my head in disbelief.

"Where we're stationed is nice," I said, "but this place is unreal."

"There's definitely lots of stuff to see and do here, but let's take care of business first."

I had already seen enough death to last me a lifetime, but some morbid corner of me was actually looking forward to checking out the inside of a morgue. My enthusiasm quickly vanished, however, as Sergeant Ketchum and I pushed our way through the swinging front doors of the graves registration building. The cold, damp air reeked of the chemicals of death and the middle-aged lifer at the reception desk looked almost as white and bloated as the bodies which he no doubt had stashed away in the back room.

"What can I do for you boys?" he asked Sergeant Ketchum.

"I'm here to identify a body."

"Name, please."

"My name is Jim Ketchum."

The lifer threw his undersized head back and roared. "Not your name, Sarge. I need the name of the damn deceased."

"Oh. Gregory Haines."

"Let's see. Haines, Haines, oh yeah, the redhead without his fucking tags. Damn, I wish all you boys would remember to wear your tags. It sure as hell would make my job a lot easier. It took us forever to figure out who the hell he was. Come on, follow me."

"I think I'll wait here, Jim," I said.

"He's not going to bite you," said the lifer, grinning.

"Let's just get this over with, okay?" snapped Sergeant Ketchum.

I hurried outside and waited in the jeep for Sergeant Ketchum. The rain had stopped and the sun was even struggling to make an appearance. The air was thick with the familiar smells of life and I inhaled as deeply as I could. I also promised myself I would never voluntarily visit a morgue again.

When Sergeant Ketchum finally came out and climbed in behind the wheel, he was obviously struggling to keep control of his emotions.

"I'll drive back, Jim—if you like."

"Who in the hell's going back?" he said as he flipped on the ignition and threw the jeep into gear. "Come on, we're going to go do some serious drinking."

"I thought we had to get right back?"

"Fuck it!"

Neither Sergeant Ketchum nor I had enough money to go to a teahouse, so we sped off in search of an NCO Club. The one we finally located put the tiny hole-in-the-wall back at our base to shame. There were clean tablecloths on all the tables, friendly, mini-skirted Vietnamese waitresses, lots of slot machines, a shiny new jukebox and a spacious dance floor. There was even a life-size color poster of a four-man, two-woman Vietnamese rock and roll band which evidently performed every night.

Sergeant Ketchum ordered and paid for the first set of beers and judging from the way he gulped his down, he was there to drink, not talk. We were on our third round and hadn't said a word to each other when an obviously drunk staff sergeant stumbled over to our table and draped his arm around Jim's neck.

"Ketchum," he said. "Well, I'll be damned! What the hell are you doing in these parts?" Jim seemed to recognize him but didn't appear to be exactly thrilled about the reunion. "Mind if I join you?" asked the staff sergeant, and without waiting for a reply, he slumped down in one of the two empty chairs at the table. "Hell," he continued, "someone told me you were dead."

"Not yet," said Jim.

"So, how's the old lady?"

"Fine," answered Jim reluctantly.

"She still milking you for every damn cent you got?"

Jim's eyes filled with anger and the staff sergeant's shit-eating grin quickly disappeared. "You got a big mouth, Ralph!"

"Hey, Jimmy-boy," said the staff sergeant, his words slurred, "you know me, man. I didn't mean nothing."

"You're worthless shit, Ralph," said Jim, his whole body eager to lash out at the staff sergeant, "and you've always been worthless shit."

"Now, now, Jim," said the staff sergeant, scared, "I don't want any trouble. I help run this place you know. Let me buy you and your buddy here a drink. What are you drinking? Beer?"

"Get out of my sight, Ralph!" screamed Jim. The staff sergeant raised his hands and waved them in surrender in front of his face, indicating once again that he didn't want any trouble. "And do it now, while you're still in one piece!"

The staff sergeant stood up as fast as his wobbly legs could perform the difficult task and then staggered back from the table until he was confident he was out of Jim's reach. "Look, Jim, I'll have one of the girls bring you over a couple of beers anyway. For old time's sake, okay? On the house."

"You keep your damn booze, Ralph. And get the fuck out of my sight!"

The staff sergeant, a lot more sober than he had been a few minutes earlier, disappeared in a flash. "Who was that guy?" I asked.

"Just someone I know. I borrowed some money from him once."

"Oh."

"The last I heard, he was some big-shot officer's driver—pimp is probably more like it."

"I thought he said he ran this place?"

"Maybe, but more than likely this is just one of the bennies he gets from being in tight with all the right people. See all these slot machines? He's probably got a part of that action, too. And shit, the son-of-a-bitch already made a fortune during my first tour converting greenbacks on the black market." He shook his head sadly. "The local gooks don't have any hard currency of their own. They get dollars from people like Ralph and use them to buy guns. And those guns end up killing Americans." He paused for a moment and looked away from me. "Who knows, maybe one of those guns killed Greg."

"By the way," I asked, "how come you were the one who had to go identify the body? He wasn't from our outfit."

"Greg was one of my aunt's boys. I know his CO and he called the major to let me know he had been killed. The old man was pretty cool about it. I didn't have to go. I just wanted to pay my last respects before they shipped him home."

He glanced down at his glass and realized it was empty. He signaled to the waitress to bring him another, and when it arrived he was still staring down at his empty glass, lost in his thoughts.

"You and Greg were pretty tight, huh?" I ventured.

"No, not really. I don't have much family, but he was a good kid, and he was one hell of a soldier. He always did what had to be done. People could count on him." He fell silent again, but when he had finished his beer, he looked over at me, his face even sadder than before. "You know, Ty, that's the hardest thing to get used to over here. All the wrong people seem to die. Scum like Ralph, they always make it home, always. The cowards, the black market guys, the drug addicts, they all go home. But really good kids like Greg, well, they just never seem to make it."

It was dark when Jim finally decided he had had enough to drink and that we should be getting back to the base. On our way out to the jeep, I convinced him that I had better do the driving. He reluctantly flipped me the keys and crawled into the passenger seat. I jumped behind the wheel and turned on the ignition.

Suddenly, two burly GI's leaped out of the night and wrestled Jim out of his seat. I hopped down and ran around to Jim's side of the jeep, but Ralph the staff sergeant, now completely sober and brandishing a switchblade knife, stopped me dead in my tracks.

"If you don't want to get hurt," Ralph advised me, "and I mean hurt real bad, then you better stay the fuck out of this." I backed up a couple of steps. "That's very, very smart," said Ralph, turning his attention to Jim.

Each of the huge soldiers who had dragged Jim out of the jeep had a firm grip on one of his arms. Jim realized he couldn't break their hold and he had stopped struggling to get free. Ralph stepped up to Jim and waved the knife slowly back and forth in front of his face. Then he kicked him as hard as he could in the groin. Jim bent over in agony and Ralph reached down, grabbed him by the hair and yanked his head skyward.

"So," said Ralph, "I'm worthless shit, huh?" Jim glared at him, but didn't answer. "I wasn't such a bad dude when you needed a thousand bucks to keep your old lady from walking out on you, was I?"

"You got all of that money back," said Jim, "and with interest."

"You really think you're hot shit, don't you? Big fucking war hero. All kinds of medals." He reached back for all the power he had in his right arm and slammed his fist into Jim's abdomen, causing Jim's knees to buckle and his face to wrinkle up in pain. "No one fucks with me, Ketchum, not even you!"

It suddenly dawned on me that neither Ralph nor his two thugs were paying the slightest bit of attention to me anymore. And then, for the first time since I had arrived in Vietnam, I remembered something I had been taught in advanced infantry training. If your enemy is armed, and you're not, and if you can get him to face you, and if you have your heavy combat boots on, then kick him as hard as you possibly can right in the crown of one of his shins. If done correctly, it's supposed to snap the bone cleanly in two.

I carefully stepped up behind Ralph and said, "Hey, fat boy." Ralph immediately whirled around and with all the force I could muster, I slammed the point of my right boot into Ralph's lower left leg. Ralph cried out and dropped to the ground like a sack of potatoes. It had actually worked. I couldn't believe it. Unfortunately, it had also opened up a whole new can of worms.

One of the giants holding onto Jim released him and came rushing towards me. I immediately took off running for the jeep. He chased me around and around the still idling vehicle until he finally ran out of breath.

In the meantime, Jim had managed to free himself from his captor and was fighting for his life in a much more dignified manner than me. He was landing most of the best blows and I starting screaming encouragement to him. "Hit him again, Jim!" I yelled. "Kick him! Kick him hard!"

The ape who had been chasing me suddenly came back to life and off we went again. This time I ran towards Jim, circled him, and headed back towards the jeep. On the way, I hurdled over Ralph, who was still crumpled up in a heap crying about his broken leg, and raced on. My pursuer had been breathing right down my neck, but when he tried to clear Ralph, he tripped and tumbled to the ground. It was all the opening I needed.

I jumped into the jeep, ground the stick shift into first gear and stomped on the gas peddle. I quickly spun the thing around and took off in the general direction of Jim. I was also headed straight towards Ralph, who thought for sure he was going to be run over, and his screams let Jim know I was on the way.

I slowed down just enough to miss Ralph and allow Jim to leap into the jeep. I floored the gas peddle, and without looking back, sped away from the parking lot. I was so pumped up with adrenalin, I kept over-correcting the steering wheel and the jeep began fishtailing all over the road.

"Slow down before you kill us," I heard Jim say, but when I finally got the jeep back under control and looked over at him, he didn't appear to be mad at me at all. In fact, he was in the middle of a big belly laugh.

"Just what's so damn funny?"

"Now that was fun!" he roared, still laughing, even though he was bruised all over and bleeding from both his mouth and nose. "And look at you. There's not a single damn mark anywhere!"

"Well, let that be a lesson to you," I said as clearly as I could.

"What did you say?"

I repeated myself.

"You're mumbling, Ty. I can't hear you. What?"

I returned his smile, but kept my mouth shut, not wanting him to know that I was busy swallowing blood, and that I had almost bitten my tongue in two while he was having so much fun.

JOURNAL ENTRY

83 DAYS TO GO

One of the really special people I've met in Vietnam is a middle-aged staff sergeant we all call Jimbo. He is a huge, muscular man with a face full of freckles and a completely bald head. He absolutely loves 'soldiering', as he calls it, and he joined the Army when he was only seventeen years old. It seems like he's been everywhere and seen everything. He is kind of the platoon philosopher and seems to have an uncanny knack for being able to put all the problems known to man into what he believes is the proper perspective. For instance, in the middle of a life and death firefight, he once crawled up to me and said, "Dying's no big deal, Nichols. Absolutely anyone can do it."

Jimbo firmly believes that, "Everything is perspective, and perspective is everything." And he drives a lot of us crazy with statistic after statistic, most of which I'm sure he makes up himself, to support his most cherished theory, that none of us have the foggiest notion of just how good we got it.

"Do you know what it means to be an American?" he once asked me. I obliged by shaking my head 'no'. "Just to be born in America," he continued, "means that you start off your life, economically speaking, in the top five percent of all the people on this earth. Now just think about that for a minute. And if you're born into a regular-type family, like me and you

were, just a middle-class family, then that puts you up in the top two and one-half percent of all the people in the whole world."

"How do you figure that, Jimbo?" I asked him.

"Look at how these people here in Vietnam live. And things are no better in most other places in the world. Look at Africa, India, China, you name it. The majority of the people in this world can't even come up with a decent meal for their kids to eat most days."

His eyes were filled with genuine sadness for those less fortunate and I told him, "You gotta stop carrying the weight of the whole world on your shoulders all the time, Jimbo."

"It's just that it drives me crazy to hear all the belly-aching that goes on around here. And it's just as bad back in the world. People really need to start figuring out just how good they got it. We're living in the best times that ever were. We got more books than any one man could ever read, medicines that keep us alive forever, and we're free to do as we damn well please."

Jimbo is the only man I have ever met who could stand up in the middle of a rice paddy in Vietnam, as he once did, admire the scenery and say with deep conviction, "It just don't get any better than this!"

Yesterday afternoon, knowing that Jimbo is scheduled to rotate in a few days, I stopped by his hootch to thank him for all the great advice he's given me over the past nine months or so. "I'm really going to miss you, Jimbo," I told him. "We'll have to stay in touch."

"Nichols," he said, "I've been in the Army for more years than I care to count, met thousands of guys and never stayed in touch with any of them, so don't be expecting any letters." I returned his warm smile. "Tell you what I will do, though. I'll pass along 'the' secret to staying sane in an insane world."

By now I have come to have great respect for Jimbo's way of looking at the world and I sat down on his bunk and listened carefully.

"You live in California, right?" I nodded my head 'yes'. "Well, then you're one of the real lucky ones, because the ocean is right there next to you."

"The ocean?" I asked.

"Nichols, when nothing seems to make any sense, you just hop in a car and head for the nearest stretch of ocean you can find. Then sit out there on the warm sand, watch the old sun go down and remember this: that very same sun has been going down ever since time began, and those very same waves have been rolling in for just as long. And that sun is going to keep on going down, and those waves are going to keep on coming in, long after you and me and all of our puny little problems are long gone and forgotten about." He sat down beside me on the bunk and put his thick, muscular arm around my shoulder. *"So, you see,"* he concluded, *"what people are always forgetting is that we, and all the things we're always worrying about, just aren't very important in the overall scheme of things."*

"It's all a matter of perspective, right, Jimbo?" I asked him, quoting his favorite saying.

"You got it, Nichols!"

CHAPTER 21

▼

FLYING WITH THE RED BARON

Nicky Anderson was greatly respected by everyone in the rifle platoon, having been a grunt himself before re-upping so he could doorgun for Wally Wakely. He loved what he was doing and was absolutely convinced that the next week was going to be the highlight of my tour, and he couldn't have been happier when he strutted into my room to give me the good news. "Guess who's going to be my replacement for the week I'm off in Hong Kong screwing my brains out?" he asked me.

"But I thought you said you were too broke to take another R & R," I replied as I continued changing the filthy sheets on my bed.

"Didn't you hear what I just said?" asked Nicky, barely able to contain his enthusiasm.

"You said you were going to Hong Kong. And by the way, did you know Hong Kong is the most expensive R & R a guy can take?

"Look at me, Ty."

"What?"

"The old man said I can choose anyone I want from the rifle platoon to take my place while I'm gone."

"So?"

"So, you stupid grunt, I'm choosing you!"

"You're kidding me," I said, stunned.

"No I'm not. You're always saying how easy I got it, flying around with Wally while you hump through the rice paddies and everything, so I'm choosing you. I've already told Wally and he's cool with it. Ketchum wasn't exactly thrilled, but even he admitted it would be a good experience for you."

"But Nicky," I said with worry, "I don't know a darn thing about doorgunning."

"It's heaven on earth, man. There ain't nothing prettier than Vietnam from tree-top level. You can see everything that's going on, and best of all, you can see what you hit."

"But I don't know if I really want to see what I hit, Nicky."

"You'll pick it up real fast, man. It's actually a lot of fun, blowing away gooks in the open. It takes a little getting used to, but once you've got the hang of it, there's nothing quite like it. Most of you grunts don't realize it, but doorgunners are responsible for two-thirds of the troop's kills."

"So what else makes it so great?" I asked, hoping for something a little less bloodcurdling.

"One of the things I really like—next to just being up there with Wally—is that it's not so damn scary. When I was on the ground, I couldn't see a thing, but I could hear the AK's going off, people screaming when they got hit, all that shit. But when I'm sitting behind my M50, I'm above it all, man. I feel a hundred times safer for some reason. I know I'm not, but it's an illusion I can definitely live with, if you know what I mean. Yeah, that's the best part of the whole damn thing—not being the least bit scared, and being up there where I can't hear anything except the helicopter blades and Wally talking on the radio."

The typical scout helicopter doorgunner in Vietnam sat behind a powerful and deadly M50 machine gun in the open cargo compartment on the side opposite his pilot. Without a doubt, he had the best view of anyone serving in the war, and he also got to wear a great-looking crash helmet, special nylon gloves and leather boots designed to resist burning, a lightweight protective flak vest and a fancy survival knife that I had always envied.

When I asked Nicky if I'd get to wear all that cool stuff, too, he smiled and said, "Let's go ask Wally. He's over at the Officer's Club, and you ain't lived until you've done some serious drinking with the Wobbly Ones!"

Rumor had it that the Officer's Club was one of the base's first building projects and it was obvious to me that a lot of time and effort had gone into its construction. Sheets of darkly stained plywood served as the walls and ceiling and created a cozy atmosphere not too unlike a dimly lit cave.

Once my eyes had adjusted to the lack of light, I was immediately impressed by the sight of all the lushly upholstered red bar stools and lounge chairs. The place even had its own ice-making machine.

After introductions all around, I sat down with Wally and Nicky and proudly ordered my first 'on the rocks' drink since I had been in Vietnam.

Wally Wakely was an easy man to like and except for a few pilots who were jealous of him, everyone did. Like most of the warrant officers on the base, he wasn't a career officer and the politics and ultimate outcome of the war were of little interest to him. He had come to Vietnam for the adventure of it, and to pursue the one great love of his life, flying helicopters.

He had Lindberg-like courage and good looks and he knew it, yet the more valor medals he collected, the more humble he seemed to become. He also never minced words and I wasn't at all surprised that the first thing out of his mouth was, "You don't know squat-shit about doorgunning, do you, Nichols?"

"No, sir, I'm afraid not."

"And I hear you're not much of a shot, either."

"I'm getting better," I assured him.

"Do you know anything about helicopters at all?"

"A little, sir."

"What's the name of the stick I hold in my left hand and use to adjust the throttle and the angle of the main rotor blades?" he quizzed me.

"The collective, I think."

"Very good," said Wally, smiling. "Now how about the one that fits between my legs and controls the tilt of the main rotor blade?"

"That's his little dick," said Nicky.

After Wally had stopped laughing, I said, "Sir, to be honest, I'm not very mechanical. I can barely get my P-38 can opener to work."

Wally and Nicky both laughed this time, and as I took another sip of my scotch, I thought about how much the best helicopter pilots serving in Vietnam reminded me of old World War One flying aces. They were young, flamboyant risk-takers without a lot of training who loved what they were doing. Some were more cautious than others, but the really good ones were willing to do just about anything to help out an American soldier on the ground.

My seven heavenly days of playing doorgunner with Wally Wakely turned out to be everything I had hoped they would be, and then some. Wally and I were always up and flying at the crack of dawn and the beauty of the lush terrain we were responsible for patrolling was breathtaking. But even more moving was the way wedges of brilliant sunlight would often strike me when I least expected it, leaving the distinct impression that God Himself had finally taken an interest in what I was doing in Vietnam.

I had been used to flying at altitudes of at least fifteen hundred feet, which protected our infantry platoon's transport helicopters from enemy ground fire, but Wally liked to get right down near the tree tops where he could do a little 'reconnaissance by fire'. He'd spot something which he thought might be a Vietcong bunker and order me to shoot it up, the hope being that someone would start firing back and give away their position. The trick was to go in close enough to get the enemy to commit himself, but not so close that Wally couldn't get the hell out of there in a big hurry if needed. And no one could get a helicopter out of harm's way faster than Wally Wakely.

Luckily for me, no matter how many times Wally descended to 'go in hot', no enemy soldier ever shot back. We saw any number of enemy bunkers, but they were all deserted by the time we got anywhere near them. Wally said I was bringing him bad luck. I told him I was bringing him good luck.

Much to Wally's disappointment, the highlight of our week together turned out to be nothing more than a dozen or so errant shots I took at a water buffalo in the open, something I had been wanting to do since my first contact with that horrible species of animal. "You weren't actually trying to hit it, were you?" he asked me over the radio.

"Naw," I lied, "I just wanted to scare it a bit."

"You don't like water buffalos, huh?"

"I hate the darn things, and they can't stand me, either. Every time I've been within a hundred yards of one, it's charged me."

"That's because they don't like the way Americans smell," explained Wally.

"Well," I said into the radio, "to tell you the truth, I don't much like the way they smell, either."

Having concluded what I considered to be a wonderfully uneventful and therefore very successful partnership, I climbed out of Wally's helicopter for what I thought would be the last time and thanked him enthusiastically for having not even come close to crashing.

"Not so fast," said Wally. "I signed us up to fly Nighthawk tonight."

"What's that?" I asked, not particularly thrilled by the idea of doing anything in Vietnam once the sun had gone down.

"The major is tired of the night belonging to Charlie, so he's got us all taking turns doing a little after-dark aerial reconnaissance."

"You mean that new gunship with the big search light on it?"

"Don't worry," Wally assured me. "It's only for a few hours, and so far it's just been a big waste of everyone's time."

The Nighthawk gunship turned out to be a converted Huey with a sniper's starlight scope and a huge searchlight. It was also armed with a nasty minigun capable of pouring hundreds of rounds of ammunition into every square foot of enemy-controlled ground.

As Wally and I lifted off into the night sky, I once again couldn't help but notice how smoothly he raised us up into the air. His every movement seemed so confident, almost as if he could do whatever it was he was doing in his sleep. He didn't seem to be flying a machine at all, but rather a living, breathing extension of himself.

He was sharing the controls with a brand new pilot who was even more in awe of Wally than me. His name was Henry Carlson and he got real nervous when Wally announced over the radio, "We're going to do a little something different tonight. I've got a hunch Charlie is already on to the routine, so let's change it a bit."

With that, Wally banked the helicopter into a steep left-hand turn and sped away from the perimeter we were supposed to be patrolling. Within minutes, he had us hovering high above a clump of tall, thick trees and when he turned on the searchlight, I could barely believe the sight below. Huddled together at the base of the biggest tree were more Vietcong than I had ever seen in one place before. There had to be at least twenty of them, maybe more, and they looked like they were having some kind of meeting. They appeared to be just as surprised to see us as we were to see them.

Then, in what seemed like one choreographed motion, the Vietcong all lifted up their rifles and began shooting. Before I could return the fire, Wally sped away from danger and calmly said, "Okay, it's all yours, Henry."

Henry, his voice breaking with excitement, thanked Wally so profusely for the opportunity that it seemed like forever before he finally got the helicopter turned around and headed back towards the clump of trees.

With the searchlight on and the minigun at the ready, Henry dove the helicopter down towards the objective only to discover that twenty-plus Vietcong had somehow disappeared into thin air. Henry circled and circled, but the enemy was no longer anywhere to be found. "Where in the hell could they have gone?" asked a frustrated Henry as he made pass after pass. "There's nothing but rice paddies surrounding those trees. They've got to be down there somewhere! Goddamn it, where are they?"

"The Lord giveth and the Lord taketh away," finally said Wally over the radio as he took back control of the helicopter, banked it sharply into the night sky, and sped us safely back to the perimeter.

Exactly eight days after my final handshake with Wally Wakely on a starlit tarmac, he lost his life, doing the one thing he loved above all else, flying a helicopter. And as I stood in silence at his memorial service and tried to tune out Major McCalley's rambling eulogy, I found myself thinking back to something I had once read in a college English class, in an Ernest Hemingway novel, about how if people bring too much courage to the world, the world has to kill them. "It kills the very young and the very gentle and the very brave impartially," wrote Hemingway. "If you are none of these you can be sure it will kill you, too, but there will be no special hurry."

JOURNAL ENTRY

73 DAYS TO GO

"Just remember you won't be alone—everyone is going to be scared shitless."

I have come to believe that those words, which were whispered to me by my father as he hugged me goodbye, apply to just about every soldier I have met in Vietnam, including those who are going back to the world with a valor medal of one kind or another pinned to their chests. But there was one exception—Crazy Willie Williams.

Corporal William Williams, all five-foot-four, one hundred and thirty pounds of him was that rare draftee in Vietnam who actually appeared to be enjoying himself. It was as if he had waited his whole life to be really good at something and it somehow turned out to be playing war. When the fighting and dying started, it was obvious to everyone around him that Willie was in his element, that this was his arena, and that he loved every moment of it. It was almost scary the way he was so totally fearless.

He came to our platoon from some grunt unit that was being taken off-line and reorganized and he apparently didn't want to be away from the action for the two months or so the whole process was scheduled to take. He claimed to be the best tunnel rat in the entire division and one night when I was standing next to him in the chow line, he told me with deep conviction, "There just ain't nothing more fun than getting hold of a gook in his own damn hole and slitting his fucking throat with my big ol' Bowie knife."

"I don't like the guy," Sergeant Ketchum told me after spending just one day in the field with Willie, "and I'm glad he's not in our squad. He takes stupid chances. He's going to get someone hurt, and he's going to get himself killed."

When a firefight breaks out over here, standard operating procedure for me and most everyone I know is to dive to the safety of the earth and then scramble for the best cover you can find. Crazy Willie, however, would always immediately, and very calmly, make a beeline to where he thought he could inflict the most damage on the enemy. It didn't matter if he had to leap-frog from squad to squad to get there, either. And once he was in position, while most everyone else was still cowered on the ground frantically trying to regroup and make sense out of all the chaos around them, Crazy Willie would start firing off clip after clip and tossing hand grenades all over the place.

"You're crazy," Harry told Willie to his face after one of those episodes, and the nickname stuck. But crazy or not, almost everyone in the platoon secretly wished they had the courage to be just like Willie.

When Crazy Willie didn't have his Superman cape on, he was really a pretty ordinary, even boring, guy. He hardly ever spoke unless the subject was war-related and he spent most of his down-time alone in his hootch, meticulously cleaning his weapons and organizing his gear for the next mission. In the evenings, he rarely showed up at the base movie and he never spent any time in the NCO Club drinking and socializing with the rest of the guys. He also didn't write or receive letters, and he absolutely hated it when anyone played their music too loud. He was in Vietnam to fight a war, pure and simple, and he seemed determined, almost driven, to do it with more guts and dash than all the rest of the platoon put together.

The only thing Crazy Willie did away from the field which was of much interest to anyone actually had more to do with his pet boa constrictor, Squeezer, than it did with him.

Crazy Willie had come across Squeezer quite by accident one evening when he and his squad were setting up a night ambush a few klicks outside the perimeter. According to eye witnesses, Crazy Willie was propped up against a tree, sound asleep, when Squeezer just crawled right up into his lap. The whole squad took off running, except Crazy Willie, who wrapped the huge thing around his neck and went in search of his squad leader to ask if he could keep it for a pet.

Squeezer had his own chicken wire cage right outside of Crazy Willie's hootch and he had to be fed pretty regularly. At first, Crazy Willie would throw him rats or mice he collected in a specially made vermin trap he moved around every night out by the perimeter bunkers. But Squeezer kept growing and growing, and soon he was a good fifteen feet long and as thick as one of Crazy Willie's muscular thighs.

"He's going to starve if I don't start getting him something bigger to eat," Crazy Willie lamented one night after a mission as me and Harry stood around with him watching Squeezer crush the life out of a rat. "He needs a rabbit, or a chicken, or a dog."

"You mean live ones?" I asked.

"Sure," said Willie. "He don't like anything that's already dead."

"Why don't you just get rid of that damn thing before it ends up eating one of us?" suggested Harry.

Crazy Willie looked over at Harry like he would have much preferred to just pick him up and toss him in with Squeezer and forget all about coming up with boa constrictor munchies for the next few months.

"It was just a joke," Harry assured Willie. "And there's no dogs or chickens roaming free around here, anyway."

"I know that," said Crazy Willie, "but that gook's farm just outside the wire is crawling with the damn things."

"Willie," I said, "you better think twice before you go messing with any of that old man's animals. When Valentine's doorgunner accidentally shot one of his water buffaloes, all hell broke loose around here. That old man is even crazier than you."

"*The Army ended up paying him ten times what the damn water buffalo was worth,*" *added Harry,* "*and he even took a shot at one of the guys who brought him the money.*"

"*Are we talking about the same gook?*" *asked Crazy Willie.* "*That little old bastard with the black teeth who is always taking a dump out in his rice paddies?*"

"*That's the one,*" *said Harry.*

"*Well, all I know is that Squeezer needs some decent grub and I plan on getting him some.*"

Sure enough, early the next week, Crazy Willie invited the whole platoon to drop by and watch Squeezer devour his first chicken. Almost everyone showed up and the atmosphere was pretty festive, considering the fact that some poor chicken was just about to be thrown to his death.

To the loud cheers and whistles of most of the guys who had gathered for the occasion, Crazy Willie tossed the chicken into the cage and everyone waited anxiously for Squeezer to do his thing. Much to Willie's surprise, Squeezer didn't move a muscle, and a full half-hour later, the chicken was still very much alive and leisurely pecking away at the ground.

"*Maybe Squeezer likes the damn thing?*" *suggested Harry.*

Then, just when everyone was about to call it a day and head back to their hootches, the chicken strolled a little too close to Squeezer for his own good, and in one explosive move, Squeezer pounced on the unsuspecting bird and methodically crushed it to death.

Having already invested almost an hour in this spectacle, most everyone decided to hang around until Squeezer finally managed to get the chicken all the way in his mouth and down into his throat.

"*That's it,*" *said Crazy Willie, taking a bow after the bird had finally disappeared from sight and become nothing more than a slow moving lump in Squeezer's upper torso.* "*It'll probably take him a good day or two to digest it, but he loved it, I could tell. From now on, it's chickens for Squeezer.*"

So, once every week for almost a month, most of the guys would rearrange their evening schedules to make sure they were there for Squeezer's next chicken dinner. No one asked Crazy Willie where he kept getting the birds, but we all knew. Then just a few nights ago, with everything nice and quiet all along the perimeter, shots suddenly rang out and flares began lighting up the black sky.

"What the heck's going on?" I asked Harry as we ran into each other on our way out the hootch door.

"You got me," said Harry as we scrambled down into our assigned bunker.

For the next ten or fifteen minutes, one flare after another lit up the perimeter and even the Nighthawk crew was scrambled to get to the bottom of things. Since no mortars or rockets had accompanied the gunfire, Harry and I both felt it would be pretty safe to make our way out to the perimeter and ask some of the guards what was going on. We were just about there when the Nighthawk helicopter shined its bright beam of light down on the ground. Lit up for all to see was Crazy Willie, staggering back towards the perimeter, with a struggling, squawking chicken under each arm.

When Willie reached the perimeter, two of the guards helped him through the wire, laid him down on his stomach—he'd been shot once in the leg and twice in the butt—and tried to get him to release the chickens.

According to one of the guards, Crazy Willie's last words before the dust-off arrived were, "Make sure someone feeds Squeezer!"

The next day, after the major ordered that Squeezer be shot and deposited in the shit-burning ditch, Harry and I went down to the NCO Club to toast the departure of one of the bravest, and craziest, guys we had ever known.

As we raised our beers, I left the toast up to Harry. "To Crazy Willie—a common chicken thief," said Harry as we clunked our cans together.

CHAPTER 22

▼

TUNNEL RATS

In the spring, our whole division began to play a bigger role in the Vietnamization of the war. Orders came down for our platoon to start spending more of our operational time helping the Army of the Republic of Vietnam prepare itself for the eventual departure of United States combat troops. We were told by First Sergeant Adams that the number of our search and destroy missions would be cut approximately in half and that many of us would soon be lecturing new ARVN recruits on American military discipline and tactics. As far as everyone in my squad was concerned, talking about how you're supposed to fight a war was definitely preferable to going out in the field and engaging the enemy. It all seemed too good to be true, and we soon discovered that it was.

It was rumored that Major McCalley was so upset with the new orders that he immediately flew up to divisional headquarters to inform his superiors in no uncertain terms that Echo Troop would be completely demoralized and left without a sense of mission if we were given any aspect of a non-combat assignment. Apparently his arguments won the day because it wasn't even twenty-four hours after the first sergeant had spoken to us that he had us back in formation again.

"I want you to totally disregard everything I told you yesterday," he said with emphasis. "The only part this platoon will be playing in Vietnamization is that starting next week, we will be sending individual squads out from time to time on joint ambushes with ARVN units."

No one said anything, but I knew what most everyone was thinking. ARVN soldiers didn't have a very good reputation among American military personnel. I personally had never fought along side them, but I had heard countless stories about their ineptitude. They were supposed to be lazy, untrustworthy, and worst of all, cowardly. It was said that the majority of them had been forced into serving their struggling new country or were in uniform only because they wanted to collect a steady paycheck from Uncle Sam.

They certainly looked the part, though, often wearing brand new jungle fatigues and combat boots. They also carried the same state-of-the-art weapons we did, but no matter how well-outfitted and equipped our government made them, the prevailing opinion was that they were simply lousy soldiers.

"This is going to be a voluntary thing to begin with," continued the first sergeant. "So, who wants to be the first squad to show some of our allies how to set up and pull off a proper ambush?"

"Day or night ambushes?" asked Sergeant Ketchum.

"Day," answered the first sergeant, "although we're going to have to take them out after dark sooner or later, too."

"We'll take a shot at it, Top," said Sergeant Ketchum.

"Good," replied the first sergeant with a thankful nod. "I appreciate your squad being the first one to step up to the plate. If our effort over here is going to mean something, we've all got to do everything in our power to make sure we leave the ARVN Army in the best shape possible when we pull out."

"Is Ketchum crazy or what?" asked Harry, who was standing next to me.

"Teaching sure beats going out in the field," I said.

"And just where do you think this is all going to take place?" demanded Harry. "In a fucking classroom? Of course not! We're still going to be out in the field. Only now we'll be standing around with a bunch of chicken-shit gooks. I'm getting sick and tired of Ketchum always volunteering us for crap like this."

"Maybe he just wants to get our squad's turn over with?" I suggested.

"And there you go again, man, always making excuses for the guy."

"I'm doing no such thing," I said as the first sergeant dismissed the formation.

"Yes you are! I don't know what's gotten into you, man."

"Nothing has gotten into me, Harry."

"Yes it has! How can you be getting so tight with a guy like Ketchum? He's damn near as gung ho as McCalley."

"He's a good guy, Harry. He really is. And don't be telling me who I can like and who I can't."

"Jesus Christ," said Harry as he flipped me the bird and began walking away, "the next thing I know he'll have his damn dick up your butt!"

Much to everyone's surprise, the two-dozen young ARVN soldiers we were assigned to train in daylight ambush techniques turned out to be attentive, hard-working and quick to learn. They met us on a bright, warm morning at the outskirts of a rural hamlet which had a sing-song name none of us could properly pronounce. A cluster of old thatched huts and dusty dirt paths served as the heart of the little village, and thin-chested, barefoot farmers and their beetle nut chewing spouses were scattered everywhere, attending their vegetable gardens and rice paddies. They seemed totally indifferent to the fact that we had invaded their ancient, unchanging world.

The first order of business was to show the ARVN's how to set up claymore mines, which were full of steel pellets and very effective at wounding or killing enemy soldiers who were strolling along a trail. Since the Vietcong were always moving in and out of peasant villages in the countryside looking for shelter and food, the footpaths they used to come and go were ideal places to set up ambushes.

With the help of Toi Nguyen, whom Sergeant Ketchum was using as an interpreter, the claymore instruction was going surprisingly well. But just as Toi had finished explaining how to best position and wire the mines, a burst of rounds suddenly rang out and everyone began diving on top of one another as we all frantically attempted to occupy the same few meters of ground.

Another couple of stray shots soon followed, one of them harmlessly hitting a tree a good twenty yards from where we were all huddled. "There!" said Sergeant Ketchum, pointing to what appeared to be a young teenage girl off in the distance with a rifle in her hand. "She's shooting at us."

When Sergeant Ketchum stood up and aimed his M16 rifle at the young girl, who couldn't have been more than thirteen or fourteen years old, she immediately dropped her weapon and took off sprinting for the center of town. "Come on, Ty," shouted Sergeant Ketchum, motioning for me to follow him. "Everyone else stay put—stay right here!"

As Sergeant Ketchum and I raced after the teenage girl, I quickly realized that even with a twenty-five pound radio on my back, I had finally found something I could top him at—I was much faster than he was. My long strides easily overtook him and I couldn't help but smile as I effortlessly swept past him. "Be careful!" he yelled after me. "And don't hurt her!"

As I reached the edge of the village, I lost sight of the young girl as she darted down one of the unpaved side streets. I slowed my pace to make sure I wasn't running into an ambush myself, and as I turned the corner where I had seen her last, there she was again—at least the bottom half of her—diving into a straw covered hut at the far end of the street.

Winded, I bent over at the waist, took my rifle off the safety and waited for Jim to catch up with me. "So, where'd she go?" were the first words out of his mouth.

"In there, I think," I said, pointing to the hut.

"Are you sure?"

"I saw somebody run in there. It had to be her."

"Okay," said Jim, who, unlike me, had already caught his breath, "I'll go take a look. Stay out here and cover me."

After cautiously entering the hut with his rifle at the ready, Jim stepped back outside and said, "There's nobody in there, Ty. You sure it wasn't one of these other ones?"

"Yes, I'm sure. She has to be in there." We then both went inside the hut, but just as Jim had said, the tiny room was unoccupied. "How can that be?" I asked. "She couldn't have just vanished into thin air. She's got to be in here."

As we continued to search the poorly lit room, Jim pointed to a couple of old thatched mats spread out on the dirt floor and said, "Turn those over."

"Why?"

"Just do it."

Using the tip of my rifle, I flipped the first one over and there was nothing but rock-hard earth underneath it. "Do you think she's hiding under a floor mat?" I asked Jim with a smile.

"Now turn over the one in the corner," he ordered me, not returning my smile.

When I kicked the second one up into the air, my eyes widened as I found myself staring down into a three or four-foot circular black hole. "What the heck is that?" I asked Jim.

"That, my friend, is the entrance to a VC tunnel. Move away from it."

"What do we do now?" I asked, quickly stepping back towards Jim.

"Do you carry a flashlight like all good RTO's are supposed to?"

"Yeah."

"Good. Then let's go have us a look."

"You're kidding?"

"No. I used to go down into these things all the time during my first tour. There were tunnels all over the place up north. That was the only way they could avoid all of our firepower. Hell, there were more NVA and VC living under the ground than above it."

"How far do you think it goes?"

"No telling. Some of these harmless looking little villages probably have miles of tunnels underneath them. They're good for scared peasants to hide in and great stop-over places for Charlie. Plus they're almost impossible to destroy. You'd need tons and tons of explosives to do a good job on most of them."

"Really?"

"Come on, we won't go in very far. Give me your flashlight. I'll go first."

"But I can't fit into that little hole with this radio on, Jim."

"So, then take it off. It's not going to be any good to us when we're under the ground anyway."

Grasping for any straw which might keep me out of a Vietcong tunnel, I said, "To tell you the truth, Jim, I'm kinda claustrophobic. I really don't think I should be going down into that thing."

"Come on," he encouraged me. "It's not that scary once you actually get inside it."

"I don't know, Jim."

"What, you afraid of one little girl?"

Out of excuses, I reluctantly shed my radio, handed Jim my flashlight and said, "Aren't tunnels always booby trapped?"

"Naw, only now and then. What you've really got to worry about is bats, rats, scorpions, critters like that."

"You're putting me on, right?" I asked, getting more nervous by the moment.

"No, not at all. You really need to keep an eye out, especially for scorpions. You get bit by one of those little guys, and let me tell you, it smarts."

"You've been bitten by a scorpion?"

"Yep. Thank god it was a small one. The big ones can kill you. Now, come on, follow me."

On closer examination of the tunnel entrance, a sturdy bamboo ladder had been shoved down the shaft and it made stepping off into the blackness a bit more bearable. Once I reached solid ground again—which didn't happen until I was a good five or six feet below the surface of the earth—Jim illuminated the first level of the tunnel with my flashlight and said with admiration, "Can you believe this place? Do you know how many years it must have taken them to do all this digging?" I was too busy looking for scorpions and bats to answer, so Jim added, "I mean, they had to take all this dirt out of here a bucket at a time. And look at this bamboo shoring. Can you imagine how much work went into that? It's really unbelievable."

As we cautiously began crawling single file on our hands and knees, I was surprised at how far my tiny flashlight allowed Jim and me to see in front of us. "How come the tunnel isn't straight?" I asked him.

"That's so the VC don't have to be more than three or four feet in front of us to keep out of rifle range. This whole thing is probably going to keep turning one way and then another. You're going to be dizzy before you're out of here."

"Is it okay to keep talking?" I asked, hoping that it was.

"Sure. But we better keep it down a little."

"I really don't like being down here, Jim," I whispered. "We're not going to get lost, are we?"

"Not if you'll stop whining and let me pay attention to what the hell I'm doing."

Sweating profusely and with the walls and ceiling of the tunnel closing in all around me, I was just about to ask Jim if I could turn around and go back when we came to a room which had to be at least six feet wide and four feet high. It felt almost spacious, considering where we had spent the past ten or fifteen minutes. Best of all, the air in it was dramatically better than what we had been breathing. As we both took a few moments to fill our lungs, Jim pointed the flashlight up at what appeared to be a wide bamboo pole which had apparently been installed as an air shaft. Pretty ingenious, I thought to myself as I stuck my head closer to the source of the fresh air. "What are these?" I asked, bumping into neatly stacked piles of God only knew what.

Jim shined the flashlight over towards me and said, "They look like sewing kits or something. Here, hand me one of them."

I passed him one of the little cardboard boxes and inside it he found plastic bags of tea, scissors, tape, a syringe, Chinese labeled antiseptics, gauze, and what appeared to be a variety of different spices and herbs. "They're first aid kits," explained Jim. "How many do you think there are of them?"

"Oh, I don't know, maybe a couple of dozen or so," I said, trying to get out of the way so Jim could point the flashlight directly at them.

"If we were to keep on going," said Jim, "I bet we would find rooms with all kinds of stuff in them."

"Like what?"

"Well, I've been in tunnel rooms stacked high with baskets full of food and water, rooms where they stored weapons and ammunition, even sleeping rooms plastered with Playboy centerfolds."

"Really? People actually sleep down here?"

"Oh sure."

"But there's no light. If you turned off that flashlight, it'd be pitch black."

"So what? It's dark once you close your eyes, anyway. What's the difference?"

"But it'd be like being buried alive. I couldn't sleep down here in a million years."

"If it kept you safe from a B-52 strike, I bet you could. Plus they probably bring candles with them. I bet they're as snug as a bug in a rug down here."

"Did you say we're not going on?" I asked, hoping I had heard him right.

"Yeah, we're not going any farther than this, not without letting someone know we're down here. Plus we don't have the right equipment. A flashlight just don't cut it. We need a couple of those head lamps that the tunnel rats use. No, we've gone far enough. I don't want to get lost anymore than you do. I just wanted to let you see what one of these things is like. Pretty neat, isn't it? And I bet there's another whole level to it, too."

"You really think so?"

"VC tunnels can get pretty elaborate. Some of them were built decades ago, when they were fighting the French. I once knew a tunnel rat who said he'd seen underground rooms where they actually operated on people. They had electricity, up-to-date surgical equipment, you name it."

"I'm sure glad we're not going any farther," I admitted.

"We'll tell the major what we found and if he wants to bring the whole platoon back, that's fine, but this one room is it for you and me."

"What about the girl? We're not going to go after her?"

"No, that wouldn't be very bright."

"But you think she's down in here someplace?"

"Oh, sure she is. But who knows where? There's probably an emergency exit or two further down the tunnel. For all we know, she may already be out of the tunnel and back at work in one of the rice paddies."

"That was really kind of weird, her standing up and taking a couple of shots at us like that. She's just a kid."

"Who knows, maybe it's personal with her now."

"What do you mean?"

"That's how war works. People start taking it personal."

"I still don't know what you're talking about."

"It's real simple. When you first get here, the enemy is just some poor slob you don't know or care anything about. But somewhere along the line, someone you know or really care about gets dusted, then all of a sudden, it's personal. You start really hating the people who killed your buddy, or in the case of that young girl, maybe her parents or her brother or her sister got blown away. Who knows. But once you start taking it personal, it's got you. It changes everything. That's why I keep friends to a minimum over here. I don't want to start taking any of this too personal."

I wanted to tell Jim that like it or not, I was his friend, but before I could speak, he backed out into the tunnel, aimed his rifle into the unexplored darkness, took off his safety, pulled the trigger and emptied a whole clip of ammunition. "What the heck are you doing?" I asked him after the dust had settled and my ears had stopped throbbing.

"Don't worry. Even if that little girl is still down here, there's no way I could hit her the way this tunnel is laid out."

"Then why did you shoot?"

"Because if that damn brat is down here, I just scared the shit out of her, and maybe she'll think twice before she shoots at an American again," he said, almost as if he was a stern father correcting a child. Then he smiled, which he did so rarely, and added, "Now let's get the hell out of here before a scorpion bites you on the butt or a bat takes a dump on your head."

JOURNAL ENTRY

68 DAYS TO GO

Earlier this evening, our hootch's mama-san stuck her head into my room and said, "Shit-man want you. Now."

"Thanks," I said, wondering what Ted Henson, the platoon's permanent shit-burner and a good friend of mine, wanted with me. I had just seen him at evening chow, and he hadn't indicated then that we needed to talk. We had been sitting with Murray Goldstein as usual and everything seemed fine.

Ted and Murray have become really tight. Where you find one, you usually find the other. Ted was the one person who really stood by Murray when he got in so much trouble for ripping Lieutenant Davenport's beloved Thompson machine gun out of his hands. When the major kicked Murray out of the rifle platoon because of it, it was Ted who talked the first sergeant into making Murray an assistant mail clerk instead of transferring him out to a line unit. Murray has never forgotten that, and he'd do anything for Ted. He even goes out and helps with the shit-burning from time to time.

Anyway, when I stepped into Ted's room, he quickly motioned for me to close the door. Ted's room is the only one in his hootch with a real door on it. He doesn't always smell all that great, and he built the door himself so he wouldn't offend anyone.

"What's up?" I asked him as I shut the door and sat down in a chair next to his bunk.

"Ty," he said, "I think we've got a real problem."

Ted is a pretty easy-going guy, and I wasn't used to seeing such an anxious expression on his face. "What kind of a problem?" I asked.

"It's Murray."

"What's he up to now?" I asked with a smile.

"No, Ty, this is serious. I think he may have really lost it."

"Murray is always losing it," I reminded Ted.

"But this time it's different," Ted assured me. "I know he's done some pretty strange things in the past, but nothing like this."

"Is he trying to set up the first ever anti-war demonstration over here again or what?"

"No, it's even worse than that. He says he saw a UFO."

"Really? When?"

"Last night."

"Where?"

"Out by the perimeter bunkers—while he was pulling guard duty."

"Well, that's not really such a big deal, Ted. Lots of people think they've seen a UFO."

"But Murray swears they beamed him up into the damn thing."

"What?" I asked, trying unsuccessfully not to laugh.

"I'm not kidding, Ty. He went on and on about it after dinner tonight. He really believes it."

"He's probably just smoking pot again, Ted."

"Could be, but I don't really think so. He swore off the really good stuff months ago."

"Well," I said, "I guess if a spaceship was going to beam anyone up from around here, it'd be Murray."

"He says he saw this bright swirling blue light and then the next thing he knew, he was on board this spaceship being given a complicated battery of physical and psychological tests."

"What kind of tests?" I asked.

"*That part he doesn't remember too well,*" explained Ted, "*except that they kept flashing all these different colored lights in front of his eyes and poking him all over with their cold little fingers.*"

"*What did they look like?*"

"*Well, he said they were really short and that they all had huge bald heads, bulging green eyes, real skinny legs and the ugliest feet he had ever seen. And none of them were wearing any clothes.*"

"*Not even the girls?*" I asked from my earthly perspective.

"*He says he couldn't tell which ones were the boys and which ones were the girls.*"

"*Is that right? How come?*"

"*Because none of them had any male or female body parts to speak of.*"

"*You're kidding? No body parts?*"

"*Nope, not that he could tell, anyway. He asked one of them about that and was told they had evolved beyond the need for body parts.*"

"*Evolved to what?*"

"*That's a good question. Kind of scary, isn't it? Murray thinks we may be the only creatures left in the whole universe who are still stuck with all these damn body parts.*"

As I sat there trying with great difficulty to contemplate life without body parts, especially female body parts, Ted added, "*It kinda makes you wonder why those poor little guys would even bother to explore the universe, doesn't it?*"

CHAPTER 23

▼

JIM'S LETTERS

It was well after midnight and I was sprawled out on my bunk putting the finishing touches on a journal entry when Sergeant Ketchum stumbled awkwardly into my room and propped himself up against one of the walls. He was obviously drunk, or high, or both, and his short, wobbly legs looked like they were just about ready to give out.

"Every damn time I come in here," he said, his words slurred, "you're writing a fucking letter."

"Actually," I said, still not completely believing my eyes, "I'm just playing around with my journal. Are you okay?"

Before he could answer, the balancing act he was trying to pull off came to an abrupt end and he crumbled to the floor right in front of me. I jumped up and struggled to get him back on his feet and onto the bunk. He still had on his dirty fatigues and mud-caked combat boots from the afternoon search and destroy mission.

"Who the hell are you writing to this time?" he demanded as he shook himself free from my grip, staggered to his feet and locked his legs in place.

"Come on, Jim," I pleaded, "just sit down on the bunk, okay?"

"What for?" he yelled. "And fuck you and all those letters you write! too." He turned and took a step towards the door, but collapsed again onto the floor.

"Here, Jim, let me help you—please," I said as I grabbed him around the waist and finally managed to lift him off the ground and get him seated on the foot of the bed.

"No sweat," he mumbled as he rummaged around in a fatigue pocket and pulled out a plastic bag full of marijuana. "Old mama-san turned me on to some really great grass. Want some?"

"No," I said, "I'm trying to keep the words on the paper."

"Well, the hell with you then!" he shouted as he attempted to get to his feet again.

I reached over and tried to keep him on the bunk, all the time wondering what in the world had gotten into him. I had never even seen Sergeant Ketchum high before, much less totally out of control. He was the most professional soldier I had met in Vietnam and for him to be in the condition he was, something had to be terribly wrong.

"Jim," I said in the calmest tone I could produce, "you're in no shape to be going anywhere. Now just sit here and take it easy for awhile, okay?"

"You sure you don't want some of this grass?" he asked again.

"Not right now," I said, out of breath from wrestling with him.

"Fuck this goddamn war," he mumbled, taking another hit off his joint.

"What's got into you, Jim? What's the matter?"

"There's nothing the matter," he shot back. "Just mind your own business!" His lower lip slowly began to quiver and he started tugging at his fatigue collar.

"Can I help?" I asked softly, suddenly realizing that Sergeant Ketchum, of all people, was about to cry.

"No one can help, man," he said, his voice breaking. "No one in the whole world." He began to cry, and when he realized he wasn't going to be able to stop, he yanked a crumpled letter out from his pants pocket and shoved it into my stomach. "Go ahead," he blurted out, "read the fucking thing!" He covered his face with his hands and sobbed uncontrollably. "Go on I said, read it!"

"Who's it from?" I finally managed to say.

"That's the problem, Ty. I don't know who the damn thing is from."

Totally confused, I began to read the letter, and it only took me a few sentences to understand why Jim was so upset. "Is this someone's idea of a joke?" I asked.

"That's what I thought at first," he answered as he took a deep breath and made another attempt to stop crying. "But this is the fourth one."

"You don't recognize the handwriting or anything?"

"No."

"Have you told the major, or the first sergeant?"

"Are you kidding?"

"You gotta tell someone, Jim."

"I just told you, didn't I?"

"But maybe the major or the first sergeant could fix you up with a Mars call to your wife or something?"

He shook his head 'no'. "I don't want to talk to her. What the hell would I say? Is it true you're screwing some sicko who's writing me all about it?" He swallowed hard, angry with himself for not being able to control his emotions.

"When's the last time you heard from her?" I asked.

"Oh, I don't know. A few weeks before these damn things started coming I guess."

"Have you written to her about it?"

"Sure. A half-dozen times, but I haven't gotten anything back."

I looked down at the letter and quickly read it for a second time. "What's he mean when he says he can hardly wait for you to die so he can get all the money?"

"I'm insured up the butt in case anything happens to me over here," he explained. "And it's all in my wife's name and handled by some lawyer friend of her mother's. Counting the ten grand she'd get from the Army, I'm worth over a hundred thousand bucks dead."

"Can't you change that?"

He shook his head 'no'. "I've got no family, Ty, nobody. Just her. My dad and brother died in a car wreck when I was eleven. After my mother went nuts, my aunt raised me for awhile, but mostly I just raised myself. When Sandy and I got serious, she became my family. I've got no one else. I guess I could change the name on my Army insurance policy, but who would I leave it to, anyway?

"You have to call her, Jim."

He stared off into space, slowly shaking his head from side to side. "No, it's all true. He knows every damn thing about her, every inch of her body, and he couldn't know the things he's been putting in these damn letters if he wasn't sleeping with her, not in a hundred years." The tears once again began rolling freely down his mud-streaked cheeks. "I guess I should have known better," he continued. "It's not like I didn't know she had this kind of thing in her. I should have never let myself believe that she'd wait through another eighteen months of this shit. She's not very strong, you know. I guess it's just as much my fault as it is hers." The tears simply wouldn't stop. "But I love her so much. Damn it, she's the only person in this whole screwed-up world I've ever loved. She means everything to me, everything. Life just wouldn't be worth living without her. What am I going to do, Ty? What am I going to do?"

JOURNAL ENTRY

63 DAYS TO GO

When you put modern weapons and all kinds of complicated machinery into the hands of hastily trained young men, you are creating accidents which are just waiting to happen. Since I've been here, I've seen guys get hurt or killed doing the stupidest things, including a fight in an NCO Club which ended up with one of the two combatants racing back to his hootch for a gun, only to be run over by a speeding jeep on his way there; two medics who were also best friends forgetting to clear their weapons before they cleaned them, resulting in one shooting the other in the groin with his .45 caliber handgun, a weapon which makes a mess you wouldn't believe; a helicopter maintenance specialist blowing himself away because he forgot to push the right button before he loaded a gunship with live ammunition; and a new recruit who got so scared during his first firefight that he pulled the pin on a grenade and threw it right into a low hanging branch just above his head. Then he watched it fall to the earth only a few feet from his position without doing a thing to escape from the blast which quickly followed.

Sadly, about one out of every five guys who die over here do so from an accident—and last Sunday was as close as I ever want to come to being one of those statistics.

It was the perfect day to break in a rookie. No rain, no heat, and best of all, no Charlie. A recent B52 strike had flattened most of the terrain we were working and we had miles and miles of good visibility for a change. Except for all the massive bomb craters we had to keep skirting, the mission looked like it was going to be a rare walk in the park.

"Why in the hell do you think the major inserted us on the face of the fucking moon?" Harry asked me as we strolled along together, almost enjoying ourselves.

"You got me," I answered. "Maybe the BDA created some bodies he wants us to identify and count."

"Are you kidding?" said Harry. "Any poor gook who was hanging around during this strike ended up in pieces too little for anyone to identify, much less count. If you ask me, he probably just couldn't stand the idea of giving us the rest of the day off just because Ketchum and Hughes are sick as dogs."

"At least Duncan has lucked out," I said.

"You got that right," said Harry as we both glanced back at nineteen year old Private Benjamin Duncan, the newest member of our squad, who was walking ten yards or so behind us and still acting like he was scared to death. "Merry Christmas, Benji," Harry yelled out. "It just don't get any easier than this. Relax, man!"

Duncan had never been out in the field before and he was understandably nervous. He hadn't uttered a single word since the lieutenant had placed him safely in the middle of the formation, but Harry's words brought a forced half-smile to his innocent young face. He may have been nineteen, but he looked sixteen, and I was glad to see him lighten up just a bit.

"Now this is my kind of war," said Harry as he lifted his heavy steel pot from his head and wiped away some of the perspiration from his forehead. "Chuck's only decent cover is that tree line way the hell over there, and it ain't even an objective."

Just as I had finished nodding my head in agreement, the dry earth all around me suddenly exploded with the sickening sound of ricocheting gun-

fire. *Time seemed to freeze as I silently cursed myself for being stupid enough to think any mission was going to be a piece of cake—especially one in which Sergeant Ketchum wasn't in the field.*

As the bullets continued to dance within inches of my right leg, I dove to the ground and quickly rolled off to my left. When the gunfire finally stopped, I was curled up on my side in the fetal position, still trying to figure out what in the world had happened. The way the bullets had walked along my side made me think that maybe they had come from above or behind me. I quickly scanned the few trees left standing from the air strike for possible snipers.

Everyone else had hit the ground, too, and Harry was the first one to low-crawl over to me. "What the hell was that?" I asked him. "A sniper?"

"No way, man. There's no snipers out here. There's not enough cover for them. You okay?"

"Yeah, I'm fine. But look at this." I showed Harry my hands. "I'm still shaking."

"That was really close, man. Maybe as close as it gets."

"It had to come from behind us, Harry."

We looked at each other. Then, seemingly at the exact same moment, we both knew what had happened. "Duncan!" we both said in unison.

And sure enough, there was young Benji Duncan, sprawled out just behind us, staring pop-eyed at me, his face red as a tomato. "Duncan!" I screamed, "get your ass up here!"

Duncan quickly scrambled to his feet but couldn't seem to make himself walk towards me. Rather than waiting for him to work up the courage, I leaped up and stormed off after him. He started to turn and run, but I tackled him and was still trying to get a good grip on his neck when Harry grabbed me from behind and pulled me away from the frightened rookie.

"I'm sorry!" shouted Duncan, "I'm really, really sorry! It was an accident! Honest to God!"

I picked up his rifle and sure enough, the safety was off and a whole clip of ammunition had been expended. I threw the gun back at him. "Duncan, you damn near walked a whole clip right up my back!"

"I don't know what happened, honest," he said. "I was just going along, trying to remember all the things I'm supposed to do, and the next thing I knew, I tripped over something."

"You fucking tripped?" Harry yelled. "Over what?"

"I don't know, I just tripped, and then, well, the gun, it just went off."

"All by itself?" I asked.

"I guess so. No, I guess I had my finger on the trigger." He lowered his head in an effort to escape looking at me. "I'm really sorry, really!"

"You had the safety off, Duncan!" I said.

"If I did, it was an accident. Honest."

"There's no excuse for walking around out here without your safety on, Duncan! That's the first rule over here! Everyone in Vietnam knows that!"

"I know, I know. I'm sorry."

"And you're supposed to have your rifle pointed into the air or ground, not at my back!"

"I know all of that. I'm so sorry. I guess I just forgot."

"You can go ahead now," Harry said to me. "Go ahead and beat the shit out of him, before I do it for you."

"Duncan," I said, trying my best to lower my voice, "I'm finally getting short, do you understand that?"

"I know that, sir."

"I don't have anymore luck left, Duncan. That was it. There's no more. That was the very last of it. And if I gotta die over here, damn it, I don't want it to be because someone forgot to do something, or because someone tripped. Do you understand what I'm saying, Duncan? I don't want to die like a dog under the wheel of a car over here."

"It'll never happen again," swore Duncan. "I swear to God, it'll never happen again!"

CHAPTER 24

▼

THE MINE FIELD

Our area of operation took in much of War Zone C and stretched from a few miles north of Saigon all the way up to Tay Ninh, which wasn't all that far from the Cambodian border, and then back across the muddy Saigon River to Chon Thanh, which was east of Highway 13.

Highway 13, which was mostly just a poorly paved two-lane road, was a familiar landmark to everyone in the troop. Whenever we heard the siren go off, followed by someone in operations yelling over the loudspeaker, "Scramble north!" we knew we would most likely be following old Highway 13 up through Ben Cat, Lai Khe, and maybe even as far north as An Loc and Loc Ninh.

The two most dangerous destinations for any mission in our troop's area of operation were known to all of us as the Michelin rubber plantation, which was just east of Dau Tieng, and the Iron Triangle, which was indeed a triangular stretch of jungle and rice paddies bordered by the villages of Ben Cat on the east, Ben Suc on the west and Phu Cuong to the south.

Both of those continually contested battlegrounds afforded the Vietcong and migrating units of North Vietnamese Army regulars with plenty of good cover to establish their base camps, which were often built atop elaborate networks of underground bunkers and tunnels.

Sympathetic local supporters seemed to outnumber the good guys by about ten-to-one and no one in the rifle platoon looked forward to spending anymore time than necessary on the ground in either of those two places. But with the heart of the Iron Triangle being only about twenty-five miles north of Saigon and the Michelin just another fifteen miles northeast of that, they were the perfect staging areas for enemy activity against the capital city of the South Vietnamese government, and whether anyone liked it or not, both areas had to be constantly patrolled.

When we weren't out humping around in the Michelin or the Iron Triangle, we would often find ourselves a few klicks outside the village of Lai Khe, which was known as 'Rocket City' because of all the enemy mortars and big 122mm rockets which rained down on it almost nightly.

Lai Khe was located right on Highway 13, near a famous stretch of road nicknamed 'Thunder Alley', where American vehicles of all shapes and sizes could pretty much count on being ambushed if they motored along it. Lai Khe was also where much of the division's support personnel were stationed and the major was always dumping us off and marching us all the way around the place in hopes of locating the very mobile Vietcong units who were responsible for the constant shellings.

Although we never really ran into any great number of the enemy while patrolling the outskirts of Lai Khe, we soon learned that something much worse was lurking out there—mine fields.

As I stood next to Sergeant Ketchum in a thick patch of waist high, sunburnt elephant grass listening on my radio to Major McCalley and one of the Cobra pilots scream epithets back and forth—they were blaming each other for the downed helicopter which was still burning and sending up a cloud of black smoke some two hundred yards to the front of the platoon's position—I couldn't help but notice that Jim's mind was somewhere else.

"What are you thinking about, Jim?" I finally asked him.

With his face full of concern and his eyes glued to the ground, he ignored my question and very carefully squatted down into a catcher's stance and began playing in the dirt. "What are you doing now?" I asked him.

"Shit!" he said, frightening me with the deadly serious way he spit out the word.

"What's the matter?"

"Don't move, Ty. Don't even take a single step. We're in a mine field."

"Mines?" Just saying the word took my breath away.

"Look at this," he said, gently exposing the prongs of an anti-personnel mine with his fingers.

"Not again!" I exclaimed.

"Quick, give me the blower," he ordered as he very carefully rose to a standing position. "And get Pinkerton back here! But don't tell him he's in a mine field—he'll panic."

I passed Jim the radio handset and as he tried to raise the major, I hollered, "Pinkerton! Get back here Pinkerton!"

Up ahead, Private Will Pinkerton, the squad's newest member and its pointman, stopped dead in his tracks and looked back over his shoulder at me. I could see by the worried expression on his young face that he thought he had done something wrong.

I waved for him to pull back, but before I could tell him that I wanted him to very carefully retrace his steps, he began jogging towards me. "Walk, Pinkerton, walk!" I yelled. "And come back the same exact way you got there!"

Frightened and puzzled, Pinkerton adjusted his pace and then came to a complete halt. "What's the problem?" he yelled back.

"There's no problem," I tried to assure him, "we just want you back here, and if you can, retrace your steps!"

"I don't understand!"

I decided to go about it a different way. "That's okay, Pinkerton! Just stay right where you are for now, okay? Don't move from that spot!"

"Alright."

"Why in the hell do that?" came thundering out of Sergeant Ketchum's mouth as the heated conversation he was having on the radio with the major continued to escalate. "Listen, One," Jim said forcefully, "it's just not worth it. Roger that, I know that, but I'm telling you, we're in the middle of a mine field down here. Don't you remember the last time we were in one of these damn things? We lost two good people!"

Jim listened impatiently to a lengthy reply from the major and then without even signing off, he fired the handset back at me.

"Now what's up?" I asked with concern.

"The son-of-a-bitch ought to be taken out and shot! He's going to get us all killed the way he goes about things. All he cares about is his precious damn helicopters."

"What about the two pilots?"

"They're burnt to a crisp. Hell, that's already been confirmed from the air. No one's moving, nothing. We can't do anything for them. Securing a downed chopper when the pilots are already dead is never worth it. Never! Charlie knows we're on our way and you can bet your ass he's waiting. Plus now we've got to go through a fucking mine field to get there!"

While I was talking to Jim, I had taken my eye off Private Pinkerton.

"What's going on?" suddenly asked the private with an excited voice, standing right next to me.

"Pinkerton, I thought I told you not to move!"

"I got kinda scared standing around up there all alone. Is everything okay, Ty?"

"What the fuck are we going to have up here, a goddamn convention?" Jim asked me as he saw Harry leave his nearby hiding place and begin strolling up to our position. Following right on Harry's heels were the platoon's new ground combat officer, Lieutenant Miller, and his RTO.

"Where's this mine field you're so worried about?" the lieutenant yelled over Harry's shoulder at Jim.

"Mine field?" fearfully blurted out Harry, coming to an immediate stop.

With all of us standing dangerously around in one big cluster-fuck, Jim pointed his rifle down at the anti-personnel mine he was straddling.

"One little mine?" asked the impatient young lieutenant. "For Christ's sake, sergeant, mark the damn thing, or blow it in place, and then have your pointman clear us a path to the objective."

"Sir," said Jim, "with all due respect, my pointman is even newer than you are and he doesn't know jack-shit about how to safely get us to that downed chopper. I'm not going to send him out to wander around in a mine field."

"Sergeant," said the lieutenant, his face flushed with anger, "the major's got aircraft on station waiting to extract that gunship and its crew. You know they can't land until we've secured the area. Now let's get on with our job."

"But we're in a fucking mine field, sir. We ought to just back out the same way we came in. Maybe we can try it from the south instead?"

"But that would take hours."

"At least the platoon would get there in one piece."

"Sergeant," said the lieutenant firmly, "I want you to clear us a path to the objective and radio me when it's safe to bring up the rest of the platoon. Now is that perfectly clear?"

Jim glanced over at me and slowly shook his head from side to side. "Yes, sir," he finally mumbled with resignation.

"Good," said the lieutenant. "I'll have my RTO inform the major."

With that the lieutenant turned and strutted back to his squad, obviously very pleased with the outcome of the conversation.

"Fuck it," said Jim as he reached into one of his ammo pouches, pulled out his compass and passed it to me. "Ty, try to keep me on a straight line, okay? I'll look back now and then for hand signals. And Harry, since you seem so damn interested in all this, mark the fucking mine."

As Harry reluctantly knelt down to deal with the mine, I said, "Pinkerton can do it, Jim. He was doing a good job when we called him back."

"I'll go back up front, Sarge," volunteered Pinkerton bravely.

"I appreciate the offer, Pinkerton," said Jim, patting him on the shoulder, "I really do. But I think I better handle this one."

"Jim," I said, knowing how he often threw all caution to the wind when he was angry, "be real careful, okay? There's no hurry."

"I will," he promised without much conviction. Then he looked into my eyes with such warmth and feeling that for the first time, I fully understood just how much we had come to mean to each other.

"Jim," I said, "why don't I tag along, just in case you need the radio?"

"No thanks my friend," he said. "This is a one-man job." He pointed off into the distance and added, "We'll use that big tree over there for our landmark, okay?"

"I want to go, Jim, really."

"I know you do, but one fool in this squad is plenty. I really don't want you out there. Just keep me on line, okay?"

I nodded that I would. "And be careful!" I yelled after him as he began moving forward, using cautious half-steps.

As Jim walked away from me, I just knew. I don't know how I knew, but I did. I had been in Vietnam long enough to have 'that feeling', that sense that something terrible was just about to happen. I wanted to race after him and have one more conversation with him, one more moment together. I wanted to tell him how much I admired and respected him, and how much his friendship meant to me. I wanted to say all the things that men who love each other always leave unsaid.

I had almost convinced myself I was being melodramatic and imagining things when Jim glanced back at me to make sure he was still on line, but instead of adjusting his course, he just stood there, looking at me.

"What's wrong, Jim?" I yelled.

"I almost stepped on another one," he finally hollered back with a smile, the fear of dying suddenly absent in him.

"Come on back!" I yelled as loud as I could.

When he waved off my concern, Harry said, "Tell him to come back again, Ty. This is fucking crazy."

"Jim!" I screamed, "No kidding! Get back here!"

He shook his head 'no' and stood his ground, looking back at me for what seemed like the longest time. Then he smiled one last time, turned his back to me and started briskly stepping off towards the objective, almost as if he could have cared less about stepping on a mine.

"Slow down, Jim!" I yelled as loud as I could. "Slow down!"

As I began to lose sight of him in the tall grass, I looked all around my position for some higher ground to jump up on, but there was none. "Can you guys still see him?" I anxiously asked Harry and Pinkerton.

Before they could answer, a loud explosion suddenly went off to our front and all three of us watched in horror as Jim's body was tossed high into the air.

"No!" I screamed, shedding my heavy radio and shoving it into Harry's arms. "No, no, no!"

"Stay here, Ty," said Harry as he grabbed me by the arm. "Damn it, he'd want you to stay here!"

"Radio the lieutenant," I ordered, "and tell him we need a dustoff ASAP! Do it now, Harry!"

With that, I threw off Harry's grip, took one last look at the tree Jim and I had agreed on as a landmark and moved as fast and straight as I could up to where the gray smoke from the explosion was still crawling up towards the high sky.

When I finally reached Jim, I wanted to close my eyes and never open them again. The gruesome sight was as bad as anything I had seen in Vietnam. Blood and guts were everywhere. I dropped to my knees and as carefully as I could, rolled what was left of Jim onto his back. Most of his bleeding chest and abdomen were covered with gaping holes and I gently removed as much dirt as I could from his intestines and pushed them back into his open stomach cavity. I thought about trying to bandage some of his wounds, but I didn't even know where to start, and I wanted to get him back to the medics as soon as possible.

All of his limbs were still attached to his body, but one of his legs was so badly mangled I was sure he would lose it to a surgeon's knife. "Jim," I said, making a conscious attempt to stop looking so scared, "it's pretty bad. I've got to try and get you some help."

Jim was too seriously wounded to talk, but his eyes were clear and he hadn't gone into shock yet. He even managed a faint half-smile as he slowly closed his eyes and then forced them open again. "This is probably really going to hurt, Jim, but I've got to lift you up and carry you back to the medics. Do you understand?"

He nodded weakly and didn't make a peep as I shoveled my arms underneath his back and legs and staggered to my feet. Once my legs were locked in place, Jim seemed to weigh almost nothing at all. With his bloody body tightly cradled against my own, I quickly set off to find help.

On the way, I kept up a steady stream of chatter, telling Jim he was going to be all right and that nobody in the squad would get home in one piece without him. I asked him over and over how he was doing, but he never answered. I stopped twice to catch my breath and readjust his weight, and the second time I noticed he had closed his eyes and that his breathing was becoming more labored.

When bright red blood began to bubble out of his mouth, he suddenly squeezed one of my arms hard with his hand. I whispered to him that I loved him and that I wasn't going to let anyone I loved die. "Hang on, Jim," I pleaded. "Please, please, hang on. We're almost there now." He squeezed my arm one last time and softly mumbled something I could not understand into my ear.

When I finally got out of the mine field and reached Harry and Pinkerton, they both helped me gently lower their squad leader to the ground. "Is the dustoff on its way?" I demanded of Harry, who was bent over Jim, trying to get a pulse.

"Where's the fucking dust-off?" I screamed at Harry.

"It's on the way," said Harry, "but Ty—he's dead."

"No he's not! No he's not!"

"Ty, listen to me," said Harry softly. "Sergeant Ketchum is dead."

Drenched in Jim's blood, I put my friend's limp, lifeless head into my lap and yelled as loud as I could, "Medic! Medic!"

CHAPTER 25

▼

THE LIFE FORCE

For weeks after Jim's death, I would wait impatiently for the last light of day and then begin to wander aimlessly around the compound. For the first time since my arrival in Vietnam, my thoughts were only of death, never of life and going home. I stopped writing letters to my parents and sister. I quit making entries in my journal. I had to be reminded to shave, and to take a shower. A sickness had overcome the very essence of me. Fever and dysentery were a part of it, and I began to lose weight. I didn't care. Life had been rendered meaningless. I wanted to suffer. I didn't want my sleep to be easy.

The sadness which had seized me sapped every ounce of my energy and made me feel cold and empty inside. Nothing really mattered anymore. It seemed to me and to all those around me that I no longer had the strength or desire to struggle with any of life's problems, much less its unanswerable dilemmas.

"You've got to knock it off," demanded Harry as he perched himself on the edge of my bunk and looked down at me. I was soaking wet, having spent the past hour standing all by myself outside our hootch in a pounding rain. "This is really crazy, man."

"Just leave me alone, Harry," I said, rubbing my eyes dry.

"At least take off all those wet clothes."

"I will."

"You know, it's too bad you can't see yourself, man. It really is."

"Why?"

"Because you look like shit!" I rolled over onto my side and turned my back to Harry. "The minute we get back from a mission," he continued, "the first thing you do is plop yourself down on this damn cot. And when you're not in here feeling sorry for yourself, you're out wandering around all over the place like a fucking ghost."

"I'm not feeling sorry for myself, Harry," I tried to explain.

"The hell you're not! You don't eat, you don't go to the movie anymore, and you haven't said a single word to me in a week."

"There's just nothing to say."

"Bullshit!"

I reached back over my shoulder and turned the lamp on my nightstand off by jiggling the light bulb socket. "Please, Harry, it's late. Just leave me alone."

"No!" snapped Harry, his eyes twitching with rage. "I've had it, and I ain't leaving here until I've said what I came to say, and if that means sitting around in the fucking dark for the next goddamn hour, so be it!"

"Suit yourself, Harry," I mumbled.

As Harry continued his harangue, I effortlessly tuned him out and found myself thinking once again about the sealed letter I had found in Jim's footlocker the night I had helped the lieutenant go through all of his personal possessions. A note in Jim's almost illegible handwriting had been scribbled on the outside of the envelope which read; "Ty, whatever it takes, please make sure this gets to my wife Sandy if something should happen to me. I know I can count on you. Thanks for everything. I wouldn't have missed knowing you for anything. You were a great friend! Jim."

At first, I desperately wanted to open the letter, sure that it contained clues as to why Jim had behaved so recklessly in the mine field on the last day of his life. It just wasn't like him to take unnecessary chances during a mission and I was convinced it had something to do with the letters Jim had continued to receive from his wife's boyfriend. I knew for a fact that Jim carried one of them around with him in a leg pocket of his jungle fatigues, and I had seen him take it out and read it from time to time, only to wad it up and angrily shove it back into its hiding place.

The more I thought about the day and the way my friend had died—and I thought about hardly anything else—the more I started to believe that Jim had decided to take his own life. At the very least, I was convinced he had stopped caring, and that he had become totally indifferent to death.

I had even considered mentioning my suspicions to the lieutenant, or to Harry, but I knew that would be the very last thing Jim would have wanted. He was an extremely private person, and to have people he didn't really know or trust digging around in the bowels of his personal life would have been unthinkable to him.

I also couldn't stop recalling Jim's final night on earth and the last real conversation we had. We were sitting together in the mess hall trying to wash down our evening chow with lukewarm day-old coffee and I had been going on and on about how old I felt, and how much I wished I could go back to being young and innocent again. "Growing up in Texas was the loneliest time of my life," Jim had suddenly said with the saddest eyes. "Most kids look forward to getting out of school for the summer, or going camping or fishing, or taking trips with their parents. Hell, I didn't even look forward to Christmas. All I ever remember hoping for was that when my old man came home from the bars, he'd be too drunk to be able to land a solid punch when he started hitting me."

"It was that bad, huh?" I had asked him.

"It was so bad, Ty, that when they told me the son-of-a-bitch had died in a car wreck, I dropped down on my knees and thanked God. I was actually happy my own father was dead. Now is that sick or what?

And it wasn't until I started dating Sandy that everything finally began to change."

"How so?" I asked him, noticing that the anger in Jim's voice started to disappear the moment he mentioned his wife's name.

Jim ignored my question and continued talking about Sandy. "You know, when she was really young—twelve and thirteen—she always used to keep her school books pressed up against her chest. Every time I saw her, even when we weren't at school, she had at least one book pressed up against her chest."

I thought that was a rather strange thing to remember and I asked Jim, "So why did she do that?"

"Well," he explained with the last full smile I ever saw on his face, "Sandy got her breasts before all of her other friends did and she was really embarrassed about it."

"How come? I thought girls couldn't wait to get breasts."

"Who knows? Girls can be weird about the damndest things, Ty. But when Sandy got her breasts, it was like bang, they were just there! I mean, one minute she was as flat as a board, and the next thing I knew, she was huge. It was really something how the whole thing just happened overnight, and I guess her girlfriends and everybody really kidded her about it. Anyway, for the next couple of years, I swear, that poor girl didn't go anywhere without at least one book to hide behind. Everybody thought she was this super dedicated student or something. It was the cutest damn thing—it really was."

As I was trying to discern if there might be any meaning in the way Jim had chosen to fondly remember his wife as an innocent young girl who used to hide her breasts behind school books, Harry suddenly grabbed me by the arm and shook me as violently as he could. "Damn it!" he screamed at me, "you haven't heard a single word I've said, have you?"

"Just what do you think you're doing?" I demanded, throwing Harry's hand off me.

"Ketchum is dead, Ty! And if you don't get over it and stop walking around out in the field like a fucking zombie, I'm telling you, you're going to be next!"

"It's my life, Harry, now just please get out of here and leave me alone."

"I told you, I'm not going until you listen to what I have to say."

"But you've been talking non-stop for the past hour, Harry. Let me sleep."

"And you haven't heard any of it, have you?"

"Okay, okay, I'm listening now. How's that?"

"Are you sure?"

"I'm sure. Just hurry up, okay?"

"Good," said Harry, locking his eyes on mine, "because I think I just may have the answer."

"Answer to what?"

"To how we go about getting you to join the living again."

"I'm among the living, Harry," I said, softening my voice and aware that he was only trying to help. "It's just that I'm not sure that I want to be, if that makes any sense."

"No you're not, Ty. You've been in that fucking body bag with Ketchum since the day he bought the farm."

"Maybe so, Harry, maybe so, but I'm just going to have to work my way through it the best I can, and you or nobody else is going to say or do anything to change that."

"I think you're wrong there, Ty, and I also think I know something that will help you."

"What are you going to do, Harry? Bring Jim back? Now if you could do that, then maybe…."

"No, Ty," interrupted Harry, "Ketchum is gone, and right or wrong, that's the way it is. All I want you to do is write a letter. One simple little letter. No big deal. Now is that too much to ask?"

"Write a letter?"

"That's right."

"To who?"

"To what's her face—Glynis?"

"Glynis?"

"That's right, Glynis."

"What's Glynis got to do with anything, Harry?"

"She's got the life force, man."

"What in the world are you talking about now?"

"Look, Ty, people come and go, but the life force always goes on. It's what makes us get out of bed in the morning and face up to another day. It's what makes us care about how we look and what we say. It's what makes us want to get out of this fucking rat-hole called Vietnam in one piece."

"The life force?"

"It's actually just another way of saying sex, man."

"Sex?"

"That's right, sex!"

"Harry, take my word for it, sex is the last thing that's been on my mind lately."

"Exactly! And that's the problem, man. You gotta get yourself reacquainted with the life force."

"And writing a letter to Glynis is going to do that?"

"Well, maybe not overnight, but it'll start you thinking about her, and I'm telling you, once you let yourself start doing that, the life force will begin to creep back into your head."

"But Glynis doesn't want to hear from me, Harry. You know that."

"Who knows, maybe she's changed her mind by now?"

"But she told me never to write to her again, and that if I did, she wouldn't even open the letter."

"I know she said that, but girls have this wonderful way of changing their minds, Ty."

"Not Glynis, Harry. She's been really hurt by this war, and now I understand just what she was talking about. The last thing I want to do is write and tell her that Vietnam is turning me into a basket case, too."

"Look, Ty, to tell you the truth, I don't really give a rat's ass if Glynis ever reads the damn thing or not. All I want you to do is just write the letter. Don't you remember how happy you were when you were with Glynis?"

"Sure."

"It was Glynis did this, and Glynis said that, remember?"

"I remember."

"It was absolutely nauseating, but life was never better, right?"

"I guess so."

"Then why not spend some time thinking about that, about the time you spent with her, you know, instead of all the crap you've been thinking about lately?"

"Look, Harry," I said as kindly as I could, "I appreciate what you're saying, I really do, but I just don't see how writing a letter to a girl who never wants to see or hear from me again is going to make me feel a whole lot better."

"It can't hurt, man. And like I said, who cares if she ever reads the damn thing or not. The important thing is just to get off your butt and write it—to give the life force a chance to do its thing. Hell, when you're done, you can tear it up and throw it away for all I care. But something tells me if you spend just a few hours thinking about the living instead of the dead, everything else will start to fall back into place."

"The life force, huh? You're full of crap, you know that, don't you, Harry?"

"All I know is that people come and go, Ty, but the life force goes on and on. If you and I disappear this very moment, no big fucking deal. But if you take sex out of the world, I'm telling you, no one in their right mind will even want to get up in the morning. Now, will you at least think about it?"

"Okay, I'll think about it."

"Good," said Harry as he stood up to leave, "and if you want to throw a P.S. in there to Glynis, tell her I want to fuck her, too."

"Get out of here, Harry."

"And if the letter doesn't work," added Harry as he began to step out of the room, "we'll give Plan B a try."

"What's Plan B?"

"Beating the fucking shit out of you!"

With Harry's departure finally secured, I forced myself to sit up in my bunk and unbutton my still soggy fatigue top. After a mighty struggle, I finally managed to pull the determined article of clothing away from my damp body and pitch it onto the floor. I fell back into my bed, closed my eyes and intertwined my fingers behind my head.

Within moments, with the rain still pouring out of the sky and a howling wind roaring in my ears, the pilgrimage began again, this time quickly taking me back to the tiny clearing in the mine field where I had found Jim's mangled and motionless body. The memories always came with a rush, and there I was again, standing over him as blood ran out of his mouth and trickled down his neck. The pain must have been unbearable, I thought to myself, but Jim's eyes remained calm, and he seemed to be struggling to say something. What was it, I wondered? And what were those final few breathless words he was trying to utter when I was carrying him out of the mine field? Were they about our friendship, or maybe something to tell his wife? Would they have been heroic and memorable words, or were they something better left unsaid?

I suddenly sat back up in my bunk and sucked in as much of the room's damp air as one breath would allow. "Harry's right," I said to myself, violently shaking my head as I tried to scramble up all the sights and sounds which were trapped inside my brain. "You've got to do something! You really can't keep going on like this. You're going to lose your mind."

I couldn't think of anything worse than filling the room with the bright light from my lamp, so I reached down under my bed for the extra flashlight I always kept there. I flipped it on, and after mindlessly painting a series of ever widening circles with it on one of the walls, I began searching for a pen and a journal with some blank paper in it. With only a tiny field of light to guide my way, I began to write:

Dear Glynis,

I've tried very hard to do as you asked, and I think the fact that I haven't written to you in more than three months is proof of that. But as much as I respect your right to completely remove me from your life, and even though I now know just how difficult it is to lose someone you really love to this war, I have decided that I am going to start writing to you whether you like it or not. You don't have to read the letters, or answer them—in fact, they might not even reach you—but I'm going to write them none the less.

The simple truth is that although I have cared about other girls—even loved one I think—only you have thrilled me. From the first moment I saw you, the feelings were completely different. When I looked at you, or heard your voice, or touched you, emotions I didn't even know existed absolutely exploded inside me. And since I'm pretty sure that happens to a person only once in their lifetime, this letter, which is going to be the first of many, is to inform you that I have decided not to let you walk away from me without putting up a fight.

When I received your letter asking me not to write again, I was hurt beyond my ability to describe it, and totally determined to do just as you wished. But the world has suddenly become a much smaller place, and one of the few things I have left to hold onto is the fact that you're still in it. So, I apologize in advance, but every chance I have from now until the day I go home, I'm going to write you a letter. They won't say much—no bloody war stories or anything like that. But they will attempt to remind you that I still love you very much, and that all I really want out of this life right now is to be able to crawl into your arms one more time.

"Well, I'll be damned," I whispered to myself as my flashlight battery went dead and I realized that my mind's eye was suddenly picturing Glynis Covington, standing alone and without clothes, in that glorious Australian field of yellow and white wild flowers, instead of

Jim Ketchum, lying motionlessly on his back, covered in his own bright-red blood.

JOURNAL ENTRY

35 DAYS TO GO

It's almost dawn and I've hardly slept at all. I'm afraid I've developed a preference for the night—for darkness. I also think I may have killed someone yesterday.

We hadn't been on the ground for more than thirty minutes when we walked right into the heart of an L-shaped ambush. They are by far the worst kind of ambushes, because with bullets flying at you from two different directions, it's almost impossible to quickly figure out the best way to react. You just have to scramble to find the best cover you can because there's little hope of breaking contact easily. And even if you are lucky enough to find something substantial to hide behind, there's usually only one option left—you have to stay put and fight back.

You also can't count on any help from the gunships or artillery because at least one leg of the L is going to put the enemy really close to you. Charlie is fully aware of all this and he knows his chances of winning the firefight greatly depend on how long he can keep us disorganized and pinned down. The greater the chaos, the better it is for him, and I've never seen the platoon in general, and our squad in particular, more confused than it was yesterday. I'm sure a big part of it was because Jim is no longer here to run things, but it took us more than six torturous hours to break contact and we were actually very fortunate it didn't take even longer.

Luckily for me, when the ambush first began, it was almost like the hand of God had grabbed me by the shoulder and flung me behind the best cover a soldier could possibly hope to have in such a situation—a massive old boulder which had probably been sitting in the same exact place since time began. And not only was it at least three-feet high and too thick for even a stray M-50 machine gun slug to penetrate, it also had a strategically placed outcropping that completely protected me from the crossfire we were absorbing.

I could hardly believe my good luck when I realized just how strong and secure my position was, and as I took my rifle off the safety, I was starting to feel pretty good about my chances for living through yet another day in Vietnam.

I've been here for almost eleven months now and been in my share of firefights, and each one has been radically different from the one which preceded or followed it. The terrain is rarely the same, the number of Vietcong opposing us always varies, the tenacity with which they fight changes from day to day, and the final outcome of the struggle rarely produces a clear winner or loser. But until yesterday, one thing has always remained pretty constant—I have rarely been able to clearly see the people who are trying so hard to kill me—at least not while they were alive.

The Vietcong are masters at hiding. Many of them fight by day and then return to their villages at night. Those who don't seem to be perfectly happy to live out in the bug-infested jungle where they create surprisingly comfortable base camps complete with fortified bunkers and elaborate underground tunnels. Not only are the VC difficult to find and incredibly resourceful, they are also capable of popping up just about anywhere and disappearing back into the jungle just as fast. When they ambush us, they always seem to be in easy to defend positions with the sun at their backs, and I don't know how many times I've stupidly stuck my head up in the middle of a firefight and tried unsuccessfully with squinting eyes to figure out just where all the shooting was coming from.

When I first got here, Jim explained to me the best way to deal with the Vietcong's maddening tactics and I have always followed his advice. He told me that the key to everything was making noise—lots and lots of noise. When I asked him what he meant by that, he showed me his M-16, and the way he had modified the barrel to make it sound as loud as possible when he was firing it. "You won't be seeing much of Charlie," he further explained, "but you'll have a pretty good idea of where he is, so even if you're pinned down and don't want to expose yourself anymore than necessary, just stick you rifle up over your head, point it at where you think the enemy is, and make as much noise as you can. As long as you're shooting at him, he's going to have his head down, and if his head is down, he's not going to be shooting back at you."

Jim also told me that if I ever saw a Vietcong in the open, to fire at his feet first, not his body. "Walk it right into him," he said. "You might end up missing, but you'll sure as hell scare the shit out of him if the dirt all around his feet starts dancing. Believe me, he'll get his butt out of there as fast as he can."

So, for almost a whole year now, I have done exactly as Jim told me. I have shot and thrown grenades at numerous enemy positions, and I wouldn't be too surprised if somewhere along the line I may have even hit someone, but I have never known for a fact one way or the other. And I have been perfectly happy to fight the war that way—completely ignorant as to whether or not I have done another human being any harm.

Unfortunately, that all changed yesterday. I was safely snuggled up behind my boulder when I happened to glance off to my left past the outcrop which was protecting my flank. Much to my surprise, two armed Vietcong were bent over at the waist in some scattered elephant grass and they were very cautiously making their way down to the foot of the 'L' where it connected at a 90 degree angle.

I only had to pivot a few feet to get them both within the sights of my rifle. But then an inner debate which seemed to last forever began. Should I shoot at their feet or their bodies? I was almost certain I could hit at least one of them, and as much as I wanted to scare them both away, I also wanted to make sure they didn't join up with the bulk of the force which had us pinned down.

Thankfully, the decision was more or less made for me. The second of the two Vietcong suddenly spotted me and swung his AK-47 around in my direction. In the frightening split second which followed, our eyes made contact and his began to blink rapidly. Before I had even finished instructing my trigger finger what to do, a burst of a dozen or so rounds from my rifle were on their way.

They didn't hit the ground around the VC's feet—they hit him—at least one of them did—I'm not exactly sure where—but his AK abruptly fell out of one hand and he grabbed his abdomen with the other. He made no noise that I could hear as he fell towards the ground and his companion made no effort to go to his aid. Instead, he sprinted away without even bothering to look back.

For the rest of the day, until reinforcements finally reached us and we were able to break contact, I kept looking over into the high grass where the VC had fallen, listening hard for sounds of life and trying to spot movement of any kind. Neither happened, and as the hours crawled by, a surprising anger began to build up inside me. I was mad at the Vietcong for putting me in a position where I had to shoot one of them; I was mad at myself for so effortlessly pulling the trigger; I was mad at being so stupid and naive when I decided to volunteer for the draft; I was mad at Jim for stepping on that mine and leaving me behind to make all my own decisions; and the list went on and on.

After the firefight had exhausted itself, the lieutenant gathered us all up and asked if we knew where any dead or wounded VC might be. I said nothing. If I had killed another human being, I didn't want him counted—I didn't want to see him—I didn't want it to be official.

Jimbo said the trick is not to hate when hate is all around you, and I think I've done that. I don't hate the Vietnamese—I really don't. But now I've killed one of them—at least I'm pretty sure I did—and that somehow changes everything. Harry says to think of it as just getting even for Jim. But this isn't about Jim, or even about the VC with the blinking eyes.

They're not the ones who are going to have to tote this memory around for eternity.

How very stupid I've been—thinking I could somehow wallow around in all this filth without even getting my hands dirty.

CHAPTER 26

▼

SQUAD LEADER

Unlike most of the men in the troop, I didn't really mind pulling perimeter guard duty once a week. The damp, heavily sandbagged bunkers weren't much for comfort, but on those all-too-frequent nights when enemy mortars and rockets began to rain down on the compound, there wasn't a safer place to be.

I had never quite been able to figure it out, but just a few minutes of incoming, as it was called, frightened me much more than spending a whole day out in the field performing the life and death duties of an infantryman. Maybe it had something to do with the fact that when I was in the field, I had at least some say over my own fate. But when it came to mortars and rockets, there was no outwitting or outmaneuvering them. Where they finally landed was just a matter of luck, a roll of the dice, and there was absolutely nothing more unnerving to me than being forced to hunker down during a rocket attack and wait for what seemed like forever to see if one or more of them had my name on it.

The time I most liked when I was pulling guard duty was the hour or so just before dawn. If I had managed to stay awake the whole night—and most of the time I did—I would reward myself by allowing my tired mind to go 'walkabout', as Glynis' Australian Aborigines called it. I knew the Vietcong were unlikely to attack with daylight only minutes away—they didn't want anything to do with gunships catching them out in the open—so I would relax my vigilance and let my thoughts wander.

I especially liked to reflect on the long history of warfare, because it never failed to remind me of just how good I had it. For instance, I found it almost incomprehensible how infantrymen on both sides of the Civil War used to line up in straight little rows and then calmly march off to their deaths. I thought about how heart-pounding scary it must have been to be up front in Pickett's charge at Gettysburg, and what courage it must have taken for cavalry officers to whip out their swords and lead their men right into the center of fortified enemy positions. I also wondered how the soldiers of the American Indian wars managed to get through all that bloody hand-to-hand combat; how the men of my grandfather's era somehow kept from going crazy in their rat-infested trenches; and how terrifying all that enemy firepower must have been to my father and all the other infantrymen of World War Two.

On what proved to be my last morning of perimeter guard duty, and with the pale early light beginning to filter its way into my bunker, a nervous voice suddenly cried out, "I'm coming in, Nichols! Don't be getting trigger happy!"

The voice belonged to one of the troop's new clerks, who I didn't know by name, and it was obvious that he didn't want to spend a single moment more than he had to out at the perimeter. "Top wants you to report to him as soon as you're done here," he informed me, his words rushed.

"You sure he wants me?" I asked, my knees creaking as I stood up for the first time in hours.

"You're Nichols, right?"

"That's right."

"Well, then you're the one he wants. He said he needs to talk to you ASAP."

"What about?"

"Now how would I know that?" he asked, quickly turning to go. "Just report to Headquarters as soon as you can, okay? He's waiting for you."

The thought which immediately popped into my head was that maybe the first sergeant had somehow found out about the letter I had sent to Robbie Cline's parents. But that had been months ago, I reminded myself. And Randy Ohida, the only other person besides Harry who knew about it, had already rotated. No, it couldn't be that. But what was it then? What could Top possibly want with me?

First Sergeant Adams was fretfully pondering a document of some kind when I quietly stepped up to his desk. He was also vigorously chewing away on a piece of gum, which surprised me because I knew it would be a crime punishable by death if the gum was in my mouth. He hated gum-chewers, and he had once told us that if he should ever find chewing gum on the bottom of one of his boots, the whole platoon would lose their PX privileges for a month. "You wanted to see me, Top?"

The first sergeant spit his gum into a wrapper, but said nothing. He got a peculiar satisfaction from making others wait and I knew it, so I spread my legs a little further apart for comfort and folded my hands neatly in the small of my back. "Take a seat, Nichols," he finally barked. "I've got a couple of things I need to go over with you—three or four things actually."

Now I was really confused. Three or four things? Maybe the major needs some more help catching up on his correspondence, I thought to myself as I sat down opposite the first sergeant and waited some more. Or maybe someone's sick back at home? But three or four things? What could they possibly be? I cleared my throat and said, "Is there something the matter, Top?"

"No, no, Nichols," said the first sergeant, breathing heavily as usual because of all the added weight he carried on his massive frame, "there's nothing the matter. In fact, I've got some good news for you."

"Really?" I said, relieved.

"That's right," he answered, tapping a pen slowly against his thick lower lip. "You're an E-4, right, Nichols?"

"Yes."

"Well, this is your lucky day, because the major wants to change that."

"What?" I asked, surprised.

"How would you like to be a sergeant, Nichols?"

"You mean get promoted?"

"Going from E-4 to E-5 is definitely a promotion, Nichols. In fact, I'd say it's a huge promotion!"

"That would be great, Top," I said with excitement, already trying to calculate how much more money I would be making.

"And I'm not talking Specialist E-5, either, Nichols. The major wants you to be a hard-stripe E-5, and give you all the duties and responsibilities which go along with that grade and rank."

"Really?" I said, slightly confused.

"That's right. Not only is the major making you a sergeant, but he also wants you to take over full operational command of Alpha Squad effective immediately. Congratulations."

"Be a squad leader?" I asked, shocked.

The first sergeant nodded his head and said, "You don't have to go before a review board or anything. The major has apparently wanted to do this for some time. He likes you, Nichols. He's taken care of everything. You're a lucky young man. Now, the next thing I want to...."

"But Top," I suddenly remembered, "our squad already has a squad leader."

"No it doesn't, Nichols," he said with emphasis, obviously not pleased that he had been interrupted. "Alpha Squad only has an acting squad leader, and there's a big difference between the two."

"Harry Watts is our squad leader, Top."

"No, he's not, Nichols! He's just an acting E-5. And the only reason he was given that position in the first place was because he happened to have more time and rank than anyone else when Sergeant Ketchum died."

"But Harry likes being our squad leader," I explained. "Why doesn't the major just go ahead and promote him?"

"That's none of my business, or yours, for that matter, Nichols. But just between the two of us, I'm not exactly surprised that the major is not the least bit interested in promoting Mr. Watts."

"Why?"

"Because as I'm sure you're aware, Mr. Watts hasn't exactly been shy about verbally ripping his commanding officer and our mission over here every chance he gets."

"But that's mostly just talk, Top."

"Maybe so, but it's the kind of talk we don't need around here."

"But Harry's been a pretty good squad leader since Sergeant Ketchum died."

"Well, everyone's certainly entitled to their own opinion, Nichols, but the reports I've been receiving would lead one to believe just the opposite. He doesn't seem to get along with anyone but you, and the other squad leaders want him replaced as soon as possible."

"The other squad leaders have been complaining?" I asked.

"That's right. Every single one of them."

"About what?"

"I don't want to get into all of that, Nichols. All you need to know is that you are the major's choice to permanently replace Sergeant Ketchum, and unless you're prepared right this moment to refuse the promotion I've just offered you, that's the way it's going to be."

"But, Top, I've only got another month to go. Harry's the one who has extended his tour so he won't have to go back and do stateside time. It doesn't even make sense to make me the squad leader. I'm not going to be here long enough to...."

"Which brings me to the next reason I asked you here this morning," interrupted the first sergeant. "I want to go over some of the pros and cons of tour-extension with you. A lot of draftees in situations sim-

ilar to yours do it, you know. It completely eliminates any stateside service once your tour of duty ends here."

"You're kidding, right?" I asked, trying unsuccessfully not to smile.

"Did I say something funny, Nichols?"

"No, but you're not really going to ask me to extend my tour, are
you?"

"Yes, Nichols, that is exactly what I'm going to ask you to do."

"No way, Top. I'm sorry, but there's no way I want to do that."

"Have you given the idea any thought at all?"

"Well, maybe a little," I admitted. "Harry and I talked about it some
when he decided to extend."

"And what were some of Watts' reasons for doing so?"

"Oh, I don't know. Mostly I think he just didn't want to do six or
seven months of stateside duty when he got done here."

"And you do?"

"Well, no, I don't, but I sure don't want to stay over here a day
longer than I have to, either."

"Why not?"

"If you were an infantryman, Top, you wouldn't even have to ask
that question." The words were barely out of my mouth when I wished
I could take them back.

"Nichols," boomed the first sergeant, "I haven't spent my whole
career tied down to this damn desk! Have you ever heard of Pork Chop
Hill?"

As the first sergeant went on and on about his combat experiences—
real or imagined—in the Korean War, I found myself wondering if
maybe I should indeed give some serious consideration to extending
my tour of duty for another three months like Harry had done. It
would mean rolling the dice a little bit longer, but there were definitely
some advantages to doing it. The war was winding down and the missions weren't anywhere as difficult as they used to be; there wasn't anyone I was really dying to get back to the States to see; I could save more
money, especially if I was going to be a sergeant; sergeants didn't have

to pull guard duty; I wouldn't have to spend half-a-year stationed God only knows where in the States shining my boots and polishing my belt buckle; once my freedom bird landed back in the world, my military service would be completely over; and maybe best of all, I would go home a hard-stripe sergeant, the rank my father had always wanted to be but never quite made during World War Two. Suddenly the decision seemed to be an easy one. "Okay, Top, I'll do it," I said the moment the first sergeant allowed me to get a word in edgewise.

"Do what?" he asked, his mind still back on Pork Chop Hill.

"I'll extend my tour."

"Well, Nichols, I'm glad to hear it," he said, sure his recollections about his glory days in Korea had helped me see the light.

"But I'd still rather Harry continue as our squad leader."

"That's out of the question, Nichols. The major wants Watts out of that position as soon as possible—no matter what you decide to do."

"You're saying Harry can't be our squad leader any longer—no matter what?"

"That's right. Now do you want the job or not?"

"Actually," I said, surprising myself, "I kind of think I do."

"Good. I'll inform the major as soon as I've talked to Watts."

"Then you're going to tell Harry?"

"Yes, as soon as we're done here."

"Can I please tell him, Top?"

"Well, I guess you can if you like."

"Thanks. I think he'll take it a little bit better coming from me."

"Okay, that's fine, but if he has any questions, you just send him right over to me."

"I will—and thank you again."

"Look, Nichols," he said with unexpected sincerity, "to tell you the truth, you've earned it. You've put in almost a full year and you've come back from a pretty serious wound. Plus Sergeant Ketchum was the best infantry sergeant I've ever been around, and he apparently thought very highly of you."

"Who told you that, Top?"

"He did."

"Really? When?"

The first sergeant smiled warmly at me, something else he had never done before, and said, "When he came in here just a few days before his death and changed the name of the beneficiary on his Army insurance policy—which brings me to the final thing I need to talk to you about this morning."

"What did Jim say?"

"Actually, Nichols, Sergeant Ketchum didn't say a word."

"I don't understand, Top."

"But he did remove his wife as his beneficiary on his life insurance policy, and he replaced her with you."

"What?" I said, my eyes beginning to fill with tears.

"That's right, Nichols."

"He left me his Army insurance money?"

"Yes. Every penny of it." My heart lurched as I tried to get my head around the enormity of what I had just heard. "Division returned the paperwork to me a few days ago," continued the first sergeant. "Everything seems to be in order. You should be getting a check before too long."

I knew if I tried to say anything, I would start sobbing. "Now get out of here, Sergeant Nichols," said the first sergeant as tears were welling up in his eyes, too. "And try your damndest to be just half the sergeant Jim Ketchum was."

I knew where to find Harry. He had run out of his beloved Marlboro cigarettes the night before, and sure enough, there he was, first in line at the PX, waiting impatiently for the doors to swing open. "I've got something I need to tell you, Harry, and I don't think you're going to like it much."

"There's no such thing as good news over here, Ty," said Harry as he glanced down at his field watch to see what time it was, "so go ahead, man, hit me with your best shot. I can take anything you've got to dish out."

"I'm serious, Harry. And I'm afraid it can hurt our friendship."

That caught Harry's attention and he turned to face me. "What are you talking about, man?"

"They're going to promote me to sergeant."

"So what? That's a good thing, stupid. Congratulations!" He gave me a hug.

"You don't care?"

"Hell no. Why should I care? I'm already an acting E-5. The only difference is that you'll be making a few more bucks than I do, but I'll just win that back from you playing cards anyway."

"But that's not all, Harry."

"There's more?"

"I'm afraid so. They're making me a squad leader."

"Really?" said Harry as he stiffened quickly. "Which squad?"

"Our squad—Alpha Squad."

"You're shitting me, right?" asked Harry, obviously stunned.

"No. The first sergeant just got through telling me."

"But I've been busting my butt trying to do a good job," said Harry, pounding a fist into his hand.

"I know."

"Did the son-of-a-bitch give you a reason or anything?"

"No, not really," I lied.

"I bet the fucking major is behind this, isn't he? I'd bet anything this is all his doing!"

"It's just a title, Harry. As far as I'm concerned, we can share the responsibilities. You know, kinda run the squad by committee."

"You know that won't work, Ty. Someone has to have the final say. When does all this become official?"

"Today, I think."

"Today?"

"That's what Top said."

"But I've already got the manifest made up and everything."

"Then we'll just go with it the way you've got it."

"Is Top still in his office?"

"He was when I left to go looking for you."

"Good," said Harry, angrily turning to leave, "I'll just go see what the fuck this is all about."

"Come on, Harry," I pleaded, grabbing my friend by the arm, "let's just the two of us talk this out for a few minutes. There's no need to go raise hell with Top. I'm pretty sure his mind is made up."

"You mean the fucking major's mind is made up, don't you?" snapped Harry.

"Let's not get into a fight over this Harry, please? Top said they weren't going to let you keep being the squad leader even if I didn't take the promotion. At least this way you can still have as much say in everything as you had before."

"I'm not letting those sons-of-bitches get away with this without giving them a piece of my fucking mind! Now let me go!"

"I'm sorry, Harry. I really am."

"The fuck you are!" he shouted back at me as he hurried off towards Headquarters.

My first decision as a squad leader was to offer Harry the job of being my RTO, which I did as soon as he returned from speaking with the first sergeant. He promptly refused, saying, "Who do you think the gooks shoot at first, man? The fool carrying the fucking radio, that's who. They want to mess up our communications and blowing away the RTO does just that. What are you trying to do? Get me killed? Do I look stupid or what?"

"But I've carried a radio for over six months," I told him, "and I'm still here. Why don't you just give it a try. I think you'll really like it."

"No fucking way," said Harry. "And the only reason you got away with it," he added condescendingly, "is because Ketchum was always there to save your damn butt."

"Are we going to keep having conversations like this?" I asked him.

"No, we're not!" he exploded. "As far as I'm concerned, we don't have to talk to each other at all!"

"I'm really sorry you feel this way, Harry."

"Go fuck yourself!"

With the exception of Harry not talking to me, I truly enjoyed my first few weeks of being a squad leader. The fact that I had always been only a couple of steps away from Jim when all the important decisions were being made helped me immensely. I didn't need to be hitting up the other squad leaders all the time for advice. I simply asked myself what Jim would have done in a similar situation and then did it.

I also worked extremely hard at never allowing fear or confusion to cross my face, even if those were the emotions I was feeling at the time. Jim had said on numerous occasions that was the key to being a good leader of men in combat situations. "If they see fear in my eyes," he had said, "then they are going to get even more scared than they already are. Never let them know you're scared—never."

It was one thing to make good decisions in the field, but unlike Jim, I wanted each and every man under my command to genuinely like me, too. I knew that was probably a weakness, but it was also a need of mine I decided not to deny, and I was extremely pleased when Marcus White, of all people, showed up in my hootch asking for a transfer to Alpha Squad.

"But we haven't really talked since that night we got stuck pulling guard duty together ages ago," I said. "Why do you want to be in my squad?"

"I'm sick of being jerked around by Hughes," he said. "He won't say it to my face, but that dude hates brothers worse than he does commies."

"How do you know that?"

"Trust me, I know."

"But I heard you were doing fine in his squad."

"I ain't killed the mother-fucker yet, if that's what you mean."

"Well," I admitted, "I do need a permanent RTO. We've been kind of passing the radio back and forth. You think Hughes would let you come on over?"

"Hell, he'll jump for fucking joy!"

"Well, it's fine with me if it's okay with Hughes. You want me to talk to him about it?"

"No, I'll do it."

"Okay. Let me know what he says."

"And you really want me to carry your radio?"

"Sure. You're supposed to be a hero, aren't you?"

"More or less."

"Well, I always make a point of trying to stay close to the right people."

"Wow, a stupid spear-chucking nigger carrying a squad radio," said Marcus, shaking his head. "Now will that be a first around here or what?"

"But you're going to have to leave all that crap behind, okay, Marcus?"

"What crap?"

"You know, the angry black man thing. If you're going to be doing that all the time, I'd honestly rather you stay in Hughes' squad. I've got enough things to worry about as it is right now."

"I am what I am, man."

"Which is a pretty good soldier from what I've been told. So can't we just leave it at that?"

"If you say so, Sarge," said Marcus, smiling and offering to shake my hand.

"I'm afraid I still can't do those complicated hand shakes very well," I admitted.

"Here," said Marcus, grabbing at my hand from a number of different directions, "it's all in the wrist, see?"

"I feel a little stupid," I said, struggling to hold my own with Marcus' long and very strong fingers.

"You pretty much look like a fool, too," said Marcus, still smiling and offering to hit elbows together.

In the field, Marcus turned out to be the perfect RTO and it wasn't long before I was relying heavily on his advice and counsel. He was more daring than me, and since I disliked the fact that I was always so cautious, we seemed to make the perfect team. Harry immediately noticed this and bit his tongue for a full week before he finally stormed up to me and said, "I thought you told me I would have some say about how things were run out here?"

"I thought we weren't talking?" I asked him.

"Well, we are now, and since I've got more time in Vietnam than anybody else in the whole fucking squad, I'd appreciate it if you would let me know what the hell is going on now and then."

"Now's as good as time as any," I said, sensing an opportunity to bury the hatchet and pointing to the gunfire we could hear coming from a distant hilltop. "We're supposed to go check that out. Any suggestions?"

"Sure," said Harry eagerly, "we're in double-canopy jungle and the major and his fly-boys can't see shit right now. Let's just find us a big old tree, pass around the smokes and water canteens, and call the fucking mission in from there."

"Kind of the chicken-shit approach to doing our job, huh?" asked Marcus, who was standing right next to me.

"Who in the fuck asked you?" Harry shot back at Marcus.

"Knock it off, both of you!" I said. "Let's just go on as far as we safely can and then maybe we'll run into a big tree to snuggle up against. How's that?"

"Who's going to take the point?" Marcus asked me.

"It looks like you and me are it," I answered. "We've got two rookies I don't know a thing about, a medic and the machine gun team to cover our rear. That just leaves you and me."

"What about this guy?" asked Marcus, pointing to Harry.

"I ain't walking the fucking point, you idiot," said Harry. "Tell him, Ty."

"Harry's getting pretty short, Marcus," I said as Marcus glared at Harry. "It's no big deal. We'll do it. I don't expect much trouble today anyway."

"And what happens if we have to link back up with Headquarters and call in arty or something?" asked Marcus. "How we going to do that if we're up at the head of the squad?"

"You've got a good point," I admitted.

"Well, I don't care about any of that shit," said Harry. "All I know is that I ain't walking no fucking point with only six weeks to go."

"How about just this once, Harry. I haven't asked anything of you since I've been squad leader, you know that. It would really help us out today."

"And it just might get me fucking killed! I told you no, and I mean no!"

"You really are a chicken-shit, aren't you?" said Marcus, still smarting over having been called an idiot.

"Fuck you, black boy!" yelled Harry right into Marcus' face.

I had never seen a man hit another man in the face so fast and so hard as Marcus hit Harry. Blood went flying in all directions as Marcus' huge fist buried itself deep into Harry's nose, smashing the bridge almost flat to the skin. Harry cried out in agony and collapsed on the soft floor of the jungle, holding what was left of his face with both hands and moaning and groaning like a man near death. I quickly dropped down to my knees next to Harry to see if I could be of any help.

"I'll go get the medic," said Marcus matter-of-factly.

"You better hurry," I said, trying to get Harry to take his hands away from his nose so I could see the extent of the injury. "I think it's broken."

"You heard what he called me, didn't you?" Marcus asked me.

"I heard."

"I didn't want no trouble."

"I know, Marcus."

"Well, I'm not sorry or nothing. I don't put up with that shit over here, Ty. I'm carrying a damn gun and risking my butt just like he is. We're fucking equal. None of that black boy shit."

"Just go get the medic, Marcus. He's in a lot of pain."

"Good!" said Marcus as he strolled off in search of the medic.

"This is all your fucking fault," Harry yelled up at me, his face flushed with the heat of humiliation.

"You shouldn't have talked to him like that, Harry. And taking the point for a few hours wouldn't have killed you, either."

"Fuck him! And fuck you, too!"

"Just be quiet until the medic gets here, Harry, okay? You're bleeding real bad."

"I don't give a shit!"

"Please stop talking, Harry. You're just going to end up saying a lot of things you'll wish you hadn't."

"You think you're really hot shit now, don't you, Ty? Just like fucking Ketchum. Little Jim Ketchum junior, that's who you want to be, don't you? Well, listen to this you goddamn nigger lover! I don't give a fuck anymore if you end up just like he did!"

"Shut up, Harry!" I screamed, grabbing him by the shirt collar and shaking him. "Shut up!"

JOURNAL ENTRY

18 DAYS TO GO

I still can't believe it! Glynis wrote back! Over the past three or four months, I must have written her a hundred letters—probably more. And then, just when I was about to give up all hope of ever hearing from her again, there it was, lying on my bunk, staring up at me after today's mission. I recognized the handwriting immediately and I can't even put into words how incredibly happy receiving that one little letter made me feel—and that was even before I opened it!

It wasn't very long, and she took the first page—all of it—just to apologize for not answering any of my letters. Apparently she knew they had been arriving at her parent's home almost daily, but she refused to let her mother forward any of them to her. Talk about will power. Yet I think I fully understand why she did what she did. We're all just doing what we have to do to get to the next day, and I have come to have great respect for that now. And to tell the truth, I think her sticking to her guns has only made me love her more!

The second page implored me to stay healthy and safe and went on and on about how worried she still is about me. But then began the words I have been hoping to hear for what seems like an eternity.

She had returned home to see her father—whose health has been failing—and decided she would open just one of my letters, but ended up reading them all in one sitting instead. Although she is very angry at me for having extended my tour of duty—she called my decision 'absurd'—she swears that she still loves me just as much as the day I left Sydney. And here's the really unbelievable part! I think she wants to marry me!

Her exact words were, "After carefully reading all your letters, each one at least twice, and after having done everything in my power to get you out of my mind and heart, I know now that it's absolutely hopeless. I'm afraid I can't possibly live without you, and I didn't want another moment to pass without telling you so. I've been a cowardly fool, Ty, and please, please forgive me for not writing sooner. Yet even now I'm terrified that something might still happen to you. But be that as it may, I want you to know I love you, desperately.

"A number of your letters spoke of marriage, and I have re-read them endlessly. You said you wanted to have children with me, and grow very, very old together. If that is still your wish, please come back to Australia and tell me so in person as soon as you possibly can, because it is my wish also. You can count on me now, Ty, you really can. I will wait forever if that is what it takes. You are the love of my life."

Wow! What an absolutely incredible letter! And she even enclosed the address of the Australian Embassy in San Francisco so I can get started on some of the paperwork required for me to return to her country.

How strange, though, that Glynis' letter would arrive today. Maybe it's really true that when one door closes, another one opens?

Harry rotated yesterday. And he did so without even bothering to say goodbye. I went over to his room, but I couldn't get him to talk to me. We haven't really had a meaningful conversation since Marcus broke his nose. But he could have said something—anything. Instead, he just kept right on packing and didn't even bother to look up

I thanked him for all his help when I first got here, and I told him how much I was going to miss him, but he didn't say a word, not one single word. It really hurt—it still hurts! Harry and I were so tight. I can hardly bear to think about it. It's like Glynis' letter was sent from heaven. Memories of Harry were saturating my brain until it arrived.

I really liked Harry. I know a lot of people didn't—Jim couldn't stand him. But Harry could make me laugh, when I really needed to laugh. And it's just awful that our friendship had to end the way it did. I swear, if I had known that taking over as squad leader was going to cause all the problems it did, I would never have done it—never. But at least he went home alive, and I'll always be thankful for that!

Now, if only I can do the same. Just eighteen more days to go if, like Granny used to always say, 'The Lord's a-willing, and the creeks don't rise'.

CHAPTER 27

▼

THE FREEDOM BIRD

I desperately wanted to be as happy and thankful as all the other lucky GI's who were boarding their freedom bird back to the world, but I wasn't. I had waited so long for the day, sometimes thinking of nothing else, but now that it had actually arrived, everything seemed so bittersweet, so anticlimactic.

I fastened my seat belt and closed my eyes. I tried to imagine what the California coast was going to look like from thirty thousand feet up in the air. I could almost see the white surf crashing up against the shore; the rolling foothills and the distant Sierra mountains; the overpopulated cities and the never-ending Central Valley. Could it all be only sixteen hours away?

As my commercial airliner slowly taxied out to its assigned runway at the Ben Hoa airport, Charlie tossed in one last poorly aimed mortar round to remind me that even though Vietnamization was firmly in place, there was still a war going on and I wasn't safely in the air yet. When a second round didn't follow, the celebration going on all around me quickly shifted back into high gear.

"I made it, Sarge!" exclaimed the young soldier bouncing around in the aisle seat next to me. He reached over and pounded me on the shoulder. "I made it, Sarge!" he yelled again. "I'm going home—I don't believe it!" He let out a deafening cry of pure joy which brought a very welcome smile to my face.

After bringing the plane to a full stop at the head of the runway, which elicited a playful chorus of boo's from almost everyone in the aircraft, the pilot began to slowly pick up speed for the much anticipated takeoff. The faster the plane rolled along, the louder the cheers, until the whole passenger compartment was wall-to-wall whooping and hollering.

When the plane finally lifted off and began gaining altitude, flop hats went flying and eyes began to water. Once it had leveled off, two long-legged and very friendly airline stewardesses began artfully struggling to escape being touched or grabbed by just about every overjoyed soldier they passed. When one of them bent down and freely planted a big kiss on the cheek of a bald staff sergeant who had to be in his fifties, the loudest roar of all went up.

As the plane sped away from Vietnam, the celebration slowly died down and I tried without a whole lot of success to turn my attention to a movie which was beginning to run through its opening credits. As I struggled to make some sense of all the conflicting emotions I was feeling, I noticed that the first lieutenant sitting in the window seat next to me seemed to be trying to do the same thing. The golden-haired officer had a First Air Cavalry patch on his shoulder and I was sure we had a lot in common, but it was obvious he wasn't in the mood to start up a conversation. He continued staring out his tiny glass porthole for the longest time, then he silently flipped the bird to all that he was leaving behind.

"Well said, sir," I said.

The lieutenant glanced back over his shoulder and I immediately wished I hadn't opened my big mouth. "It was all a big fucking joke, Sergeant," said the lieutenant softly, returning his moist, glassy eyes to the nonexistent view outside his window. "And it was on us."

The 'No Smoking' sign finally went off and most everyone around me began to light up. Someone offered me a cigarette and I politely declined, explaining that I was trying to quit. I was up to three packs a day and determined to kick the habit before I got back to the world. I had tried everything, including cutting way back and never buying my own, but that had only turned me into a dreaded mooch and made the cigarettes I did smoke taste even better. I knew that quitting cold-turkey was my only hope.

As I was trying to ignore my craving for a cigarette and also come up with something to say which might comfort the obviously hurting lieutenant seated next to me, I suddenly found myself thinking all the way back to a conversation I had with a truly kind chaplain the day after Jim died.

I had never thought of myself as a religious person, but there I was, less than twenty-four hours after Jim's death, walking into the base chapel and knocking on the chaplain's door. When all the small talk and a lengthy prayer had ended, and with me feeling no better than when I first walked into the chapel, the chaplain asked, "Have you ever read the Bible, Ty?"

"Only parts of it, sir."

"Well," he explained, "in it there is much about human suffering, and how important it is to God that each of us, while we are in the world, suffer." When I told him I didn't think God should be in the business of making people suffer, the chaplain added, "I know it's difficult to understand now, but the more a person suffers on this earth, the more special he or she is in God's eyes."

"Why is that?" I asked.

"Because suffering is one of the few things which can make us more compassionate, more sensitive, more charitable, more capable of loving our fellow man. In other words, it makes us more Christ-like, and more acceptable in the presence of God."

"Then you're telling me it's good that I feel so awful?"

"Something like that. And the sooner we can pick up all the qualities which only suffering brings us, then the sooner we can get off this earth and move on to much bigger and better things."

"So," I said, trying hard to make sense out of what I was hearing, "you're saying that the guys who skate through this life, the ones who don't do much suffering, the ones who get all the breaks, the ones who don't have to die young in a stupid war, those aren't the lucky ones?"

"That's right. In fact, if you're not suffering in this world, and if you aren't aware of all the suffering which is going on around you, then you're probably not doing much with the life God gave you."

The chaplain said a number of other things that morning, but the one sentence I really wanted to share with the lieutenant was, "Something must drive us out of our own self and into the world—and that something is suffering."

Unable to bring myself to bother the lieutenant, I closed my tired eyes, spread my legs out as far as the seat in front of me would permit, and turned my thoughts to Toi Nguyen, the commander of the Vietnamese Kit Carson Scouts who had served Echo Troop so faithfully, and the last person to hug me goodbye when I left our base for Ben Hoa. I wondered what would happen to Toi, someone who had worked so long and hard for the Americans, if Vietnamization didn't work? What if the South falls apart once we're all gone, I asked myself. What if the North does finally win in the end? Will Toi and all the hundreds of thousands of others just like him be considered traitors? Will they all be taken out and shot? Will they put Toi's wife and daughters into concentration camps?

I forced all the questions without answers out of my head and recalled instead Toi's last words to me as we embraced for the final time. "Do not worry about me, my friend," he had said with the same wonderful smile which had helped him endure decades of hardship and struggle. "I will be fine, and someday you will come visit me in a free Vietnam."

When the freedom bird finally landed at Travis Air Force Base in California, the hot afternoon sun was out in full force and waves of heat were radiating up from the asphalt airstrip. The celebrating immediately started all over again, with deliriously happy soldiers with bulging eyes and straining necks gathered around every available window to get even the tiniest glimpse of home.

With everyone shouting and jockeying for position to be among the first to deplane, I settled back in my seat and said a silent prayer to a God who still had me thoroughly confused. I humbly thanked Him for getting me home in one piece and promised to get back to Him later about all the other questions I had on my mind.

"Shall we stand up and get the fuck off this thing?" suddenly said the sad-eyed lieutenant seated next to me.

They were the first words the man had spoken since he had flipped off Vietnam and I was happy to hear them. "I think I'll just wait here until the line thins out a bit, sir."

The lieutenant nodded that he understood and held out his hand for me to shake. "Take care of yourself, Sergeant."

"Good luck to you, too, sir," I said, shaking the lieutenant's strong hand.

"I think I've already used up all my luck," he said. "How about you?"

"And then some, sir."

"I just want you to know you're the best military traveling companion I've ever had."

"But I didn't say a word, sir."

"Exactly. And not one war story, either. You know what that tells me? That and that combat infantryman's badge you're wearing?"

"No, sir."

"It tells me that it was hell for you, too, but that we're both going to be okay." Complete strangers, we smiled and looked at each other as if we were brothers. "You have yourself a good life, Sergeant."

"I will, sir. You, too."

With that the lieutenant stood up, slithered in front of me and quietly disappeared forever into the aisle of youthful humanity rolling its way towards the front exit. For reasons unknown to me, I decided I wanted to be the very last person off the aircraft.

As I sat there avoiding the stampede, it dawned on me that just like the lieutenant, there were any number of people I had met in the military whom I would never be seeing again. I nostalgically went over a few of their names and faces, but quickly stopped myself. All we would ever have in common was our year in Vietnam, and I suddenly never wanted to see any of them again.

"Once you walk off this plane," I whispered to myself, "you've got to leave it all behind you. Forget what Jimbo said about a war never being over just because it ends. Don't be marching in Veteran's Day parades for the next fifty years. Frame it. Give it a beginning, a middle, and an end." And I promised myself I would truly do everything in my power to do just that.

When I finally stepped out onto the mobile staircase, I looked up at the bright sky and then down at the tarmac. There was no red carpet, no welcoming committee, no cheering crowds, no band playing.

As I silently made my way over to the buses which had been chartered to take us into San Francisco for in-country processing, I couldn't help but notice an old aircraft hangar off in the distance with a 'Welcome Home' sign made up of old rusting metal letters fastened to its side. The 'm' in Welcome, and the 'o' in Home, had fallen off from lack of care.

CHAPTER 28

▼

HOME

When my taxi cab coasted up in front of the Phi Beta Chi fraternity house, I couldn't get over the fact that so many improvements had been made to its exterior. It no longer looked like it belonged in a Victorian-era haunted house movie and even the tons of dead oak tree leaves which always used to litter the unkempt yard had been raked up. The whole place had been tastefully painted and landscaped, and for a moment, I even wished I had gone ahead and pledged when I once had the chance.

I climbed out of the taxi, paid the driver and threw my duffel bag over my shoulder. As I began walking up to the front porch, even more hard-to-believe changes became apparent. The decades-old roof had been re-shingled and all the broken windows had been replaced. A large paper banner with the words 'Welcome To Hell Weekend' also hung over a beautifully carved wooden door which even had a fancy brass doorknob on it.

What has gotten into these guys, I thought to myself as I knocked on the door. At least all the loud voices, laughter and cussing I could hear going on inside sounded familiar.

I knocked a second time and when the door opened, there stood a skinny young man who seemed to go into shock once he spotted the military uniform I was wearing. "Man," he stammered, "I think you got the wrong fucking place."

"I'm looking for a friend."

"Sorry," he said. "This is Hell Weekend. If you're not a brother or a pledge, you can't come in."

"His name is Steve Cheever."

"You know Steve?" he asked, very surprised. "The president of Phi Beta Chi?"

"That's right. Is he here?"

"Yeah, he's here, but you still can't come in. Only brothers and pledges."

"You tell him I'm here. I'll wait."

The young doorkeeper, whom I assumed was a pledge, took another up and down look at my uniform and shook his head. I dropped my duffel bag on the porch and said pointedly, "My name is Nichols, Ty Nichols. Now please get your skinny ass in there and tell Steve I'm here."

"Alright, alright, take it easy. But you have to wait here."

As he went back into the house, I took out a cigarette I wasn't supposed to be smoking and was beginning to light it when the front door suddenly exploded open and Steve leaped into my unprepared arms. "Ty, I'll be goddamned!" he yelled as he squeezed the breath out me. A number of the fraternity brothers peeked their heads out the door to see what all the commotion was about. "What in the hell are you doing here? The last time I talked to your mom, she said you had re-upped and she didn't know when you would be getting home."

One of the fraternity brothers, growing impatient with the reunion, stepped out onto the porch and said, "Come on, Steve, the marshmallow race, remember."

"Just a minute, Dave, okay?" said Steve. "This guy is like a brother to me and I haven't seen him in damn near two years."

"Don't let me hold something up, Steve," I said.

"It's no big deal, man, just the marshmallow race. I'm in charge of the damn thing again this year and they're about ready to go in there."

"I just dropped by to ask you a favor, Steve. A pretty big favor, actually."

"You just name it, Ty. Anything for you, man. You know that."

"Damn it, Steve," said Dave, "come on, everyone's waiting in here."

"Look, Ty," suggested Steve, "why don't you come on in and let me get this race out of the way and then we can talk, okay? I've got a hundred and one questions to ask you."

"I'm not exactly dressed for a frat party, Steve."

"No problem, man," said Steve as he threw his arm around my shoulder and escorted me into the house.

Once inside, Steve could see that I was really impressed by the fresh coat of paint, lush carpet and all the new furniture. "Not bad, huh?" he asked me proudly.

"What has happened to this place, Steve? When I left, it was a dump, inside and out."

"We more or less burned it down one night after a party."

"Really?"

"And everything turned out to be insured. Is this a great fucking country or what?"

As I continued to look around, it quickly became obvious that at least one thing hadn't changed—there were drunk and almost drunk fraternity brothers everywhere. I also couldn't help noticing that my uniform was drawing a lot of attention.

"Who the hell let in John Wayne?" called out one of the brothers.

I ignored the remark and followed Steve through a connecting dining room which led to a well-lit backyard. It was overflowing with more inebriated brothers, most of whom were harassing a group of about fifteen pledges. The pledges were trying very hard to act calm and collected, but none of them were very convincing.

"Did I ever tell you about the marshmallow race?" Steve asked me.

"No, I don't think so."

"Why do I keep thinking it was one of the reasons I could never get you to pledge?"

"You're thinking of Queer Weekend."

"Oh, that's right," said Steve, smiling. "Anyway, you're going to love the marshmallow race. It's my favorite part of Hell Weekend. Stay right here and you'll have a bird's-eye seat. It'll only take me a few minutes."

Steve strutted out into the middle of the yard and at the very top of his lungs, yelled, "All right, quiet everyone! Quiet!" The rowdy, beer-guzzling crowd wasn't that easy to silence, so again he screamed, "Quiet, everyone! Damn it, be quiet!"

Once Steve had everyone's attention, he said, "Dave, where's the marshmallows?"

Dave, grinning from ear to ear, held a large plastic bag of jumbo marshmallows up over his head and waved it for all to see. The gesture drew a loud round of applause from all of the assembled fraternity brothers.

"Good," said Steve. "Now who's got the finish line?"

Two smiling fraternity brothers off in the distance stretched out a rope and waved to Steve.

"Let's get it on!" shouted one of the spectators. His words encouraged more applause and a chant of, "Do it! Do it!"

Steve waved back to the two fraternity brothers in charge of the finish line and motioned for Dave to toss him the bag of marshmallows. Dave lobbed them over to Steve, who opened the package with his mouth and began stringing them along the starting line. He made sure that each marshmallow he placed on the grass was a few feet away from its neighbor. His task finally completed, he wolfed down a few of the leftover marshmallows and strolled back out into the center of the yard.

"Okay," he hollered, "pledges, listen up! I want each one of you to pick out a marshmallow and stand behind it. Let's go! Move it, move it!" He waited patiently until all the confused pledges were finally in place and the laughter coming from the fraternity brothers had died down. "Good," he continued, "now drop your pants! All of you! And your underwear, too!"

There was an instant protest from the pledges, but it quickly subsided as Dave stepped forward and threatened them all with a crack from a vicious looking paddle which had once been a boat oar. "Come on," yelled Steve, "get 'em off! We don't have all night. And as soon as you have, I want you each straddling your marshmallow. One foot on each side, understand?"

With all the nervous and embarrassed pledges nude from the waist down and standing over their marshmallows, Steve began to very matter-of-factly explain the rules of the race. "Now, listen up. I'm only going to go through this once and if I was you guys, I'd pay close attention to what I say. It's real simple. I'm going to yell out 'on your marks, get set, and go'. When I say 'go', you are each to squat down and pick up your marshmallow between the cheeks of your ass."

Most of the pledges shook their head and muttered to themselves, but none of them offered any real protest. A few were even smiling and eager to get under way. "Now," continued Steve, "while holding tightly onto your marshmallow, you are to run, or waddle, to the finish line. If for some reason along the way you should have the bad luck to drop your marshmallow, you must pick it up, bring it all the way back to the starting line and start all over again. Any questions?" The vast majority of the assembled brothers were almost hysterical with laughter. "And oh, yes," added Steve with emphasis, "I almost forgot. The loser of the race eats all of the marshmallows!"

That announcement brought a smile to my face and the loudest roar of the night from the brothers. "Okay," yelled Steve, "now here we go! Everybody ready? Okay! On your marks! Get set! Go!"

The majority of the pledges quickly managed to get their marshmallows under control and began waddling off towards the finish line. Cheered on by the screaming brothers, they all seemed to be doing pretty well, with the exception of one poor young man who had no luck whatsoever in picking up his marshmallow and had been left squatting at the starting line. He was mercifully joined by two other pledges who had dropped their marshmallow and been forced to start all over again.

The three of them finally got out onto the course and began fighting it out for last place. It turned out to be a photo finish, and while everyone was arguing over who would have to eat all the soiled marshmallows, Steve made his way over to me and put his arm around my shoulder.

"You don't really make one of them eat the marshmallows, do you?" I asked.

"Naw, although last year some pledge did eat them just for the hell of it."

A drunk brother suddenly staggered over to Steve and me and with slurred words, said, "Hey, solider-boy, you kill yourself any of those damn dinks?"

"Get the hell away from us, Wayne," said Steve.

"I just want to know if he killed any dinks, Steve."

"You're drunk, Wayne," said Steve.

"Come on, soldier-boy, tell me how many dinks you killed."

"Get lost, Wayne," said Steve as he spun his fraternity brother half-way around and gave him a two-handed shove in the back. "Sorry, Ty. He's just had too much to drink."

"No problem," I said.

"Come on," said Steve, "let's go back on inside and get ourselves a couple of beers and do some serious visiting."

Steve took me upstairs to his room and handed me a beer from his own private refrigerator. We pulled out a couple of chairs and sat down at a table which appeared to have been recently used for a lengthy game of poker. Food-stained betting chips, empty beer cans and sticky playing cards were scattered everywhere.

"Have you been home yet?" asked Steve.

"No. I came here right from in-country processing in San Francisco. That's why the uniform. With Mom back in Vermont staying with my sister, there was no real reason to go home."

"Hey, Ty, I was so sorry to hear about your dad, man."

"Well, he always had a lot of trouble with his heart. It wasn't like it was totally unexpected I guess."

"Your mom took it really well. You would have been proud of her."

"That's what I hear. I got a couple of letters from her that sounded pretty upbeat. Plus she's got a lot of real good friends. And Sharon will take great care of her. She'll be fine."

"They wouldn't let you come home for the funeral, huh?"

"It would have been a big hassle for quite a few people, and I'm not much on funerals anymore. Plus I only had a few weeks to go, so I decided to just stick it out. I'm going over to the graveyard after I leave here."

"I know you and your dad were never really that close, but …"

"We resolved most of that in a couple of letters just before he died."

"Oh, well that's good, man, that's really good," said Steve, sensing that I wanted to change the subject. "Anyway, so tell me, what's it feel like to be back? I mean, it must be pretty exciting, huh?"

"It's nice."

"Only nice?"

"Okay, really nice."

"Did you bring home any souvenirs or anything?"

"No, not really."

"No tobacco pouches made out of some gook's tits or anything like that? I hear a lot of guys come home with those?"

"No," I said, trying not to show my disappointment in my old friend.

"Too bad. I'd sure like to see one of those."

"Look, Steve," I said as politely as I could, "it's great seeing you and everything, but I really need to talk to you about that favor, and then I probably should be getting on my way."

"What's the big hurry, man?" Steve asked as he returned to the refrigerator for another beer. "Anyway, it was really hell over there, huh?"

"Sometimes."

"So, how you feeling?"

"Pretty good."

"Did your side heal up and everything?"

"Yeah."

"I about shit when I heard you had been wounded. And my mom said your parents thought you had actually been killed when they first saw that telegram they got from the Army."

"They wrote me a letter about that. I guess in World War Two, getting a telegram from the War Department only meant one thing. I'm sorry they had to go through that."

"Anyway," said Steve, once again sensing that I wanted to change the subject, "you sure look different."

"I lost some weight."

"No, I mean you look, you know, older."

"I am older."

"I guess you know all about Amy and Denny Davies, right?"

"Yeah."

"Can you believe she actually married that clown? Someone said she's already pregnant."

"He's not such a bad guy."

"I wish I had his money, that's for sure. But it really doesn't bother you, huh?"

"No. I'm happy for her."

"Okay, man, if you say so." After an uncomfortable silence, he added, "I swear, man, I've got a hundred and one questions to ask you."

"Shoot."

"Well, first of all, why in the hell did you extend your tour for those extra three months? I thought you had gone nuts or something when I heard that."

"I just didn't want to do any stateside time. If I had come back when my year was up, I would have had to do at least six months at some base in the States. That would have meant lots and lots of saluting and shoe shining and keeping my hair cut."

"I hear you, man." There was another lengthy pause as we both realized we didn't have all that much to say to one another. "Sorry I didn't write more often," he said finally. "You know me. I'm not much of a letter writer."

"That's alright."

"There just wasn't that much to report, if you know what I mean. Nothing much changes around here. You know that."

"I understand, really."

"Anyway, how you showin' getting that Bronze Star? That really made your dad proud, you know that, don't you?"

"They give everybody medals, Steve. If you're over there long enough, it's hard not to get one."

After we both squirmed around in our chairs for a few seconds, Steve said, "Well, I just can't get over how different you look, man. And I guess after everything you've been through, watching a bunch of stupid pledges run around with marshmallows up their asses probably seems a little silly?"

"A little."

"So, how about another beer?"

"No thanks."

"Anyway, so the war's over for you?"

"Almost."

"Almost?"

"Steve, I really need a favor from you."

"Anything, man. You know that. You and I go back a long ways."

"I need to borrow your car. Dad totaled his when he had the heart attack and I don't have much cash on me. Mom has all my money, and I don't want to bother her right now with stuff like that."

"Well, sure," said Steve, hesitating. "I mean, what's a best friend for?"

"I'll need it for a few days, maybe as much as a week."

"No problem, man," he said, swallowing hard. "I can use my old man's wheels." He took out his car keys and flipped them to me. "It's got a full tank of gas."

"I really appreciate this, Steve. You were always a good friend."

"So, where, where you taking it?"

"To Dallas."

"Dallas?"

"That's right?"

"You mean Dallas, Texas?"

"Yes."

"What the hell are you going there for?"

"To visit a friend."

"And it can't wait?"

"No, I'm afraid not."

"And you think it'll take almost a week?"

"Probably more like five days. Four to drive, and one to visit. I'll get back as soon as I can—and I'll take real good care of the car."

"Well, he sure must be one a hell of a friend, you know, to want to take off for fucking Texas the first day you get back from Vietnam."

"He was, Steve. He really was."

CHAPTER 29

▼

DALLAS

412 Rockrose Road, the return address on all the letters Jim had received from his wife while he was in Vietnam, turned out to be a little rundown flattop tract house in a dusty suburb of Dallas. The street it was on was dotted with deep potholes and littered with trash and dead leaves which no one apparently had the time or energy to pick up and put in a garbage can. Every other home seemed to have an old car in need of tires or other repairs parked in front of it and almost all of the lawns looked like they hadn't been watered or mowed in ages.

I wheeled Steve's car up into the dirt driveway of Jim's house and got out to take a closer look at the 'For Sale' sign which was staked in the front yard. Then I walked up to the porch, cupped my hands in an attempt to block out some of the bright reflected light, and gazed into the kitchen window. Still unable to see clearly, I used the palm of my hand to wipe a circle of the glass pane clean.

The house was obviously unoccupied and had been for some time. There was no furniture, carpets, nothing. A large colony of ants had to be nearby because orderly columns of them were marching in and out of the kitchen. I decided to walk next door and see if someone there could help me.

I knocked a half-dozen times on the door of 416 Rockrose Road before an elderly, sleepy-eyed Spanish lady finally cracked it open, made sure the chain was snugly in place and peeked out at me. Her face was a map of deep lines and hard times.

"Excuse me," I said, "but could you please tell me if Mr. and Mrs. Jim Ketchum used to live next door?" I pointed to the empty house.

"No English," said the old lady as she pulled a shawl up around her neck.

"Jim Ketchum," I said slowly. "Next door?"

She shook her head, apologized with her very tired eyes and shut the door.

Disappointed, I decided to give 408 Rockrose Road a try. I was just getting ready to knock when a middle-aged woman with a face full of sun-wrinkled skin and a cigarette dangling from her lips pushed open the screen door. She had a bottle of bright-pink nail polish in one hand and an applicator in the other.

"Can't you read?" she asked, pointing out a 'No Solicitors' sign in her front window. "No damn salesmen!"

"But I'm not selling anything," I said as she placed the handle of her nailbrush between her nicotine-stained teeth and slammed the door shut. "Please," I said, raising my voice, "this is important."

"Go away or I'll call the cops!" she yelled from inside the house.

"I'm a friend of Jim Ketchum," I yelled back. "Do you know where I might be able to find his wife?"

Just as I was ready to give up and try one of the houses across the street, the door swung open again and the woman said, "You're a friend of Jimmy's?"

"That's right," I said, sighing with relief. "We served in Vietnam together. We were very close friends. I'm looking for his wife, Sandy. It's very important that I talk to her. I have something to give her."

"Well, I'm afraid you're a little too late for that. The bitch moved, and believe me, I wasn't the only one happy to see her go."

"How long ago?"

"Oh, I guess it's been three or four months now. All I know is that the minute she and that worthless boyfriend of hers got their hands on Jimmy's money, they got themselves hitched and took off for greener pastures."

"Do you happen to know where they went?"

"Your guess is good as mine, honey. They sold Jimmy's house to some investment people for fifty cents on the dollar and were out of here the next day."

"And you don't have any idea where she might have gone?"

"No, not a clue. Some other state, probably. But Jimmy wasn't even cold in the ground when they were making all their big plans, though, I can tell you that."

"I've got a letter he wanted me to give her," I explained. "I promised him that I would get it to her. I've come a long way to make sure she gets it."

"Honey," said the woman as kindly as she could, "Sandy ain't ever coming back this way again. She hated everything about her life here. She used to park herself in my kitchen and go on and on about it for hours at a time. She wanted out of here so bad she could taste it. And if you want to know the plain truth, there's nothing in a letter from Jimmy that Sandy would be interested in hearing anyway. It's sad, but that's just the way it is. When she got Jimmy's money the first thing that girl did was run out and buy herself a fancy new pickup truck. It was the biggest damn pickup truck I ever saw. It must have cost a fortune. It was fire-engine-red, with tires big enough you could have put them on a tractor, and I know for a fact that she thought more of that damn truck than she ever did of Jimmy." She stepped out onto the porch to be closer to me. "You know, honey," she continued, "Jimmy was such a nice boy. When he mowed his lawn, he'd always mow mine, too. My back has been bad for years. And he'd also fix things for me. That boy could fix just about anything."

"Would you happen to know her new husband's name?" I asked.

"Corey. Yeah, I'm pretty sure that was it."

"No, I mean his last name?"

She thought for a moment and said, "No, you got me there. Sorry, all I know is that she called him Corey. Big guy. Mean. Stupid looking, too."

"What about her parents? Would they know where she is?"

"Look, honey, I never heard Sandy talk about anyone but herself. If she's got people someplace, she never mentioned it to me."

"Well," I said, not knowing what to do next, "thank you anyway."

"I sure wish I could have been more helpful, honey. But I'm afraid finding Sandy would be about as likely as coming across a diamond in a cow turd."

"You're probably right," I reluctantly admitted, my shoulders sagging. "Thanks again."

We exchanged smiles and she waved goodbye, but as I started to walk away, she called out after me, "I don't mean to pry, but was you with Jimmy when he died?"

I looked back at her and said, "Yes, I was."

"Good. That's good. No one should have to die all alone, without no family or friends around."

"Ma'am," I asked, "would you happen to know where Jim is buried?"

"Of course. Everybody from around here gets buried in the same place, Camellia Lawn. It's about twelve miles east of here." She pointed off towards some foothills. "A really nice place. Lots of trees and grass. It's not very big, but if you stay on the same road that got you here, you can't miss it. There's a big statue of Jesus right out in front of it."

"Thank you."

"And in case you're wondering, Jimmy got a proper funeral. The Army came out and did a right nice job."

"I'm really glad to hear that. Thank you."

"My pleasure," she said as she smiled warmly and waved goodbye again.

I went back over to Jim's old house and plopped down on one of the front porch's dusty steps. How are you going to be able to keep your promise now, I asked myself, suddenly almost as sad as the day Jim had died. And even if you could find her, she probably wouldn't want to hear what the letter has to say anyway.

I thought about opening the letter, reading it, and just throwing it away. But then it crossed my mind that maybe I could locate Sandy through the investment firm which had bought Jim's house. A phone number was on the 'For Sale' sign. Maybe she had left a forwarding address with them? But why would she do that? She's already got the money from the house. And even if you do find her, then what? Do you tell her what a low-life you think she is? Do you throw the letter at her? Do you spit in her face? No, Jim wouldn't have wanted any of that. He loved her. He really did. And she must have loved him at one time, too. There's got to be a part of her that's really special, or Jim wouldn't have been so crazy about her. Nothing is ever totally black and white. If nothing else, Vietnam has at least taught you that. There's always two sides to every story. And that Corey guy will get his. What goes around always finds a way of coming around in this world. Who knows, maybe that's Sandy's punishment—spending time with human garbage like that?"

"Young man, young man, wait a minute!" called out Jim's next door neighbor. She hurried over to me as fast as her aching back would permit and handed me a bundle of freshly cut garden flowers. "I'm afraid they ain't much, just something I had growing out in the backyard, but if you get out to see Jimmy, I'd sure appreciate it if you'd put them on his grave for me. I don't drive anymore. He's right on top of the biggest hill."

"I sure will," I said as I stood up and took the flowers from her. "That's very kind of you. Thank you very much."

She clumsily reached out and hugged me, pressing the sweet-smelling flowers up against my chest. "Seems like there's always another war for you poor young boys to die in. You'd think we'd all wise up, wouldn't you."

"Yes, Ma'am," I said, hugging her back, "you'd think we would."

CHAPTER 30

▼

CAMELLIA LAWN

The wind had come up a bit and I tightened my shirt collar snugly around my neck as I began the surprisingly steep climb up to Jim's grave. Dusk had forever been my favorite time of day and I was glad the sun hadn't completely disappeared when I arrived at Jim's marker. It was a simple white cross with his name and the dates August 18, 1945—March 4, 1969 engraved on it.

I sat down in the lush green grass atop the hill and propped the flowers from Jim's neighbor up against the base of the marker. I crossed my legs Indian-style and pulled a blade of grass out of the earth covering Jim's body, stuck it in my mouth and stared out at as beautiful a sunset as I had ever seen.

"You said Texas sunsets were as pretty as the ones in Vietnam," I said to Jim, "but I never believed you. Well, I do now."

I sat in silence until the sun went down behind a distant hill and then the words finally began to come. "Well, Jim, I tried to find her, I really did. But she's gone, and I don't know where to look. A really nice neighbor of yours who gave me these flowers says she doesn't think your wife will be coming back this way again. To tell you the truth, Jim, I don't think she will, either. But you know, my Granny used to say that we're always getting it all mixed up anyway, that we spend most of our lives busting our butts trying to get people to love us, when what's really important is loving others. So I don't know, but I think maybe you were way ahead of the game, loving your wife so completely the way you did. I hope so."

I took a few moments to look all around me and then said, "They gave you the high ground, Jim. I'm really glad they did that. Remember how you used to always tell me that life, just like war, is all about finding a way to take the high ground?"

My voice began to break so I looked away from Jim's grave marker and watched as a slow-moving old man in dirty work clothes bent over and used a cigarette lighter to torch a tall mound of dry grass clippings at the foot of the hill. A gust of wind blew into the fire and hurled the dancing embers upward on an air current which eventually passed right over me. A few of the ashes fell into my lap and as I picked them up and pressed them between my fingers, I thought back to something Jimbo had said, that the ashes of war are mankind's greatest shame.

With the little fire at the bottom of the hill still snapping and crackling, I said, "Well, Jim, I guess I should try to get you all caught up on things. You know, you're not going to believe this, but after we lost you, the major actually gave the squad to me. Now is that a hoot or what? We're talking the same guy here who dove into a pile of shit the first time we met. Do you remember that? I was so completely in awe of you. You weren't afraid of anything, and I was afraid of just about everything. How I lived through those first few months I'll never know, but I do know I couldn't have done it without you—not in a hundred years.

"I had no idea how hard your job was until I had to start doing it myself. When I'd make up the manifest and try to figure out who was going to walk where, I had to worry about who was taking drugs, who was married and who wasn't, who was most likely to freeze, all that stuff. And to tell you the truth, I never really got very good at it, and how you did it so well for so long is beyond me. I did get pretty good at keeping the squad out of trouble, though, and although a couple of guys got hit while I was in charge, no one was killed. I'm very proud of that, Jim, I really am.

"Being a squad leader—having all that responsibility—it really helped me grow up. I think it even made me a better person—stronger, more confident, maybe even a little wiser. But I'm afraid it also ended up coming between me and Harry. I had to ask him to walk the point one day, just for a few hours, and he went absolutely ballistic. Anyway, one thing led to another, and he never really spoke to me again. Can you believe that? We were such good friends. And it still hurts when I think about it. We didn't even say goodbye to each other when he went home. I know you never much liked Harry, but I really did, and I still feel awful that our friendship ended the way it did. I was just try-ing to do my job the best I could. Towards the end, he was telling everyone I had turned into another Jim Ketchum. I don't think he ever realized it was the biggest compliment he could have given me.

"The war settled down quite a bit after you left, Jim. The rules of engagement changed and towards the end of my tour, we got in another major who wasn't anywhere as gung ho as McCalley. We still got in over our heads every once in awhile, but it was nothing like when you were with us. All everyone talked about, even the officers, was Vietnamization and what unit was going to be sent home next. I really felt bad for poor old Toi Nguyen. Remember him? You know, right to the bitter end, he refused to believe America had given up. I often worry about what will become of him and his beautiful family now.

"Let's see, who else would you be interested in hearing about? Oh, yeah, you remember Marcus White, that real angry black guy? Well, we got to be pretty good friends—he even transferred over to our squad. He was darn near as brave as you, Jim. It's kinda sad, but the last thing he told me when he rotated was that he wasn't really going home—he was just going back to another war zone.

"McCalley went home in one piece of course. Someone tried to frag his hootch a few weeks before he left and a lot of people thought Harry was behind it. Who knows, he probably gave himself another Silver Star for surviving the attack.

"Remember Murray Goldstein? He made it, thank God. I always admired the way he yanked that Thompson submachine gun out of that crazy shake and bake's hands and slammed it into the ground. It's too bad the world isn't full of guys like Murray. I think we'd all be a lot better off if it was.

"Ted Henson, the shit-burner, made it, and so did Terry Pierce, the guy who used to get all those perfumed letters. Benji Duncan wasn't so lucky, though. You probably don't remember him. He was the one who fell over his own feet and almost walked a whole clip up my back. Well, a couple of months later, he tripped over a booby trap wire, and, well, that was that.

"Oh, I almost forgot, do you remember giving me Richie Nunn's stateside address and telling me to send him a little letter thanking him for being such a good RTO and friend if anything should ever happen to you? Well, I did it, and I got this really great letter back from him going on and on about all the wonderful times you two had together, especially the flag football games that used to be held behind the hootches where you were the platoon's quarterback and he was the guy you always threw the ball to when the game was on the line. I guess that was before my time, but Richie said those games, especially the ones against the doorgunners and the mechanics, were like little wars, and that you had a rifle arm and could read his moves like no one else. He said some of those games and the touchdown passes he caught from you were among the best memories of his whole tour. Anyway, he was so sad to hear about your death, but he has fully recovered from all his wounds now and he married that really cute girl he was always writing all those letters to, and they're as happy as can be. Don't be surprised if he comes and visits you someday soon. He said he loved you like a brother, and always will."

I sprawled out on my back and placed my hands behind my head. The vast Texas sky was still fighting to retain some of the sun's orange afterglow and the darkening clouds seemed to be in a great hurry to get where they were going. "The other night, Jim, when I was driving through New Mexico or someplace and trying to keep from falling asleep at the wheel, I decided to try and count up all the times you saved my life. Do you remember the time that Vietcong jumped up out of a bunker and shot at me point blank from about ten yards away? I'll never forget the look on his face. He was just a kid, he couldn't have been a day over sixteen, and I swear he was even more scared than me. But I just stood there like an idiot, too shocked to even raise up my rifle. Thank God he tried to shoot at my head and couldn't keep his AK from pulling upwards after he fired off the first round and missed. You know, if you hadn't shot him, I don't think I would have ever got around to doing it myself.

"And do you remember how you got me back to Headquarters Squad and onto the dustoff the day I got hit? And the night we had to leap-frog all the way back to the base when the darn claymores didn't work and our little two-man night ambush blew up in our faces?"

I took a deep breath and sighed. "Aw, Jim, what the hell I am doing on top of a hill in the middle of Texas? Do you realize I've said a prayer for you every single night since the day you died, and I don't even know enough about God to know if you're having a great time someplace else, or if you're just going to be a long time dead?"

For the first time since Jim's memorial service in Vietnam, I began to cry. I quickly wiped my eyes dry and sat back up. "I do have something really special to tell you, though, Jim. Do you remember me going on and on about Glynis—that girl I met in Australia on my R & R? Well, I think I may have really lucked out. She said she would never answer any of my letters, no matter what, but I just kept writing and writing and about a month before I went home she finally wrote back. Believe it or else, she swears she's still crazy about me and she's waiting for me in some little outback town that I can't even pronounce. I don't have the foggiest idea what I'm going to do for work when I get there—she's a teacher—but that ten thousand dollars you left me is really going to help us get started. I almost fell over when the first sergeant told me you had changed things around and named me as your beneficiary just before you died. You didn't have to do that, but I can't thank you enough, and I promise I'll really put it to good use.

"Glynis said not to bother to show up unless I was planning to marry her, but that's all I've ever really wanted to do since I first laid eyes on her anyway, so I can't tell you how much I'm looking forward to seeing her again. I squared away most of the paperwork and everything with the Australian embassy in San Francisco before I came home, and all I've really got to do now is say goodbye to my mom and sister and then get on a plane to Sydney. From there I have to catch a ride on a train to a place called Adelaide to meet Glynis and then it's off into the outback. And for what it's worth, Glynis and I have already decided that if we ever have a little boy, we're going to name him either James David Nichols, or David James Nichols, after you and her brother. We agreed not to fight it out until the time comes."

I reluctantly got to my feet and gently patted the top of Jim's grave marker. The tears began to flow down my cheeks again, but this time they were welcome and I made no effort to wipe them away. "I've got to be going now, Jim. But someday I promise to come back when I can stay longer. And I'll bring Glynis, okay? I've told her so much about you, and she's so thankful I had you to look out for me." My voice kept breaking, so I paused for a moment to clear my throat. "I'm so very, very sorry you had to die over there, Jim," I finally continued, "and it makes no sense to me whatsoever that I've got a whole life ahead of me and all you end up with is this little piece of ground out in the middle of nowhere. You were ten times, no, a hundred times, the soldier I was, and yet I'm alive, and you're dead. There's so much I don't understand, but starting from this moment, I'm going to try and get on with my life and make something good come from it. Maybe sometimes the answer to something is that there just isn't any answer? But at least I know that it's all free time now."

I thanked Jim again for helping me get through all those scary times in Vietnam when I didn't have the courage or knowledge to help myself, and I told him that I loved him. Then I took out my pocket-knife, knelt down on one knee, scratched out the deepest hole I could on top of the grave, and dropped in the unopened letter Jim had written to his wife.

I packed down the dry Texas earth until it was rock-hard and told Jim one last time how much I loved him. Then, without looking back, I hurried down the hill as fast as I could, thankful beyond words for my life, for having known Jim Ketchum, and for the wonderful girl waiting for me half-a-world away.

About the Author

Daryl Fisher is the Features Editor for his hometown newspaper, the *West Sacramento News-Ledger*. He and his wife, Mary Lynn, have four children, Carrie, Ty, Paul and Kyle, and a grandson, Riley. Daryl served in Vietnam from July of 1969 to July of 1970, where he attained the rank of sergeant. He was also awarded the Purple Heart and the Bronze Star for valor.

Daryl has written a weekly humor column called *"My Back Pages"* for almost two decades and has published a collection of his 100 favorite columns under that title. *This is his first novel.*

978-0-595-43782-5
0-595-43782-6

CPSIA information can be obtained at www.ICGtesting.com
Printed in the USA
BVOW041432100213

312793BV00002B/187/A